In Ed Sheehan's novel, *Spy Diplomacy,* is filled with nail-biting action, terrifying bravery, and heart-wrenching twists and turns.

The inimitable style of this author keeps the reader satisfyingly on the edge of the seat and sagging in brief respite as the story deepens into the foreshadowing of a lifelong career of service to country -- in a very unusual way. Another Ed Sheehan thriller.

Barbara McClary, award winning children's author, published biographer

I0685123

ED SHEEHAN

Spy Diplomacy
A Pat O'Sheen historical thriller

By

Ed Sheehan

ISBN-13: 9781732448537

Dedication
To my high school sweetheart, wife, and first editor,
and our three kids and three grandkids

Spy Diplomacy

Chapter One
Expatriate

Army Captain Pat O'Sheen's flight arrived at the Charles De Gaulle airport in Paris before sunset. He was in France to apprehend or kill an American expatriate, John Diffley. Pat went through Army basic training with Diffley at Fort Benning in Georgia. Diffley finished third behind Pat and Mike Burkowski on the sniper range, second behind Pat on the pistol range, and Diffley, who out-weighed Pat by forty pounds, was the only one to defeat Pat in hand-to-hand combat. O'Sheen and Diffley were both fearless warriors during the Vietnam War. Diffley left the army and disappeared before the army could arrest him for war crimes for the decimation of civilians in a Vietnamese village. Pat knew that many villages were taken over by the Vietcong. The villagers had to cooperate with the Cong or die. Their cooperation angered many South Vietnamese (ARVN) soldiers and the American soldiers fighting side-by-side with them.

On one occasion, Pat had stopped his Special Forces unit and the ARVN forces fighting with them from taking revenge on one village. In the battle outside the village, Colonel Truong and his troops were surrounded by the Cong forces. The trees that Pat and Mike Burkowski set up in were perfectly positioned to help defend Colonel Truong's troops. Truong and his troops thanked Pat and Mike for saving them, but Truong's forces were angry at the villagers for not warning them. Pat talked to the village leaders with Colonel Truong and managed to calm everyone down. Pat could understand how things could get out of control.

But Pat wasn't after Diffley for war crimes. Seven months ago, a French corporation's chief executive officer (CEO) was assassinated by a sniper in Paris. The sniper left fingerprints. A French agent recognized the professional nature of the hit and contacted other foreign intelligence agencies across Europe. They were able to match the fingerprints to other high-level assassinations. The fingerprints could not be matched to any of the European databases so the French agent sent the fingerprints to the CIA. The FBI matched the prints to Army Sergeant John Diffley.

President Ford's administration didn't want to disclose that an expatriated American sergeant was the assassin, and Ford made finding

1

Diffley the CIA's top priority. A CIA agent found Diffley in Barcelona, Spain. When two CIA agents tried to apprehend him, one was killed and the other was crippled for life. After that, America released Diffley's identity and his military photograph to Interpol, the international police organization.

Police cornered Diffley in a small house in Madrid, Spain. Diffley escaped by killing six Madrid police officers and wounding four. He disappeared off the face of the earth again. He was seen again a few days ago near Paris.

***

Pierre Boudreaux, at the age of twenty-five, was the youngest man in the relatively short history of the Prefecture de Police in Paris to be considered for a promotion from a street cop to a homicide detective. While waiting for the powers in the hierarchy to approve his promotion, he and his more experienced street partner, Jacque Hebert, were given a special assignment. They were to assist an American Special Forces officer, Captain O'Sheen, capture an expatriated American, John Diffley, whose picture was at the top of Interpol's most-wanted list.

Pierre Boudreaux expected to meet a large man in an Army Special Forces uniform, and he expected to spend hours in meetings in preparation for cornering and capturing the fugitive. Instead, he and Jacque met a man casually dressed in black pants and a black turtleneck sweater who was about Pierre's age. The man was less than six feet tall, slim, mildly attractive, and who walked toward them with long, graceful strides that exuded an air of self-confidence. His short hair was parted on the left side and he held a carryon bag and had a black leather folder held under his left armpit. He approached Pierre's older and larger partner, Jacque, and introduced himself as they shook hands, "Hey, I'm Pat O'Sheen."

Jacque's response was a cold, "Bon Jour, monsieur. I am Sergeant Hebert."

To Pierre's surprise, O'Sheen spoke in French and replied in Jacque's French-Mediterranean accent with a sincere, long-winded, apologetic show of appreciation for the help.

His normally hard-ass partner's sour attitude changed immediately. Jacque cordially motioned with his left hand to introduce Pierre, "This is…"

Pierre interrupted. He had recognized the American's southern drawl when he first said hello. O'Sheen impressed him and he wanted to make a good impression.

"Hey there. I'm Pierre Boudreaux. It is a pleasure meeting you." He drawled the greeting in his best "Gone with the Wind" movie southern accent. Pierre was about Pat's height, thinner, had black hair, a thin black mustache, a handsome angular face, and dark brown eyes.

He succeeded in getting a warm smile and a harder than expected handshake that relaxed slightly as O'Sheen looked deeply into his eyes, holding eye contact for way too long. O'Sheen held Pierre's right bicep as they shook hands, seemingly a more friendly gesture than he had given Jacque. Pierre held the stare. O'Sheen didn't speak.

Pierre tried to think of something clever to say when O'Sheen asked Jacque in French, "Where is our vehicle." *So much for pleasantries!*

When they got to the police cruiser, Pierre again tried to impress the American by opening the back door for him while Jacque proceeded as usual to the driver's door. His reward was a firm hand above his left hip and a gentle pressure that forced Pierre to take the back seat. O'Sheen got into the front seat beside Jacque.

When Jacque started the car, O'Sheen requested, "Un Momentito, por favor."

Pierre wondered, *Spanish*? Pat pulled something from the black leather folder under his arm and handed it back to Pierre.

Pierre looked at the map with a blue line leading from the airport to an area that was circled on the map about an hour southwest of the airport.

Pat continued in French, "Pierre, are you familiar with the circled area?

"The area is dangerous. Not a safe place to go into at night with only one police cruiser and no backup." Pierre told Jacque the area of France that was circled on the map.

3

Pat said that he needed to get there as quickly as possible. Jacque frowned but started in that direction.

Pat instructed Pierre, "Find a safe place on the map for y'all to park. I will walk into the neighborhood alone."

Jacque wondered if the American cowboy was planning to go into the dangerous neighborhood alone for surveillance purposes or to apprehend the target.

Jacque radioed dispatch with their destination and requested two back up units.

Pat handed a picture to the back seat. Pierre recognized the Interpol picture, "We've been briefed on the target."

Pat handed back another picture.

Pierre admitted, "I don't recognize this man." When Pat handed back another picture, Pierre said, "I don't recognize this man, either."

Pat exclaimed, "**They are all the same man. Study the pictures**." Pat immediately regretted the tone of voice he had used with the young police officer in the back seat. Pat had not wanted local police backup in Paris, but the CIA had insisted in case the mission turned sour with international complications.

Pierre was stunned—his ego slighted. The sun had set, and the light through the windows had dulled to a soft, pleasant amber. He pulled a flashlight from his belt and focused the light on the pictures. He had been trained in disguises. But, if this was the same man, he had a special talent. It took him a few minutes looking at the first two pictures to discover that the key was in the man's eyes. He looked at the next picture and saw it immediately. He couldn't see O'Sheen's eyes from the back seat, but he recalled O'Sheen's hazel eyes from the first encounter when O'Sheen had over-emphasized eye contact. He realized that he had just received a valuable training lesson from the American.

Pierre and Pat discussed the details of the pictures and the warrior skills of the target.

***

Jacque had trouble concentrating on the road while listening to the exchanges between O'Sheen and his young partner. Jacque recognized the teaching technique that O'Sheen was using on Pierre. His aggressive and now dead captain had tried to grill the technique into

4

Jacque's head. Two years ago, his captain's lack of fear and devotion to his job led to his violent death. Jacque's enthusiasm for the job, and for life itself, had waned after his captain's death. He understood Pierre's fascination with the American.

When Jacque parked the cruiser near the fugitive's hideout, O'Sheen asked, "Do you have my weapon?"

Jacque knew that giving him a loaded weapon was against regulations, but he had orders from the highest level. He handed O'Sheen the Glock 19 minus a magazine.

Pat calmly requested, "The magazine, please."

Jacque handed him the magazine and was surprised when O'Sheen extracted cartridges from the loaded magazine, seemed to weigh them in his hand, replaced them in the magazine, and rammed the magazine into the handle of the pistol.

Jacque queried, "You are not very trusting, are you?"

Pierre watched from his back seat as O'Sheen raised his left hand and lowered the collar of his turtleneck sweater, exposing a 3-inch long scar, starting slightly next to his carotid artery and proceeding to the soft tissue on the top of his back. O'Sheen said, "I learned to always check my ammunition."

Jacque quickly handed O'Sheen the second magazine. O'Sheen looked at him expectantly.

Jacque knew that silencers were as illegal in America as they were in France, but he retrieved it from the cruiser door pocket and surrendered it.

O'Sheen screwed the silencer into the barrel of the Glock, opened the door, and jumped from the police cruiser. "Wait here. Do not follow me or pursue this man. He is too dangerous. If I don't return in thirty minutes, wait for back-up, and please send my body home to my wife."

Jacque noticed that it was said matter-of-factly. *'Send my body home to my wife,* and pick up a loaf of bread and some milk on the way.

Jacque watched O'Sheen trot off toward the target. The man got his adrenaline pumping. He wanted to follow, but he couldn't leave his junior partner alone in the cruiser on the edge of this neighborhood.

He picked up his radio to report in when Pierre suddenly jumped from the back seat and ran after O'Sheen.

"Damn it," Jacque cursed in English. He made his compulsory report before leaving a police vehicle unattended, grabbed the short, double-barreled shotgun from the dash, and headed for the bungalow. Pierre and O'Sheen were almost out of sight.

***

Pierre had trouble following the fast and stealthy O'Sheen. He realized that his boots were too noisy on the street. O'Sheen slowed his pace to allow him to catch up, probably because his boots might attract unwanted attention. He followed O'Sheen's zigzag pattern for six blocks, even though the target was only four blocks from the parked cruiser. He squatted down next to O'Sheen behind the rusted carcass of an old Peugeot, fifty feet from the bungalow. The small two-room bungalow had only one exit: the front door.

Pat told him, "This guy can afford to buy loyalty. Stay here and **watch your back**."

Pierre watched as Pat approached the front door. He watched him try the knob and then drop down to his knees. Seconds later, he stuck a small instrument into the lock, stood up and slowly opened the door. Pierre was anxious as O'Sheen entered the house.

Suddenly, a large man crashed through the front window, diving to the small front yard with glass from the window flying in all directions. Pierre rose to his feet with his pistol in a two-handed extended position, ready to fire if necessary. He heard the distinctive click of a revolver cocking behind him—*behind him where O'Sheen had said, 'Watch Your Back'*. He spun around as he dove to the ground, realizing that his effort was unlikely to save him. He heard the pistol report and felt the bullet nick his head above his ear. He heard another loud report— too loud for a pistol. He spun his gun toward the report and saw Jacque spinning the shotgun in his hands toward the house. The man that had shot Pierre was lying at Jacque's feet. Pierre tried to lift himself up and spin toward the house, but he dizzily fell back to the ground.

***

Pat heard the man crash through the front window and was running to the front door when he heard the two shots coming from where he had left Pierre. He recognized that the second report was from a shotgun. Pat feared the worst for Pierre. With his silenced pistol held in outstretched arms, he approached the front doorway and saw his target aiming his pistol toward Pierre's position.

The poof from his silenced pistol was inaudible above the loud report from Diffley's pistol. Pat's shot was accurate. The expatriate's head snapped to the side before he collapsed to the ground.

**

Pierre sat up and saw the man who had crashed through the window fire his pistol, and he heard Jacque's body hit the ground behind him. The head of the man who shot Jacque jerked sideways, and he crashed violently to the ground. He saw O'Sheen in the front door and saw another armed man coming around the far corner of the house from O'Sheen's right. He was too far away to warn O'Sheen. If he fired at the man, the report from his pistol could be a dangerous distraction for O'Sheen, and he was too far away to fire accurately He crawled on his knees over to Jacque's still body and sat up in a position to protect him.. He watched O'Sheen back up into the house while the man came running toward Pierre's position. O'Sheen had accomplished his objective. The expatriate was down. *Was O'Sheen going to abandon him and Jacque?*

The man slowed his approach and walked by O'Sheen's position with a pistol in his extended left hand aimed at Pierre. Suddenly, the pistol flew from his hand. The man grabbed his bloody hand in agony. He looked around totally baffled. He had not heard a shot. Unable to see the threat, he spun around and ran like a wounded deer away from the scene.

Pierre turned back to Jacque's body to access his injury. It was bad—very bad. The bullet had entered his right eye and exited from his right temple, probably fatal. Pierre ripped a piece of his partner's shirt off and used it to apply pressure to the wound. Still dizzy from his own wound, he fumbled to retrieve the radio from his belt. He was about to scream for O'Sheen when a hand reached down and retrieved his radio.

The man who had caused all this mayhem knelt down beside him. The whites of his eyeballs were blood red, frightfully satanic. A very angry and disoriented Pierre swung his free left backhand toward O'Sheen's nose. A strong hand seized his fast-moving backhand and stopped the feeble attempt. The effort made the weakening Pierre fall from his knees to the ground, and the pain burst from his head wound.

He put his hand above his ear and applied pressure in an attempt to slow the flow of his blood.

Pat grabbed Pierre's radio, pushed the talk button, and in French said, "Two officers down." He gave their location knowing that despite the dangers of this neighborhood that the declaration of "Two officers down" would elicit an immediate response from the two back-up units that Jacque had requested.

Pierre heard two "poofs" from O'Sheen's silenced pistol before he passed out.

Chapter Two
Pierre

When Pierre woke up, Captain O'Sheen was sitting next to his bed in the hospital room. "Jacque?" was Pierre's first raspy spoken thought, barely audible.

Pat said as he stood and approached Pierre's bed, "I believe the bullet missed his brain. He is still in surgery."

O'Sheen raised the back of Pierre's bed up and handed him a cup of cool, refreshing water. Pierre felt the pain over his left ear and reached up to feel the bandage. He knew he was lucky to be alive as he drank the refreshing water. O'Sheen was acting differently, like a friend and not like the warrior that he met at the airport earlier. But the next words out of O'Sheen's mouth were accusatory.

"I asked you to stay in the car. Why did you follow me?"

Pierre wondered himself, but his mind was in no condition to formulate a plausible answer.

O'Sheen didn't press him. They remained silent.

Pierre broke the silence, "O'Sheen, why didn't you go in with more force? We could have arranged for an American-style swat team."

Pat answered, "Pierre, we were lucky to find Diffley's location. He has never stayed in one place for very long. If we came in with more force, he would have been gone from that bungalow before we got there.

Pat sighed. "I didn't want to involve the Prefecture de Police at all, but my superiors were afraid of a possible 'uncomfortable' outcome." Pat held up both hands with two fingers extended and swiped the air in a quotation mark mime around the word "uncomfortable". I needed a weapon, maximum speed, and political cover for myself if too many casualties occurred. If you had stayed in the vehicle, you and Jacque would not have been shot."

Pierre winced. Pat lowered his gaze and became introspective.

Pierre realized that by following Pat, he was responsible for Jacque's injury. The realization brought Pierre to the lowest point of self-esteem of his career.

Pat cleared his voice and added, "And if you and Jacque had not followed me, I would probably be dead." He looked into the policeman's eyes and said, "Thank you, Pierre."

Pierre didn't know how to respond. He couldn't believe the man talking to him was the same warrior with red eyes who killed Diffley.

They sat in silence.

Pierre broke the silence again and switched to English, "Pat, do you have family? Wife...kids?"

His question in English and the informal address was rewarded with a warm smile, "Yeah, I have a lovely wife who was my high school sweetheart and a three-year-old son. My wife calls me Eddie."

"Your family sounds perfect. Why do you put your life in jeopardy like you did tonight?"

Pierre watched as Pat reflected again before answering. "Pierre, I will live a long and happy life if it is God's will. I could be killed in a car accident on the way back to the airport here in Paris. God gave me special talents. Should I bury them in a field?"

Pierre recognized the reference to one of Jesus' parables in the Bible—the fearful servant of a strict master burying his money talents that were entrusted to him in a field, rather than risk losing them in an investment.

"Pierre, what about your family?"

"I'm engaged. We're getting married in two months." Pierre considered the night's events and the inspirational insight that he had just received from the American warrior and added, "God willing."

Pat was impressed with Pierre's ease in their English conversation. But more importantly, he recognized that this Frenchman was now a part of his life. Pat had saved his life, and he was now responsible for him. He slid his left hand under Pierre's down-turned right palm on the mattress and placed his right hand over the back of Pierre's hand.

Pierre was flabbergasted. Tonight, he had watched a true professional at work. Pierre had made an error in judgment; perhaps a deadly error for his partner, Jacque. Yet this man, a man he just met a few hours ago, was suddenly treating him like the brother that he never had. His cousins grew up with brothers and sisters as daily companions. As an only child, Pierre had been jealous. Meeting a brother-figure on this bizarre night was somehow both unsettling and comforting. He sensed a long-lasting friendship with this man. *God willing*!

He was uncomfortable with Pat holding his hand at first. This man wasn't the same man who had red eyes at the fire-fight.

Pierre instinctively withdrew his hand from Pat's when his captain walked through his hospital room door with a doctor. The doctor started checking Pierre's vital signs, while his captain answered the question that was anxiously pasted across Pierre's face.

"The bullet missed Jacque's brain. He lost his right eye, but his condition has been raised from critical to serious."

The captain looked at Pat with daggers in his eyes. "I almost lost two of my best officers tonight because of your recklessness. We have six dead bodies that must be explained."

Six! Pierre could only remember two—the one Jacque killed with the shotgun, and Diffley, whom O'Sheen killed. He jumped to Pat's defense. "Captain, O'Sheen asked us to stay in the police cruiser. He told us to wait for back up if he didn't return in the next thirty minutes. And then he asked us to send his body home to his wife." Pierre sighed loudly. "I just couldn't sit there and let him go in without back up, and I acted against his instructions and without consulting Jacque. I am responsible for Jacque's and my injuries."

Pierre's captain looked at him sternly, and then his look changed to approval conveying that he would have provided backup to the American, too.

Six dead bodies! The number was still sinking into Pierre's consciousness. O'Sheen must have fought off one hell of an attack after Pierre had slipped into unconsciousness.

Pierre watched Pat hand his captain an incident report that he must have written while waiting for Pierre to come out of surgery. His captain read the report and asked for clarification, "You intended to approach the target alone. Yet, you allowed Pierre to catch-up and join you. Why didn't you send him back to Jacque and the police cruiser?"

Pat calmly answered, "Our approach was detected. We had at least two hostiles following us. Alone, Pierre was unlikely to make it back to the police car alive. He was safer accompanying me. I traveled a long way to apprehend the extremely dangerous target. My assessment, under the circumstances, was that Pierre was a very capable asset for both of our survivals."

Pierre objected, "I didn't detect anyone following us."

Pierre's captain ignored Pierre and nodded his head in agreement. Pierre was shocked. His captain never accepted homicide incident reports on the first submittal. Pierre knew that he would be able to review the report later.

His captain said, "I need you to come to the prefecture in the morning and meet with my superiors."

Pat nodded. He was proud of Pierre for taking blame for Jacque's injuries.

Pierre caught Pat's eyes again before he left. The admiration that had exhilarated him earlier was evident in O'Sheen's eyes again, but there was something more permanent in those eyes. Pierre hoped that he would see the peculiar American again. He watched Pat walk out his hospital-room door, but hopefully not out of his life.

Chapter Three
Blood Money

It was dawn when Pat walked back into the hostile neighborhood where he killed Diffley. The cab driver dropped him off a quarter-mile away—refusing to get closer. Pat tipped him twenty dollars, and offered him another fifty if he waited for an hour for his return. The African cab driver agreed.

Pat held his fully loaded, silenced Glock against his right thigh. Some of the men in neighborhood eyed him with suspicion, but Pat walked confidently up to Diffley's door that was unlocked and he entered the house. He locked the door after he entered. The house had been ransacked. Diffley had been a very active assassin for hire. He had to keep a lot of money in the house. He had probably bought his neighbors loyalty, and they had already ransacked the house for any remaining money. At least Pat didn't have to waste time looking in the usual places. Pat started searching in the bedroom. He removed throw rugs from the floor and started tapping every square foot of tile with the heel of his boot while tapping the walls with the butt of his Glock.

The mattress was askew on the double bed. Pat leaned it against the wall and started tapping the butt of his Glock on the tile below the bed frame. He smiled when he heard a hollow sound under one of the tiles. After locking the bedroom door, he pulled a hunting knife from his boot and worked a tile loose. When he lifted it, he saw the corner of a suitcase under the floor. After removing three more tiles, he lifted the suitcase out and lowered it to the floor outside the bed frame. He unzipped the bag and saw that it was filled with money, negotiable bonds, and securities. Now the challenge was to get the suitcase out of the neighborhood.

He exited the bedroom and set the case by the front door.

He peered through the smashed out window that Diffley dove through the night before. Three men stood in the small yard across the street, about thirty feet from the widow. No weapons were visible. Pat held the silenced Glock against his right thigh again and moved into the opening and yelled, **"Hey?"**

When they looked at him through the hole in the window, Pat said in French, **"You three boys go find someplace else to play."**

The one standing with his left shoulder facing Pat starting swinging a pistol around his right hip and upward. Pat shot the man in his right bicep. He shot the two other guys in their right biceps in the next three seconds . . . equal pay for equal work. The silencer suppressed the noise of the gunshots. The three young men ran off to play somewhere else.

Pat stuck his head out the front door and pulled it quickly back in behind the door frame as a shot echoed through the neighborhood. In his peripheral vision he had seen one man near the corner of the house to his right. No one to the left. He switched the gun to his left hand and came out low. He shot the pistol out of the man's hand. The bullet ricocheted off the pistol and creased the man's right temple, and he fell unconsciously out into the open. Pat looked to his left as he pulled his head back in through the doorway. There was still no one on the left side of the house.

He had entered the neighborhood from the rear of the house and from the right side where the man lay unconscious. He didn't want to leave by the same route. He picked up the suitcase with his left hand and with the Glock in his right hand as he exited the door, turned left, and peered around the corner of the house. He zigzagged his way out of the neighborhood without another hostile encounter. Ten men in the neighborhood had paid a price for his two visits. Perhaps the neighborhood was a little less dangerous.

Pat was slightly surprised that the African cab driver was still waiting for him, even though he had only been gone for thirty minutes. He pushed the case into the back seat and climbed in behind it. The driver drove the hour back to his hotel. It was almost nine a.m. in Paris.

Pat had the cab driver wait at the hotel while he put the case under the bed in his room and changed into his army uniform. He had the cabbie drive him over to the Paris Prefecture de Police. Pat had no idea how long he would have to spend with Pierre Boudreaux's supervisors reviewing the action from the night before, so he settled the final fare with the cab driver and tipped him fifty dollars. He got a receipt.

Pat's meetings lasted for a little over an hour, and in the end, the six homicides were classified as "justifiable". Pat learned that Pierre was released from the hospital and would arrive at the prefecture around eleven, so he waited. Jacque was still in ICU but his status had been upgraded to "fair".

After Pierre filled out his incident report, he was given three days of sick leave. Pat offered to buy Pierre's lunch. Pierre's car was still in the parking lot from yesterday, and since Pierre was still on prescription pain medicines, Pat drove. They ate at Pat's hotel and charged the meal to his room to be paid by the U.S. Army. Over lunch, Pierre convinced Pat to spend the night at his apartment. Pierre wanted Pat to meet his fiancé.

Pat checked out of the hotel and put his carry-on bag and the suitcase in Pierre's trunk. Pierre didn't ask why Pat now had two bags, and Pat didn't tell him that one was filled with Diffley's blood money. They stopped and bought two bottles of French wine on the way to Pierre's apartment.

By the time they walked into Pierre's apartment, it was two-thirty, which was eight-thirty A.M. in Langley, Virginia. Pierre let Pat have the privacy of the phone in his bedroom to make a credit card call to the CIA.

"Gene, Pat O'Sheen here." He updated the CIA supervisor on his mission resulting in Diffley's demise.

"Gene, can you have someone contact Diffley's relatives to see if anyone wants his remains?"

Gene was surprised by Pat's compassion. "I'll get someone to handle it."

Pat didn't tell Gene about Diffley's money. "Do you know if Pete is in the building?" Pete was Pat's closest friend in the CIA.

"He was earlier. I'll put you through to the switchboard. Have her page him. Congratulations on a job well done."

The switchboard operator picked up, "May I help you?"

"I hope so. I'd like to talk to a half-oriental guy named Pete. I've forgotten his last name."

"I can page him. Who should I say is calling?"

"Pat O'Sheen."

"Hold, please."

Pat said, "Wait. What's his last name?"

"You will have to ask him. Please hold."

Pat smiled. The ploy to learn Pete's last name was worth a try.

Seconds later, "Pat, how are you?"

"Good, Pete. And you?"

"Fine. How's your new mission going?"

"Successfully completed. That's why I'm calling. Pete, can you call me from a secure phone for a private conversation?" Pat assumed that the calls on CIA phones were recorded.

When the answer came back affirmative, Pat gave him Pierre's phone number.

Pat opened the bedroom door and went out to talk to Pierre. He told Pierre that he was expecting a return phone call. Ten minutes later, the call came. Pat took it in the privacy of the bedroom.

"What do you need, Pat?"

"Pete, on this assignment, I found a suitcase full of ill-gotten money. I'm not sure what to do with it."

"Have you told anyone else about it?"

"No. You are the first."

"What continent are you on?"

"Europe. Why?"

"Pat, I'm going to give you the name and phone number of a banker in Zürich, Switzerland. I suggest you deposit the money there."

"Does the CIA have a slush-fund account there?"

"Not that I know of. You will have to open your own account."

Pat sighed, "That doesn't sound ethical."

Pete chuckled. "I guess that depends on the agent. Most agents have a slush fund. I only use mine for government business. The department is too slow to come up with cash when you need to have it in a hurry. If the expense is legitimate, the CIA will reimburse you when you have to use your slush-fund money.

"Pat, do you remember that the MI6 agent in Australia came up with thirty thousand to pay the Cambodian underground to help us get the six POWs to Thailand?"

Pat countered, "Yeah. But Cory Webb is a millionaire."

Pete said, "I bet he used his government slush fund.

"Pat, if you stay in this business, you will eventually have to rely on that money in a pinch."

Pete was making good sense. "Okay. Give me the banker's name and phone number."

"Have you got something to write on?"

Pat didn't, but he wasn't going to tell Pete about his audio-graphic memory. "I'm ready."

Pete gave him the information, "Don't call him until after ten in the morning Zurich time. I'll get with him before then and tell him to expect you.

"How much money is it?"

"I haven't had time to count it. Some of it is in negotiable bonds and securities."

"Give me a guess."

Pat said, "Maybe fifty thousand."

"Wow! That's a respectable start for your first solo assignment. I suggest that you use some of the cash to get to the Zurich bank and back to where you are now without leaving a paper trail. Congress doesn't give a damn about the special needs of field operatives like us."

Pat understood the warning.

Chapter Four
Kathie

Pierre was watching a soccer game (called futball in Europe because it's played with the feet, whereas American football is played more with the hands). He turned the volume down on the TV as Pat entered the room. "I called my fiancé on the other line. Kathie will be here in about an hour."

Pat nodded and smiled. He let Eddie take complete control. Everyone called him Eddie before his Army buddies started calling him Pat on his Saint Patrick's Day birthday. Eddie created a separate Pat personality to handle the killing in the war. Eddie's personality was much better at socializing.

Pierre held up a beer bottle in his left hand, "There's cold beer in the fridge. Help yourself."

Pat did.

When Pierre opened the door for Kathie, she screamed, **"What happened to your head?"** Despite her shocked tone of voice, her French sounded delicious.

"It's just a nick." Pierre brought her into the room. "I would have been killed if it wasn't for this man.

"Kathie Benton, this is Captain Pat O'Sheen, U. S. Army."

Pat returned her sweet smile, took her extended hand, and bent down and kissed the back of it.

He released her hand as he smiled back into her beautiful blue eyes that were only slightly below the level of his eyes. "Please, call me Pat." He added for Pierre's benefit, "Actually, my wife has always called me Eddie since we fell in love in high school. I answer to Eddie, too."

Her smile widened and her eyes beamed with delight. She turned her pretty eyes on Pierre, "What do you call him?"

"Pat."

She looked back at O'Sheen, "Then my calling you Pat will be less confusing, if that is all right."

Pat nodded, "Your logic makes perfect sense."

She remarked, "Your French doesn't sound American."

Pat looked at her long blond hair, "And you don't look French; more like Scandinavian."

She chuckled, "You're right. My parents moved here from Sweden when I was two."

Pierre was pleased that the two of them hit it off so well. "I'll open a bottle of wine."

She said, "I set the Chinese take-out food on the balcony. I'll get it."

When she came back in with two take-out boxes, she looked at Pat, "I hope you like Chinese?"

"I do. I learned to speak it when I was nine."

Kathie did a double take at the answer, "You can speak Chinese, too?"

"My best friend in the third grade was Chinese. His parents couldn't speak much English."

They ate the Chinese food while consuming more than normal amounts of French white wine.

When Pat looked at his watch, Kathie asked, "Do you want to call Dale?"

Pat smiled at her insight, "I usually call her around noon in Alabama, which is fifteen minutes from now."

"You can call from our . . ." she tried to correct herself, ". . . from Pierre's bedroom."

Pat failed to totally suppress his chuckle, probably due to the beer and wine.

He said, "Kathie, I would like you and Pierre to talk to her. How good is your English?"

Kathie hadn't considered that Dale couldn't speak French with Pat speaking it so comfortably, "I can handle it."

Pat looked at Pierre, "Does your kitchen phone have a speaker?" Pat knew the technology was available in France and that a police officer might need it.

Pierre nodded and stood up, a bit shaky at first, and pointed to one of three buttons on the base of the countertop black phone.

Pat dialed "O" like he did on the phone in Pierre's bedroom when he called the CIA. He gave the operator his Army calling card number and his home number—Dale's number. He hadn't yet activated the speaker feature on the kitchen phone.

"Hi, Hon, it's Eddie."

"I can tell. I was expecting to hear from Pat. I hope he didn't get his ass shot off again."

Pat laughed, "Not this time. Pat completed his mission successfully."

Dale let out a whoop that Kathie heard from three feet away, even though the phone was held to Pat's ear. The joy immediately endeared Kathie to Pat's wife. But she couldn't help but notice that Eddie O'Sheen talked about Pat O'Sheen in the third person. She looked at Pierre. Pierre hadn't noticed, being too enthralled with Pat's side of the conversation.

Dale said, "Where are you?"

Pat looked at the police officer, "I'm at Pierre Boudreaux's apartment in Paris, France."

"Why can you tell me where you are now, but not before you went there?"

"Because Pat's mission is complete. It is no longer top-secret."

"Who is Pierre Boudreaux?"

"Pierre is a police officer with the Prefecture de Police in Paris. Kathie, his fiancé, is here with us."

"Why are you with them in Paris?"

"Pierre helped me apprehend an American expatriate. Pierre was shot during the effort, but he's okay now. I'm putting you on speaker phone."

Dale heard a couple in the back ground over the speaker phone. She had a million questions that were just thwarted by him putting her on speaker.

Pat nodded to Kathie. She jumped right in as Pat expected her to, "Hello, Dale. I am Kathie Benton. Pat has shown us a picture of you and Scott. You have a lovely family." Her English was beautifully accented.

"Well, thank you, Kathie. When are you and Pierre getting married?"

"In two months, after I get my degree in Dental Hygiene."

They talked for over a half hour, with Pierre and Pat managing to get a few words in once in a while. It was like they all were old friends who hadn't seen each other in a long while and were catching up with each other's lives.

Pat finally cut it short, "The Army is probably going to complain about the big phone bill. We better all say good bye for now."

Kathie went first, "Bye, Dale. It was great talking to you."

"It was great talking to y'all. Bye, Pierre."

"Good bye, Dale. I hope we get to meet soon."

Dale said, "Captain O'Sheen, you need to arrange that. I've always wanted to visit Paris. Now we have a good reason."

She changed subjects, "Eddie, when are you coming home?"

"I'll be leaving here in the morning, but I have a little side trip to make. It should only delay me for a day or two. I'll keep you informed. I love you."

"I love you, too. Thanks for calling."

Chapter Five
Slush Fund

Pat's plane arrived in Zurich, Switzerland, at eleven a.m. He had arranged for a rental car and drove to a lunch meeting with the banker, Carl von Finck. After he retired to his bedroom in Pierre's apartment when Kathie left the night before, he had counted the money, mostly French francs and Spanish pesetas. Assuming the pesetas exchange rate was about the same as francs, the bag contained the equivalent of about $60,000 dollars. He counted the bonds and securities by type, but didn't know their value.

Pat had called Pete's banker from the airport in Paris and told him how much cash he had. Von Finck suggested they meet for lunch across the street from the bank to make sure they were "compatible". Pat assumed that meant that Finck wanted to decide if Pat was a crook. Pat wore his Army uniform to the luncheon. Pat didn't speak German and the Swiss man's English was a little hard to understand, so they conversed in French.

Over lunch, Pat told Carl about the hired assassin, Diffley, who was killed during the attempt to apprehend him, and that two Parisian police officers had been shot during the incident. He admitted that he found the blood money under the floorboard of Diffley's bungalow the next morning. Carl seemed comfortable with the source of the money.

Carl changed the subject, "How do you know Pete?"

Pat noticed that he didn't mention Pete's last name. "We worked together several times rescuing POWs during the Vietnam War."

"Was he a soldier at the time?"

"No. He worked for the U.S. government."

Carl noticed that he didn't mention what branch of government. He liked Pat, "When do you want to bring the money to the bank?"

Pat side-stepped the question. "I also have some negotiable securities and bonds that I haven't calculated the value of yet."

22

Pat pulled two sheets of paper from his pocket. He handed Carl the top sheet that had the description of the three types of negotiables securities. After Carl looked at it, Pat said, "How long will it take to get me a current value on each of those?"

"Can you give me an hour?"

"Yes. I'll bring the money to the bank in an hour if that works for you?"

"Muy bien."

Pat stood up, reached in his pocket and put four ten franc copper coins on the table, "Will that cover lunch?"

Carl handed one coin back. "Three will cover the lunch and the tip."

Pat smiled and headed for the door. He was already starting to like Carl.

Pat left in the opposite direction of the lot where his rental car was parked. The bank was in the heart of the high-rise Zurich business district. Pat had an hour to kill. He did a lot of window shopping, always looking more at the reflection in the window than at the items on display to be sure that he wasn't being followed. He shopped his way around to the parking lot and his rental car. He opened the locked trunk with a key, pulled out the case, and walked the three blocks to the bank. He arrived fifteen minutes early for his meeting.

He walked up to an information desk and said in French, "My name is Pat, I have an appointment with Carl von Finck."

She didn't ask Pat's last name. Pete told Pat that the banks in Zurich protected the privacy of their clients. She called Carl's secretary.

Minutes later, Pat rode up the elevator with Carl to his office on the seventh floor. Carl closed the office door after they entered and sat behind his desk with Pat across from him. He handed over the folded sheet Pat had given him after lunch. Next to each negotiable security was an amount followed by CHF (Swiss franc).

Pat was surprised at the large numbers; the first one was the lowest at 1,860 CHF. There were 43 of those notes in the suitcase. He asked, "What is the current exchange rate to U. S. dollars."

Carl had anticipated the question and smiled, "One dollar is worth 1.62 Swiss francs."

Pat did some quick calculations in his head and estimated that all the negotiables were worth about two-hundred thousand dollars. He said, "Do you have a copy of the bank's privacy policy that I can read while you count?"

Carl opened a file drawer in his desk, pulled out a document about six pages thick and handed it to him.

Pat stood up and held up the case, "Where do you want to count this?"

"Open it and set it on the floor by my desk here." He pointed to the floor.

Carl was impressed when he looked in the open case, "Did you group and band them?"

"No, I found it that way. Diffley was a sergeant. The U. S. Army teaches us to be neat and organized."

Carl put the eight stacks on the center of his desk above a ledger pad. He selected the smallest denomination of Spanish pesetas, wrote the description on the pad and started counting. Pat started reading the bank's secrecy agreement. They both finished at about the same time.

Carl handed Pat the ledger of his count. Pat said, "I had trouble with the bonds sticking together. You need to count them again."

"Do you agree with the others?"

"Yes."

Carl counted the bonds again, "I got sixty-three that time."

"That's what I got the second and third time."

After another half an hour, the account was set up and the money deposited. Pat could access the account from a Touch-Tone phone or by calling Carl during banking hours.

As they shook hands, Carl said, "What are you going to do with all of that money?"

Pat shrugged, "Use it as a government slush fund. I don't want the blood money on my hands."

Carl nodded. He believed Pat.

"Did you find out who paid Diffley the money?"

Pat shook his head. "No. That is not my area of expertise or job responsibility."

Chapter Six
Home at Last

Pat's return flight to Paris wasn't leaving Zurich until six, so he drove his rental car up into the Alps. It was summer, but there was still snow on some of the peaks. The beautiful scenery took his mind off his qualms about depositing so much blood money in his personal account. He got out of the car at a scenic overlook with an internal struggle going on between Eddie and Pat. Pat had control. After enjoying the view from the overlook, Pat saw a high mountain point about a mile to his left and about two-thousand feet higher than the overlook. Pat marched off on a small trail toward the snow covered peak.

Pat concentrated on navigating the trail instead of stopping periodically to enjoy the view. When he reached the apex and was sure he was at the highest point of the peak, he swiped the snow off with his right foot exposing rock. His breathing was still heavy and his heart rate still elevated, which was the purpose of Pat's uphill hike. He sat down on the rock so that Eddie could enjoy the view.

Eddie took over as his eyes panned the gorgeous view. It was rare for Pat to voluntarily give up control without outside influence from Dale or close friends. Eddie could see Zurich and the lake to the northwest. He thanked God for his beautiful creation and vowed to never use the blood money he just deposited in the bank unless it was necessary to help Pat perform his government missions.

Pat slept on the commercial flight back from Zurich to the Charles de Gaulle airport in Paris. The trip to Zurich and back was paid in cash out of the blood money. He had used his Army card to book red-eye flights back to Washington, D.C. He slept most of the way on the flight over the Atlantic Ocean.

The CIA didn't need him to return to Langley, so he rented a car and drove to Fort Bragg, North Carolina. He stopped at his apartment before reporting back for duty. Dale, dressed in an orange halter top and blue hot pants, jumped into his arms when he walked through the door. Her blond hair was teased up and her smile made her face more beautiful. Scott hugged his leg. After giving Dale a passionate kiss, Pat picked up Scott and hugged him, knowing that it was past his naptime.

Dale asked, "Have you had lunch?"

"Yes, I stopped at a Burger King."

They sat down on the couch. Scott ran into his room and brought out the rocks that he collected while his daddy was gone—pebbles really. He put them in his dad's hands. Pat smiled and put them on the cheap wooden coffee table in front of the couch and spread them out.

Scott enthusiastically said, "Which one do you like best?"

Pat studied the pebbles. He picked out one that was marbled in gray, black and brown, another one that had a yellow hue, and one that had a unique angular shape. He set them apart.

Scott's eyes beamed up into his dad's bemused eyes. Pat could tell the three were his son's favorites. Scott repeated, "Which one do you like best?"

Pat picked the one with the yellow hue.

Scott's face broke out into a big smile, "That's my favorite, too." He climbed up into his daddy's lap and hugged him. Scott heard his dad's heartbeat and let his ear remain on his chest, listening. Minutes later, he was asleep.

Dale smiled at Pat when she noticed his eyes scanning lustfully down her halter top, her bare midriff, her hot pants, and bare thighs. While he carried Scott to his bedroom, she went into their bedroom.

Pat laid Scott in his bed. He spent a few minutes smiling down at his sleeping son, his heart welling with love and pride. He walked out of his son's bedroom and silently closed the door. He could smell Dale's approach behind him. He turned around to her sexy smile. His eyes canvassed her body through her semi-transparent negligee.

Afterwards, when both of them caught their breath, Dale hugged her naked body to her husband's side, her thigh lying across his groin. "I think you just impregnated me." She looked up into his eyes.

Pat was surprised, "Why do you think that?"

"It's the right time in my menstrual cycle, and as much as you ejaculated into me, at least one of the sperm should succeed in finding my egg."

Pat chuckled. Dale had matured from the teenager he fell in love with. They both were addicted to their sexual encounters, but intercourse was not something they talked about openly. Pat didn't know what to say.

Dale said, "Do you want another kid?"

Pat didn't hesitate, "I hope the next one will be a girl."

Dale sat up exposing her ample, bare breasts, "Really, I would love to have a girl."

She moved her thigh off his groin when she felt it growing. She smiled and watched it grow. They made love again.

Chapter Seven
Major

It was almost half-past three when Captain O'Sheen walked into Major Ray Kramer's office. Ray was ten years older than Pat and much better looking. Ray looked at his watch as he stood up, "Traffic problems?"

"No. I stopped at home to see Dale and Scott. Dale and I had some catching up to do." Pat had been ordered to report to Kramer's office immediately.

Kramer chuckled at Pat's honesty. O'Sheen's disdain for military protocol would never allow him to become the general that his intelligence, leadership, and warrior skills screamed out for.

Ray walked around his desk and while shaking Pat's hand said, "Congratulations on your successful mission in Paris."

Pat said, "I wasn't on a mission in Paris. I was visiting a friend."

Ray knew that Pat had never been to Paris before, but if Pat thought the mission was still top-secret, he would let it go.

In the silence that ensued, Pat said, "So, why was I ordered to report here immediately?"

Ray knocked on the door that adjoined Colonel Jerry Swayze's office. He stuck his head in and told him that Pat was here.

Ray walked back behind his desk, opened his middle drawer and withdrew a small felt covered box. Ray had choreographed the whole scene in his mind.

Colonel Swayze entered the room and congratulated Pat on the successful mission in Paris. Swayze was four inches taller and heavier than Pat and Ray. He was at least twenty five years older than Pat with black hair that was greying at the temples, making him look more distinguished. It made sense to Pat that his C-Os would know about his secret missions.

Ray walked around the desk and handed the felt box to Jerry. Ray made a production of removing Pat's "captain" insignia.

Jerry pinned a new insignia's to Pat's collar and another next to the honoraria above the left pocket on Pat's chest. He smiled into Pat's eyes, "Congratulations, Pat. You have been promoted to major faster than anyone since World War Two.

Ray stepped forward, "Congratulations, Pat. I no longer out-rank you."

Jerry said, "Pat, you have been ordered to report to General Haig's office at the Pentagon."

Pat was honored by his promotion and pleased that Dale's family budget would be increased. "Ray, why does General Haig want to see me?"

"I think he is going to transfer you to military intelligence."

Pat chuckled, "My dad once told me the term 'military intelligence' was an oxymoron."

Jerry laughed, "Maybe General Haig thinks you can change that negative image."

Ray added as an incentive bonus, "Your friend John Romano is working at the Pentagon now."

Ray wasn't surprised by the spark in Pat's eyes. He knew Pat and Dale loved Cap Romano. John Romano was a captain when he flew his helicopter into a hot fire fight in Nam to rescue O'Sheen and Burkowski. Cap was missing in action for almost two years when O'Sheen and his sniper partner, Mike Burkowski, rescued him from a POW camp. Two years later, Pat and Dale had rescued Cap from the deepest depths of depression in a psych ward in Louisiana.

Pat said, "When am I supposed to report?"

Ray smiled, "You have earned a few days off. Let me know when you are ready to leave, and I'll get Jerry to coordinate it."

Pat looked at Colonel Swayze, "I'll be ready on Monday."

Ray was surprised, "That soon?"

"I'm anxious to find out what I will be doing next."

Pat walked through the front door of their apartment. Dale and Scott heard him enter. Dale had to run toward the door to keep up with Scott. Pat turned away from them to close the door. When he turned around, Scott had his arms up in air. Pat lifted him up and smiled at Dale as he hugged Scott.

Dale noticed, "Ohmygod, you have been promoted to major?"

Pat chuckled and nodded.

She laughed, "You're moving up the ladder really fast. I'm not sure that I will ever want to be the First Lady."

Pat guffawed. The laugh was contagious and Dale joined in. Even Scott joined in.

"Where did you learn to laugh like that?" Dale managed to say between laughs.

Pat replied, "From Cory Webb while I was in Australia. You are going to love Cory and his wife, Teresa."

Over a drink, Pat told her about having to go to D.C. to see General Haig and his possible reassignment to military intelligence.

He said, "When was the last time you were in D.C.?

"Sixth grade. Nixon was the Vice President. We actually saw him when we toured the Capital Building."

"I have a few days off. Why don't we load up the Maverick (Ford) and all drive to D.C. for a visit?"

"I'd love to."

"I'll tell Major Kramer that I'll call Debbie, General Haig's secretary, first thing on Monday morning."

***

The O'Sheens stayed in a motel in Virginia and spent the weekend touring Washington on two very hot July days.

On Monday afternoon, Pat reported to General Haig's office.

Pat enjoyed talking to Debbie while he waited in General Haig's reception area. Debbie was a very pretty brunette with blue eyes. She was almost ten years older than Pat. She congratulated him on his promotion, but didn't treat him any differently. She liked Pat. Rank wasn't important to her.

Her phone rang and she punched a button, listened and said, "Pat, you can go in."

Debbie returned Pat's grin. Debbie took notice that he wasn't nervous like most people who entered General Haig's office. Pat wasn't nervous at all. She remembered him calling from CIA headquarters and asking her if he could talk to Al, referring to the general. She wondered how big O'Sheen's balls were—and not just metaphorically. Pat was not a handsome hunk, but the American hero was a real man in every respect.

General Haig, who was about thirty years older than Pat and looked like a tough General, was rounding the desk as Pat entered the room. He waved off Pat's salute and offered his hand. "Pat, the president asked me to thank you for handling Sergeant Diffley for us."

Pat was still in his Eddie mode and just nodded while he shook Haig's hand. Eddie wasn't proud of the fact that Pat had killed Diffley.

Haig was reminded that O'Sheen didn't gracefully accept accolades, and that Pat had been the first soldier that he was aware of to turn down the Medal-of-Honor. He said, "Congratulations on your promotion."

"Thank you, sir. Did you influence that decision?"

Haig was surprised by the directness of the question. He did influence the promotion. The Army needed warriors like O'Sheen. But, he didn't answer the direct question. He directed Pat to sit on a leather chair in front of his desk.

To Pat's surprise, Haig sat on the chair next to him, instead of behind his desk.

"Pat, you have a unique talent for languages. Do you speak any of the Middle Eastern languages?"

"No, sir. I've picked up a little Hebrew from my Jewish friends."

"How long do you think it would take you to learn Persian and Arabic?'

Pat wasn't bragging, "Depending on the teaching aids and assuming I can spend full time on it, I can learn to speak a language in a few months.

Haig's eyebrows raised in doubt.

Pat added, "I've never learned to read and write in anything but a Latin alphabet, so I don't know how long it would take to me to learn to read and write Arabic."

Pat was intrigued with the challenge and prodded, "What do have in mind, sir?"

Haig was surprised again by such a direct question. He answered this time, "We are planning to assign you to military intelligence. The

CIA may eventually want your help in the Middle East and North Africa. The CIA has the best quick-track language training, so we plan to send you to Langley."

"Can my wife and son live with me near Langley while I train there?"

Al Haig really liked Pat—the warrior was also a dedicated family man. He would like to have him on his staff for his blunt-spoken leadership skills, but the country needed his skills on the front lines. "Yes. I have arranged for a car to take you to Langley this afternoon. You will meet with Gene again at CIA headquarters. You can look for living quarters for your family while you are there."

"I just need a ride to my hotel room across the river. I drove my family up from Bragg in our personal car on Thursday for a couple days of vacation in the D.C. area. I'll drive my car to Langley and find a temporary hotel room in McLean."

General Haig said, "Pat, the fact that you might do some work with the CIA is classified "need-to-know". If anyone wants to know what you are doing at Langley, language training is the only reason you are there. That goes for your wife, too. Do you understand?"

"Yes, sir." Pat knew that Haig was friends with the CIA director, and he assumed that was why the general was handling this personally.

The general stood up.

Pat stood, "General Haig, I would like to see Major Romano while I'm here in the Pentagon. Is there enough time for me to do that?"

"I'm sure John would like to see you, too. Get Debbie to track him down for you."

Chapter Eight
More training

Dale said from across the front seat of their Maverick, "Why are you going to CIA headquarters to learn Persian and Arabic?"

"General Haig says that it is the quickest place to learn a new language."

Pat further explained, "Our government thinks the Middle East is heating back up. The Shah of Iran is getting a lot of dissent from his people. Egypt and Syria are sable rattling again. In Libya, Gaddafi is becoming a real pain in the ass. I guess Haig just wants me ready to gather intelligence if it becomes necessary.

"Dale, in a lot of our foreign embassies, the military attaché is a diplomat who is usually in military intelligence. They may eventually want to move us to one of the embassies."

Dale insisted, "When Scott is older, I want him to go to school in America."

Pat nodded. He expected even more objection to moving overseas. Dale was getting used to being a military wife. He changed the subject, "I saw Cap at the Pentagon. He wants us to come over to his apartment on Friday night. We didn't get much time to talk, but I think he might have a new girlfriend."

Dale's eyes brightened, "I haven't seen him since his promotion to major. I can't wait."

She added, "Doesn't it seem awkward calling him Cap now that he is a major?"

Pat agreed, "Yes. I think his military friends call him John now. Maybe we should follow suit and see how he responds."

"I am so happy that Cap . . . that John is doing so well. He asked you to pull him out of another hole in the psych ward in Louisiana, and you did. I am so proud of you." She slid across the front seat of the Maverick and laid her head on his shoulder. Scott stirred from sleeping in her lap, but went back to sleep immediately. He inherited that trait that from his dad.

"I had help from you and Scott to help Cap." Pat was as happy as he could remember since the worst day of his life day when he watched his sniper partner, Mike Burkowski, being shredded to pieces by six or seven AK-47s. He wrapped his right arm around Dale and sighed as he drove up the George Washington Memorial Parkway toward McLean, Va. and the CIA headquarters in Langley

***

Pat's Iranian teacher suggested learning Persian first because it uses the same script as Arabic, but has four more letters in its alphabet. His teacher, Ramin Madani, spent seven hours a day with him, five days a week. Ramin was a retired professor and still lived near Georgetown University. Pat knew he wasn't a full time CIA employee because he didn't have a CIA attitude.

Pat and Dale moved from a motel into a subleased apartment in Georgetown on September 4, two days before Dale's birthday. They spent the two days unpacking and rearranging the furniture.

Pat left Langley for home early on her birthday, caught the Metro, and stopped at a bakery to pick up the cake that he had ordered. He and Scott enjoyed singing "happy birthday" and watching Dale blow out the candles. Pat gave Dale a new stereo for her birthday. The old, outdated one was broken in the move. Dale loved music.

After Scott went to bed, they sat on the couch. Dale said, "You gave me another birthday present."

"I did?" He saw the glow in her face and guessed, "Are you pregnant?"

Dale laughed. "The way you read my mind is scary. Yes. The doctor confirmed it this morning."

Pat threw his arms around her, "What a great present for me on your birthday."

He leaned back with his face aglow. "When is it due?"

"April. I told you that you probably impregnated me the day you got back from Paris."

A month into the language training, Pat invited Ramin over for dinner at their apartment. He declined the first invitation, but accepted the second invitation a couple weeks later. During Dale's delicious lasagna meal, Pat translated a lot of Dale's conversation into Farsi (Persian) to start introducing the language to her and Scott. Ramin had to correct him many times. As expected, Ramin enjoyed being with Dale.

In the weeks following the dinner, Pat was able to take more control over his lessons. Instead of conjugating verbs and learning sentence structure and vocabulary, Pat moved Ramin to mostly teaching through conversations in Farsi. They started walking the CIA grounds while Pat pointed out the trees, grass, ponds, streets, parking lots and spaces, and over lunch, talking about every cafeteria item they saw and every type of food. Ramin was amazed that he rarely had to remind Pat the Farsi name for most things.

Ramin was a Muslim and he recommended that Pat start learning the Muslim prayers if he ever wanted to go undercover in a Muslim country. After a few weeks of saying the mid-day prayers, they started going to a mosque together on Fridays for noon prayers.

By Christmas, Pat had completed his Farsi lessons and was learning Urdu, the other primary Persian dialect, and the main dialect in Afghanistan. He learned to speak Urdu and Arabic in the next three months, but he was still having a difficult time learning how to read the script, and worse yet, trying to spell and write it. But communicating was Pat's first priority. He had never learned to read or write Vietnamese, Chinese, or the Cambodian Khmer script, but he communicated in the languages like the locals in those countries. His special talent was audio-graphic, not photo-graphic.

Dale had their daughter, Amanda Anne O'Sheen, on April 10. Pat was able to witness the birth of his second child, like he did when Scott was born.

Dale's mother and dad drove up. Griff only flew when absolutely necessary because he had too many close calls when he flew so much for the Department Of Defense. Mary stayed to help Dale for three weeks. She stayed the third week that Pat's deceased mother had gladly taken when Scott was born.

Scott was fascinated with his baby sister, and sat on the couch next to his father when he laid her on his lap so that she could look up at him. Pat hugged his son to his side as his daughter grabbed Scott's offered fingers. Life didn't get any better than this.

Barbara, Pat's older sister, had a nursing conference in Boston that third week that Mamie (Dale's mom) was there. Their dad, Bill O'Sheen, flew up to Boston with her. They stayed at their brother Bob's house. Bill O'Sheen's plan was to fly to D.C. on Saturday to see his new granddaughter.

The phone rang in O'Sheen's apartment a little after ten on Wednesday night. Dale said, "Who could be calling this late?"

Pat shrugged and answered the call on the wall phone in the kitchen.

"Eddie, it's your brother Bill."

Before Pat could say hello, his brother said, "Dad has had a heart attack up in Boston. He is in the hospital."

Pat said loud enough for Dale and her mother to hear. "Dad had a heart attack in Boston? How bad is he?" Dale and her mother both put their hands on their hearts with worried looks on their faces.

Bill said, "Barbara was with him. Dad asked her to get his nitroglycerin pills from his dopp kit. Barb . . ."

Pat interrupted, "Why does he have to take nitroglycerin pills."

Bill knew his baby brother was getting hyper. "Eddie, Barbara was the only one who knew he had acute angina. She recognized that he was having a heart attack. She told Bob to call 911, and she found his pills in his suitcase and gave him two of them. The ambulance arrived four minutes later. He is going to be all right."

Pat said to Dale and Mamie, "Bill said Dad is going to be okay."

Dale took in a deep breath.

Mamie said, "Eddie, you should go to him."

Pat accepted Mamie's advice. He spoke into the phone. "Bill, are you going to Boston?"

"Yes. I'm driving up on Friday."

Pat said, "I'll fly to Boston on Friday."

Bill had only spent significant time with his baby brother twice since their mother's funeral. "Eddie, why don't you take the train into Penn Station in New York and ride up in my car with me to Boston."

Pat's brother Bill was six years older than him and was one of his main mentors. After Bill went to the Naval Academy, they rarely got time to spend much one-on-one time with each other. Barbara had reported that Dad's heart attack was mild. The drive to Boston would allow six one-on-one hours. Pat and Bill worked out a plan to meet at Penn Station.

Mamie called Griff when Pat got off the phone and told him about the heart attack. He decided to drive up to D.C. the next day, Thursday, instead of Friday to pick up Mary. Pat appreciated that Griff would be with Dale and the kids while he was up in Boston.

Bill's Triumph TR3 was parked at the curb when Pat exited the terminal building at Penn Station. He saw Bill get out, and Pat hurried toward him with a huge smile on his face. As Pat approached, he saw Bill's long face.

He dropped his bag, "What's wrong, Bill?"

Moisture filled Bill's eyes—a rare occurrence. He hated to be the one to break the news and devastate his younger brother. "Dad had a massive heart attack last night that he didn't survive."

Eddie stood there frozen, his mind unwilling to accept the news.

Bill took two steps forward and wrapped his arms around his tearful brother as tears started streaming down his cheeks. Eddie held his oldest brother for over a minute while trying and failing to get his emotions under control.

Pat compassionately took control from Eddie and released from the hug. "Barbara and Bob must be devastated. Let's get on the road."

Bill was surprised at Eddie's sudden recovery. He said, "I made reservations for us to fly up. Is that okay with you?"

"Yes. When does our flight leave?"

Bill looked at his watch and then into his brother's eyes "We have almost two hours." Bill drove to the LaGuardia airport.

Pat said, "What airline? I'll pick up our tickets while you park."

On the plane, Bill and Pat were both quiet.

Bill, who was about Pat's size but with black hair and blue eyes, finally said, "Eddie, are you okay?"

"Bill, Eddie is not quite ready to handle this yet." Pat faced his confused brother. "We haven't had much time to talk since I went to Nam. In the Army, they started calling me Pat on my birthday during my first tour of duty in Nam. Eddie couldn't handle killing other human beings, so he created me, Pat, as his alter ego. I can kill when necessary without remorse. My sniper partner and I killed several hundred enemy combatants and rescued over two hundred P-O-Ws. I got in the habit of taking over from Eddie when his emotions get the best of him, and I took over several minutes after you told him that his dad died."

Bill's jaw dropped more and more as Pat made the disclosure. "Are you saying that you are not my brother?"

"I am your brother. I just have a different personality than the Eddie you grew up with."

"You are freaking me out. Have you seen a psychiatrist?" The concern was clear on Bill's face.

"Yes," Pat said. "After the withdrawal from Saigon, I went to Fort Polk to visit an army friend who was a patient in the psych ward. His psychiatrist told me that creating an alter ego to handle the horrors of war made good sense to him. I drive Dale a little crazy at times. She still prefers Eddie, but she has learned to love me, too. I sure as hell love her and our kids."

Bill's eyebrows rose, "I have never heard you cuss before."

"You mean Eddie." Pat smiled. "Eddie doesn't like it when I curse, so I only do it to make a point. I did in this case to help you understand the difference between Eddie and me."

"This is nuts." Bill shook his head. "You talk about Eddie like he is a totally different person. Can you switch back to him?"

Pat stared at his brother and Eddie was surprised that Pat let him take over. Eddie's eyes filled with moisture.

Eddie said, "I'm sorry, Bill. Pat is overly protective of me during emotional times. He takes over at will. He has to agree to let me take back over."

Bill saw the transformation back to his baby brother. "Doesn't Pat drive you crazy?"

Eddie chuckled. "I am used to him. So is Dale. I'm surprised that he exposed himself to you. I am not sure why he did." Eddie went retrospective for a minute. Bill was used to Eddie doing that.

"You talk about Pat like he is someone else. He talks about you the same way." Bill was bewildered.

Bill said, "Eddie, you need to handle our father's death without Pat's help."

38

"Maybe we shouldn't tell Barbara and Bob about Pat just yet. Okay?"

"Sure. I'll let you handle that."

"Thank you, Bill."

Chapter Nine
Replacement

As the plane started its approach into Boston, Eddie said, "Bill, I would like Father Muller to handle the funeral services."

"I would like that, too." He knew Muller married Eddie and Dale, and he buried their mother.

Eddie said, "If Barbara and Bob agree, I'll call Father Muller tonight. I've stayed in touch with him over the years. Muller helps me keep Pat straight."

Bill chuckled at how Eddie talked about his alter ego in the third person.

Bob picked them up at the airport. They shared hugs and tears outside the baggage claim area. Bob was two inches taller than Pat and Bill and outweighed them by more than thirty pounds. He was only sibling that had red hair and freckles.

While driving, Bob said, "Barbara was with Dad when he had the second heart attack. I'll let her tell you about it."

Bill said, "How is Barbara handling it?"

Bob admitted, "Better than I am. How are you, Eddie?" Eddie had always been the most sensitive of the sons.

"I'll be alright, Bob." Eddie replied.

When they got to Bob's house, Eddie noticed that Barbara's husband, Joseph, and their twelve-year-old son, Daniel, were already there. Barbara threw herself into Eddie's arms first. She was eight years older than Eddie and a very attractive woman. Bill moved in and joined in the hug. Then Bob and Joseph moved in, and they all cried in each other's arms.

When they all broke from the hug, Bob said, "Now that we got that out of the way, let's have a drink and celebrate Dad's life."

Barbara raised a hand to stop Bob. She looked at Bill and then at Eddie. "I want you to know that Dad didn't suffer. He had some pain during the first heart attack, but he had no pain during the second one. His heart stopped, and he was already unconscious when I called the code blue. They opened up his chest up to massage his heart, but there was a hole in it the size of my thumb. He died quickly."

Tears started rolling down Eddie's cheeks. "Oh Barbara. That must have been awful for you."

Barbara's eyes moistened, but tears didn't flow. "I'm a cardiac nurse. I've seen a lot of patients die. Seeing Dad die was the toughest." She had told herself that she was going to be strong for her younger brothers . . . particularly for Eddie.

She grabbed a Kleenex and handed it to Eddie. "Let's have that drink now."

Eddie called Father Muller in Birmingham after their first drink. He could do the funeral service on Wednesday, which was agreeable to everyone.

Bill called Ridout's Funeral Parlor in Homewood, Alabama. Barbara called Uncle Eddie McMullen on their mother's side of the family in Pittsburgh. Uncle Eddie offered to inform all the other relatives in Pittsburgh. Bill called Uncle Joe O'Sheen, and he agreed to handle notification on their dad's side of the family.

Eddie called Dale and was surprised when Griff answered the phone.

"Hi, Eddie. Mary called me and I drove to D.C. I am so sorry about your Dad. Mary and I will miss him."

"Thanks, Griff." Eddie told him about the funeral arrangements.

"Eddie, let Dale and the kids ride with Mary and me back to Birmingham. You can fly to Birmingham from Boston with your brothers and sister. Talk to Dale about it. I'm handing the phone to her."

On Sunday, Eddie flew with Barbara and Bob's families to Birmingham with the coffin. Bill flew to New York. He and his girlfriend, Susan, were flying to Birmingham on Monday. Barbara's husband's car was at the airport, and he took Eddie to Dale's parent's house. Dad's car was parked at the airport, so Bob drove it to Dad's house and he and his wife and two kids stayed there.

On Monday morning, Barbara and Eddie went to Elmwood Cemetery and arranged for their father's interment next to their mother. Bob picked up Bill and Susan at the Birmingham Airport.

At Eddie's request, Bill picked up Dale at her parent's house.

He thought it a strange request until Dale said, "Bill, Eddie wants me to tell you about his dual personality."

"Ah! So that is why he wanted me to pick you up."

"Yes," Dale said. "He said he told you that his army buddies started calling him Pat on his birthday on Saint Patrick's Day in Vietnam. Eddie couldn't handle killing people in the war, so he created an alter ego, Pat, to protect his troops. When he came back from his first tour of duty, I knew the war had changed him. I thought I had lost the innocent boy I married. But he morphed back into Eddie and told me about his alter ego, Pat. When he left for his second tour of duty, I was really scared that he would permanently become Pat.

"He still won't talk about the war. Over the years, I've learned about what he did from his friends. His best friend in the Army was Mike Burkowski. They became best friends while going through a year of training together, and they fought side-by-side in the war. Shortly after they returned to Nam for their second tour of duty, a CIA agent approached Pat with information on a POW prison camp in North Vietnam. Mike told me that Pat planned a rescue mission, which he had trouble getting the brass to approve. Pat's plan was for the two of them to infiltrate fifty miles behind enemy lines, kill the guards, and evacuate the POWs by helicopter. The plan called for Pat to sneak into the POW camp at night and rig the guard barracks with explosives. Somehow Pat succeeded in doing that. After the barracks blew up, Pat and Mike killed the rest of the thirty six guards. They communicated to an aircraft carrier that the camp was secure and to send in helicopters to evacuate the eighty-five POWs.

"Pat got shot in the butt during the rescue, but he refused medical treatment until the POWs were airlifted out. He passed out from loss of blood, and was unconscious for over a day on the aircraft carrier and almost died twice.

"Eddie called me from the aircraft carrier. I asked if he was Pat or Eddie. He said, 'Eddie. Pat got his butt shot off.' He downplayed his injury. Mike told me that his blood pressure got so low that they had to put him into a coma."

Bill interrupted, "I can't believe my baby brother did all of that."

"He didn't. Nor did the Eddie that I married. Pat O'Sheen did it. Eddie tells me there is no way he could do what Pat does.

Dale continued, "Two months later, Pat planned a much bigger rescue farther behind enemy lines. This time there was a Viet Cong Army base next to the much bigger prison. Pat planned pretty much the same scenario except Pat timed blowing up the barracks with an airstrike on the Cong base. Special Forces units came in on the first helicopters to help subdue the sixty prison guards. The Special Forces units only had to kill four guards and five surrendered. Mike Burkowski told me that he only killed about a dozen guards. There were three guard barracks at this prison. Pat could only plant explosives on the two outside barracks. Mike told me that somehow Pat took over one of the guard towers and used a fifty caliber Russian machine gun and a couple of grenades to annihilate most of the guards in the center barracks. Then he ran into the commandant's quarters, killed three guards and wounded the commandant. When Special Forces Sergeant Linski entered the commandant's quarters, Pat was sitting on the couch next to a beautiful Vietnamese girl and was drinking a beer."

Dale saw Bill's incredulity. "That certainly wasn't your baby brother or the Eddie I married."

Bill agreed. He had pulled into a parking space in Homewood Park to hear the rest of the story.

Dale smiled her approval. "On their third tour of duty, Pat disobeyed orders and went on another POW rescue with the South Vietnamese Army near the Cambodian border. He didn't take Mike with him because he didn't want Mike to get in trouble by disobeying orders. They rescued nine South Vietnamese soldiers and one American soldier.

"While he was on that mission, I called army headquarters in Vietnam, because I hadn't heard from Eddie in almost a month. I was told that he was on an assignment, and when I asked, they said that Mike wasn't with him. I asked them to get a message to Burkowski.

"Mike called me later that day. He tried to hide it, but I could tell that he was angry that Pat didn't take him with him.

"Two days later, Pat called me. I cussed him out for not contacting me and for not taking Mike on the mission. Pat got mad at me and told me that I better get used to the idea of being married to both him and Eddie. I told Pat to never call me again—to find Eddie and have him call me. Then, I hung up on him. I was afraid that I had lost Eddie forever.

"But, Eddie called me back thirty minutes later, all full of apologies. He gave Jesus the credit for Pat letting him take over.

"The next day they announced that a peace treaty was signed in Paris; that the war was over and Eddie was coming home. But Pat volunteered to stay in Nam after all the troops left to train South Vietnamese snipers, and Mike stayed to help him. I was pregnant with Scott, so he came home a couple of months later."

Bill said, "I'm sorry, Dale. I didn't know that my brother was putting you through so much hell."

"Bill, Eddie was the one who went through hell during the war. It sounds worse in this condensed version than it really was. My husband is still Eddie when he is at home. After Scott was born, he was Eddie for the next two years. Then North Vietnam attacked South Vietnam again. Mike Burkowski volunteered to help with the evacuation of the embassy during the fall of Saigon. Pat volunteered to cover Mike and was put in charge of a twenty man sniper force."

Bill put up a hand to stop her. "Are you saying that Eddie and Mike were snipers?"

Dale nodded. "I didn't know that he was a sniper until after the fall of Saigon. Does that sound like your baby brother or the Eddie I married?"

Bill shook his head in disbelief.

Dale continued, "During the evacuation, Mike was killed outside of Saigon in a tree near Pat. Only Pat and one other of the twenty snipers got out alive. Pat still can't talk about Mike. He won't talk about the war at all. That is why I'm warning you not to ask Eddie about the war."

Bill asked, "Pat told me some of this on the flight from New York to Boston. He said a psychiatrist told him that creating an alter ego to handle the horrors of war made sense."

Dale nodded, "After Mike was killed, Pat took me to visit one of his friends who was in a psych ward in Fort Polk. Pat called him Cap, because of his rank. I need to explain who he is.

44

"Cap flew his helicopter into a hot zone and pulled Pat and Mike out, saving them and four men in their unit. It was on his second tour of duty when a CIA agent approached Pat and showed him pictures of a POW camp. Pat recognized Cap Romano in one of the agent's reconnaissance pictures. Cap was the reason Pat and Mike volunteered for that first POW rescue mission.

"During that first rescue, Pat pulled John Romano out of locked, water-filled hole that he had been in for almost a week. Cap was almost dead.

"When we visited Cap at Fort Polk, he told me that he was about to give up and drown in his hellhole when an angel appeared to him and told him that Pat O'Sheen was coming to save him." Dale got goose bumps and shivered, unintentionally authenticating her story.

Bill assumed the hellhole was the reason Romano was in the psych ward. "Where is Cap now?"

"He is a major now, and he works in the Pentagon. Pat pulled him out of another hellhole . . . no, actually Eddie pulled him out of the psych ward with Scott and my help. Cap was able to ween off his heavy drugs, and a month later he was out of the psych ward.

"But on the first day, I visited Cap, the doc was fascinated with the positive effect that we were having on Cap. The doctor wanted Eddie to be temporarily reassigned to help him with Cap and other patients in the psych ward. Eddie and I agreed.

"On the first day I met Cap, the doctor sent Eddie off to the bathroom to see how Cap would behave without him around.

"When Eddie was gone, Cap told me that Pat and Mike were the best sniper team in Nam. I didn't believe him and said something naive about Eddie not being capable of killing anyone. Cap chuckled and explained that killing is what soldiers do in war.

"Cap's psychiatrist overheard me telling Cap about my husband's split personality. Cap told me that it made perfect sense for my husband to create an alter ego to deal with the horrors of war. I was surprised when Doctor Creighton agreed with him.

"The doctor intercepted Eddie on the way back from the bathroom and got him to talk about the war, and more importantly, he got Pat to tell him about Mike Burkowski getting killed. I was watching from a distance and could see tears running down his face.

"A couple weeks later, Craig Dolly, the only other surviving sniper who Pat got out of Nam on evacuation day, was killed in a car accident. Eddie went into another deep funk and Pat took over. That was when I started falling in love with Pat."

Bill's eyebrows rose.

Dale giggled. She enjoyed Bill's confusion. His confusion meant that he was starting to understand. It took years for love to carry her from confusion to understanding. "A month later, Cap rode with Eddie and me to my parents' house in Birmingham. Your dad had dinner with us. Then we took Cap to Fort Bragg where Pat reported for his next assignment. Cap was treated by the psychiatric department up there."

She looked into Bill's eyes with moisture in hers. "I have two incredible husbands. You have an incredible brother. Let's go see him. I'll let you decide what you want to share with Barbara and Bob, but convince them to not to ask Eddie to answer questions about the war."

Bill started the car, backed out of the parking place, and smiled as he drove toward his dad's house. He was absolutely sure of one thing—his baby brother had a very exceptional wife.

On Tuesday night, Rideout's Chapel was overflowing for the rosary and the visitation. Eddie made it through without a lot of tears.

The large crowd for the funeral mass at the large Our Lady of Sorrows church was overwhelming. It had been crowded at Pat's mother's funeral on the exact same date three years before. Dale's cousin, Amy Mahon, watched the kids at Griff's house.

Father Muller knew all of the O'Sheen family very well and his eulogy was personal and tearfully moving. He closed with, "Our Parish lost a great friend, and the O'Sheen family lost a magnificent patriarch. The Lord took Bill O'Sheen to his heavenly home to join his wife, Anne. But God sent a new soul, Amanda Anne O'Sheen, into the O'Sheen family and into the care of Eddie and Dale O'Sheen. We will welcome her into our Catholic family at her baptism here today at one p.m. All are welcome.

"There will be a procession leaving in ten minutes to the graveside ceremony at the Elmwood Cemetery."

Father Muller left the altar to console the O'Sheen family sitting in the front two rows.

It was Father Muller who convinced Dale to have Amanda's baptism on the same day as Bill O'Sheen's funeral. He presented it as a practical matter—the family would already be assembled from around the country. Father Muller didn't consider Bill's passing as a sad event—death was as much a part of life as birth was. Birth was the beginning, death was just a transition to everlasting life. Baptism was the first of many steps in a path to achieving everlasting life in paradise.

The Our Lady of Sorrows (OLS) Altar Sodality and the bereavement committee served lunch to the O'Sheens and many of their relatives in the OLS Youth hall. Most of the senior citizens knew Bill and/or Anne O'Sheen. Eddie knew many of them. Mary, Dale's mother, knew most of them.

More of the people attended Amanda's baptism than Dale expected. By two p.m. she was exhausted and Eddie took her to her parents' house. Pat and Mary took care of his kids while Dale took a nap.

Eddie agreed to bring Dale to Dad's house by seven p.m. Bill and Bob were buying steaks, and plenty of beer and booze. Dale wasn't in the mood for an Irish wake party, but Dale's mother offered to take care of her kids. Eddie and Scott fed Amanda a bottle of milk. Scott was fascinated with his month-old baby sister.

The wake party went smoothly until after dinner. By then, Uncle Mickey and Bobby McCoy were pretty drunk. When things got heated, Dale announced that she had to leave to breast feed Amanda. Barbara hugged Dale and whispered a "thank you" for stopping the argument—she knew that Dale wasn't breast feeding. Eddie and Dale drove back to her parents' house.

Chapter 10
Iran

Dale and Pat went back to D.C. Pat had a good grasp of reading Arabic by June, and he was reassigned to the 303rd Military Intelligence Battalion at Fort Hood, Texas.

Pat was put through a three week military intelligence training course. After the training, he and Dale were on their way to the American Embassy in Iran. They were allowed to visit her family in Birmingham for several days and left their Ford Maverick at Dale's parents' house.

On the way to Iran, they stopped to visit Pierre and Kathie Boudreaux in their apartment in Paris. It was the first time that Dale met them in person. Pat and Pierre were not surprised that Kathie and Dale hit it off with each other immediately. Kathie adored Amanda—it was obvious that she wanted to get pregnant.

Pierre understood what working under a military attaché in a foreign embassy meant. Pat was becoming a spy. He didn't vocalize his understanding, because Pat avoided the subject. Pat did share with him that he had learned to speak Persian and Arabic.

Pierre could speak several European languages because most European countries were not much bigger than States in America, and except for Germany and the other Slovakian countries, the languages were Latin based like the French he grew up with. He had learned most of the languages when he was young. There were a lot of Arabs and North Africans moving into southern France to work the vineyards. French families, because of the birth control pill and abortions were no longer procreating enough offspring to harvest all of the grapes. Pierre never considered that he should learn Arabic. But the fact that Pat had learned it so quickly was motivating.

It was unusually cold outside during their visit to Paris, but Dale wanted to go up the Eiffel Tower during her first visit to Paris. Kathie baby-sat Amanda. Scott loved climbing around in the tower despite the cold wind, and he was starting to develop a cold when they got on a commercial flight to Tehran. He screamed as the plane climbed in elevation. Pat had a piece of gum in his mouth. Pat's eustachian tubes leading from his throat to equalize the pressure in his inner ears were small, and he always had problems with pressure in his ears from quick changes in elevation. Chewing gum helped. He put the gum in Scott's mouth and told him to chew it. Dale looked at Pat reproachfully. When the pressure was relieved from Scott's inner ears, he smiled up at his daddy. Dale smiled at Pat, too, despite his poor example of proper hygiene.

A young man about Pat's age named Jim Reese, who introduced himself as a low-level diplomat, picked them up at the Tehran airport and took them to a small house a few blocks from the embassy where they were going to live. While Pat and Dale were touring the small two-bedroom house, Jim walked next door and returned with his pretty wife, Norma Jean, and their three year-old daughter. Dale's eyes lit up when she answered the front door. Minutes later, the two wives were talking like they had been close friends for years.

Pat asked Jim about Colonel Neal Williams, who was Pat's new commanding officer (C-O).

Jim refused to offer an opinion, but a look of sympathy on his face expressed more than any negative words could have voiced.

Jim invited them over to his house for a welcoming party to meet some of the embassy staff.

After Dale and Pat unpacked their bags and moved the furniture around three times to meet Dale's approval, a teenage baby sitter that Norma Jean arranged knocked on the front door. She was the daughter of one of the embassy staff. She spoke adequate English. Amanda was already in bed. Scott warmed to her immediately. Dale worried, but they were just going next door for a little over an hour.

Pat and Dale arrived at the Reese's house at seven for the party. The small house was crowded. Apparently, everyone was curious about the new major joining the embassy staff.

Jim made a special effort to introduce Pat and Dale to the embassy staff individually. One, a marine corporal, Justin Johnson, who was in charge of embassy security, quizzed Pat with excessive scrutiny. Pat immediately liked him. Pat asked him why his new boss Colonel Williams wasn't at the party. Johnson shrugged in a way that indicated he didn't care much for Neal Williams.

Most of the men that Jim introduced him to were Americans. But Pat chose to mingle with the two Iranian staff members who stood away from the Americans. When he started speaking to them in Farsi, they warmed to him. They were reluctant to talk politics, but they were friendly to Pat, and were complimentary of Pat's beautiful wife.

Jim Reese watched O'Sheen's interaction with the Iranians with interest.

Dale was happy when they put Scott to bed that evening. She liked the women at the party. She liked how the men accepted her husband. Some of her fear of moving to a foreign country subsided.

She said, "Eddie, I thought Iran was a third world country living in poverty. Tehran looks like the old cities in northeast America. The men walking the sidewalks dress like Americans. I didn't see many women, but only a few of them covered their faces with a veil."

Pat offered, "In Muslim countries, the women don't have many rights. I told you about wearing a scarf over your blond hair and not to wear sleeveless blouses and skirts or shorts that expose too much skin. Apparently, Muslim men haven't learned how to handle their hormones."

Dale started unbuttoning her blouse, "Have you?"

"Not with you." He started to unbuckle his belt.

Chapter 11
The Embassy

Pat entered the embassy and encountered an Iranian woman receptionist with the most beautiful hazel eyes that he had ever seen. Pat was in uniform.

She said in English with a heavy Iranian accent, "May I help you?"

Pat said in Farsi, "How long have you been working here?"

She smiled at Pat's perfect Farsi, her teeth were crooked, but her smile lit up her gorgeous hazel eyes, "Who are you?"

"I am Pat O'Sheen. What is your name?" Pat stretched his hand across the desk

Her smile slackened a bit, but she placed her right hand in his. "Colonel Williams is expecting you."

Pat gently squeezed her small hand. He thought about bending down to kiss the back of her hand, but didn't. He asked again, still speaking in Farsi, "What is your name?"

"Cleo."

Pat said half-jokingly, "Is your full name Cleopatra?"

Her smile widened, "Yes. My dad took my mother to see the pyramids in Egypt shortly before I was born."

Pat said, "The name suits you. Cleopatra is probably the most famous queen of all times."

She blushed a bit. "I'll let Colonel Williams know you have arrived."

"Thank you, Cleo." Pat sat down in the reception area.

Colonel Williams kept Pat waiting for over twenty minutes. Cleo looked at him sympathetically when she finally told him that he could go in.

Pat entered the door without knocking. Williams ignored him, pretending to do paper work on his desk. Pat sat down in a chair in front of his desk and slouched in it like a rebellious teenager.

Williams looked up at the disrespectful soldier and hesitated when his eyes encountered a steely-eyed glare. He averted his eyes from the glare, "O'Sheen, I've read your file. You were a hot-shot in Nam, but this is Iran. You have no status here. I am your C-O and you can't sneeze here without asking my permission."

Pat faked one of his Grosspoppi's extended sneezes. "Ah . . . Ah . . . Ah . . . Ah shoo."

Williams looked back up into O'Sheen's eyes expecting a smirk. Instead, he encountered the same steely glare. This time, Williams tried to handle the glare, realizing that he was already losing control of O'Sheen. "Are you going to be a problem, O'Sheen?"

"Colonel Williams, why didn't you come to the embassy party to welcome me last night?"

"Major O'Sheen, I'm a busy man."

Pat said, "I found it interesting that no one at the party had one nice thing to say about you. Why did you make me wait in the reception area for over twenty minutes?"

Colonel Williams started rising out of his chair; O'Sheen stood up much faster.

William's said, "Major, I will not tolerate insubordination."

"Colonel Williams, I was sent here to find out what was going on between the people of Iran and the Shah's regime. I will do that by spending most of my time getting to know the Iranian people. I am not here to serve you. If you want to get along with me, you better stay out of my way."

Williams started around his desk his hands balled up into fists. He wasn't going to let a subordinate treat him with such disrespect. As he rounded the desk, he was surprised to see O'Sheen smiling.

Pat warned him, "Colonel, you don't want to mess with me. I won't hesitate to put you down or send you to a hospital. I don't fear military discipline."

Williams stopped his advance. What he heard about O'Sheen was accurate—the son-of-a-bitch was fearless.

Pat projected his right hand lightning fast toward the Colonel's stomach. Williams attempted to tighten his abdomen to handle the blow—a blow that never made contact. He looked down and saw Pat's hand open up in an offered hand shake.

He looked back up into O'Sheen's bemused eyes and understood how he made it to the rank of major so fast. He stepped back, smiled, and shook Pat's hand, "Welcome aboard, Major. Your reputation is not exaggerated."

"Thank you, Colonel Williams. I've always hated military protocol."

The colonel chuckled, "You made that perfectly clear. Please, call me Neal."

"My friends call me Pat." He released from the handshake, glad that the first confrontation ended amicably.

Williams sat down on Pat's side of the desk, indicating that he was willing to talk.

Pat sat down, "Neal, what can you tell me about the Shah's stability?"

"Do you know who Ruhollah Khomeini is?"

Pat replied, "He is a Muslim cleric who was exiled by the Shah for preaching support for the rule of Islamic law and for his opposition to the Shah."

"That's right. You've done some homework. Khomeini's oldest son, Mostafa, died last October under suspicious circumstances. Khomeini supporters blame SAVAC, Iran's secret police, for his death, which instigated militant protests. The Iranian military lacks the training to confront civil unrest and a recent protest ended in bloodshed, which resulted in a lot more popular support for the protesters. There is some talk of an Islamic revolution."

Pat asked, "Do you know who the major players are?"

"That's not in my area of expertise. You need to talk to our station chief, Hal Middleton."

"Okay. I'll do that. Thanks for the help, Neal." Pat stood.

"Anytime." Neal rose to his feet.

Pat formally saluted and left the office. Neal chuckled about the formal salute. O'Sheen was very peculiar. Neal liked his no-nonsense attitude but controlling him was going to difficult.

Cleo noticed the smile on O'Sheen's face, which was rare for anyone leaving the colonel's office. Pat asked her to check to see if Chief Middleton was available.

She made a call and said in Farsi, "Major O'Sheen, his secretary said he was in a meeting, but that he should be available in an hour. Do you want her to make you an appointment?"

"Yes. Where is his office?"

She liked the sexy new American. "I will show you."

They went up a set of stairs to the second floor and entered a large room with five desks. Cleo stopped at first desk by the door, "Major O'Sheen, this is Mrs. Middleton."

Pat said in English, "I know. We met last night. Hi, Kay."

"Hi, Pat. Are you learning your way around?"

"Yes. Cleo has been very kind."

Cleo smiled, "I better get back to my desk." She walked away.

Kay said, "Hal is in the Ambassador's office."

Pat saw Omid from last night's party and waved. Omid waved Pat over.

"Hello, Omid." They shook hands. Pat said, "If I remember correctly, you serve as interpreter and translate Persian documents." Pat sat down in a chair next to Omid's desk.

Omid sat down, "You have a good memory. You met a whole house full of people last night."

"Yes, but only two Iranians. Where is Amir?"

"Monday is his day off. How is your first day going?"

"Very good."

"Then you haven't met with Colonel Williams yet."

Pat chuckled, "I just left his office. We got along just fine after he got to know me."

"Well, you are the first. It must be the military connection, although the last military man in your position requested a transfer."

Pat changed the subject and the language to Farsi. "Omid, are you a Shi'ite Muslim?"

"Yes."

"Do they let you go to a mosque for noon prayers?"

"Only on Fridays. Why do you ask?"

"I would like to go with you."

54

"Pat, you would feel very uncomfortable if you don't know the prayers."

"The mosques in the United States say the prayers in Arabic."

"We do, too." Omid smiled. "You are the first Muslim that America has ever sent over here."

Pat didn't correct him, "Can I go with you?"

Omid smiled. "Yes. I go with Amir. I don't think he will object."

"Thank you."

Pat changed back to English, "Where is the bathroom?"

"Down the hallway on the left."

Pat stood up and headed for the hallway.

Omid mused at the unusual American as he walked athletically away.

When Pat reentered the room thirty minutes later, Marine Corporal Justin Johnson, head of security, was there. Pat shook his hand and they shared amenities. Before they could talk more, the door to the ambassador's office opened. Station Chief Hal Middleton saw O'Sheen and beckoned him in.

The ambassador was standing next to his desk. Hal handled the introduction. "Ambassador Andrew Sullivan, this is Major Pat O'Sheen."

He stepped forward and shook Pat's hand enthusiastically— diplomatically. "Welcome, Major O'Sheen. I am glad that you are coming aboard."

Pat locked eyes with him, "Thank you, Sir. I look forward to working for you."

Sullivan broke with formality, "May I call you Pat?"

"Yes sir."

"Pat, please sit down." He pointed toward the couch.

When Pat sat down, the ambassador and the station chief sat down in two upholstered chairs across from him.

Sullivan started the conversation, locking eyes again with Pat, "Hal has updated me on your file. Your military achievements are remarkable. Hal also explained your CIA connection."

Pat looked at Middleton, wondering if he should have disclosed the connection. Hal smiled. Pat accepted that the decision was made way above his pay grade.

Ambassador Sullivan continued, "Pat, Hal told me that you are fluent in Farsi. How do you intend to proceed?"

Pat replied, "I want to mingle with Iranian civilians and try to meet the main organizers behind the protests. I . . ."

Sullivan interrupted, "Pat, the word will get out that you work at this embassy. I think your expectations may be unrealistic."

"I plan to be open and upfront that I am U.S. military and work at the embassy. After that, I realize it may take a while to earn their trust."

Sullivan shook his head in doubt, "Don't do anything to jeopardize this embassy."

"Sir, you can be assured that I would never do that. I will keep Mister Middleton and Colonel Williams informed on my progress."

Sullivan changed subjects, "How did you and Neal get along?"

"Very well, sir. He was a bit uptight at first."

"Pat, Neal is a friend of mine. Our wives were very close friends in Laos. He is having marital problems which has made him ornery, and we need to cut him some slack."

Pat said, "He and I got along fine. You don't need to worry about that."

Sullivan raised his eyebrows in doubt, but stood up and said, "I've got to prepare to leave for a lunch meeting."

Pat recognized that he was being dismissed and stood up. He liked the old ambassador.

On the way out, Pat gave Omid a friendly slap on the shoulder, waved at the marine, Colonel Johnson, and smiled at Kay Middleton as he walked into the hallway. He knew they would all talk about him after he left. That was expected with new employees in business and in government. Pat felt good about passing his first day of judgement. Pat handed the reins over to Eddie. His next task fell under Eddie's expertise.

Chapter 12
Pray

Cleo smiled at Pat as he approached her desk.

Pat returned the smile and pointed to the door, "Is Neal in?"

When she nodded, Pat approached the door.

Cleo panicked, "I have to announce you."

Pat turned and assured her, "That won't be necessary with me, unless he has someone in his office." Pat looked into her eyes for an answer.

She said, "He's alone. But please let me announce you."

Pat noticed the door was cracked open a few inches this time. He knocked and opened the door without waiting for a response. He leaned in, his hand still on the doorknob, "Neal, I need some advice. Can you spare a few minutes?"

Cleo's jaw dropped when she heard the Colonel Williams say, "Sure, Pat. Come in."

Pat noticed that Williams was now in his dress military uniform. He sat down across the desk from him, "Neal, this is the first time my wife has traveled overseas with me. We have a four year old son and a nine month old daughter. I'm concerned about them adjusting to this environment."

Neal glared at Pat, "Did Andy tell you about my family problems?"

Very perceptive! Eddie didn't return the glare like Pat would have. "He mentioned it without offering any details. I had already noticed the lighter tanning around your ring finger where you used to wear your wedding band. The ambassador made it very clear to me how much he respects you."

Neal was disarmed by the compliment. He raised his left hand and for the first time paid attention to the effects of removing his wedding band. He was surprised that O'Sheen had noticed it.

Pat continued, "My family is very important to me. More important than my military career."

When Neal didn't respond, Eddie continued, "Do you and your wife have children?"

"We have two." Neal couldn't believe how he involuntarily answered the question. His dander started rising.

Pat looked around the room, "Do you have pictures of your kids." He knew he had hit a sensitive nerve.

Neal glared at Pat, but O'Sheen refused to lock eyes with him again. He realized that O'Sheen was trying to be his friend. No one had tried that for almost a year. Almost involuntarily again, he rolled his chair back and opened his middle drawer. He withdrew an 8 x 10 framed picture and handed it across to Pat.

Pat looked at a picture of a good looking boy about ten years old and a pretty blond girl about six. "They are beautiful. You must miss them something awful."

Williams shield cracked open, "I do. I had to put the picture in the drawer because seeing it tears me apart. My wife refused to bring the kids to Iran, which made me angry. She knows what it means to be a military wife. That was a year ago. Now the bitch has asked for a divorce." Moisture entered his eyes. He couldn't believe he was sharing with this stranger.

Pat said, "I can see that you still love her. My wife has already accused me of putting my country ahead of my family."

Neal looked up into Pat's eyes. This time O'Sheen maintained eye contact with warmth expressed in his eyes. Neal found it hard to believe that this was the same man who had confronted him so challengingly first thing this morning. He looked down at his watch, "I have an appointment for lunch."

Pat didn't want to lose momentum, "Ambassador Sullivan cares deeply for you. I think he would have you reassigned so that you can rejoin your family rather than keep you captive here to prove your loyalty to him."

Neal said a little testily, "I thought you came in here **for** advice, not to **give** advice."

Pat said, "You gave me the advice I was seeking. I will do my best to make sure I never lose my family by putting my career first. Thank you, Neal." He stood up, saluted, and left the room.

Neal mused while watching the unpredictable O'Sheen gracefully walk out of his office.

Pat talked to Cleo until Neal walked out for his lunch appointment.

Neal exited his office and said as he walked past, "Thanks, Pat."

Cleo's jaw dropped. Pat chuckled at her surprise.

Pat walked to a window that looked out of the front of the embassy.

Cleo walked up next to him and watched as the ambassador and the colonel climbed into the back seat of a sedan. She said, "You seem to like him."

"I do. He has had a tough year without his wife and kids here. I am not sure that I could handle that."

"Did you know him before coming here?"

"No. I just met him this morning."

Cleo squeezed Pat's forearm and smiled up at him.

Pat looked at his watch on the way up to the second floor. It was almost noon. He caught Omid before he left his desk.

"Omid, I need an interpreter."

"It is time for Zuhr (midday prayers) here in the embassy."

"May I join you?"

Omid smiled. "Yes."

Pat followed Omid to the hallway and in through the next hallway door on the right. The room was empty except for one small palazzo pub table against a side wall. There were two Iranian men in the room. Omid introduced Pat.

Omid walked to a corner and selected two rolled up prayer rugs from a pile. He handed one to Pat, "You can use Amir's prayer rug."

Pat accepted the rug, "Thanks. What about wudu?"

As if on cue, Cleo walked in with a bowl of water. She was shocked to see Pat. She set the bowl on the skinny palazzo table.

Pat removed his shoes and socks. Being new to the group, he performed wudu ritual washing first. He bowed his head for several seconds, then he cupped his right hand and dipped it in the bowl and lifted out some water, poured the water over his forehead and wiped his hand down his face.

He lifted some more water out with a cupped left hand, poured the water on his right forearm and wiped his left hand down to the tips of his right fingers. He repeated that on his left forearm and hand.

He wiped his hands on the hair on the front half of his scalp, wiped the top of his right foot from the toes up to his ankle with his right hand and repeated with his left hand on his left foot. He stepped aside so Omid could perform his purification.

Pat unrolled his rug on the floor and faced in the general direction of Mecca. Omid unrolled his rug next to Pat, and faced Mecca. Pat had to turn his rug slightly.

When they were all washed and lined up, Omid announced in Arabic, *"I intend to say 3 Sunnah, 3 Fard, 3 Sunnah, 3 Nafl Rak'ahs of Salatul Dhuhr for Allah facing al-Ka'bah."*

They all raised their hands to their ears and started with the first Rak'ah (unit of prayer) saying together,

Allahu Ackbar (Allah is the greatest)

They placed their right hand over their left, below their navels. *Subhanakallähumma wa bi hamdika wa tabarakasmuka wa ta'ala jadduka wa la ilaha ghairuka* (O Allah, glory and praise are for you, and blessed is your name, and high is your majesty, and none is worthy of worship but you.)

They bowed down and said, *Allahu Ackbar* again and then some more prayers in Arabic.

They put their hands on their knees and said more prayers, stood upright and said more prayers, got prostrate with forehead, nose, palms, knees, and toes touching the floor and said, *Allahu Ackbar* again, and some more Arabic prayers.

They sat upright with knees bent, hand on knees, said a short prayer, went prostrate as before and said, *Allahu Ackbar* again, then repeated the following Tasbih three times:

Subbana rabbiyal-a'la (Oh Allah, glory be to you, the most high).

60

They prayed two more Rak'ahs and rolled up their rugs. Pat and Omid went back to Omid's desk.

Pat said in Farsi, "Can I buy your lunch? I am not familiar with Iranian cuisine. Where were you planning to eat lunch?"

"I normally eat in the cafeteria in the basement."

Pat shook his head, "Can you show me someplace to eat away from the embassy, preferably with good Persian food. I'll buy."

Omid smiled and accepted.

Pat stopped at Kay's desk. "Kay, Omid and I are going out to lunch. Omid has agreed to give me some advice for moving through Iran. We may be gone for an hour or more."

Pat walked next to Omid to a family-owned restaurant four blocks from the embassy. Omid had been there before and made three or four meal recommendations. There were no pork dishes of course. When the waiter took the order that Omid recommended, Pat held onto the menu. He started reading it to Omid starting from the top. Omid corrected his pronunciations, and explained the food in each menu item. They were halfway through the menu when their lunch was served. They talked about the people in the embassy over lunch. Pat finished going through the menu after lunch and then started asking about sacred sites and popular places to see in Iran. Two hours after they left the embassy, Omid became uncomfortable being gone for so long and suggested that they return. Pat agreed.

When they got back to Omid's desk, Pat asked Omid where he could buy a prayer rug. Omid told him of a place near Pat's neighborhood.

The ambassador saw Pat and called him into his office. Pat was concerned when the ambassador closed the door after Pat entered.

Chapter 13
Close of the first day

Ambassador Sullivan motioned for Pat to sit on the couch again, and he sat in the same chair as before. "Pat, I heard that you shared midday prayers . . ." He got stuck trying to come up with the word. "What do they call them?"

"Omid calls them Zuhr. In Arabic they are called Dhuhr."

"So you speak Arabic, too?"

"Yes sir."

"Any other languages?"

"I'm fluent in Vietnamese, Khmer, and Chinese. All three of those languages are similar. I'm fluent in French and I can handle Spanish and Italian because they are all Latin based languages."

"You're not pulling my leg are you?"

"No sir.

Pat added, "Farsi, Urdu, and Arabic are all similar."

"When did you become a Muslim?"

"I'm not. I am a devout Catholic, sir. But, I love the Muslim daily prayers. I believe in praising God in every way possible. And, when in Rome . . ." Pat said no more.

There was nothing in the file that said Pat was religious—just a warrior. Fascinating. It was like O'Sheen had two separate personalities. Sullivan released a rare chuckle. "If you ever decide to get out of the Army, you should consider diplomatic service."

Pat chucked, "Sir, sometimes I'm not very diplomatic."

"So Neal tells me. But, you sure made one hell of an impression on him."

"I like Neal, sir. I think he needs to get reassigned to where his wife will agree to join him. I believe that he still loves her, and I know he loves and misses his kids."

Sullivan stared at the sophisticated young man who didn't hesitate to say what was on his mind. "It seems you have learned a lot about my people here on your first day in the embassy."

"You have a great crew, sir. I'm sure that you have earned their loyalty."

The ambassador stood, "I hope to earn yours. If you feel the need, you can come directly to me at any time."

"Thank you, sir." Pat knew a dismissal statement when he heard one. When Sullivan didn't follow him to the door, he turned, "Do you want me to close the door?"

"No. Leave it open."

Pat spent the rest of the afternoon organizing his office. He read the tabs on the files, but didn't take the time to open many of them.

Pat stopped and purchased a Muslim prayer rug on his walk home. He had to negotiate the price for the one he wanted. He was learning more of the Tehran accent and the local Farsi with each encounter.

When Pat walked through the front door, he dropped the prayer rug to the floor and stretched out his hands as Scott ran and jumped into his arms. For some reason, the picture of Colonel Williams' children flashed through his mind. Dale wasn't right behind Scott to greet him as usual. He was about to ask Scott where she was when he saw her walking toward the door.

She smiled and shrugged, "I was in the bathroom."

Pat switched Scott to his left arm and kissed his sexy wife.

Dale thought that it was Eddie and not Pat who came home. She expected Pat to take over on the first day of a new job in a foreign country. But she also knew that Pat was learning to imitate Eddie.

She looked down at the partially rolled up throw rug on the floor and smiled. "How did you know I wanted a small rug for the kitchen?"

Pat chuckled, "It's not for the kitchen. It's a Muslim prayer rug."

"A Muslim prayer rug? Why would you buy that?"

Pat said, "Because I had to borrow one to say midday prayers in the embassy today. And I'm going to a mosque on Friday and will need one." He walked past her toward their small living room.

Dale knew that Pat was in control. Pat didn't talk about his work. She needed Eddie tonight, not Pat."

Pat carried Scott to their small couch. "Is your sister taking a nap?"

"Yes. She sleeps a lot."

Dale watched from behind as Scott did his magic on Pat. Pat became totally absorbed with his son.

She calmed, "I'll get dinner ready."

He looked over his shoulder, "Thank you, Hon."

She smiled. Pat never called her "Hon", only Eddie called her Hon.

They both put Scott to bed before they ate a late dinner.

When they sat down at the small kitchenette table, Dale probed, "How was your first day?"

He looked at her with concern, "I want to hear about your day first."

Pat was not that sensitive to her needs, "Eddie, I really like our neighbor, Norma Jean Reese. She knocked on our door this morning after you left and invited us to go with her and her three year old daughter, Jessie, to a park a few blocks away. The park was beautiful and had swings, a slide, and a sand box for the kids. I felt like I was back in America. Scott and Jessie loved playing with each other. Apparently, there are no other American kids their age living near here. Norma Jean is very happy that Scott is here to play with her daughter, and I am happy that we have such good neighbors."

Eddie glowed with relief at the great news. "How did you get food to cook supper tonight?"

"Norma Jean has an old car and drove us to a market. They spoke some English there, and Norma Jean knows some Farsi. The merchants were very nice to us and doted over Scott, Amanda, and Jessie. To be honest, I was quite shocked. Living here is going to be much more pleasant than I expected."

Pat smiled and let out a big sigh of relief.

She knew his worry about her was satisfied and said, "Now—how was your first day?"

He gave a short reply, "It started out rocky, but everything worked out. I had a very good day." He saw her skepticism. "Dale. Pat and I both had a very good day."

Dale knew she had to press Eddie to get more. "Why did it start out rocky?"

"My new boss made me wait for twenty minutes to see him. I could see the lighted buttons on his secretary's phone and knew he wasn't on a phone call. When I went in, he was a grumpy and rude. I wasn't surprised based on what some of the people said about him at our welcoming party at the Reese's last night. But Pat was able to straighten him out."

Dale's eyebrows rose, "How did he do that?" She was used to Eddie referring to his alter ego in the third person.

"When Colonel Williams told Pat that he couldn't sneeze in Iran without his permission, Pat faked one of Grosspoppi's sneezes."

Dale chuckled, "That sounds like Pat."

He continued, "Pat demanded to know why he was kept waiting for twenty minutes. Williams came storming around his desk with his hands balled up into fists. Pat warned Williams not to mess with him. He was ready to knock the Colonel's teeth out, and the Colonel knew it. But, I managed to calm Pat down and instead of punching him, Pat offered a handshake. Williams accepted it. Then he sat down on Pat's side of the desk and told Pat to call him Neal."

"Wow!"

"After that meeting ended amicably, Pat met with Ambassador Sullivan and Station Chief Middleton. Do you remember Hal and Kay Middleton from last night?"

"Yes. Kay was very nice."

Pat said, "She works in the embassy.

"Anyway, the ambassador told Pat that Neal had marital problems and to cut him some slack. I went back to see Neal."

"You, not Pat?" She was getting better at determining which one of his personalities he was in.

"Yes. Pat turned things back over to me."

"Voluntarily?"

"I think so. He has been doing that more often lately."

Dale said, "I'm starting to love him more and more."

"Not more than me, I hope."

"Not **more** than you, but **because** of you."

"Well, he loves you, too."

Dale smiled, "Which means he is starting to love you."

Eddie laughed, "Pat and I have been getting along pretty well lately." He involuntarily fell into a spontaneous, boisterous laugh. His laugh exceeded the levity of the conversation.

Dale said, "What is so funny?

"If this place is bugged and someone is recording this conversation, the embassy will send me to a psych ward."

Dale burst out laughing and they hugged.

Pat told her about getting Neal to talk about his family and about telling the ambassador that he should get Neal reassigned to a place where his wife and kids will rejoin him.

Dale smiled, "You may be the nicest guy in the world."

Chapter 14
Rita

Neal Williams met Rita almost twenty years ago in Columbus, Georgia, after he finished basic training at Fort Benning. They met in a crowded restaurant while waiting in the bar for a table. Neal suggested that Rita and her girlfriend have dinner with him and his army buddy to save table space for the other people waiting. The pickup line worked and the rest was history.

Rita's father died from cancer two years ago while they were stationed at the embassy in Laos. She felt terrible about not being home for his last days. They took their kids to Laverne, Georgia, for the funeral. Rita and the kids stayed in Laverne with her mom for a few weeks after Neal returned to Laos.

When the Laos Ambassador, Andrew Sullivan, accepted the ambassadorship in Iran, Neal volunteered to go with him over Rita's objections. Rita and the kids stayed at her mom's house in Laverne while Neal set up a homestead in Tehran. When Neal called to make arrangements for them to fly to Iran, she informed him that they weren't coming—that she had already registered the kids for school in Laverne. After a few months, she started begging Neal to ask for an assignment somewhere else. She still refused to let her kids live in a Middle Eastern Muslim country. Neal refused to ask for a reassignment. He had to remain loyal to Andy Sullivan for his diplomatic career. Months later, she told him she wanted a divorce, hoping that would force him to recommit to their failing marriage. Neal got very angry, and now would only talk to her for a few seconds when he called to talk to the kids. Talking to Neal about his career choice to stay in Iran was off limits.

Neal looked at his watch—eight p.m., which was nine-thirty a.m. in Laverne. He called Rita. Her mother answered the phone and said the kids were in school. She was surprised when Neal asked to talk to Rita.

Rita came on the line lacking enthusiasm, "Hi, Neal."

Neal took a deep breath, "Hi, Rita. I miss you and the kids something awful." He used the same words Pat had used that morning.

Rita noticed the "you" in front of "the kids". His attitude sounded totally different from his normal tone to her when he called the kids. Her woman's intuition sensed something happened to Neal that changed his attitude . . . something that was bringing him back to her.

A tear streamed down her cheek "We miss you, too." She said. "Are you coming for a visit?"

Neal said, "I want to tell you about today before I answer that."

The tone of his voice concerned her. Maybe her woman's intuition was wrong, "Why?"

Neal spoke so softly that she had to listen closely to hear every word, "A new Army intelligence officer, Major Pat O'Sheen, started working for me here at the embassy this morning. Our first encounter almost came to fisticuffs. I'm not sure if he or I backed off first, but he earned my respect in the first few minutes. I knew that Pat was declared a war hero many times in Vietnam and that he had a reputation for fearlessly speaking his mind, even to generals. He smiled and shook my hand as if I had been his long-time friend.

"He left my office to meet the other members of the embassy staff. He returned to my office before lunch, stuck his head in the door, and asked if I had a few minutes to give him some advice."

Neal stopped, not sure if his wife wanted to hear any more of his story.

Rita sensed a passion in her estranged husband's story. "What happened?"

Neal was encouraged and continued, "Pat, his wife, and two young kids just flew into Tehran yesterday. He was worried because this was his wife's first time to live overseas.

"Rita, I knew that Pat had just come from a meeting with the ambassador, and suspected he was bringing up family matters because Andy had told him about our problems. When I asked Pat, he admitted that Andy had mentioned it. O'Sheen had the gall to tell me that he hoped he would never put his career ahead of his family—a backward way of accusing me of doing just that. I got mad at him, but I knew he was right."

Neal took a big breath to build up more courage. "I love you, Rita. I've been such a fool. Do you think that you could ever forgive me?"

Rita started sobbing, "I love you, Neal. And, God knows how much I miss you." She struggled to find her voice. She had almost given up hope that this moment would ever happen. "I think O'Sheen was an answer to my prayers. Thank him for me."

Neil said, "I will. And, I'm going to talk to Andy and see if I can get flights to Fort Benning. Is that okay?" He thought about saying that he'd get a motel room.

She got control of her sobs before answering, "Yes. My bed is so cold at night."

Neal sighed at the invitation. "I'll call you when it's tonight over there; when I can talk to the kids. And I'll let you know what Andy says."

They talked for five more minutes. When they disconnected, Neal called the ambassador's quarters.

Andy was thrilled at the news, "Come to my office first thing in the morning and we will work out the details."

"Thanks, Andy."

The next morning, after starting the ball rolling for his trip to America, Neal looked in the open door to Pat's office and saw him going through a thick file on his desk. When he started to walk through the door, Pat stood up and saluted. Pat was making a special effort to recover from his disrespect during their first encounter.

Neal said, "Saluting me is not necessary, Pat. I just came in to thank you. But more importantly, my wife asked me to thank you."

A big, sincere smile spread across Pat's face. "You talked to her last night? Do you want to tell me about it?" He walked around the desk.

Neal was a bit surprised by Pat's interest. He turned and closed the door. When he turned back, he asked, "Pat, are you a religious man."

Pat shared, "Yes. I was planning to become a priest before I met Dale and fell in love with her. Why do you ask?"

"Rita believes that your showing up here was an answer to her prayers to save our marriage."

Pat chuckled, "Neal, I just say what I feel—what I believe. Sometimes it gets me in big trouble."

Neal sat down and Pat turned a chair toward him and sat down. Neal told him almost verbatim his conversation with Rita. Pat didn't interrupt his monologue.

Neal finished, "From me and my family, thank you, Pat."

Pat smiled warmly and stood up, "Neal. I believe you and your wife will work it out. I am very happy for you and your family."

Neal stood up, "Pat, you have no idea how much I appreciate what you have done for us." Neal left the room with moisture in his eyes.

Eddie conveyed to his alter ego, *did you learn anything from that, Pat?*

Eddie got a sharp pain in his gut that lasted less than a second. He smiled at Pat's understanding.

***

Ambassador Sullivan answered his phone, "Yes, Kay?"

"Andy, General Haig wants to talk to you." Her voice betrayed her surprise.

"Really? Put him through." He hung up and picked up when it rang again.

Andy answered as he always did. "Ambassador Sullivan."

"Andy, its Al Haig."

"Hello, Al. How is my old boss doing?"

"I'm not old."

"I meant my past boss."

"I haven't passed away yet, either. You mean your former boss."

Andy laughed, "I see that you are still a stickler for choosing the right words."

"Words have meanings, Andy. Using wrong words can get you in big trouble."

Andy laughed again, "I have missed your tutelage, Al. To what do I owe this unexpected pleasure?" Andy had enjoyed working for Haig when Al was the White House Chief of Staff. Haig had extremely high standards.

Haig said, "Have you met Pat O'Sheen, yet?"

"I met with him twice yesterday. He's quite a remarkable young man. What is your interest in him?"

"I sent him there. Andy, he is one of a kind, the best warrior I've ever met and a brilliant linguist."

Andy said, "My staff has already testified to his remarkable language skills."

"Andy, he is also very innovative. I want you to make sure he is given a lot of latitude over there to do things his way. Don't let anyone stifle his creativity."

"That is extremely high praise for a major. Al, is he a relative of yours?"

"No, I wish I could claim his genes."

Sullivan couldn't believe the accolades that Haig was heaping on the young soldier.

Andy added to the accolades, "Al, O'Sheen is very outspoken. He isn't afraid to say what's on his mind." He explained, "One of my close friends, Colonel Neal Williams, is his C-O over here. Pat got in Neal's face when they first met, challenging his authority. O'Sheen warned Neal to stay out of his way. The affront won Neal's respect."

General Haig smiled. O'Sheen was goal oriented and never gave a crap about military protocol.

The ambassador continued, "Al, when I met Pat, I told him to give Colonel Williams some slack because he is going through some family problems. Pat went back to Colonel Williams' office and chastised him in a diplomatic way, saying that he would never put his career ahead of his family. As a result, Williams called his wife last night. I think O'Sheen might have helped save their marriage."

Al said, "I knew he was a warrior. I had no idea he had a soft heart."

"He does, Al. Pat has already won the friendship of many of the Iranians in the embassy by saying the midday Muslim prayers with them. Pat did all that on his first day here. Where in the hell did you find him?"

Al knew that Andy was sufficiently impressed with O'Sheen and would give him enough leeway. He answered Andy's question, "A CIA agent in Vietnam found him. Most of what they did together is still classified, but the agent found a jewel in the dung hole of that war.

"Andy, Pat has already impressed two Presidents. He turned down the Medal-of-honor from President Ford—that is still classified. It won't be long before President Carter needs his talents. Take care of him.

71

He has no political ambitions, and therefore he lacks your diplomatic tact. You may have to excuse his insolence from time to time."

Sullivan never put up with insolence. "I won't allow him to disrupt the agreements we have established with the Shah's regime. Al, why did you send him here?"

General Haig understood the ambassador's concern. "Andy, O'Sheen is an asset we need to develop. He has a unique ability to see the big picture and then put all of the pieces together.

"One more thing, Andy. We never had this conversation. The reason for my call is that most information on O'Sheen is classified unless cleared in advance."

"Yes sir. I understand."

Haig disconnected.

Sullivan sat there stunned. He was impressed with Pat, but he had no idea that the young major had already impressed people in the top levels of the U.S. military and presidents of the United States. The words *turned down the Medal-of-honor* echoed through his mind. *Why would a soldier do that?*

Chapter 15
The Imam

Pat wore civilian clothes as he spent the next day walking the streets of Tehran, visiting some of the beautiful areas that Omid had suggested, and some of the rough, ugly neighborhoods that Omid warned him to avoid. Pat talked to several people in every place he visited.

By noon, Pat started to mimic the local dialect and his skin was dark enough that after noon no one suspected that he was a foreigner. He moved into the poor neighborhoods that Pat found more informative, where the people weren't concerned with Islamic revolution, but did hate the Shah, blaming their miserable plight on him. They were ripe for manipulation.

When Pat returned home, Scott didn't run to greet him. He heard voices on the back porch. He smiled, happy that Dale made friends so easily. He went into the bathroom and relieved his bladder, then he walked onto the back porch. Norma Jean was sitting next to Dale, and his intrusion interrupted their conversation. Her husband Jim Reese was sitting in a chair next to his wife. Pat knew that Jim had followed him through Tehran until he went into the rough neighborhoods. Jim was good at surveillance, but Pat was on high alert in a strange country and picked up his surveillance early that morning. He had no reason to lose Jim's tail.

Scott ran up the two back stairs and jumped into his daddy's arms.

At the same time, Dale jumped up and hugged him. She immediately knew that it was Pat who returned home and not Eddie. She said, "Norma Jean took me to a place to buy wine. Do you want a glass?" When Pat nodded, she headed for the kitchen.

Pat reached into the small play pen and picked up Amanda who was smiling from ear to ear. Pat sat down in a chair next to Jim Reese with Mandy on his lap.

Jim asked, "How was your day?"

"Very good. You know how my morning went. My afternoon was similar, except I talked to the poorer people of the city during most of the afternoon."

Jim picked up his wine glass. He was embarrassed, "You knew I was following you?"

"I didn't mind. We all have to answer to someone. Who do you answer to?"

"Hal Middleton, and of course, we all answer to Ambassador Sullivan."

Pat smiled. Jim cleverly avoided revealing who had told him to tail him. Pat had already surmised that Jim was CIA, not just a low level diplomat as he had first introduced himself.

Jim said, "Pat, there are some sections of town you should avoid, particularly on foot."

"Omid told me which ones. I wondered if you would follow me into them."

Jim smiled, "One stranger on foot in those neighborhoods is noticeable. Two would have stood out too much, putting us both in jeopardy."

Pat chuckled. Jim was definitely CIA trained.

Dale walked out with his glass of wine. Dale sat down where they both could see Scott playing with Jesse in the back yard.

Jim asked, "Well Pat, did you learn anything from the locals today?"

Pat smiled at Dale when she looked at him. "I learned that the Shah isn't very popular in Tehran. The poorer people were more open about their hatred for him. Was he ever very popular?"

Jim shook his head, "He was never very popular with the Islamic clergy because of his secular rule and the modernization of Iran—westernization if you will. His reforms alienated the landowners and didn't really help the plight of the working class as planned. He is definitely losing the support of the masses. But the SAVAK have maintained control. I understand that there are over two-thousand political prisoners in jail."

Dale changed the subject, "Pat, Jim and Norma Jean are both from Kansas."

Norma Jean jumped in, "Jim and I met at the University of Kansas."

Pat chuckled. Enough business talk. They talked of personal subjects over two glasses of wine. The women didn't learn much new. They were just updating their men.

The next morning, Pat arranged for a pool car. Ambassador Sullivan walked into Pat's office, and Pat stood up to greet him.

"Pat, my wife and I would like to invite you and your wife to join us for dinner. Are you available tomorrow night?"

"Yes, sir. We will have to ask someone to watch our kids."

"Bring them along. We have a fifteen-year-old daughter who will watch them."

Pat smiled, "Sounds great. What time?"

"Plan to get here between seven and seven–thirty."

"We will. Thank you, sir. I am honored."

"We are looking forward to meeting your family." Andy left Pat's office.

Pat drove to places too far to walk to in a timely manner, so he could get more familiar with Tehran and its people. He got home a little later than normal, and Dale was already cooking dinner.

After sharing hugs, Pat said, "The Ambassador invited us to the embassy for dinner with him and his wife tomorrow night."

"Really! I'll ask Norma Jean if she can keep the kids for us."

Pat shook his head, "The ambassador has a daughter who will watch them. Scott will get a kick out of seeing where I work."

"I will too. But what should I wear?"

"How about your blue evening dress?"

"I thought you didn't want me to wear sleeveless dresses over here that expose too much skin."

"We are going to the U.S. Embassy, not out on the town."

The next morning, Pat considered wearing his military uniform to the embassy. He knew that if he did, Omid and Amir would not let him accompany them to the mosque. He wasn't afraid to go to the mosque alone in his uniform. He wanted to gage the attitude of the Iranians toward Americans.

Dale walked into the bathroom and saw Pat standing in his briefs, with his cute butt and muscular back toward her, staring into their tiny closet. She put her arms around his waist, her hands on his flat abs and hugged him from behind. "Good morning."

Pat crossed his hands and put the palms of his hand on the back of her hands and pressed them tighter to his abs, "Good morning."

Dale freed her hands and ran them up to his muscular pecs, "Can you be late for work this morning?"

Pat grabbed her right wrist and ran her hand down to his groin, "I can't show up at work like this."

Pat made sweet, tender love to his wife. She didn't restrain her vocals when she reached orgasm. He tried to restrain his voice when her climax caused his, knowing that the walls in the house were thin.

Minutes later, Scott twisted their bedroom doorknob.

Pat heard him and pulled up the sheet to cover their naked bodies. Scott opened the door and ran into the room, worried about his mom's groans.

Scott saw his daddy and climbed up on the bed smiling. He was not used to seeing his dad in the morning.

Pat put on civilian clothes. Pat could enter the mosque in his military uniform anytime in the future without offending Omid and Amir. Pat went up to talk to them before going down to his office.

When he walked back down to his office, Pat said, "Good morning, Cleo."

Cleo smiled at him, "Good morning, Pat."

Neal's door was all the way opened this time. When Pat stuck his head in the door, Neil smiled at Pat and waved him into his office. "Good morning, Pat. Please close the door."

"Good morning, Neal." Pat closed the door and sat down across from Neal.

"Pat, I'm flying to Germany on Sunday and catching a military flight to Fort Benning."

Pat knew Laverne, Georgia was close to Fort Benning. "I hope everything goes well with your wife and kids."

"Thank you.

"Pat, General Swanson asked for a progress report on you. Apparently, you know him?"

"Yes. He commanded a couple of POW rescue missions I worked on."

Pat didn't want to talk about the rescues, which reminded him of his best friend Mike Burkowski getting killed. "What did you tell him, Neal?"

"I was pretty vague and told him that you were getting to know the people in Tehran and learning how to get around. You need to tell me more about what you are doing, in case he asks again."

Pat debated with Eddie about how much to expose. Eddie won the two-second debate inside his head. Eddie said, "You told him right, Neal. My goals are to determine the stability of Shah's regime and to be able to pass for a local Iranian in case that ever becomes necessary. There is no doubt in my mind that devout Islamists are against the Shah. I've been here less than a week, so I'm just getting started. I am going to the mosque with Omid and Amir at noon. I hope to learn more there."

Neal was shocked, "You're going to the mosque for midday prayers?"

Pat was surprised that Neal hadn't heard that he had been sharing midday prayers with the Muslims in the embassy. "Neal, I learned all five of the Muslim daily prayer rituals from my Arabic teacher in Virginia. I've already shared mid-day prayers with the Muslims here in the embassy."

Pat changed subjects, "When are you getting back from America?"

"Two weeks from Monday, if all goes well. Sooner if it doesn't"

"Well, good luck." Pat stood up and left Neal's office.

Pat, Omid, and Amir got to the mosque just minutes before the start of prayers. The back of the room was full, so Omid led them up the right side to the front. Pat rolled his prayer rug out next to Omid's, and Amir laid his to Pat's right. Friday was the Muslim day of assembly, instead of Saturday for Jew's, and Sunday for Christians. Pat knew the prayer ritual changed on Friday, with the Jumu'ah prayers replacing the Zuhr.

The muezzin chanted out the second adhan (call to prayer). Three minutes later, the imam stood and said, "Al-hamdu li'llāh. " (Praise belongs to Allah) and gave his first of two sermons. In the service, he invoked peace and blessings on Muhammed and read part of the Qur'an and interpreted it. Then the imam admonished the congregation to be pious and said a prayer on behalf of the faithful. The imam sat down. The congregation prayed in silence.

Two minutes later, the imam stood again, said, "Al-hamdu li'llāh. " He gave a short second sermon very similar to the first and at the end named one of the faithful who had died, and two who were recently put in prison. A grumble passed through the mosque.

Then the imam led the congregation in reciting two Rak'ahs instead of three, like in the Zuhr prayers said on other days.

The imam noticed a new man in his congregation and approached Amir and Omid at the end of the service.

Omid handled the introduction, "Imam Sahib, this Pat O'Sheen."

The imam smiled and offered his hand, "You have an American name."

Pat smiled and shook his hand, "Yes. I just arrived in your country on Sunday."

"You don't sound like an American."

"I initially learned Arabic to say the Muslim prayers, and then kept studying Islam. Farsi was easy to learn after learning Arabic."

"I assume you work at the embassy with Omid and Amir. What do you do there?"

"I work for the military attaché, Colonel Williams. I am a major in the U. S. Army."

"Ah! So you are a military intelligence officer. What intelligence are you hoping to gather?"

Pat was growing fonder of the imam with every exchange. Imam Sahib had not yet diverted his eyes from Pat's. Pat smiled, knowing the imam was gathering intelligence, too. "I am hungry. I will buy your lunch if you will join me, and we can continue talking."

Pat extended the invitation to Omid and Amir. They declined, saying that they had already eaten.

Imam Sahib had never met an American before who prayed Muslim prayers in his mosque, and who answered his inquiries so honestly without reservation. Sahib was fascinated and agreed to have lunch with Pat.

They walked to the same restaurant Omid had taken Pat to on Monday. The restaurant owner and his wife knew the imam and gave them personalized service. Before and while eating lunch, Pat and the imam talked of their childhoods, their educations, Pat's war service, their families and children, and many other subjects about their pasts. The imam was easy to talk to and showed a real interest in Pat. After eating, they talked about politics, the Shah, and Islam. After another thirty minutes, the imam had to depart for other commitments.

Chapter 16
Dale's entrance

Back at the embassy, Pat told Neal about his lunch with Imam Sahib.

When Pat stood up to leave, Neal said, "I look forward to meeting your wife and son at dinner tonight."

"I didn't know you would be there. I'll warn Dale." Pat laughed when Neal started laughing. "Is anyone else coming?"

"I'm not sure. Hal and Kay might be there."

"Neal, Dale is wondering what to wear?"

"I think a cocktail dress would be appropriate."

"Maybe once we get here. But what about on the walk over?"

"Pat, take a pool car home and drive her over here." Neal had not yet met Dale and was wondering how hot she looked in a cocktail dress if Pat was worried about her walking the few blocks to the embassy.

"Thanks, Neal. Would you call and approve it?" Neal had to approve Pat's use of a pool car.

"Sure."

Pat wanted to try to meet the Iranians that lived near his neighborhood. Most of the Muslims near his neighborhood would not be working today, on their Islamic day of gathering.

Pat wandered around the neighborhood having short conversations with men playing with their children in the streets. He saw four men sitting on a front porch. Pat stopped and said, "Allahu Akbar." He got a weak response.

Pat announced from the street, twenty feet from the front porch, "I just moved my family into the neighborhood. I am hoping to find friends here."

Three of the guys were sympathetic and turned to look at a big man who Pat surmised was the owner of the house and the leader of the family. The man, who was about Pat's age, reluctantly stood up and approached Pat. He was four inches taller than Pat and had an aggravated look in his eyes. "When did you move here?"

Pat managed to say meekly, "Six days ago. I'm sorry if I infringed on your privacy. I will move along."

Acceptance was portrayed in the man's eyes without entering the features on his face. The smile that followed was forced.

A teenager trotted down from the porch and interrupted by addressing Pat, "Didn't I see you eating lunch with Imam Sahib today?"

Pat hadn't noticed him at the restaurant and knew he was going to have to improve his visual skills. "Yes. I am very impressed with your imam."

The big man's facial features softened, wondering who this man was who already knew the imam. "Please come up on my porch so we can talk in the shade—out of this hot sun."

The teenager, maybe seventeen years old and trying to grow a beard, offered Pat his seat. Pat accepted. The teenager sat on the top step of the porch.

After the leader sat down, he asked, "Where did you live before you moved here?"

Pat turned it around on him, "You have a slight Arabic accent. Where are you from?" By his reaction, Pat knew that the guy was used to questioning, not being questioned.

The Arab answered, "I was born in Saudi Arabia." He repeated his question more forcefully, "Where are you from?"

Pat smiled, "America. I work at the U.S. Embassy."

The man was surprised. His guest sounded local. "Were your parents Iranians?"

"No. Do you work with SAVAK?" Pat knew by the way he was being questioned that the guy was law enforcement.

The man's eyes bore into Pat's for more than thirty seconds. Pat's eyes didn't yield contact.

Pat smiled into his inquisitors eyes and stretched his hand out, "My name is Pat."

Amusement filled the SAVAK agent's eyes. He admired Pat's timing to break the ice by introducing himself, and realized that he was dealing with a very savvy American intelligence agent—someone he needed to get to know better as part of his job. He smiled and shook Pat's hand, "My name is Jamil."

Jamil asked, "How long have you lived here?"

"Almost a week. I am already learning to love the Iranian people."

Jamil's jaw dropped a bit, "You speak Farsi like a local. What do you do at the embassy?"

"I work for the military attaché. I'm a major in the U.S. Army." Pat knew that Jamil was going to investigate his background. Lying or even slightly hedging would ruin his credibility.

Jamil said, "So you work in military intelligence?"

Pat nodded. His honesty was rewarded with a smile.

The older, silent man sitting on the porch cleared his voice for recognition. Pat had already surmised that all of the men were kin.

Jamil complied with the elder's wish, "Pat, this is my father."

Pat spun in his chair and shook the offered hand. The man looked to be in his mid-fifties. His eyes expressed kindness and interest in Pat.

He said, "My name is Abad. How did you learn to speak Farsi so well?"

His Saudi Arabian accent was much more recognizable than his son.

"I have a knack for languages, sir. Once I learn to think in a language and not have to interpret from English, I can speak it very quickly. I picked up the local dialect by talking to a lot of my neighbors, which is why I am walking around to meet more neighbors today."

Pat changed the focus off himself again, "Is this also your son?" Pat faced the man sitting next to Abad.

"Yes. Pat, this is my son Muhammed."

Muhammed reluctantly offered his hand. Pat shook it enthusiastically, "You have your father's attractive eyes, like your little brother's." Pat smiled at the teenager on the steps. He smiled back, proud to be recognized.

While Pat talked to Jamil's family, Jamil barked an order through the screen door.

Minutes later, Jamil's wife came out with a tray carrying a pitcher of tea and four cups. Her eyes captured Pat's for several seconds as she exited the door and then panned his body, as Pat's eyes scanned hers.

She wore a hijab that covered her hair and lower face, with only her eyes visible, and a chador that went all the way down to her feet. Pat couldn't imagine her looking more enticing if she had come out in hot pants and a halter top. Muslim men apparently didn't have a good grasp on the male psyche. Imagination sparks a man's desire more than exposure to female skin and hair.

Pat spent another thirty minutes on the porch, much of it bantering back and forth with Jamil. Pat liked him and he could tell the feeling was mutual. But it was the observant, mostly silent father, who really captured Pat's attention. He wasn't a fan of the Shah.

Pat walked back to the embassy and drove a pool car back to his small house. Scott greeted him in his nicest clothes. Pat showered and dressed in black pants, highly-polished black shoes, and a long sleeve white shirt.

Dale was in her blue cocktail dress as he exited the bathroom. She turned her back to him, "Zip me up."

Pat second-guessed his earlier thoughts about women being more enticing being covered up. He could tell that Dale was nervous about the dinner with the ambassador. He hugged her from behind. Scott watched from the doorway.

Dale said again nervously, "We don't want to be late. Zip me up."

The guard at the gate recognized Pat and stooped down to see the boy and the woman sitting next to him. He smiled at the beautiful woman and the child in her lap.

Pat chuckled, "Open the gate, Jim."

Jim stood back upright, "Yes sir."

Pat pulled up to front door of the embassy, jumped out, opened Dale's door, picked Amanda off her lap, and offered his hand to help Scott and her out of the car.

Dale realized that Eddie was nervous, too. She had never been to any high level government social gatherings.

The Marine lieutenant snapped to attention as Pat and Dale approached, but his eyes weren't on the superior officer, they were on his beautiful wife.

Pat said, "Hello, Chris."

He looked at Pat for the first time and said, "Hello, Pat."

Pat said, "Chris, this is my wife, Dale."

Dale offered her hand. Chris took it in two of his. "It a real pleasure to meet you, Mrs. O'Sheen."

"What is your last name, Chris?"

"Millikan, ma'am."

"I thought you looked Irish. Where are you from?"

"Near Cincinnati, ma'am."

"It is very nice to meet you, Chris."

"My pleasure."

Chris released her hand. Pat introduced Scott.

Chris shook the boy's hand and turned back to look at Dale. "Who is this precious one asleep in your arms?"

"This is Amanda."

Chris said, "I'll escort you to the ambassador's living quarters." He held the door open for them, led them to a door leading to the private quarters, and knocked on the door.

The ambassador opened the door, "Pat, please come in."

Scott led the way. Pat said, "Ambassador Sullivan, this is Scott and my wife, Dale."

"Hello, Scott. He offered his hand, and Scott grabbed his index finger, shook it, and smiled.

The ambassador turned, "Dale, it's so nice to meet you. Please call me Andy." He shook her offered hand.

His wife walked up next to him. "Pat and Dale, this is my wife, Jane."

She was an eloquent lady in her late forties with black hair. She was dressed in a modest, black cocktail dress.

She extended her hand, "Pat, my husband speaks very highly of you." She shook Pat's hand with a firm grip. "Who is that beautiful girl asleep in your arms?"

"Amanda."

She extended her hand again, "Dale, it is so nice to meet you. I love that blue cocktail dress."

"I love your dress, too. I wanted to wear black, but Eddie wanted me to wear this one."

She saw confusion in Jane's eyes. "I'm sorry. Eddie's Army buddies in Vietnam started calling him by his middle name, Pat. I met him in high school, and I still call him by his first name, Eddie."

Jane smiled, "So, you married your high school sweetheart?"

"Yes, ma'am." Dale's face beamed.

Neal approached. He understood why Pat didn't want to parade Dale through the streets of Tehran in that dress. The strapless dress was held up by its tightness around an hourglass figure. Dale was hot, very hot, and had that "pretty girl next door" manner—not fake glamour.

Pat said, "Dale, this is my C-O, Colonel Neal Williams."

Neal took Dale's hand, bent down and kissed the back of it. "I'm not surprised that Pat married such a beautiful woman."

Dale blushed.

Jane slapped Neal's arm, "You never kissed the back of my hand."

Neal laughed, "Andy could fire me if I kissed the back of your hand. Pat can't." Everybody joined in his laughter, including Hal and Kay who were both approaching. Pat's admiration for Ambassador Sullivan increased.

Andy started to handle the introduction, "Dale, this is Hal Middleton, our station chief, and his wife, Kay."

Dale said, "We met at the Reese's house."

A girl approached. Andy introduced her, "Jenifer, This is the O'Sheen's son, Scott, and their daughter Amanda."

She curtsied somewhat formally and said "Hello" to the adults. She smiled at the boy and said, "Hi Scott."."

Scott said, "Hi, Jenifer."

Jane said, "Jenny, show Scott your playroom."

Dale took Amanda from Pat and followed the kids down a hallway and into a bedroom made into a playroom that contained Lego building blocks, puzzles, and a TV with a VHS tape player that Dale had only seen in stores. A collection of tapes were stacked in the cabinet under the TV.

Dale said, "Jenny, bring him out if he calls for us."

"Okay, Mrs. O'Sheen. You can put Amanda down in a play pen in the next room. I will keep an eye on her."

Dale leaned over with Mandy in her arms and put her free arm around Jenny. "You are so sweet. Thank you."

Jenny smiled into Dale's eyes.

Andy said, "Pat, would you like a drink?"

Pat nodded, "I don't guess you have any bourbon?"

"Yes, I do." He led Pat to a cabinet and pulled out a fifth of Maker's Mark.

Pat smiled, "How can I get my hands on a couple bottles of these?"

"I'll give you one before you leave tonight." When Pat looked surprised, Andy added, "We can at least provide some of the comforts of home when we drop someone's family off in a foreign country."

Pat thanked him.

Dale added a breath of fresh air by drawing the conversations away from embassy business and politics. She wanted to know what to visit in Iran, what she should wear, and how she should act when out with her husband. As usual, Dale was the center of attention.

After an excellent lamb dinner cooked by the embassy staff, Jane brought out a hijab. She showed Dale how to put on the hijab to cover her hair and veil her face.

Neal suggested that she wear the hijab when visiting religious shrines. Kay agreed.

Chapter 17
Mass

The next day, Pat went out shopping with Norma Jean and Dale to buy Dale a hijab to veil her face. Dale already had a few headscarves. Norma Jean suggested that Pat stay out of the women's store . . . that it might not be appropriate. Pat saw two men sitting on a bench. He approached and said, "Hello. Are your wives shopping in there, too?"

Scott looked at his dad oddly. Pat smiled at him, realizing that Scott rarely heard him speak in Farsi.

The younger man nodded.

The older man, who looked like the younger man's father, said, "Yes. We always wait out here." He addressed Scott, "Hello, young man. What is your name?"

Scott thought the man addressed him, but he didn't understand. He looked up at Pat.

Pat interpreted, "Scott, he said 'Hello, young man. What is your name?'"

Scott smiled at his daddy and then at the man, "Scott O'Sheen."

The man looked at Pat, "Scott O'Sheen? Is that his name?"

"Yes. We just moved here from America. I am Pat O'Sheen."

The young man said, "You sound like a local."

"Thank you. I have already learned to like Iran very much. The people here are very nice."

The older man said, "A lot of Iranians don't like Americans."

"Is that how you feel?"

"I have nothing personally against you, but your country supports the Shah."

"Father, hush."

The father's look reprimanded the son. "The Shah put your younger brother in prison."

Pat interrupted, "I have met a lot of Iranians that feel as you do. What is your other son's name?"

The son said, "Why do you want to know?"

"I work at the American Embassy. Perhaps I can help in some way."

The father smiled, "What do you do at the embassy."

"I work for the military attaché. I am in the army."

The father told his son to slide over, and he slid over making room, "Pat, please sit down so we can talk."

Scott jumped up on his dad's lap. He smiled at the bearded man.

The father smiled and pretended to snatch Scott's nose, holding his thumb between two knuckles, and presenting it to Scott like it was his nose. He said, "I got your nose."

When Pat interpreted, Scott reached up and felt his nose. He laughed and said, "Uh, Uh." He leaned over and felt the man's beard.

Pat said, "No, Scott."

"It's okay, Pat. I love kids."

The man introduced himself and his son. He gave Pat his younger son's name and explained that he was jailed six months ago for saying that he opposed the Shah to the wrong man. The boy was only twenty-years-old: nineteen when he was arrested. The man explained some of the difficulties in finding out anything from the prison system.

Dale and Norma Jean exited the store, Norma Jean holding Amanda in her arms and her daughter's hand. Dale was carrying a bulky bag containing her purchases. They both wore scarves covering their hair. Pat waved at them. Scott jumped from Pat's lap and ran to Jessie. The three men stood up as they approached.

Pat introduced everyone around. The son interpreted Dale's English to his father. Pat interpreted the father's Farsi to Dale and Norma Jean. Pat took Amanda from Norma Jean and was rewarded with a hug.

Minutes later, a pregnant lady walked out of the store. The son walked over to her. He introduced his wife to the Americans. She spoke some English. Both of their English was a bit hard to understand, but Dale took Amanda and was soon in a conversation asking her when her baby was due and making small talk about kids. When they parted company, Pat promised the father that he would look into his imprisoned son's situation.

They got up early on Sunday morning. Pat had learned, with the help of Cleo, of a warehouse where they could go to Mass. It was several miles away and Jim Reese let them borrow his car. Pat had a hard time finding the warehouse. Sunday was a work day for Muslims in Iran, so all of the warehouses in the area had cars around them. Pat drove through a couple of parking lots without stopping.

Dale said, "How do you know that wasn't it?"

"I think I'll know when it's the right one."

Pat pulled into the next warehouse, drove by the front door and said, "This is it."

"Eddie, how do you know? Does God talk to you?" She wouldn't be surprised if he said *yes.*

Pat guffawed the laugh that she knew he learned from an Australian.

As they walked to the front door, Pat pointed. Dale saw a white, small wooden crucifix lying flat in the grass. She knew they were in a Muslim country, but she didn't like learning that Catholics had to celebrate Mass in hiding.

They were late, so the priest was reading the Gospel when they entered the makeshift church. The priest stopped in the middle of a sentence when he saw strangers enter. Everyone turned around and looked warily at the strangers.

Pat told Dale under his breath. "Genuflect and make the sign of the cross." He lowered Scott to his feet. Scott genuflected with them and made the sign of the cross. The congregation smiled. A child can't be trained to fake so innocently.

The priest continued reading the Gospel.

There were less than a hundred people sitting on folding metal chairs, and the priest said Mass on a wooden alter made of plywood stretched on top of two wooden sawhorses.

The mass was in Farsi, but Dale understood what was going on, like the Latin Masses she couldn't interpret without an English Mass book when she was growing up. Of course, she didn't understand a word of the priest's sermon.

During the sermon, the priest looked over at them several times. Dale's instinct was to smile at him. She was wearing a scarf, like most of the women in the church. None were wearing a veil to cover their face. The children of the adults were half of the congregation.

At communion, Pat moved up next to Dale holding Amanda on his right hip as the priest placed the Sacred Host on Dale's tongue. The priest made the sign of the cross on Amanda's forehead, returned Scott's smile, placed his right hand on his head and blessed him. Pat received the Host on his tongue.

When the priest gave the final blessing and said in Farsi "Go out with love to serve the world." The congregation started moving toward Pat and his family before the priest left the altar. Instead of walking down the center aisle, the priest hurried toward Pat and his family.

Scott was intimidated by the approach of so many people and reached up to his daddy. Pat picked him up. Dale was intimidated and moved behind Eddie. Pat switched Scott to his left hip and put his arm around Dale's shoulders.

The priest hurried up to them, "Stay back, my friends. You are frightening their children." Everyone went silent and froze in place.

Pat smiled at the priest, stepped forward and offered his hand. The priest accepted it, "Welcome to our congregation. I am Father Divari."

Pat grinned, "I'm sure everyone here would like to know who we are. May I address the congregation?"

"Yes." The priest seemed pleasantly surprised by the offer.

Dale guessed that Pat had taken over from Eddie. He put Scott down and Dale took Scott's hand.

Pat grabbed a chair, turned it around and stood up on it. The folding chair tried to fold under his weight, but Pat pressed his heels down on the front of the seat to stabilize it.

Pat scanned the murmuring crowd. He spoke in Farsi with authority, "Apparently, this congregation doesn't get many visitors. I tried to arrive early, but this was a hard place to find. I regret discovering that Catholics in Iran have to celebrate Mass in hiding, like the early saints had to hide to celebrate Mass in the catacombs of Rome.

"My name is Pat O'Sheen. I just arrived with my family from America last Sunday."

There was a soft grumble. Pat tried unsuccessfully to locate it. One guy spoke out, "You don't sound American." Pat smiled at the man and tried to memorize his face.

"I work for the military attaché in the American Embassy. I am in the U.S. Army. My wife's name is Dale, our son's name is Scott, and our daughter is Amanda. They don't speak Farsi, only English. We look forward to meeting you. Please try not to frighten our son." Pat stepped down from the chair and approached Dale, who was still standing next to the priest.

A lady about Dale's age had approached her. She said in barely understandable English, "Dale, my name is Shirin. Welcome to Iran."

"Thank you, Shirin. Is this pretty girl your daughter?"

The girl standing next to Shirin was about ten. She smiled, apparently understanding some English. She said, "Yes," and grabbed her mother's hand.

The priest introduced Pat to the men who had gathered around him.

The O'Sheens finally got back to their car about forty minutes later.

Chapter 18
Acting Military Attaché

Pat reported to the ambassador's office first thing on Monday morning.

Kay told Pat to go straight in. Pat knocked on the door and stuck his head in. Andy waved him in. This time he didn't get up from his desk.

"Pat, I just got a call from the Iranian defense minister's office. He wanted to meet with Neal, but I explained that Neal was out of the country. You and I are going to meet with them at their office at ten. You need to go back home and get on your dress uniform."

Pat said, "I have a dress uniform hanging in my office. Why do they want to meet with us?"

"I don't know. But, it must be of some importance if they didn't want to discuss it on the phone."

Pat nodded, "What time do we need to leave here?"

"Nine-thirty."

"I'll be ready."

Pat and the ambassador met with the Minister of Defense, Rashid Fahad, and the SAVAK director, Nasser Moghadam. They both had military backgrounds and were impressed with the numerous ribbons, combat and skill badges, and unit awards that covered Pat's dress uniform. They were also impressed that Pat never averted his eyes from the eyes of the one addressing him, and that he spoke Farsi like a Tehran native.

After the preliminaries, they got down to business. They knew that Pat had only been in the Middle East for a short time, so they addressed the ambassador.

Fahad said, "Andy, I'm sure you know who Saddam Hussein is?"

Andy nodded, "The vice president of Iraq."

Pat added, "And the commander of their military."

They all stared at O'Sheen, surprised at his input.

They were more surprised when Pat asked, "Are Saddam's troops causing problems on the border near your oil fields in the south?" Pat had heard it from Jamil, the SAVAK agent in his neighborhood.

Nasser said, "Yes, how do you know that?"

Andy stared at Pat in shock, "Pat, how could you possibly know that. You have only been here for a little over a week."

Pat shrugged, "I understand the psyche of people like Saddam Hussein. I have studied people like him for years." Pat did not want to mention Jamil and cause him problems, "My question about skirmishes on the southern border was only conjecture."

Eddie couldn't pull Pat back, "You have good reason to be concerned about Saddam Hussein. He participated in a failed coup d'état years ago and had to flee to Egypt. Now he has much more power in Iraq. His cousin, President al-Bakr is in poor health, and I understand that Saddam may already be the de facto leader. Saddam will probably be in total control within a year, without having to attempt a coup d'état this time. Once he is in control of the Ba'ath party, Saddam will have all of those who oppose him killed. That is the type of man he is."

Nasser smiled at Major O'Sheen. He wondered if O'Sheen understood Saddam's psyche because it was not unlike his own. He looked at Andy and admitted, "Our thoughts are very much like Major O'Sheen's. We are asking for your help to clarify Saddam's intentions."

Andy said, "We don't have diplomatic relations with Iraq. I'm not sure how we could help you."

Nasser looked at Pat.

Pat said nothing, waiting to see how diplomacy worked . . . or how it didn't work.

Nasser looked back at the Ambassador, "Your CIA works closely with Israel's Mossad and England's MI-6. Except for the KGB in the Soviet Union, they are the three best intelligence agencies in the world. You can help us without having diplomatic relationship with Iraq."

When Ambassador Sullivan didn't offer a response, Pat did. "I will see what I can find out and get back to you by the end of next week."

Ambassador Sullivan glared at Pat again.

Defense Minister Fahad noticed the ambassador's glare and said to the major, "Who will verify your intelligence?"

Nasser glared at Fahad. Pat realized that Nasser hated dealing with diplomats as much as he did.

Pat offered, "Colonel Williams will be back by the end of next week. He can give you his analysis on the intelligence I gather."

Pat stood up. "I am not a diplomat. I will wait outside while you decide the course of action you want me to take." Pat walked toward the door.

Nasser stood up, "I agree with Major O'Sheen. America's involvement should be a political decision." He followed O'Sheen out the door and closed it behind him.

Fahad looked at Sullivan whose face was red. He offered some solace, "Andy, O'Sheen is obviously a warrior who doesn't aspire to become a diplomat."

Andy apologized, "I'm sorry, Rashid. This is O'Sheen's first embassy assignment. I don't yet know him very well, nor did I coach him on when to speak and when to just listen."

"No apology necessary, Andy. I found his direct approach very refreshing. He has an amazing grasp of Middle Eastern history and its politics for an army major who just arrived here. Is he capable of gathering enough intelligence to report back to us by next week?"

"Honestly, Rashid, I don't know. I hope to be able to give you a better answer in a few days."

In the hallway, Nasser smiled at O'Sheen. "Major. You stuck your neck out pretty far in there. Your career as a diplomat may be short lived."

Pat chuckled, "I have no desire to become a diplomat, Director Moghadam. Please call me Pat."

"Then why are you here in Iran, Pat?"

"I am in training. The military brass wants me to have a better understanding of potential hot spots in the world. I believe that Saddam Hussein may be the first to create one of those hot spots."

Nasser was starting to understand. "How long have you been speaking Farsi?"

Pat answered honestly, "I started learning it about six months ago. The army recognized that I have the ability to learn new languages quickly."

"Obviously. Pat, you sound like you have speaking Farsi since your childhood."

"Thank you." Pat noticed Nasser was comfortable using the familiar address. He decided to take advantage of the opportunity. He pulled out his wallet and extracted a small piece of paper. He handed it to the director of national security.

Nasser looked at the name on the paper, "Who is this?"

"Nasser, he is the son of a man who has become my friend. The son is twenty years old. He was arrested about six months ago. How can I find out where he is being held and get permission to visit him?"

"Pat, let me check it out. I'll have someone call you at your embassy."

The ambassador came out of the minister's office alone. "Major, are you ready to go?"

"Yes sir."

The ambassador said, "Nasser, it was good to see you again."

"It was my pleasure, Andy." Nasser turned, "Thank you for your offer of assistance, Pat."

Pat shook the offered hand. "It was a pleasure meeting you, Nasser."

Pat followed Andy down the hallway as Nasser went back into the minister's office.

The ambassador was quiet on the way back to the embassy, so Pat remained silent.

Chapter 19
The Mission

When Pat and the ambassador got back to the embassy, Andy ordered Pat to come up to his office. Pat sat on the couch and Andy sat in his usual armchair.

"Pat, we haven't worked together before, so I can't really criticize you for what you said in the meeting."

Pat smiled, "But you think I went too far and said too much?"

"Yes. I . . ."

Pat interrupted, "I do owe you an explanation, Sir."

When the ambassador seemed willing to listen, Pat continued. "Do you know who Ruhollah Khomeini is?"

"Yes. He is an Islamic scholar whom the Shah exiled from Iran over a decade ago."

Pat clarified, "Almost fourteen years ago, and he has lived in Iraq for most of those years. Khomeini has a tremendous amount of influence with the Shia Muslim majority in Iraq. Vice-president Saddam Hussein is a Sunni Muslim, and he has already asked Khomeini to leave Iraq. But Khomeini is very popular with the press in Iraq and has stayed in Iraq in defiance of Saddam's request."

Andy interrupted, "How do you know all of this?"

"Andy, you need to keep this confidential." Pat stared at the ambassador.

Andy nodded, intrigued.

Pat trusted him, "I learned to speak Farsi and Arabic at CIA headquarters in Virginia. During the six months I was there, I spent countless hours going through the CIA files on the Middle East and North Africa. I mostly concentrated on the hot spots of Iran, Iraq, and Syria."

Pat wasn't used to speaking about classified information. "Andy, what I am about to tell you is highly classified. The only reason I am telling you this is because of our meeting this morning, I think you need to know what I am planning. You cannot tell anyone that I told you this, not even General Haig. Do you understand?"

Andy was even more intrigued. "Yes."

Pat took a deep breath, not sure how much he should disclose of the top-secret information. "You probably know that President al-Bakr of Iraq is a Shi'ite Muslim. So is President Assad of Syria. As I said in this morning's meeting with Fahad, al-Bakr is ill. He does not want to turn his country over to Saddam, who is a Sunni Muslim, so he is in the process of trying to broker a deal with President Assad of Syria to merge the two countries, giving control to Assad."

Andy's jaw dropped, "You have got to be shitting me?" *How could a major in the army have more access to intelligence than a Middle Eastern ambassador?*

Pat replied, "I'm not shitting you. There is some speculation that Khomeini is behind this merger. That makes sense to me, because he is going to have to find a new country to live in if Saddam takes total control of Iraq.

"If Khomeini is exiled from Iraq, he will try to get the Muslims here in Iran to revolt against the Shah. That is my goal here, Andy, to evaluate how influential Khomeini is with the Shia majority of Muslims in Iran."

Andy shook his head, trying to take it all in. "So that is why you say the midday prayers with the Muslims here?"

"Yes. And it is why I went to mosque with them on Friday and then took the imam to lunch."

Andy was amazed, "You have been here a week and have already had lunch with Imam Sahib?"

"Yes. He was quite informative. And he agrees with hundreds of people I have talked with in Tehran. Everyone knows who Khomeini is. The older ones who remember him when he lived here all revere him.

"Andy, if the rest of Iran is like the Muslims I've met in Tehran, you are sitting on a powder keg that is about to explode if Saddam takes control in Iraq and expels Khomeini.

"I assumed when I was sent here that I would have to go into Iraq sooner or later. The meeting this morning has made it sooner."

The ambassador countered, "What do you hope to learn in Iraq?"

Pat looked out the window for a minute to collect his thoughts. "I need to go into Iraq to find out how soon Saddam will take control."

Andy said, "Pat, you may know the history. But you need a better grasp of current political reality. You could cause an international incident for America if you are caught in Iraq spying for America. Pat, you have been here less than two weeks. Give yourself more time to get your feet on the ground."

Pat understood the ambassador's concern. "Andy, based on our meeting this morning, I think Nasser will help me forge papers to travel through Damascus, Syria, into Iraq. It may be my only opportunity to get SAVAK's help to go into Iraq and not be connected to America if I get caught."

"If you get caught, it will be your head that rolls . . . literally."

"If that happens, I trust that you will make sure Dale and my kids make it back to America safely."

Andy stared at Pat, whose eyes showed no more emotion than his tone of voice. It was like O'Sheen had two personalities; the fearless warrior sitting in front of him, and the man who expressed such love for his wife and kids on Friday night, and the kind man who would encouraged Neal to get back with his wife. He was starting to understand why a young, fearless officer like Pat had so many ribbons on his dress uniform and medals for valor.

Pat clarified, "Of course, I'm going to have to run my plans by your friend, General Haig."

Pat stood up, "I'll keep you informed, Andy."

"You might want to run your plan by Hal."

"I'll have to clear that with Haig first."

Andy stared at Pat's back with a higher level of respect as he left the room.

Cleo was a bit disarmed by how striking Pat looked in his dress uniform. He smiled at Cleo but didn't stop to say "hello". She was surprised when he closed his door. He had never done that before. Pat wasn't acting normal. She wondered what was going on.

A minute later, she answered her phone. It was Pat. "Cleo, I need a secure line."

When Pat hung up, she secured the line and connected Pat.

Pat dialed the number from memory.

"Aye?"

"Aye, Cory. I'm sorry to bother you at home."

Cory Webb recognized Pat's voice. "Pat, you have yet to do anything that has bothered me. What do you need?"

"I'm calling from Iran. I have been assigned to the embassy here. I am planning to go into Iraq undercover. I am hoping to get help from MI-6."

Cory was surprised, "Pat, a request like that has to go through channels."

"Cory, the United Kingdom still has diplomatic relations with Iraq. America does not. I'm going into Iraq rogue—not as an American."

Knowing how fast Pat learned to speak the Khmer language of Cambodia before his successful POW rescue there, Cory asked, "Can you speak Arabic well enough to hide that you are American?"

"Cory, I've learned to speak Farsi like a local this week. I will spend a few days with the locals in Bagdad before I contact your agents. I will not be a threat to them. They will still be able to screw any women they want."

Cory laughed. "I wasn't sure if America was savvy enough to turn you into a spy."

Cory got serious, "Pat, what you are requesting is politically complicated."

Pat said, "That is why we have to keep the politicians out of it."

When Cory didn't respond, Pat said, "Cory, I don't want you to hurt your status with MI-6 for trying to help me."

Cory just snickered this time. He knew Pat was manipulating him. But Pat was also cleverly giving him the words that he could convey to MI-6. "Can you tell me what are you hoping to learn in Iraq?"

Pat shared his thoughts about Khomeini and an Islamic revolution in Iran if Saddam Hussein gets control and kicks Khomeini out of Iraq. He didn't share the top-secret possible merger between Syria and Iraq.

Pat concluded, "Cory, I want to learn if the people of Iraq will support Hussein if he forces President al-Bakr out of power."

Cory looked at the clock on his wall, "It is almost seven-thirty in the morning in London. "It will be a few hours before I can get back to you."

"Thanks, Cory. Say hello to Teresa for me."

"You say hello to her." Cory handed Teresa the phone.

"Hello, Pat. How are you?"

"Never better, Teresa. How are you?"

"Very good. I was hoping that you called to say you are bringing your family here for a visit. I want to meet your family."

Pat smiled, "I like that idea. I believe we are closer to you here in Iran."

"Iran? What are you doing there?"

"The army assigned me to the embassy here."

"Do you have Dale and kids there with you?"

"Yes."

"I can't wait to meet Dale in person." Teresa cut their conversation short, "I have something on the stove. I'll give you back to Cory. It was great talking to you."

Pat gave the embassy number to Cory.

Pat changed back into his civilian clothes and walked to the same restaurant he took the imam to on Friday.

When he walked into the restaurant, it was full, with four men waiting for a table to open up. He was about to turn to leave when the owner approached him and said in Farsi. "Pat, come in. I have one seat available, if you don't mind sharing a table with my nephew?"

Pat said, "It will be my pleasure, Youssef."

As it turned out, Youssef's nephew ran the clothing store next door. During the introduction, Youssef told his nephew that Pat ate with Imam Sahib there on Friday.

They had a long, friendly conversation over lunch.

Late that afternoon, Cory Webb called and said that MI-6 agents were willing to meet with him in Iraq. Now all Pat needed was General Haig's blessing. It was still too early in the morning in America to call Haig at the Pentagon.

Pat walked home to have dinner with Dale and the kids. Dale knew it was Pat and not Eddie who came home. Scott didn't recognize the difference—he was just thrilled that his daddy was home.

After dinner, Pat told Dale that he might have to be out of the country for a week.

Dale asked, "Where are you going?"

Pat shook his head.

Dale countered, "Don't tell me it is another 'top secret' assignment."

Pat shrugged. He didn't want to get in an argument.

Dale decided not to press the issue. She knew she couldn't win with Pat. Instead, she leaned down and kissed Scott, who had fallen asleep on Pat's lap.

Pat stood up and carried Scott to his room, put him to bed, and kissed his forehead.

Dale was waiting in the hallway when Pat came out of Scott's room.

Pat was a little embarrassed when she smirked at the grin that Scott put on his face. He hugged her as she moved into his arms.

When she looked up into his eyes with love, he said, "I have to go to the embassy to call America."

Dale grimaced, "About your top-secret project?"

Pat nodded.

Dale knew the routine, "Will the project put you in danger?"

"Not in any more danger than you will be in if you keep riding around with Norma Jean on the streets of Tehran. Driving is safer in America."

Dale chuckled. She couldn't argue about the perils of driving in Tehran. Pat always pointed out that the highways were more perilous than his missions. The driving comparison always calmed her fears about his missions, despite the fact that Pat had so many bullet holes in his body. But, he got most of them in the Vietnam War.

She said, "Make me a promise."

"If I can. What is it?"

Dale grinned, "Let me see your bare buttocks where the bullet passed through before you leave on your mission."

Pat smiled at her quirky way of asking him to get naked. He kissed her tenderly and said, "I love you."

Dale felt the swelling of his groin as he pressed against her. She said, "I thought you had to call America."

"It's just eight in the morning there. We have time."

Dale feigned confusion, "Time for what?"

Pat stepped back, crossed his hands in front of him and pulled the polo shirt over his head and threw it on the floor. He knew that his body turned Dale on. "Time for whatever you want to do."

Dale was turned on by the tight abs and the growing bulge in his pants. She put her hands on his bare chest and pecked a kiss on his lips. "What do you have in mind?" She knew what they both had in mind.

Pat grabbed her shirt tails and pulled it up and over her head.

She unfastened her bra and threw it down next to his shirt. She smiled up into his eyes "Now what?

Pat pulled her against him, "Let's go the bedroom."

Dale pushed away and marched to the bedroom, getting more turned on with each step.

Chapter 20
Bureaucracy

At the embassy, Pat arranged for a secure line. He dialed the country code for America, the area code and number, and hit the speakerphone button, expecting the connection to take at least a minute. He walked to the door and slit it slightly open to see if anyone was in the area to listen. There wasn't anyone. Pat closed the door and wondered if he was becoming paranoid.

The connection started ringing as he walked back to his desk. A sweet voice answered, "General Haig's office."

"Hello, Debbie. It's Pat." He picked up the receiver to take it off speaker.

"Hi, Pat. Are you calling from Iran?"

"Yes. How do you keep up with all the people that call there from around the world?"

"I don't. But I do keep up with you."

Pat chuckled, "I bet you say that to all the guys."

She laughed without trying to stifle it.

Pat took that as a sincere sign of fondness for him. "Is Al available?"

She chuckled again, "You are still the only one below the rank of colonel that calls him Al."

Pat said, "I won't be a major for long."

"I don't doubt that." She knew General Haig was very high on Major O'Sheen.

"Debbie, I will be busted back to the rank of captain for showing disrespect by calling a general by his first name."

The turn-around response forced Debbie to laugh again.

She reduced her laugh to a chuckle and replied, "I'll check to see if 'Al' wants to talk to a lowly major who is about to be busted back to captain."

Pat got serious, "Debbie, tell General Haig that I have some critical information. I am calling from a secure line. Make sure his line is secure."

The change in Pat's mood concerned Debbie. "Hold on, Pat."

General Haig picked up, "Hello, Pat. Is there a problem?"

Pat assumed Debbie had recognized his mood change and conveyed it to Haig. "Sir, Andy and I met with Fahad, the Iranian defense minister, this morning. They have had some skirmishes with Iraqi troops on the border near the Iranian oil fields. They have asked for our help in finding out what is going on."

It took Pat ten minutes, fielding all of Haig's questions, to explain what he had learned from talking to Iranian intelligence, his theory on Khomeini, and an impending Islamic revolution in Iran against the Shah if Hussein takes total control in Iraq.

Haig leaned back in his chair. O'Sheen's bleak scenario was one that he had never heard from the "experts". No one had ever expressed concern that the Islamic scholar, Khomeini, might influence the precarious balance of power in the Middle East. He would have been very skeptical if any other soldier who had only been in the Middle Eastern theater for a couple of weeks came up with such a wild theory.

Haig said, "Pat, no one else has voiced concern about Khomeini. I hope you haven't spooked Fahad with your theory."

"No sir. I haven't even alluded to it. But in asking for our help, I believe SAVAK might supply me papers and IDs to go into Iraq to keep America out of my insertion. I want to infiltrate Iraq as a Syrian."

"What would you hope to accomplish in Iraq?"

Pat responded immediately, "To get an idea if the Iraqi people will support Saddam if he initiates a coup d'état against President al-Bakr."

Haig leaned forward, knowing that Pat's concern was based on his interaction with the citizens in Iran. "Pat, you have only been over there for a few weeks. Our diplomatic relation with Iraq are improving. If they catch an American spying on them, it could upset years of effort by our State Department."

Pat replied, "I'm going in disguised. If I get caught, they won't be able to connect me to America, and you can substitute someone else's fingerprints in my military file."

"Pat, if you get caught, they will probably kill you."

Pat said, "If that happens, Ambassador Sullivan has assured me that he will get my family back to America safely."

Haig never doubted Pat's courage. He just wasn't convinced of the importance of Pat's cause. He didn't want to risk such a valuable asset like Pat O'Sheen without more intelligence.

Haig said, "Pat, I need time to evaluate your request. I'm not inclined to approve your insertion into Iraq at this time."

Pat increased the stakes, "I also want to get with MI-6 and our CIA assets in Iraq to get an update on the merger talks between Iraq and Syria."

Haig was shocked, "How do you know about that?"

"I read it in the CIA files while I was at Langley learning Farsi and Arabic. But that intelligence was gathered too long ago. I need an update on that intelligence."

"Who gave you access to those classified files?"

The question surprised Pat. "I assumed that you had given me the clearance, sir."

Haig assumed it was the CIA director. "Like I said, Pat, I need time to evaluate your request."

Pat expected the bureaucratic nonsense. General Haig had called him "Pat" during the whole conversation. He responded in kind. "Al, my plan is to go into Iraq no later than Saturday. Apparently, I'm not articulate enough to convince you of the threat Hussein and Khomeini present. The State Department needs to concentrate their diplomatic efforts to forming a relationship with Saddam Hussein. Hussein understands the threat Khomeini's radical Shia Islamic philosophy presents to world. He also knows that if he assassinates Khomeini in Iraq, he will have a Shia revolution in his country.

Haig said, "Pat, Hussein doesn't control Iraq."

Pat replied, "If our CIA knows about al-Bakr's plan to merge Iraq with Syria under Assad, they should at least suspect that Hussein will learn of it and learn that Khomeini is behind it."

Khomeini was low on Haig's radar of people who could cause a diplomatic crises. "Pat, you are to stand down until I get back to you."

Pat didn't respond.

General Haig broke the silence, "Do you understand my order, Major?"

Pat didn't respond.

Haig gave Pat another thirty seconds to acquiesce. He knew he was dealing with an opinionated, passionate personality who openly disdained bureaucratic protocol.

Pat finally said, "You need to get back with me no later than Friday, Sir. I understand the risks to my life in Iraq. To me, that risk pales in comparison to the bigger picture—the long-term risks to our country without a strong Shah in Iran. The CIA assets in Iraq could help accelerate my analysis, but I will find out what I need without their help."

Haig held his handset in front of him and looked at it like it was at fault. For some reason his advice to his friend, Ambassador Sullivan passed through his mind, 'O'Sheen is very innovative. I want you to make sure he is given a lot of latitude over there to do things his way.'

Haig compromised, "O'Sheen, you can make your plans. But you are not to go into Iraq without receiving my approval. Do you understand?"

"Yes sir." Pat did understand the order. He had until Saturday to decide if he was going to have to disobey it.

Pat had already arranged for a meeting with Nasser. The next morning, the Director of SAVAK, Nasser Moghadam, agreed to provide Pat with forged documents to go into Iraq through Syria. Pat had carried a briefcase into Nasser's office at ten o'clock. SAVAK needed to take Pat's picture for the forged IDs and visas.

After amenities, Pat asked, "Do you have a sink and a mirror nearby?"

Nasser opened a door to his private bathroom.

Pat said, "Nasser, I'm going to change my appearance so my forged papers can't connect me to the American embassy here. It shouldn't take me much more than ten minutes."

Pat made his nose larger and the crown straighter to look more Syrian. He pinched in the outside of his eyelids just a little to make his eyes look smaller. He put in prosthetics over the molars of his lower and upper teeth on both sides to swell his face. Then, he colored the fast-drying paste on his nose and the putty on his eyes to match his skin.

106

He closed his briefcase and walked back into Nasser's office. Nasser was sitting at his desk. He looked up and did a double-take. He stood up, walked around his desk, and looked at O'Sheen from all angles.

He smiled, "Your eyes look almost the same, but the transformation is amazing. So you really are a spy?"

Pat chuckled, "In my army, we prefer the term military intelligence officer."

Nasser looked closer, "The color is a little off in places."

Pat knew his wife would agree. "It will work for the photo IDs. Nasser, I would like to go into Bagdad as a Syrian. Can you handle the IDs for that?"

Nasser smiled with admiration. "I think so. Follow me."

Twenty minutes later, the pictures were taken. Pat decided on the name Sayid Hanna with a fictitious address in Damascus. Pat removed his makeup in Nasser's bathroom. Nasser informed him the IDs would be ready the next afternoon or the morning after that, which suited Pat just fine.

After lunch, Pat received a call from a SAVAK lieutenant in his office at the embassy.

The lieutenant said, "We have a prisoner, al-Rashid, who we will release to your custody if you will come and sign him out."

"Me? I'm not an Iranian citizen."

The man said, "In Iran, if you sign out a prisoner, you are responsible for his conduct for the next six months. If he commits any crime, you will be arrested as an accessory. Apparently, whoever ordered him released to you, trusts that you will keep him out of trouble."

Pat realized that the sign out procedure was a clever, no-cost, effective way to assign a probation officer to a released prisoner. "Where are you located?"

Pat pulled out a business card from his wallet as he listened to the instructions.

When they disconnected, Pat dialed the number on the business card and asked for Rashid.

Rashid was overwhelmed with emotion at Pat's news about his son's release.

Rashid picked Pat up at the embassy, and they retrieved his son from the prison. Pat had just made lifelong Iranian friends in Tehran.

Chapter 21
Qom

The next morning, Pat got a pool car and drove thirty miles south through Qom to Kashan. Kashan had a nice museum, a good place to meet and talk to intelligent people. Mostly though, Pat just wanted to distract his mind away from his impatience with General Haig, who had not yet called to approve his incursion into Iraq.

After an interesting morning talking to Iranians in Kashan, Pat stopped at a crowded park in Qom. When he walked into the park, he realized that there were about a dozen chess matches going on. More than half of the spectators were gathered around one match.

Pat walked up to that group. A man turned slightly toward him and greeted him.

Pat returned the greeting and asked, "Is the city champ on this table?"

"Yes. Where are you from?"

"Tehran." Pat was not looking at the man, but was studying the chess board. The older of the two chess players moved his knight. Pat shook his head and whispered to his new acquaintance, "Bad move. He is trying to go on offence at the wrong time. Is he the city's best player?"

"No. The other man is. But I thought it was a very clever move."

Pat shrugged, "After that mistake, I could checkmate him in five moves."

The guy looked skeptically at Pat. They watched in silence as the game sped up, both players on offence, the champ knowing that his opponent's checkmate was one move behind his. Five moves later the game was over.

The man next to Pat looked at him, "You know your chess. Why don't you challenge the champ? It will cost you 1000 rials *(about fifteen dollars).*

Pat smiled at the realization that this was a gambling event.

Pat said, "How do I offer the challenge?"

"Put your money on his table before anyone else does."

Pat put his money down first, sat down, and offered his hand across the table.

The man smiled and accepted the handshake. "You are not Iranian. Where are you from?"

Pat was surprised, "Why do you think that I am not Iranian?"

The champ changed to English with a Boston accent and said under his breath, barely audible. "Because you offer your hand like an American."

Pat realized that he was dealing with a covert American agent.

The agent saw that his chess challenger understood.

The men around were loudly calling other men over to watch the match. Pat's acquaintance was taking bets, not on the winner, but on how many moves the newcomer from Tehran could survive.

Forty-five minutes later, they agreed to declare the game a stalemate—no winner. The small crowd cheered, and many of the observers patted Pat on the back.

Pat picked up his rials and said loudly over the noisy crowd an offer to buy the local champion a glass of tea.

The man nodded and stood up, "Come with me."

As they started walking, the man asked in English, "What is your name?"

Pat diverted in English, "How should I offer my hand so I don't come across as an American?"

"You should not offer it to a stranger until he introduces himself and gives you his name."

The man stopped. There was no one nearby. "They call me Caleb."

Pat thought, *no last names. Definitely CIA.*

"Pat O'Sheen." They shook hands.

Jamil corrected Pat's handshake, "Just one up and down, not multiple times like they do in America."

He said, "So you are the new military intelligence officer at the embassy?"

"Yes. What do they call you in Boston?"

Jamil was impressed that Pat picked up his Boston accent

They were crossing the street toward a small restaurant and Caleb switched back to Farsi, "So, what are you doing in Qom, Pat."

"I'm just out meeting the Iranian people and getting the lay of the land."

"Your Farsi is very much localized for someone who has been here such a short time."

"Thank you. I have talked to almost a hundred locals. You sound local, too."

Caleb said, "My dad was born and raised in Qom. He went to college in America where he met my mother. I have many relatives here."

"How long have you lived here?"

"Twenty years. I met my wife here, and we have three kids. Qom is my home. I own a small local winery."

When they sat down in the restaurant, Caleb ordered two teas and some fruit.

He said, "Pat, it sounds like you are doing research if you have already talked to so many Iranians. What are you trying to learn?"

"Two things mostly: the first is how the people feel about the Shah."

"What have you learned so far?"

Pat considered how much he should say, "In Tehran, they tolerate him. The more devout Muslims don't like his westernization programs and could become hostile toward him if they had a strong leader. This is my first day out of Tehran. How do you feel about the Shah?"

Caleb didn't answer directly, "You described the feeling of people all across Iran fairly accurately. If you are concerned about a revolution, you are barking up the wrong tree. The Shah's military and the SAVAK are too strong."

"Even against a strong opposition leader?"

Caleb shook his head, "If someone starts to become too prominent, the Shah will deal with him harshly."

Pat nodded, "Exile him like he did Khomeini, or kill him like Khomeini's son?"

Caleb chuckled, "Yes. You have done your homework. You said you were trying to learn two things. What is the other?"

Pat shrugged, "How the Iranian people feel about Khomeini."

"Pat, the older ones will remember him, and many still hold him up on a pedestal. But the younger people have probably never heard of him."

"The younger people I talked to in Tehran knew of him. A couple of university students I talked to have even read some of his teachings."

Caleb seemed surprised. He turned around and called across the room, "Abud?"

A teenager trying to grow his first beard stood up and walked over, "Yes?"

"Abud, do you know whom Ruhollah Khomeini is?"

"He is an Islamic scholar whom the Shah exiled from Iran a long time ago."

Pat asked, "Is he still alive?"

"Yes. He lives in Iraq."

Caleb was surprised, "How do you know this?"

"I learned it in Madrasa *(school)*."

Caleb dismissed the boy.

He said to Pat, "I still think you are barking up the wrong tree. Khomeini hasn't stirred up any opposition to the Shah in the last decade, and the Shah will never let him back in."

Pat said, "Khomeini is happy living with his Shi'ite brothers in Iraq. Caleb, do you know who Saddam Hussein is?"

"Of course."

"Vice president Saddam Hussain politely asked Khomeini to leave Iraq. President al-Bakr is ill and Saddam is poised to take his place. When he does, he won't be so polite the next time he asks Khomeini to leave."

Caleb concluded for him, "And you think that Khomeini will start stirring up opposition to the Shah?"

Pat nodded, "Khomeini will be a man without a country."

Caleb conceded, "You might be right."

Caleb looked at his watch, "I need to stop by my winery on my way home."

Pat reached for his wallet.

Caleb gestured with his hand, "I have already had them put the bill on my tab."

Pat objected, "I offered to buy you tea. You accepted."

Caleb responded. "Pat, you had an opening to beat me in the chess game and didn't take it. Why?"

"Because you left the opening intentionally to see how I would react. Winning that way doesn't appeal to me. You knew who I was when I sat down across from you."

Caleb laughed, "I always thought the term military intelligence was an oxymoron, but in your case the two words fit together very well."

Pat stopped at a beautiful shrine on the way out of Qom. It turned out to be the Fatima Masoumeh Shrine. The second holiest Shia shrine in Iran.

Inside, Pat learned that Fatima Masoumeh was the sister of the eighth Imam, Ali al-Rida, and the daughter of the seventh Imam, Musa al-Kadhim. In Shia Islam, women were often revered as saints if they were close relatives to one of the Twelve Imams.

Chapter 22
Preparation

The next morning, Pat stuck his head in the station chief's office, "Good morning, Hal."

"Hi, Pat. Come in and relax for a while."

Pat shook his head but took two steps into the office, "I don't have but a minute.

"Hal, do you know a guy named Caleb from Qom?" Pat saw the surprise in his eyes despite Hal's effort to quickly hide it. Pat wondered if Hal would deny knowing Caleb.

Instead, Hal said coolly, "Why do you ask?"

"I played chess with him in Qom yesterday. He is very intelligent and will be a great asset during and after the Iranian revolution." Pat turned and walked out the door, waving the back of his hand over his shoulder.

Hal jumped to his feet to call Pat back into his office, but he held his tongue. Pat had come into his office to confirm his suspicion that Caleb was a CIA operative. Hal knew he had just unwittingly confirmed Pat's suspicion. There was no way to take it back.

Pat suspected that Hal would be talking to Caleb before the day was over, if not before the hour was over. Caleb was the first person to understand Pat's theory of Khomeini being forced to instigate a revolution against the Shah of Iran. Caleb would share that theory with Hal. Pat hoped that Hal would pass it up the line to CIA headquarters. It was a big stretch to hope that his theory would make it up to director of the CIA and then to General Haig before he would have to disobey Haig's direct order not to go into Iraq on Saturday. But perhaps it would give him some cover when he returned to Iran from Iraq.

Pat stopped at Amir's desk.

Amir looked up from the document he was translating and smiled, "Hi, Pat. We've missed you at midday prayers."

Pat smiled his appreciation, "I've been traveling. I'll be there today."

Pat stopped at Kay's desk by the door.

Kay looked up, "You look happy today, Pat."

Pat raised his eyebrows, "Is that unusual?"

"No. You always bring a little sunshine into the embassy."

Pat didn't feel like sunshine. If Haig didn't call by tonight, his planned incursion into Iraq should be delayed. He had already decided to not let that happen. He walked to his local bank and transferred money from his Swiss bank slush fund. He was informed that the funds wouldn't be available for his use until tomorrow, which was okay with Pat.

Pat said midday prayers with the Muslims at the embassy. After lunch with his Muslim friends in the embassy cafeteria, he was restless and becoming more and more impatient. He made a decision and called the airlines. He made a reservation for an early flight on Sunday from Tehran to Damascus under one of the alias names on his forged documents that Nasser had prepared for him. He called a different airlines and made a reservation from Damascus to Bagdad on Sunday night under the name Sayid Hanna. He hoped to learn the Syrian Arabic accent enough during his long layover to pass as a Syrian. If he was caught spying, he didn't want Iran or America to be implicated. Of course, he could be captured and broken. Pat had heard that everyone could be broken under intense torture. Senator McCain, an American POW war hero, admitted that he was broken in the "Hanoi Hilton" prison in North Vietnam. Pat O'Sheen would not let that happen to him. He would die first.

Dale knew it was Pat who came home that night. Scott didn't know or didn't care. He loved his daddy, and Pat loved him as much as Eddie did. Amanda was already in bed.

After they had dinner, and while Pat put Scott to bed, Dale pulled the bourbon out from under the counter. She could tell that her husband was stressed and needed comfort. She needed some stress relief, too. She smiled at Pat as he walked into the kitchen and handed him a drink. She held up the bourbon bottle that Pat got from the ambassador at the embassy, conveying that it was almost empty.

Pat nodded his understanding and accepted the drink. He put the drink on the counter without taking a sip and put his hands around Dale's small waist, conveying the idea that his comfort didn't come from bourbon.

Dale squirmed away, "I want you to talk to me." She picked up his drink and handed it back to him. They sat down on the small couch.

Dale asked, "Pat, am I going to see Eddie before you leave on this mission?"

Pat answered honestly, "I don't think so."

"Then it must be dangerous."

Pat replied, "I don't anticipate any physical danger. The bureaucracy in Washington may ruin my army career because they haven't approved my mission yet."

Dale glared at Pat, "Don't you dare ruin Eddie's military career, I will never forgive you."

Pat said, "Dale, I don't expect you to understand, but Eddie does. I have to do what is best for America to prevent the need for our soldiers to be forced into another war."

Dale understood Pat's passion to protect American soldiers since his first tour of duty in Vietnam before Mike was killed. She summarized Pat's motive softly, almost inaudibly, "So another Mike Burkowski doesn't have to die."

Pat looked into Dale's eyes realizing that she was starting to understand. But he didn't want to talk about Mike—not tonight.

Dale saw a hint of moisture enter Pat's eyes. He started to stand up. Showing emotion embarrassed him. She put her hand on his shoulder and used it as support for her to stand up.

She said, "I have to pee." It was a delaying tactic to give Pat time to overcome his emotional response to Mike Burkowski's memory.

Pat sipped his drink as his mind focused on Dale's warning for him not to ruin Eddie's military career. He loved Dale and couldn't ignore her warning. Maybe he needed to pull back. He could defend his delay to Nasser for another week while blaming it on the American bureaucracy. He started to relax until Dale walked up in her transparent negligee. She sat down next to him and kissed him.

Pat started to kiss back passionately.

Dale pulled back, "Pat, you need to relax. I taught Eddie how to relax while making love to me. Is he smarter than you?"

Pat managed to hold his laugh to a chuckle, "Teach me."

She leaned into him and kissed him tenderly.

Pat overcame the urge to throw his arms around her, pick her up, and carry her to the bed.

Dale smiled up into his eyes. He was being obedient. "You need to unfasten your belt."

Pat obeyed willingly, unfastened his belt, and started to unzip his pants.

Dale stopped him, "Don't unzip your pants. I want to do that"

Pat was amused and getting more and more aroused by her tease.

She kissed him more passionately this time. Pat wasn't sure if it was acceptable yet, but he cupped her right breast in his left hand. Her kiss became more passionate, and her hand grabbed his knee and then slowly slid up his thigh to his groin.

Chapter 23
Permission

The next morning, Pat drove up to Karaj where he visited the Morvārid *(Pearl)* Palace, which was designed by the Frank Lloyd Wright Foundation. He thought that it would be a good place to meet and talk to intelligent Iranians. It was.

From there, Pat drove up to Qazvin, about a hundred miles northwest of Tehran. Qazvin was once the capital of the Persian Empire. Pat got there in time for midday prayers at Masjed Al-nabi (the Soltani Mosque): one of the most glorious mosques of antiquity in Iran. He talked to a few old men after prayers. The Farsi accent was slightly different than in Tehran. But so far, he hadn't found different attitudes toward the Shah or Khomeini anywhere.

Pat had lunch where one of the men recommended that he eat, and then he drove back to the embassy. He had a message to call General Haig at nine a.m. EST.

Pat went home for dinner and then went back to the embassy.

He secured a line and called the Pentagon, "Hello, Debbie. It's Pat."

She answered bubbly. "Hi, Pat. The general is expecting your call. Hold on."

Haig picked up, "Good morning, Pat."

"Good evening, sir."

Haig chuckled at the way Pat always referred to the time difference. "Pat, I was hoping to get some intelligence out of Iraq to save you from having to go in, but the CIA hasn't had any luck communicating with their agents. MI-6 has confirmed that President al-Bakr is still in poor health. Are you still wanting to go into Iraq?"

Pat wanted to make it crystal clear that he was ready to go in, even without approval "Yes sir. Nasser, the head of SAVAK in Iran has already made my forged documents. I am going into Iraq from Damascus disguised and under the Syrian alias, Sayid Hanna."

Haig said, "Spell that alias name for me." Pat did.

Haig sighed, "Pat, I believe you have the savvy to pull this off. Let me know when you finalize your plan to go in."

Pat thought about waiting until tomorrow to tell him. But he decided on upfront honesty, "Sayid Hanna has a flight reservation from Damascus to Bagdad Sunday evening."

Haig said, "So you were planning on going in even if I didn't approve?"

Pat remained honest, "I'm not sure, sir. For my wife and kid's sake, I didn't want to jeopardize my career. I wasn't going to make that decision until tomorrow night."

Haig smiled and shook his head. Pat's admission that the only thing that might hold him back from disobeying his orders was concern for his family was a rare display of honesty. O'Sheen was one of a kind.

Haig said, "Have you got a paper and pencil?"

Pat picked up a pencil with no intention of using it. "Yes sir."

He gave Pat two CIA agents' alias names in Bagdad and instructions for finding them. "Pat, commit that to memory and destroy the paper."

Pat smiled knowing that he could repeat it all word-for-word a year from now in Haig's voice, "Yes sir."

"Take care of yourself, Pat. And call me as soon as you get back to Tehran—or if you have problems in Iraq."

"I will. Thank you, Sir."

Dale noticed the smile on her husband's face when he came home. "Your call to Washington must have gone well?"

"It did, Hon. Pat is not going to have to put my career in jeopardy. His mission was approved."

"Would he really have jeopardized your career?"

"I think so. I wasn't trying to discourage Pat. Our mission is very important." Dale smiled at the way Eddie always referred to Pat in the third person.

Dale thought it might have been Eddie when he first walked through the front door. She had already put the kids to bed. She watched

118

as Eddie went into the kid's room and kissed Scott on the temple. Scott got a little smile on his face and went right back to sleep. He kissed Amanda without waking her.

The next morning, Pat went to Ambassador Sullivan's office to talk to him about Iraq. "Has General Haig talked to you about my insertion into Iraq?"

Andy admitted, "He asked my opinion about the timing and wanted my thoughts on your Khomeini theory."

"Did he ask if I told you about al-Bakr and Assad negotiating to merge the countries?"

"No. And I didn't bring it up."

Pat nodded his approval and said, "Thank you, Andy."

"Pat, when are you hoping to go in?"

"I'm leaving for Syria Sunday morning."

Andy's eyebrows raised and his eyes widened, "When I talked to Al, he didn't sound inclined to let you go into Iraq."

Pat offered, "I think he realized that I was planning to go in with or without his permission."

Andy was incredulous, "You would have disobeyed a direct order from General Haig?"

Pat shrugged, "Fortunately, I didn't have to make that decision."

Andy showed concern, "So, if I give you a direct order, I can't count on you to carry it out?"

"Andy, I can be opinionated and hardheaded, but I am usually right. I'm not into mutiny, so you can count on me to do the right thing." Andy relaxed until Pat continued. "Even if your order is misguided."

The ambassador glared at Pat, "That was the most ambiguous answer I have ever heard."

Pat chuckled. With a big smile on his face, he said, "You won't have to put up with my flippant attitude for very much longer, Andy. I should finish my research here in another month—six weeks tops."

Andy grimaced, "I didn't mean to convey that I don't want you here."

Pat stood up, "I know that, Andy. You are the best ambassador I've ever worked for."

When Andy smiled, Pat turned and walked toward the door.

Andy ran his memory through Pat's file and said loudly, "I'm the only ambassador you have ever worked for."

Pat guffawed as he continued walking out the door.

Andy joined in the contagious laughter. Pat was never boring, and he was a man Andy definitely wanted by his side for as long as possible.

Everyone at the five desks in the open area outside the ambassador's office turned toward Pat, the contagious laughter put smiles on their faces, and some of them joined in his laughter.

Pat said, "We have a great boss." He pointed his thumb over his shoulder and saw agreement in their faces.

Andy heard and appreciated Pat's comment.

Instead of sitting back behind his desk, Andy sat in the armchair next to the couch where he first talked to O'Sheen. He considered the unique young man who somehow managed to get his way with General Haig, one of the highest officials in the United States. Yesterday, Hal Middleton told Andy how Pat had manipulated him into exposing a very deeply ingrained CIA agent in Iran. Hal wasn't happy about it at the time, but Andy knew he could trust Pat. O'Sheen was an extremely capable asset who would always be difficult to control. He was anxious to find out what Pat would learn in Iraq. He didn't buy into Pat's Khomeini theory and had shared that opinion with General Haig. But O'Sheen's total commitment to his mission forced Andy to start reconsidering the unlikely theory. As Pat once told him, only listening to conventional theories wasn't wise.

Pat went to the bank and withdrew the slush fund money he had transferred in cash, mostly in Iraqi dinars. He said midday prayers at the embassy and then went into his office and closed the door. He made the sign of the cross and asked for God's guidance in Iraq. He didn't pray for his safety—he never did. Since his first say in Vietnam, he always put his life totally in God's hands.

Chapter 24
Unlikely encounter

Dale put the finishing touches on Pat's disguise before he caught a cab to the airport.

Pat got off the plane from Tehran in Damascus with his carryon bag. After clearing customs, he went into the men's room, pulled his Syrian IDs from his underwear, peed, and put his fake Iranian IDs in their place. He bought a magazine and found a group of talkative young men waiting to board a plane and sat down near them. They were all talking about some business convention in Cairo. After about twenty minutes of listening to them while pretending to read his magazine, Pat was starting to think in Arabic—instead of English or Farsi. He had discovered a long time ago that to speak a language fluently, it was necessary to think in that language and not translate back and forth.

Pat started reading an article in the magazine in earnest. It was about Umayyad Mosque, also known as the Great Mosque of Damascus located in the old city of Damascus. It stated that it is one of the largest and oldest mosques in the world and is considered by some Muslims to be the fourth-holiest place in Islam. Every mosque had a claim to greatness.

Pat read that after the Arab conquest of Damascus in 634 AD, the mosque was built on the site of a Christian basilica dedicated to John the Baptist, who was honored as a prophet by Christians and Muslims alike. A legend dating to the 6th century holds that the building contains the severed head of John the Baptist. The shrine of John the Baptist (Yahya in Arabic) was still inside the mosque's prayer hall. The mosque is also believed by Muslims to be the place where Jesus (Isa) will return at the End of Days. The Shia Twelver Muslims believe that Jesus and the twelfth Imam will return together in order to fulfill their mission of bringing peace and justice to the world. *Jesus and the twelfth Iman? Why did Muslim radicals hate Christians?*

121

Pat looked at his watch. Depending on traffic, he might be able to make it to the mosque for midday prayers. He paid for his ticket for his next flight to Bagdad, checked his bag, caught a cab and barely made it to the mosque in time for noon prayers. After prayers, Pat managed to engage a few men in conversation. When Pat said that it was his first time in the mosque, the oldest of the men offered to give him a tour. Pat agreed and the other men walked away.

The man called Pat by his covert name. "Sayid, let me get my cleaning crew started first." He walked to a corner where a small group of women stood who Pat had mistaken for wives of the men he was talking to. He gave them instructions while pointing around the mosque as he spoke.

The old man was patient during the tour as Pat asked a lot of questions. Almost an hour later, Pat went to a restaurant nearby that the man recommended. He sat at a counter and struck up a conversation with the man sitting next to him. The man didn't ask where Pat was from, so Pat was comfortable that he had almost mastered the Syrian Levant Arabic accent, whose syllables stress patterns similar to the Arabic he had learned at CIA headquarters. It should get him through customs in Bagdad with his forged Syrian papers.

Pat had the restaurant call him a cab. He slept on the short flight to Baghdad. After clearing customs, he went to a rental car counter where he rented a car. The man behind the counter made him reservations at a hotel that he recommended near the British Embassy, supplied a map, and gave him directions. The hotel had a restaurant, so Pat ate a late dinner that wasn't very good and went to bed. *So far, so good.*

In the morning, Pat showered, being careful to keep his disguise fairly dry, and he ate breakfast at the hotel. He had the hotel desk call him a cab. He gave the cab driver two addresses and asked him to take him to the closest one first. He had phone numbers for the two agents, but they may not have been informed that he was coming, and Pat didn't think that they would meet with him based on a phone call. The cab driver had the same Arabic accent as the people at the rental car counter and the people at the hotel. Pat asked him what places he should see while visiting the city, and he kept the driver talking so he could learn the slightly different letter pronunciations, syllable emphasis, and semantic slang. There was a definite Persian influence that Pat recognized in the dialect. Pat had to ask the driver to explain some of the terms, as he had with the old man at the mosque in Damascus, and the people at the car rental agency and hotel in Bagdad.

The first address they arrived at was a one story complex with six front doors with stoops that were only about fifteen feet apart—cheap living quarters. No one answered the door at the unit number that Pat was given. Thirty minutes later, they arrived at the second address, which was a modest single-family dwelling in a well-kept neighborhood. No one was home. At least Pat knew how to drive to the addresses now, and it was obvious where the senior agent lived.

On the way back to the hotel, they ran into a traffic jam that only let them move forward three blocks in a half hour. Pat didn't mind. He was learning to speak the local dialect from the driver.

But when the driver looked at his watch, he became impatient, and minutes later started getting angry. He yelled, **"The traffic shouldn't be like this at this hour."**

Pat leaned forward from the back seat, "Rashid, do you have another fare to pick up?"

Rashid admitted, "Yes, in twenty minutes. I'll never make it. I need to radio it in."

Pat said, "If it is near here, I don't mind sharing the ride back into the city."

Rashid looked in his rearview mirror at Pat, "He is ten minutes east of here. Are you sure you don't mind?"

Pat said, "Apparently, there was a miscommunication on my appointments. I am in no hurry."

In the rearview mirror, Pat saw the appreciation in the driver's eyes.

Rashid said, "Thank you. I will discount your fare."

Pat smiled and leaned back, hoping that he would enjoy the company of another man to talk to in this horrendous traffic jam.

Rashid turned left at the next intersection. The going was slow, but it was easier moving crossway to the traffic than it was heading into Bagdad. Rashid looked at his watch every five minutes, too nervous to talk to Pat, but not yet panicked.

They pulled up to a gated, guarded community surrounded by a high concrete wall with six or seven strands of barbwire on six-foot tall steel posts on top of the ten foot high concrete wall. The guards recognized Rashid and waved him through. Pat was starting to understand Rashid's nervousness. This fare was a very important man and obviously one of Rashid's regular morning pickups.

Pat said, "Who are we picking up?"

"The Iraqi minister of defense." Rashid was less nervous.

Pat was more nervous. *Lord help me!*

They pulled up to a large stone house. Rashid got out and walked toward the front door. A tall, thin man in a dark tailored suit came out the front door, walked across the large porch and down four steps to a cobblestone sidewalk. He stopped and talked to Rashid. Rashid pointed his thumb over his shoulder at the cab, apparently explaining why a man was in the back seat of his cab.

Rashid turned around and approached the cab alone. He opened the back door and said, "I'm sorry, Sayid. I need you to get out of the cab so that I can search you for weapons."

Pat climbed out smiling, glanced at the defense minister, and turned around. Rashid did a thorough pat down, apologizing the whole time.

Pat said, "You don't need to apologize, Rashid. I understand." The Defense Minister was close enough to hear them.

Pat anticipated the next request, pulled his IDs from his back right pocket, and handed them to the driver. Rashid smiled his appreciation.

Pat held his breath as the defense minister took a quick look at the IDs. He approached Pat and said, "Mister Hanna, a man in my position must take precautions. I am sorry. I am Defense Minister Khairallah." He offered his hand.

Pat shook it up and down once, "It is honor to meet you, sir. An unexpected pleasure. I apologize for the inconvenience I have caused you."

Khairallah shook his head, "You haven't caused it. The traffic around here often causes inconveniences. It was kind of you to share your cab."

Pat said, "I offered to share it because Rashid has been so kind to me. This is my first time in Bagdad, and he has been very helpful. He was distressed that the traffic would not let him pick you up on time. And based on his nervousness, I suspected that you were someone important. My reward is in getting to meet you."

After they were in the cab, Khairallah asked, "What brings you to Baghdad, Mister Hanna?"

"Please call me Sayid. I am a structural engineering consultant. I was hoping to get some business here to fix some bridges, but apparently, there was some miscommunication between my company and the two people I was to contact here."

Pat changed the subject to deflect from his pretentious profession. "Rashid has made several suggestions on places to see while I'm here, so I'll go touring while my office in Damascus tries to straighten out the miscommunication with the people I was scheduled to contact."

Khairallah ignored Sayid's business problems and suggested, "You should see the al-Jawadain Shrine."

"Rashid suggested that. I'll plan to visit there after midday prayers."

Khairallah offered, "They hold midday prayer service at the shrine if the weather is good. They should have them today."

Pat nodded, "Thank you. I may do that. But first, I have to call my office from the hotel."

"Where are you staying?"

When Pat told the defense minister, he said to the driver, "Rashid, drop Sayid off at his hotel first. It is on the way to my office."

There were a couple minutes of silence.

Pat took a risk, "How is President al-Bakr? I heard that he was ill before leaving Damascus."

The minister treated it like a normal question, not the probing question of a spy. "He has been bedridden for almost a month now. The vice-president is having to perform most of his duties."

Pat said, "I hate to hear that. Your president is very popular in Syria because he is a close friend with our president."

Khairallah softened his statement, "He has been bed-ridden before, but not for this long. He has a team of doctors that say he will live for many more years."

Pat could tell that he was lying. "Good." Pat smiled as he should at the good news. But he was really smiling because he was happy that he would not have to bother the CIA agents or MI-6 agents. He had learned what he needed from Saddam Hussein's top military advisor.

Pat risked one more question, "Will Saddam Hussein become president if al-Bakr doesn't survive?"

Khairallah nodded, "Most likely."

Now all Pat needed to meet the objective of his mission was to get the pulse of the Iraqi citizens' attitudes toward Saddam Hussein—like he had already accomplished with the citizens of Iran toward the Shah and Khomeini.

Chapter 25
Confirmation

Pat left his hotel and drove to the al-Jawadain Holy Shrine. It was crowded and he had to park a half-mile away. The bazaar (market) near the shrine had many shops and places to eat and was very crowded. Pat assumed most of the crowd were tourists to the shrine.

Pat approached two men who looked like brothers and were about his age, "Can you tell me where they have the dhuhr (midday) prayers?"

The older of the two said, "We were just about to go there. You may go with us."

They stopped at a large fountain to perform wudu (ritual washing). They walked around the shrine and Pat saw a huge grass field. The men took off their shoes at the edge of the field, walked to the center, which was filling up with people who stood side-by-side. Everyone was facing in the same direction, toward Mecca. Five minutes later the prayers started with someone leading over loud speakers.

After prayers, Pat introduced himself to his new acquaintances. He used his Syrian accent.

He said, "This is my first visit to Iraq. Are you from here?"

The older one, Muhammad, answered, "Yes. Where are you from?"

"Damascus. I was hoping to get some recommendations on what to see in Iraq while visiting."

The younger one spoke for the first time, "We are in a hurry to get to a restaurant before it fills up with the prayer crowd."

Pat offered, "I'll buy your lunch if you will let me join you."

The brothers looked at each other and nodded. They hurried through the crowds and were seated at a table in what they said was their favorite restaurant in the bazaar.

Pat asked, "Do you come here often."

Muhammad said, "It is kind of ritual for us to come on Jamal's birthday."

Pat looked at the younger brother, "Well, happy birthday, Jamal."

The quiet brother nodded his head, "Thank you."

Pat looked at the menu. The brothers didn't. They both ordered the same meal.

When people find what they really like at a restaurant where they only visit occasionally, they usually order the same meal every time. Pat knew it was a veal dish and said to the waiter, "I'll make it easy on you and have the same."

The brothers recommended the same places to visit in Baghdad that the cab driver had, and then they recommended more places in other parts of Iraq.

Pat guided the conversation to the president's health and then to Saddam Hussein. The brothers both assumed that Saddam would take over and didn't expressed opposition—not like the opposition he heard against the Shah from some citizens of Iran.

The veal was a different type of spicy than Pat had tasted before. Pat considered it so good that he wanted Dale to learn how to duplicate it. Pat considered it the best meal he had tasted in the Middle East and expressed his appreciation to the brothers for recommending it.

The brothers appreciated his accolades.

After they finished lunch, Pat asked, "Are you going into the shrine?"

The older brother said, "We went in earlier. We are going home to celebrate Jamal's birthday with our families.

Pat looked at Jamal, "You are fortunate to have such a loving brother."

Jamal nodded and his face glowed in agreement.

Pat stopped at a store and bought a pack of Turkish cigarettes. Dale discouraged his smoking, but most of the men in Iraq smoked. Smokers tended to gather together and talk as they smoked. He was in Iraq to talk to people.

He walked back up to the shrine. There weren't many benches to sit on and relax. Most people sat on the low walls around the many fountains. Pat retrieved a cigarette from his pack and sat down next to an older man who was smoking. He searched his pockets.

He asked the man, "Do you have a light?"

The man lit Pat's cigarette with a butane lighter. They struck up a conversation.

Pat learned that the Holy Shrine was holy to Shia Muslims, not Sunni Muslims. Pat assumed that most of the visitors were Shi'ites. Pat guided the conversation to the conflict between Shi'ite and Sunni Muslims. The man accepted the reality that Saddam Hussein would be their next president, even though Saddam was a Sunni Muslim. He expressed no aversion to Saddam.

Pat spent the rest of the day talking to dozens of men at the shrine. None of them were opposed to Saddam running the country, although several expressed their wish that Saddam was a Shia and not a Sunni Muslim.

Pat had accomplished his mission. Saddam was taking over. He would exile Khomeini, and Khomeini would start a revolution against the Shah of Iran. Pat knew he was right, but he doubted that anyone in America would believe him. He knew that he was considered a novice in Middle Eastern intelligence.

Pat walked the half-mile to his car and climbed behind the wheel. He had not been followed all day, so the defense minister didn't suspect that he was a spy. He was only a mile from the house of the senior CIA agent that the cab driver took him to early that morning. The agent might be expecting him. Pat drove to the house. This time there was a car in the carport.

The sun had set, but it was not yet fully dark. Pat pulled into the driveway and tooted his horn once. When a corner of a blind in a front window pulled back as someone glanced out, Pat blinked the lights to high beam and back down. He climbed out of the driver seat and walked to the front door.

The door opened seconds after he knocked on it. A fifty year old man, two inches shorter than Pat opened the door and glared into Pat's eyes. The man's right hand was held to his right thigh. Pat assumed his right hand held a gun.

Pat said in English, "I'm Pat O'Sheen. If you have talked to your office, you know why I'm here."

The man said gruffly, "Come in."

Pat stepped through the front door feeling uncomfortable with the man's attitude.

When Pat was inside, the man started raising the gun toward Pat's chest. Pat snatched the Glock 17 out of the man's hand with his left hand. The older man stepped aggressively toward Pat. Pat put his right hand on the older man's chest and pushed him backwards. The back of the couch kept him from falling to the floor. The agent knew he had lost control.

Pat ordered as he kicked the door shut and raised the barrel of the man's pistol. "Sit down."

"Where do want me to sit?"

Pat grinned at him, "In your favorite chair."

The man walked around the couch and sat down in an armchair.

Pat sat on the couch and said in Arabic, "So you don't know who I am?"

"I know that you are not Major O'Sheen. They faxed me a picture of him."

The disguise! Pat opened his mouth and removed the prosthetics capping his molars. "I'm not going to remove my nose or eyelid molds."

The guy said, "They should have told me you would be disguised."

Pat dropped the magazine out of the Glock and ejected the chambered bullet. He put the items on the corner table between them.

The agent smiled and extended his hand, "I'm Youssef. Joseph or Joe in America."

No last name. Pat shook his hand.

Joe said, "How can I help you?"

"Joe, are you aware that President al-Bakr is bed-ridden?"

Joe nodded, "It is not the first time."

"But he has been in bed for a month? Saddam Hussein is practically running the government now."

"Who told you that, Major O'Sheen?"

"The Iraqi defense minister, Khairallah." Pat told him about the cab ride and his unexpected encounter that morning.

"That is an incredible story. Where did you learn to speak Arabic? You almost sound like a local."

"At CIA headquarters." Pat told him about going through the CIA classified files. "Joe, did you write the report on al-Bakr and President Assad of Syria getting together?"

Joe was silent.

"Joe, Saddam would be the big loser if the countries merge. Do you think Saddam is holding al-Bakr hostage while he solidifies his hold on the country?"

Joe admitted, "I guess that is a possibility, even though they are cousins."

Pat and Joe discussed Khomeini. Joe didn't know as much about him as Pat. Pat shared his theory on Saddam forcing Khomeini to leave Iraq, and Khomeini starting an Islamic revolution against the Shah of Iran.

Pat finally said, "Well, I guess I won't find out more than Khairallah told me this morning. I think I'll go back to Iran tomorrow." He put the prosthetics back in his mouth and stood up. He didn't blame the agent for not trusting him.

Joe walked him to the door.

Pat made plane reservations for the next afternoon from his hotel room.

The next morning, he ate breakfast at the hotel and then walked to the British Embassy. He asked to see the MI6 agents and was able to meet with one of them. He learned nothing new. He did share his Khomeini theory with the agent—the more eyes watching, the quicker its development would be recognized.

Chapter 26
Argument

After clearing customs in the airport in Tehran, Pat called Dale on a payphone.

"Hi, Hon."

"Hey. Where are you calling from?"

"The airport in Tehran. I'm back from my mission."

"Whoopee. That was quick."

"I'll be catching a cab home in a minute. I don't want you to shoot me when I walk in the front door in my disguise."

"Thanks for warning me. I love you."

"I love you."

Pat was rewarded with a hug and kiss from Dale when he walked through the front door.

Dale looked up and studied his face, "Your disguise held up very well."

"Yes. But I'm anxious to get it off and wash my hair in the shower." Pat headed for the bathroom.

Dale gave him a few minutes alone in the tub/shower, and then slipped open the curtain enough to climb in. His manhood reacted instantly, which always amazed her. She wondered if all men were so easy.

Forty minutes later, Pat asked, "Is there any bourbon left?"

"Yes." Dale wasn't sure if it was Eddie or Pat that she had just made love to. She thought it was Pat, who was learning to be more patient to enjoy the prolonged experience.

Pat climbed out of the bed and while getting dressed in a running suit and tennis shoes said, "I have to go to the embassy and call General Haig while it's still morning in America. But I want a drink first."

He watched as Dale put on a robe. She giggled at how much he loved seeing her naked body.

Pat walked into Scott's room. He was sleeping on his back. Pat bent down and kissed him on the forehead. Scott's eyes popped open and he threw his arms up. Pat picked him up and hugged him. "Thank you for taking care of mommy for me while I was gone."

Scott chuckled.

Pat said, "I've got to go to the office for a while, but I'll be here when you wake up in the morning. Okay?"

"Okay." Scott said sleepily.

Pat laid him back down and kissed Amanda without waking her.

Dale was finishing making two drinks when Pat entered the kitchen. Pat's forged passports were sitting on the counter next to her. She looked into his eyes. Pat looked down at the passports and back up into her eyes.

She saw his disapproval. She thought he should be more open with her about his missions, "So you went into Iraq as Sayid Hanna. Are you a spy?"

Pat hedged, "I am a military intelligence officer."

"What would have happen if you were caught in Iraq with fake documents?"

Pat shrugged, "I wasn't in danger of being caught." He picked up a drink, retrieved a pack of Turkish cigarettes from a drawer and walked out onto the small back porch and sat down.

Dale picked up her drink, knowing that Pat was miffed and followed him out and sat down on the chair across from him. She wasn't sure if he was Pat earlier, but she was sure he was Pat since he saw the passports on the counter.

Pat pulled out a Turkish cigarette and lit it, confirming he was in his Pat mode.

Dale calmly asked, "Are you mad at me for looking at your fake passports?"

Pat shook his head back and forth very slowly, "I am very mad at myself for leaving them where you could find them."

"I am your wife. I have a right to know who you are and what you do."

Pat grimaced and looked into her gorgeous, light brown eyes. He said, "You don't want to know what I do, and you should never try to probe into my missions. You won't like what you learn."

Pat should have left it at that, but he didn't. "I let Eddie take control at times because I love you and the kids, and I know you love Eddie more than me. But, I can't allow you to interfere with my missions. If you do, I will have to keep Eddie and you out of my life."

Dale glared angrily at him.

Pat knew he should apologize, but instead he returned her glare.

Dale glared at him, "If you do that, I will keep the kids out of your life." Dale jumped to her feet and ran into the house and slammed the door.

Pat took a sip of his drink. He knew he took the anger at himself for being careless with his fake IDs out on Dale. He couldn't imagine life without Dale and the kids. But he had more to consider than his own happiness. He chugged the rest of his drink and walked through the house toward the front door. He heard Dale crying in the bedroom. Eddie tried to take over, but Pat drove him back as he walked out the front door—he had to report to General Haig. He ran at full speed the half-mile to the embassy, trying to run off his confusion and frustration. Frustration because he knew he had just screwed up big time with Dale, who he loved more than life.

He walked up to the embassy gate. The guards signed him through.

He got a secure line and called Haig.

"Hello, Debbie. It's Pat."

"Hi, Pat. General Haig is in conference. Are you calling from the embassy in Iran?"

"Yes. I just got back from a trip. Al wanted me to let him know when I got back to Iran. It is late over here. If he wants me to call him tomorrow, just leave a message here at the embassy."

"Okay, Pat. I'll tell him."

Pat walked slowly back home. He had no idea what he should say to Dale. He let down his control, hoping that Eddie would start to take over. Eddie didn't, because Eddie wanted Pat to suffer for upsetting Dale.

Pat sat down on his front porch stairs. He was not afraid to face an invading army in Saigon, but he was afraid to face Dale after his inexcusable tirade. He ran phrase after phase of apologies through his mind. They all sounded lame. The more excuses he came up with, the worse they sounded. Pat was not a humble guy.

Eddie finally took over. He didn't want to prolong Dale's pain— Pat might sit on the porch all night.

Eddie stood up and walked through the front door. He went straight to their bedroom. Dale was wearing a granny gown. She looked up from a novel she was reading. He could tell that she was still angry and hurting.

Eddie sat down on the edge of the bed and looked gently into her eyes, "Hon, Pat is sorry."

Dale knew she was talking to Eddie, "Why are you telling me he is sorry? Is he afraid to apologize to me?"

Eddie chuckled, "Yes. He is terrified. He sat on the front porch for twenty minutes trying unsuccessfully to come up with the right words to apologize. I think tonight was the first time he has ever experienced fear."

Dale squelched a smile, and then her anger returned, "He threatened to keep you and me out of his life."

Eddie assured her, "He can't do that."

Dale was exasperated and declared, "Eddie, I hate to tell you this, but he has more control over your life than you do. Otherwise, we would not be having this conversation."

Eddie considered the truth of her declaration. "Dale, I created Pat to survive in Vietnam. I know how to make him miserable to get him back in line . . . like I did tonight."

Dale said, "I don't expect to understand what is going on with Pat in your head. Why don't you just un-create him?" She knew that un-create wasn't a word, but there weren't words to explain what was going on in her husband's head.

"Do you want me to?" He knew that Dale loved Pat. "Are you that mad at him?"

"Yes. Get rid of him if you can."

Eddie felt a sharp pain in his stomach.

Dale suggested, "When your army commitment is up this time, let's move back to Alabama. You can get a job as an engineer making much more money than you make now. We can buy a house with a white picket fence, and I can drive the kids to school in a station wagon with fake wooden sides. Then you can get rid of Pat."

A severe pain hit Eddie in the gut with only the slight earlier warning. He grabbed his gut and doubled over.

Dale threw the covers off and wrapped her arms around him, "Eddie, what's wrong?"

The pain subsided, "It was just a stomach cramp."

Dale said, "I hope you didn't get food poisoning in Iraq."

Eddie sat back up and distracted her with where she left off. "When we were dating, you said you didn't want a house with a white picket fence and a station wagon."

Dale smiled, "You never forget anything I've ever said."

Eddie couldn't think of a response. Dale knew about his audio-graphic memory.

Dale admitted, "I was younger and wanted something more exciting than a white picket fence and a station wagon, but not as exciting as what you and Pat are doing. We have kids. I am ready to settle down."

Eddie still had nothing to say.

She challenged, "Admit it. You can't expel Pat from your mind."

Eddie admitted, "Dale, I don't want to. This world needs Pat, and I love what we do together."

Dale glared into his eyes, "That was Pat talking."

"No, Dale. That was me talking. I may never be able to just sit on a couch all weekend, drinking beer and watching sports. Pat will make me as miserable as I made him tonight for hurting you. Every time I see a news report that I knew Pat and I could have helped abort, Pat will make me feel guilty. I will become a miserable person and a terrible husband and father.

"Dale, I approve of Pat's missions. I know this is what God wants me to do. It wasn't my choice, but He has given me some very unique talents to protect American soldiers."

Dale said, "And you need Pat to do it?"

"Yes. He still has a lot to learn to earn your respect. He is only five years old."

Dale didn't know whether to laugh or cry, "What are talking about?"

"I just created him in Nam five years ago. And like most young kids, sometimes he throws a temper tantrum when he doesn't get his way."

Dale laughed, "Well, I don't put up with temper tantrums."

Eddie smiled, "Scott has already learned that. Pat got his first lesson tonight. He is a fast learner."

Dale hugged him. It was confusing to live with a man with two personalities. "Well, he better learn to appreciate having you on his side when dealing with me."

Chapter 27
Haig

Pat didn't get to the embassy until nine a.m. He had a message to see the ambassador.

He walked up to the second floor, "Good morning, Kay."

Kay smiled, "Good morning, Pat. Andy is expecting you."

Pat said hello to everyone as he walked by the desks in the outer office. The ambassador waved Pat into his office from his chair, "Good morning, Pat. Come in and close the door."

Andy didn't get out of his chair from behind the desk as he normally did, "Please, sit down."

Pat wondered what was up. Andy wasn't acting normal.

Andy said, "I thought you were going to be gone for at least a week. Did something go wrong?"

"No, quite the contrary. Everything went perfectly. I found out all I hoped to learn quicker than expected."

Andy relaxed. "General Haig called. He is also concerned why you are back so soon. He wants us to call him immediately."

Pat said, "It's nighttime in America, too late for him to still be in the Pentagon."

"I know. I just got off the phone with him twenty minutes ago." Andy picked up the phone, "Kay, make that secure call for me."

Pat was surprised that everyone was so concerned about his infiltration into Iraq. "Andy, has something happened that I don't know about?"

"Not that I know of. But I do wonder why Haig is so concerned."

Andy's phone beeped. He picked up the receiver.

Pat could hear the phone ringing in Andy's ear and the male voice that said "hello".

"Al, Andy here. I have Major O'Sheen with me."

Pat heard Haig say, "Hold on. I'm going to switch phones." The phone seemed to go dead.

Haig picked up the phone in his home office, "Andy, put Pat on speaker."

Andy punched a button, "Can you hear me?"

Haig ignored the ambassador, "Pat, can you hear me?"

"Yes sir. Loud and clear." Pat mimed for Andy to turn down the volume.

"Pat, what went wrong? Why are you back in Iran so soon?"

"Nothing went wrong, Al. Everything went perfectly. I found out all I hoped to learn quicker than expected."

"How?" Haig didn't believe anyone could gather reliable intelligence in three days.

"Sir, I had a long talk with the Iraqi Defense Minister Khairallah. I learned what I was looking for straight from the horse's mouth." Pat heard Haig shuffling papers. He assumed that Haig was confirming the name of the Iraqi defense minister. Not even Pat could remember the name of every official in every government in the world.

Haig said while he was searching through papers, "How did you meet him?"

Pat repeated the cab story from the beginning, the CIA agents not being at home, the cab driver being upset by the traffic jam, and Pat's offer to share the cab ride back to town.

Haig had quit shuffling papers. "And his other fare was the defense minister, Khairallah?" Haig's pronunciation of the name was almost unrecognizable.

"Yes sir."

"And he just jumped in the cab with you?"

"No sir. He had Rashid, the cab driver, search me for weapons, and then he studied my forged papers."

"So you almost blew your cover."

Pat took over from Eddie. "No, I didn't come anywhere close to blowing my cover. I was able to ask him everything I wanted to know without arousing any suspicion. He answered all my questions."

Haig recognized that Pat got defensive—maybe aggressive was a better word. Haig said, "The defense minister can follow your fake ID back to Iran."

"No he can't, General Haig. I used a different name with different forged papers to fly from Tehran to Damascus and back." Pat's tone was getting testy.

Andy noticed insolence building and motioned his hand up and down for Pat to calm down.

Pat calmed, "General Haig, I went through Damascus into Iraq disguised. I spoke with the defense minister in a Syrian Arabic accent. There is no way he suspected that I was an American spy. I spent two more days in Iraq and wasn't followed."

Haig knew that O'Sheen was difficult to control. He challenged the testy attitude, "How did you learn a Syrian Arabic accent?"

Pat accepted the reasonable question, "I scheduled my flights so that I could spend enough time in Syria to learn their accent."

Haig was skeptical, "You learned a Syrian Arabic accent in one day?"

"Yes sir."

Haig thought, *bullshit*. But then he considered how quickly Pat learned Farsi and Arabic.

Pat interrupted Haig's thought process and said with a bit of ire, "General Haig, aren't you at all interested in what I learned in Iraq."

Andy couldn't believe O'Sheen's insolence.

Haig controlled his ire, "What did you learn, major?"

Pat wasn't intimidated by the "Major" address, "Minister Khairallah told me that President al-Bakr has been bed ridden for over a month and that Saddam has taken over most of the duties of running the government."

Haig sighed, "We already know that, major. Al-Bakr has been bed-ridden several times before. Did you learn anything new?"

Pat said, "He has never been bed-ridden for over a month. I trust my instincts, General Haig. Saddam is holding al-Bakr captive to keep him away from President Assad of Syria while he consolidates his control over Iraq."

"I'm sure Khairallah didn't tell you that?"

"He didn't voice it, but it was written all over his face. He knows he is backing the right horse."

Haig summarized Pat's argument, "So you think Saddam Hussein is about to take over Iraq?"

"Yes sir. He will be in total control before the end of summer. And then he will exile Khomeini. Khomeini will start a full scale revolution against the Shah of Iran before Christmas."

Haig sighed, "Khomeini has been out of the loop for over a decade. No one here believes that he will ever be a player again."

Haig said, "Andy, what do you think?"

"Al, Khomeini still has a big influence over Shia Muslims in Iran. But the Shah will crush any attempt at a revolution before it can get any major support from the citizens of Iran."

Haig asked, "Pat, do you disagree with Andy?"

"Sir, when Saddam kicks Khomeini out of Iraq. Iran is going to turn into a bloody hellhole."

Haig knew how long Andy had been in Iran. Pat had learned an incredible amount of intelligence in just a month, but he was new to the arena. "Pat, you need to have more intelligence to convince me that Khomeini is going to be a serious problem. Khomeini is not on any of our intelligence radars."

Pat understood, "I'll keep working on it, Sir."

"Pat, do you have anything else to report?"

"Nothing that can't wait until I investigate further. I know it is past your bedtime in Washington."

Haig chuckled after they disconnected.

Andy glared at Pat. "Pat, you will never be a diplomat if you don't learn how to cushion your opinions."

Pat snickered as he stood up, "Andy, I'd rather die than become a diplomat. I'm glad that America has people with your temperament and tact to handle that."

Pat added, "Andy, you need to call the SAVAK director, Nasser, or Defense Minister Fahad. I think it was a SAVAK agent that followed me to work this morning, so they know I'm back from Iraq and will want a report from me." Pat left the ambassador's office without waiting for a reaction. He knew that Andy didn't quite trust him yet.

Pat walked down the stairs and down the corridor to his office. Cleo's face brightened as he approached her desk. Pat smiled and asked, "When will Neal be back?"

"The day after tomorrow."

Pat started to turn toward his office. For reasons he couldn't later rationalize in his audio recall, he turned back and asked in Farsi, "Cleo, when are you getting married?"

Cleo jumped up from her chair, "Who told you I was getting married?"

Her reaction confirmed the truth of his question. "Have you set a date?"

"Next month."

Pat could tell that she was elated with anticipation, and he was thrilled by her elation, "When can I meet your fiancé?"

"Would you like to come to our wedding?" She was excited by Pat's interest.

Pat wasn't sure how to handle the invitation, "I would be honored, if your fiancé approves." Pat understood the Muslim male dominated culture. Her fiancé would probably not welcome an American whom he didn't know to his wedding. He turned away and walked to his office to keep her from trying to affirm an invitation she was not able to control.

Chapter 28
Report

Pat started writing up the details of his visit to Iraq. Paperwork wasn't his forte, but he understood its importance. His phone rang. It was the ambassador.

"Pat, you were right. I just got a call from Nasser. He and Fahad know you are back from Iraq. They are going to be here at ten-thirty. You need to come up to my office to discuss what to tell them."

Pat walked up to the ambassador's office, considering how to convey his intelligence diplomatically. Pat didn't want to embarrass his friend, Ambassador Sullivan.

He sat down across the desk from Andy.

Andy started, "Pat, I don't want you to bring up your Khomeini theory with the Iranians."

Pat didn't respond.

Andy was upset that Pat didn't readily agree. "Pat, like General Haig told you, we need more intelligence before we can support your Khomeini theory."

Pat nodded, "Can I tell the Iranians that Saddam Hussein is about to take control of Iraq, and that he will try to instigate a conflict with Iran in the next few weeks to put fear into the Iraqi people to help him consolidate his control?"

Andy's eyebrows rose, "You didn't mention that to Al."

Pat replied, "Haig was only worried about my identity as an American being compromised. Nasser sent me into Iraq to find out why Saddam was causing skirmishes on the southern border. I am going to have to give him my opinion, Andy."

The ambassador knew he couldn't control what Pat would say. It was too late to cancel the meeting. "Pat, don't offer your opinion unless asked."

Pat warned, "Nasser will question me directly, and Andy, I will answer him with my opinions honestly."

Andy nodded, he had no other option.

Kay walked in and announced the Iranian visitors. Andy came around his desk as Pat stood up. They shared amenities with Nasser and Fahad and sat down on the couch and armchairs—the visitors on the couch.

Nasser looked at Pat, "You weren't in Iraq for long. Was your identity compromised?"

Pat stifled his chuckle and answered the question for the third time, "No, Nasser. It went better than expected. The forged papers you provided to me passed the highest levels of scrutiny."

Andy interrupted the conversation and presented Pat's belief that Saddam Hussein was taking control of Iraq. Andy inserted every diplomatic uncertainty and ambiguity.

Pat admired Nasser for patiently listening through all the diplomatic bullshit without interrupting. Pat should learn from Nasser's patience.

Defense Minister Rashid Fahad accepted Andy's diplomatic explanation.

Nasser didn't. "Pat, you were only in Iraq for three days—not long enough to learn anything meaningful."

Pat addressed Defense Minister Fahad, instead of Nasser. "Rashid, do you know the Iraqi Defense Minister Khairallah?"

Fahad admitted, "I know of him but have never talked to him. Why do you ask?"

"I talked to him for thirty minutes. The information I'm bringing back to you came out of his mouth."

Fahad didn't believe the young American, "How did you meet Khairallah."

Pat went through his cab story again. He complimented Nasser, "The fake ID's you gave me stood up under Khairallah's scrutiny.

"Khairallah told me that al-Bakr has been bedridden for over a month, the longest time ever, and that Saddam has taken over most of his duties. He was gloating because he is Saddam's right hand man. I believe that Saddam is keeping al-Bakr out of the public eye while he consolidates his power."

Pat hesitated to allow questions.

Fahad said, "We cannot verify your claim of meeting Khairallah." He believed that the young American major was manipulating them in an attempt to further his career.

Pat glared at him. "Fahad, I am not surprised that you doubt me, because you don't know me. But I never lie.

"As far as the border skirmishes are concerned, I think Saddam is hoping to egg you into a major retaliation into their territory. I talked to dozens of Iraqis. They all fear the Shah's powerful military supported by America, and they will support Saddam's takeover of Iraq if he convinces them that the Shah is a threat to their sovereignty."

When no one responded, Pat added, "I don't think you want Saddam Hussein as a neighbor."

Fahad was skeptical of the young, low-ranking major, "You are speculating about Saddam's motives for the border skirmishes."

Pat understood his skepticism. "Saddam is a Sunni Muslim. A majority of Iraqis are Shia Muslims and would prefer to have a Shia president. But they all know that Saddam controls the military, and they will rise in support of him against a military threat from Iran."

Nasser argued, "Almost all Iranians are Shia Muslims."

Pat said, "Yes, and the Shah exiled the most famous Iranian Shia Muslim—Khomeini. He lives in Iraq. Saddam asked him to leave once, but Khomeini is happy living with the Shia Muslims in Iraq, and he is popular with the Iraqi press, so he has stayed in Iraq."

Ambassador Sullivan interjected forcefully, "We are getting off the subject." Pat was too close to exposing his Khomeini theory to the Iranians.

Nasser nodded agreement, "Pat, I've learned about your two successful POW rescues in Vietnam. I would like to hear your opinion on what to do about the skirmishes on the border."

Pat didn't hesitate, "I'd pull my troops back off the border except for an adequate number of scouts to warn of an incursion by the Iraqis."

Fahad said, "We won't do that. A country that doesn't protect its borders is not a country at all."

Pat said, "I'm not suggesting that you don't protect your borders. I'm just suggesting that you outsmart Saddam. I would send a thousand soldiers into the oil fields as workers, and I would stock armaments and army uniforms nearby. When the scouts warn of an Iraqi incursion into Iran territory, I'd mobilize them and surround the Iraqi troops on three sides with overwhelming fire power, inflicting as few casualties as possible and force them to retreat back across the border. I would make sure to have it all on film, proving that they invaded your territory. I would present the film to the United Nations. Have enough medics in your forces to bandage the wounded and escort them back to the border. Hire your best undertakers to embalm their dead. Let the United Nations handle the negotiation to return their bodies to their families in Iraq. Saddam will lose prestige and al-Bakr may be able to take back control of Iraq. Like I said earlier, you don't want Saddam Hussein as a neighbor."

Andy was mesmerized, "That is brilliant!" He was embarrassed at his expletive.

Rashid Fahad stared at Andy and realized that he was hearing Pat's idea for the first time.

Pat said, "Rashid, I just came up with that suggestion without forethought. It may be one possible way to try to outsmart Saddam. I haven't been to the area of the skirmishes. I'm sure you can come up with a better plan."

Nasser hid his smile. O'Sheen handed the reins of control over to Rashid very cleverly. Pat was learning to be a diplomat. O'Sheen was definitely someone Nasser wanted to have on his side in the future.

Rashid looked at Pat with a new level of respect, "You are warning us not to get suckered into Saddam's scheme?"

Pat answered immediately, "Yes sir. When we talked last week, you asked for our intelligence input on the border problem. When I was in Iraq, I also talked to CIA and MI-6 agents. They didn't know about the border skirmishes, but they didn't disagree with my analysis of Saddam's possible motivation.

"Neal Williams, our defense attaché, whom you know well and have good reasons to trust more than you do me, is supposed to be back here in the next couple of days. I will update him on the intelligence I gathered. You should get his opinion."

Nasser chuckled, unable to disguise his amusement this time. Pat was rapidly learning how to handle diplomats.

146

Rashid looked at the SAVAK director, not understanding the humor in his chuckle.

Nasser deflected Rashid's curiosity, "Pat, thank you. We will take your advice under consideration. Andy, when Neal gets settled back in from his trip to America, have him contact us." Nasser stood up. Rashid reluctantly stood up. Pat wasn't sure which one of them held more power now, but he had no doubt who was the most intelligent and would have the most power down the road.

Pat stood up and said, "I'll walk you to the embassy front door." Pat wanted to talk to Nasser alone.

Andy stood up and walked down the stairs with them to the front door. O'Sheen was too close to disclosing his Khomeini theory in the meeting. O'Sheen told Haig that he wouldn't discuss his theory with Iran without more research. Andy didn't trust O'Sheen to honor his commitment to Haig.

After they shared amenities and the Iranians exited the embassy. Andy said, "I'm hungry. Have lunch with me."

Pat knew that he had disclosed opinions to answer the Iranians questions that Andy had never considered. Andy had no military experience. Pat owed him an explanation.

Pat smiled and said, "I'm starving. Are you buying?"

"Yes. We'll eat in my quarters."

In the ambassador's quarters, the ambassador disappeared for a few minutes, using the need to go the bathroom as an excuse. But Pat heard him telling his wife that he needed to talk to his luncheon guest in private. *His luncheon guest—not Pat O'Sheen.* Pat chuckled. His recommendations to the Iranian officials had thrown Andy's diplomatic balance off kilter.

Andy instructed Pat to sit down at the dining room table. Pat took an end chair which didn't make Andy happy. Pat hid his amusement.

Andy sat down on a chair next to him, instead of the other end of the table.

He said quietly, "Pat, you should have discussed your military strategy with me before our meeting."

"I didn't have a military strategy before our meeting. I was surprised when Nasser asked for my military opinion. I had to respond to Rashid's naive response that a country that can't protect its borders is not a country at all. He was taking Saddam Hussein's bait. I just suggested that he turn the bait against him."

"You did that brilliantly. But you should not have offered it without discussing it with me first."

Pat stared at Andy without responding. Apparently, opinions from lower level diplomats were not allowed to be expressed outside the State department without approval.

Andy added to his criticism, "You brought up Khomeini. You told Haig that you would not discuss your theory on Khomeini until you had more research to support it."

Pat said coldly, "I didn't disclose my theory. I planted a seed in Nasser's mind."

Pat turned the questioning around. "Why did you follow us downstairs when they left the embassy?"

Andy was wary of O'Sheen's more aggressive attitude. He got defensive, "You have no right to question my motives. I was just being friendly."

"Bullshit. You wanted to make sure I wouldn't share my Khomeini theory with Nasser."

Pat stood up. "Andy, I will follow your guidelines and the guidelines of my military superiors. But I will not be anyone's puppet." Pat turned and walked out of the ambassador's quarters.

Andy was stunned. He had invited Pat to lunch to offer Pat the Military Attaché position in Iran. Neal Williams had called him and said that he and his wife were getting back together, and that he would come back to Iran for only a few weeks. He asked for a transfer to Cairo, Egypt or anywhere in Europe. Andy wanted O'Sheen to take his place.

But Andy just learned again that he couldn't control O'Sheen. Pat was brilliant. In only a month, he had a firm grasp of what was happening. By infiltrated Iraq, O'Sheen had earned Nasser and Rashid's respect. Earning their respect was the closest anyone could get to gaining access to the Shah. O'Sheen could be a great asset to Andy's diplomatic career. He decided to never use a confrontational approach with Major O'Sheen again.

Chapter 29
Normalcy?

Eddie was trying to make Pat feel guilty for his treatment of the ambassador, but Pat wasn't buying it.

Pat returned Cleo's contagious smile as he approached his office.

Cleo said in Farsi, "You missed midday prayers."

Pat nodded, "I was tied up in meetings."

She said, "My fiancé wants to meet you."

Pat asked, "Just me or my family?"

Cleo's face glowed, "Your family. I would love to meet your wife and kids."

Pat sighed. Eddie took over, "Sounds great."

Cleo's smile grew, "I'll work out a meeting."

Pat sat down on the corner of Cleo's desk, "Have you been up to the Imam Reza Shrine in Mashhad?"

"Not since I was a child. But I remember how magnificent it was. Are you thinking about taking your family up there?"

"Yes. But I'm going up there on government business. I will need a pool car."

Cleo offered, "I can make reservations for you. When do you want to go?"

"After lunch tomorrow."

Cleo offered, "There are a lot of beautiful sites on the way up there. You won't arrive until after midnight if you leave after lunch and drive there. I can write up an agenda for you and your family."

Pat kissed the tip of his right forefinger and pressed it to her forehead, "Thank you."

He went down to the cafeteria and ate a late lunch that one of the servers heated up for him in a toaster oven.

When Pat got back to his office, his phone rang. Cleo said that Nasser Moghadam of SAVAK was calling. Pat wondered if he wanted to talk about Khomeini. He took the call.

"Hello, Pat."

"Hello, Nasser. Do you have questions about what we discussed this morning?"

"Yes. Can you come to my office tomorrow afternoon, alone?"

Pat assumed that Nasser knew embassy phone calls were all recorded, "I'm leaving town tomorrow for a few days. I may be able to change my priorities. What is this about?"

Nasser measured his words carefully. "Pat you mentioned Khomeini this morning. I would like to talk to you about him—off the record."

"I can't talk to you about him."

"Why not?" Nasser sounded offended.

"I've been ordered by my superiors not to share my naive theories until I gather more evidence to convince my government of his threat to Iran."

Rashid understood Pat's message, "Is that why you are going to be out of town tomorrow."

Pat said, "I can't discuss that at this time."

Rashid smiled. Pat's cautious answer was a definite "Yes".

"Pat, would you please let me know when you get back to Tehran?"

"I will."

Pat was pleased that Nasser was concerned about Khomeini based on the seed he planted in the meeting that morning. Nasser was smart and alarms were going off in his head. Pat's explanation that he couldn't talk about Khomeini would focus Nasser even more on Khomeini. Pat's work in Iran was almost done. He no longer needed to convince American diplomats that he needed to espouse his Khomeini theory to Iran. But he did need to convince America that Khomeini's radical Islamic philosophy could destabilize the Middle East.

Dale greeted Pat as he entered the front door. She rarely beat Scott to the door. She could tell by the hug and kiss that Eddie, and not Pat, came through the door.

Eddie picked up Scott, "What did you do today?"

Scott surprised him, "I learned to talk to some of the kids in preschool. Some of them don't talk like we do. They talk like you do sometimes."

Eddie looked at Dale, "Preschool?"

Dale explained, "Norma Jean suggested I try it. Her daughter goes there twice a week in the morning. She enjoys the break."

"Did Amanda go too?"

"No. She is too young."

She walked to the kitchen. Eddie followed with Scott in his arms. Dale started making them a drink.

Scott asked his daddy in Farsi, "Did you have fun today?"

Eddie chuckled and answered in Farsi, "Yes. I have fun every day. Some days are more fun than others.

"How about you. Did you have fun today?"

"Yes." Scott said it quickly while nodding his head emphatically.

Eddie approved of the preschool. He knew Dale was worried that he wouldn't. But Eddie understood that a mother needs a break from her twenty-four hour a day job. He wanted Scott to learn foreign languages, which is much easier for young children.

Eddie asked Dale, "Did you meet the teacher in the school?"

"Yes. And I met her assistant."

Eddie wanted more, "And you are sure that Scott is safe going there?"

"Yes. They were very friendly to me. I'm sure you know that some Iranians don't like Americans." She handed Pat a drink.

"Have you had problems?"

"Eddie, most people here are polite to me. But I can tell the difference between politeness and friendliness."

He liked it when she called him Eddie and he hugged her. She had just confirmed some of his research.

They sat down on the couch.

He changed subjects, "I am going to visit a shrine northeast of here to talk to the people there. It is a long drive. I would like you and the kids to go with me."

"Really! I would love to go with you. I haven't been more than ten miles from here."

Eddie said, "You would have to wear a hijab to cover your hair and to veil your face at the religious shrine."

"Oh crap. I forgot." She jumped up, ran off, and came back with her purse.

She smiled seeing Scott asleep with his ear to Eddie's chest. She sat down while opening her purse. She pulled out a small piece of paper and handed it to her husband.

He looked at the telephone number, didn't recognize it, and looked at Dale for an explanation.

Dale chuckled. She rarely had the upper hand. "The first time you went shopping with me here, I bought two scarves and a hijab to cover my hair and face. You waited outside the ladies store on a bench. You met a father and son."

Pat said, "This is not the father's number."

"No, it's not." Dale gloated.

She did a "Heh, Heh" to stall Eddie's impatience. "If you remember, we met the son's pregnant wife when I came out of the store. I saw her again today. She talked to me like I was her best friend."

Pat understood where Dale's frivolity was leading, He tried to gain the upper hand. "I remember her. She was very attractive. Are you suggesting that I call her for a date?"

Dale stared into her husband's eyes. He knew. "You have already figured out that this is al-Rashid's number. Why didn't you tell me that you got him out of prison?"

"I liked his family. He was arrested for opposing the Shah when he was nineteen. I told his dad I would try to help. I gave his name to one of the high ranking Iranian officials, and asked him to let me visit him. They were willing to release him from prison if I signed for his release." Pat didn't tell her about his liability for signing the release papers.

"Why didn't you tell me?" Dale was so proud of him.

Eddie shrugged, "Pat was obsessed with his infiltration into Iraq at the time."

Dale burst out laughing. She still found it hilarious when Eddie talked about Pat in the third person. Her laugh woke Scott up.

Dale took Scott into her arms, "Mr. O'Sheen, you're a very complicated work of art."

152

She stood up to put Scott to bed, "Don't you ever doubt that I love you."

A warm feeling filled him. "Likewise."

Pat dialed the number.

A male voice answered, "Allahu Akbar."

Pat recognized the voice, "Al-Rashid? Pat O'Sheen."

"I'm glad you called. My dad wants me to help you by telling you about the attitude of the students toward the Shah."

Not a convincing motivation, "Your father? What about you? Do you want to help me?"

"With qualifications. Major O'Sheen, I'm back at the university. My dad says that he will disown me if I get you in trouble."

"I can take care of myself, Al-Rashid. I want to talk to you, but not on this phone line. Do you have any free time in the morning?"

"I don't have any classes between nine-thirty and eleven."

They arranged a meeting place.

Chapter 30
Shrine

Al-Rashid shook Pat's hand with a big smile on his face. "Major O'Sheen, I owe you for getting me out of prison."

Pat smiled, "You have already thanked me for that, al-Rashid. I want to know if the students at the university are planning demonstrations against the Shah."

"Why do you want to know? Will you warn Director Moghadam?"

The question exposed a lot. Students were not well enough connected to know that Pat knew Nasser. There was a high level official in the Shah's regime providing information to the students—fueling their zealousness.

Pat lied, 'I don't support the Shah. Are the students hoping to establish an Islamic Republic?"

Al-Rashid was impressed with the American, "I have heard that you are a Muslim. We will not establish a republic. We will establish an Islamic theocracy to rule the state."

Pat managed to force a smile, "Based on Khomeini's doctrine?"

Al-Rashid was surprised, "You know who Khomeini is?"

Pat said, "I've read many of his writings. Do you hope he will come back to Iran?"

"He will, after we drive the Shah out."

"You will die trying to drive him out."

"My death as a martyr will encourage more Muslims to rise up against him."

Pat admired his zealousness. It reminded him of the Viet Cong in Vietnam and the guard talking about his family on the back porch of the POW barracks that Pat blew up. He detested their philosophy, but admired their zeal.

Pat had heard all he was going to learn and stood up.

154

Al-Rashid stood and offered his hand. "Will you join our cause?"

Pat shook his hand and answered honestly, "Al-Rashid, I'm a student of history. The people who live in a country controlled by a religion rarely prosper. The American founders who wrote our constitution outlawed religious control. I think the people of Iran will suffer if you succeed in forming a theocracy."

Pat walked away, worried that his honesty might make him a target of the Khomeini extremists. Al-Rashid may give him a pass because he was grateful for getting him out of jail. But Pat recognized that al-Rashid's zealousness might overrule his gratefulness. Pat was glad that he was leaving the area in a few hours with his family. Al-Rashid confirmed Pat's theory about the Islamic extremist's commitment to depose the Shah. But Pat knew it would still be a hard sell to convince the powers in America.

Pat, Dale, and kids left Tehran two hours later in an embassy pool car. Dale and Scott were happy to see new terrain. They were particularly thrilled to see the mountains that were glowing in the sunshine.

Dale remembered, "Isn't Neal Williams coming back today?"

"That was his plan."

"I would think you would want to be there to greet him to see how things went with his wife and kids."

Pat looked at Dale who was holding Amanda on her lap, and then looked back at the road. "Neal and Andy are long-term friends. They can work out the transition better without my interference."

"What transition?"

"Neal's wife refused to come to Iran. That was a year ago, and their marriage was falling apart. Before he went home, he requested a transfer if he succeeded in reuniting his family."

"Because you encouraged him to get back with his family."

Pat looked over at Dale.

She smiled, "Military wives communicate. State department wives do, too. We know more about what you do than you could imagine." Her husband went silent.

Dale tried to wait him out until she sensed that Pat was taking over. "I never talk about your missions. If that is why you quit talking, you don't need to worry about that."

"Don't I?"

"No."

Scott struggled to stand up, "Look." He pointed at a large volcanic looking mountain.

Pat slowed. He took a left at the next road. It was a small, poorly maintained road.

Dale asked, "Why did you turn onto this crummy road?" She worried that he was upset.

"Because Scott wants to see that volcano."

She said, "Eddie, I never talk to anyone about your missions. Even if you told me more about them, I wouldn't. You loved Mike and trusted him, didn't you?"

Pat let up on the gas pedal and looked over at her.

She looked over at him and was alarmed at his glare.

Scott pointed, "There's a sign."

Pat looked forward and read it. He turned right on a volcanic, crushed-rock road.

Dale said, "You trusted Mike, and you can trust me."

Pat concentrated on driving as they climbed the steep, rocky road up the mountain. They encountered two cars coming down. Pat stopped to let them by.

Dale was looking down off the edge of the road. If the car went over the edge and tumbled down the slope, none of them would survive. "Are you sure this is safe?"

Pat replied, "They made it. I will make it." He pressed the gas pedal and continued up and around the volcanic mountain.

They got out in a small parking lot near the top. Pat picked Amanda up off Dale's lap and exited the car. Scott followed him out and walked up and looked off the edge of the mountain. In the low humidity, they could see for a hundred miles. Scott said, "Wow!"

Pat agreed, "Wow is right."

Dale moved up next to them, "This place is so beautiful. Did Cleo tell you about it?"

Pat put his arm out and Dale moved into his side. He put his arm around her. "Cleo suggested it, but she said it was out of the way. When Scott pointed it out, I couldn't resist."

Scott walked back toward the volcanic crater. Pat handed Amanda to Dale. He caught up with Scott and walked next to him, his left hand near the back of his neck. There were no guard rails. The crater was a thousand feet across.

Scott walked toward the edge.

Dale objected, "Eddie."

Pat grabbed the top of Scott's T-shirt with two fingers as Scott walked up to the edge and looked down into the crater. The vertical drop was only about ten feet and then sloped down another two hundred feet to the bottom. If Scott fell off, he would tumble down the slope ten or twenty feet. Friction would stop his slide. If Pat fell off, he would probably tumble all of the way to the bottom. Newton's law: mass and velocity creates momentum. Scott and Pat's velocity would be equal, but Pat's weight would increase his momentum so much that he could tumble all the way to the bottom.

Dale walked up to the edge and backed away. She almost panicked when Scott moved forward, his toes inches from the edge. Pat moved forward with him, two fingers gripping the top of his shirt. The toes of Pat's right foot extended over the edge.

Dale backed farther away, experiencing vertigo. "Pat, bring him away from the edge." She knew it was Pat that wanted their son to be "macho" . . . not Eddie. The human male species had very little common sense.

Scott looked up at his daddy and smiled. Neither one of them had any fear. Scott reached his hand up. Pat grabbed it, knowing that would help Dale relax.

They made a few more interesting stops on the way up toward Mashhad.

At the stops, Pat moved a distance away from them to smoke and talk to locals. Dale understood that this was a research trip for her husband. They were all having a marvelous time, all paid for by American tax dollars. It was almost midnight when they checked into a hotel almost two hours from the shrine.

The next day, they had to park a half-mile away from the shrine. Pat was upbeat about the walk, explaining that they all needed the exercise. At the shrine, Pat explained that it contains the mausoleum of

Imam Reza, the eighth Imam of Twelver Shiites. He had to explain the meaning of "Twelver Shiite" and that the twelfth Imam would return with Christ to save the world. He explained that the mosque was largest in the world by dimension and the second largest by capacity.

The shrine was gorgeous and fascinating, but Dale and Scott were ready to leave after two hours. Eddie didn't spend enough time with them, but instead, talked to men in smoking groups. Dale talked to a few abandoned mothers like her who spoke some English. Scott spoke some Farsi with their kids.

Pat and Dale walked back toward the car. Dale wasn't her normal friendly self. Scott was holding his dad's hand.

Eddie asked Dale, "Are you mad at me?"

"No. You told me you were coming up here on business. But, you left us alone. I tried to mingle with the people who could speak English . . ."

Pat interrupted, "I never let you out of my sight. Scott was enjoying himself."

Dale couldn't counter that argument.

"Eddie, no one was threatening. But, as I said before, a lot of the people here don't like Americans. I can't speak without them knowing that I am an American. I was . . . uncomfortable."

Her perception reinforced Pat's concept, "You looked over at me numerous times. You knew where I was. If you wanted to leave, you could have told me."

Dale repeated, "I knew that you didn't come up here on vacation. I wanted to let you do your job."

Pat put his arm around her.

She muttered almost under her breath, "Whatever that job is."

Pat heard her and smiled. *Behind every great man was a great woman.*

Chapter 31
Fight

Colonel Neal Williams corralled Pat as he walked into the embassy. "Pat, come to my office."

Neal closed the door after they entered his office. He spoke up immediately, "Pat, you are causing a lot of controversy over here."

Pat had been in the military long enough to understand that some officers were not capable of command and were assigned to the State Department. Pat knew that he probably fit into that category—not because he couldn't lead, but because he wouldn't automatically follow his leaders without question.

"Neal, I'm just doing what I was sent here to do."

"Well, Major, You need to learn to obey your superiors."

"I do when their orders don't interfere with my mission."

Pat changed subjects, "Colonel, was your visit with your wife and kids successful?"

Neal went back to the original subject, "Andy is my best friend. He wants you …"

Pat interrupted, "Was your visit with your wife and kids successful?" He knew his question pried into Neal's personal life.

The colonel didn't answer directly and combined the two subjects, "I'm being reassigned to Cairo. Andy is considering you for my replacement here."

Pat knew the answer to his question based on Neal's reassignment, but he wanted Neal to admit it, "Are your wife and kids going to join you in Cairo?"

"Major, you should not pry into the personal life of a superior officer. That borders on insolence."

Pat jumped up off his chair and walked toward the door, confirming his insolence.

Williams said, "Major. I didn't give you permission to leave."

Pat spun around and said calmly, "Neal, you can work with me as a friend or against me as a superior officer; your choice." Pat left the room.

Neal was shocked. Andy wanted his opinion on whether he should offer Pat the military attaché job. Andy was worried that he couldn't control Pat. Neal agreed to confront Pat. Based on the confrontation they just had, he knew that Andy couldn't control O'Sheen. Neal doubted that anyone in the world could control O'Sheen.

Neal had already talked to Nasser and the director of SAVAK sang Pat's praises. O'Sheen was making him look bad. Neal needed to cut the insolent major down to size. He could do that with the ambassador. Pat had offered him a choice. He decided to work against O'Sheen as a superior officer.

Pat took Dale out to eat early on Friday night. Norma Jean kept the kids.

Pat took her to his favorite restaurant where he often ate lunch. She wore a scarf to cover her hair. Youssef saw them enter and hurried to the door. "Hello, Pat. Is this your wife?"

Dale could follow a conversation that far in Farsi. She smiled.

Pat spoke in English, "Yes. Dale this is Youssef, the best restaurateur in Tehran."

Dale bowed slightly, "I am pleased to meet you." She knew better than to offer her hand like a westerner.

Youssef showed them to a table. Pat took the chair where he could see the door.

When they sat down, Dale said, "He treated you like a celebrity."

Pat chuckled, "Youssef treats everyone he has ever met like a celebrity. So does his wife. That is why their restaurant is so successful."

Dale replied, "I was hoping the food would be good."

"You will love it."

Pat noticed three men walking into the restaurant. The oldest and largest one stared at Pat like he recognized him. Pat got a slight warning pain in his stomach. Pat didn't think he had ever seen the man before, but he wished that his visual memory was as good as his audio memory.

Dale noticed the change in her husband, "Eddie, you invited me on this date. Don't let Pat take over."

Pat smiled at her.

A waiter approached them with a menu. Pat handed it back and ordered for both of them—two different meals that they would share. He ordered the best white wine to come out of an Iranian vineyard— according to his Iranian friends, it was from Caleb's winery in Qom. It was priced above their normal budget. Pat ignored the stare from the man in the front corner table. Pat would not let him disturb his date with Dale. He just had to concentrate on not letting Dale know that he took over from Eddie and spoil her rare night out in Tehran. He moved to the seat to his right, next to Dale with his back to the restaurant, but his peripheral vision was able to see the man at the corner table by the door.

Eddie and Dale spoke back and forth in English. Dale loved the wine and was thoroughly enjoying herself. Dale loved her meal. Half way through, they swapped plates. Dale loved the second plate even better. She was getting giddy enjoying the meal and a night out, and she was talking louder under the influence of the wine.

When the wine was gone, the waiter approached, picked up the empty bottle, and asked if they wanted another. Dale didn't understand what he said, but his intent of selling another bottle of wine was universal. She shook her head. She grabbed the waiter's arm and told him that she wanted to talk to the chef.

Pat translated for the waiter, who smiled at her and went into the kitchen.

As they took the last few bites of their meals, Youssef's wife came out of the kitchen and approached the table. Pat noticed the big guy in the corner get up and approach. Pat picked up the table knife and lowered it to the napkin on his lap. He turned his chair toward the front door and the approaching man. Youssef moved back from the cash register.

The big man interrupted, "Americans are not welcome here. I hate Americans." Dale didn't understand the man's Farsi, but she was alarmed at his tone of voice.

Pat replied in Farsi calmly, not wanting to alarm Dale further, "Then you should move away from us and leave us alone." Pat moved the napkin off the knife in his hand that was not visible over the table from Dale's angle.

Dale calmed at her husband's calm response. The big man stepped forward. Youssef's wife screamed out a name.

A slight smile crossed Pat's face as he glared at the man.

The smile disarmed the man and he stopped. A man his size came out of the kitchen with a large meat-cleaver. Youssef ran into the developing fray. He confronted the man face on, even though the man outweighed him by sixty pounds. Youssef ordered the man out of the restaurant, declaring that he had too much to drink. The big man looked at the man his size approaching with the large knife from the kitchen. He glared at Pat and left the restaurant with the two younger men who looked like his sons.

Everything calmed down. Dale asked Pat, she knew it was Pat by his focus. "What was that all about?"

Pat heard the quiver in her voice, and he took her shaking hand, "A drunk."

Dale understood more than that. "That hates Americans?"

Pat couldn't lie to her and nodded.

Dale was shaking, "Maybe the kids and I should stay in our apartment."

Pat looked in her eyes, "Why?"

"Because there are a lot of people here that don't like Americans."

Pat challenged, "You were never afraid to drive and shop around Birmingham."

Dale glared at him, not understanding the connection.

Pat clarified, "There were several negroes in Birmingham who hated white people. That didn't keep you locked in your house. There are some people in Iran who don't like Americans. Don't judge the people here based on the actions of one anti-American drunk."

Dale smiled at him. It was hard to negate his logic. She relaxed.

Pat didn't. He paid the bill and said to Dale, "You may want to go to the rest-room. It is a ten minute walk home."

When she nodded, he pointed to it.

While she was in the rest-room, Pat surveyed the street out front expecting to confront the big man, but he wasn't there. Maybe his sons talked their inebriated father into going home.

Pat talked to Youssef while he waited for Dale.

Pat and Dale exited and turned left on the sidewalk. Pat walked beside her on the street side of the sidewalk. The traffic on the street was still heavy and slow. When they were fifteen feet from the end of the block, Pat saw the younger son peek around the corner.

Pat put his arm in front of Dale and stopped her. "Get behind me."

"Why?"

Pat stepped forward in front of her as the three men rounded the corner. Pat spoke in Farsi, **"Stop where you are."**

They slowed but kept moving forward.

Pat said calmly, "Believe me guys, you don't want to mess with me."

They slowed some more and spread out. The big guy's right hand was made into a fist, telegraphing his first-planned sucker punch.

Pat could have landed the first blow, but he wanted to make sure that Dale knew that he was fighting in self-defense.

The big guy threw his right fist as anticipated. Pat blocked it by throwing up and out his left forearm. Pat's right hand darted out, the middle knuckles extended, and he popped the guy in his larynx.

The older son had already started moving around Pat's right, not toward Pat, but toward Dale. Pat kicked sideways catching the son hard on his right hip, knocking him into the street. There was a screech of tires, a thud, and breaking glass.

Pat didn't look to the street, but squared off against the younger son, who looked to be about eighteen. The kid backed away, raising his hands with his palms facing out, making it clear that he wanted no part of Pat.

The father was backing up with his right hand to his throat, trying without success to gasp in some air. He voluntarily went down on his butt. The younger son knelt down next to him, "Papa?"

Pat looked into the street. The other son was lying on his back in front of a car, holding his broken left arm. His head was cut."

Pat said to the kid, "Your father will be able to breathe in another minute or two. I didn't hit him hard enough to kill him. You need to tend to your brother in the street."

The kid looked to the street, jumped to his feet, and ran to his brother.

Pat turned and grabbed Dale's right elbow that was shaking badly, "Let's go."

"We can't just leave them like this."

Pat said, "That is exactly what we are going to do."

They walked home at a fast pace.

Pat made them drinks.

Dale said, "If they identify you, you will be in trouble."

"I have diplomatic immunity. In any case, it was self-defense."

"Good God, Pat. You put two of them down in a matter of seconds." She took a two big swallows of her drink.

"Dale, they stepped into one of my areas of expertise. You heard me talking to them as they approached. I warned them that they didn't want to mess with me." He took a small sip of his drink.

"I think the one you kicked out into the street was coming for me." Dale started shaking again.

Pat moved forward and held her. After a minute he said, "He probably only moved toward you to distract me to give his dad an advantage."

She couldn't believe how calm he was. She said, "Thank you, Pat."

She had calmed, "I'll go next door and get the kids."

Chapter 32
Police

Pat answered the phone in the kitchen at eight the next morning (Saturday). The male caller said, "Major O'Sheen, please hold for the ambassador."

Andy came on, "Pat?"

"Yes sir?"

"Nasser and a SAVAC agent are here with two policemen."

Pat said, "Tell Nasser I'll be there in ten minutes."

Andy expected Pat to ask why, "So you did get in fight last night?"

"It wasn't actually a fight. We'll talk about it when I get there. I'm bringing Dale and kids."

"Why?"

"Dale was a witness."

Pat walked into the bathroom where Dale was applying makeup. "Wipe your lipstick off and get your scarf. We need to go to the embassy. I'll get Scott ready to go."

Dale said, "They found out already?"

"Yes, and you were a witness."

On the walk to the embassy, Dale asked, "What do you want me to tell them?"

"I want to you to tell them the truth about what you saw."

"Tell who?"

"Nasser Moghadam is there. He is the director of SAVAK."

"Oh shit, the director?"

Pat stopped and turned to Dale, "You know about SAVAK?"

"Everyone in Iran knows about SAVAK. They must really be pissed if the director is at the embassy."

"No. Just the opposite. Nasser is a friend of mine."

Dale's voice rose a half octave. "You are a friend of the director of SAVAK?"

"Yes."

Dale was impressed. Her husband knew the top people in the military and in the government in America, and already knew some of the top Iranian officials—and he was just a major.

Pat started walking again. He was carrying Scott to make better time. Dale was carrying Amanda and had to hurry to keep up, which told her that her husband was nervous.

Pat checked them in at the guard gate. Pat knew the guard. Scott pointed and asked the guard, "Is that a gun?"

The guard smiled and looked at Major O'Sheen.

Pat told Scott, "Yes. That is Sig Saur P226 pistol."

Scott said, "Can I see it?"

Pat nodded to the guard.

The guard pulled it out of the holster, checked that the safety was on, and showed it to Pat's young son.

Scott reached for it. The guard pulled it back out of his reach.

Pat put his hand forward, "May I?"

"It's against regulations, Sir."

"I know. I won't report you if you don't report me."

The guard smiled and handed Pat the pistol. Pat checked the safety and turned the grip to Scott.

Dale wasn't happy.

Scott reached out his left hand. Pat handed it to him while holding it. It was too heavy for one hand.

Pat said, "Grab it with two hands."

He did, but it was still too awkward and heavy.

Pat handed it back to the private, "Thank you, Mark. I'll clean that for you on the way out."

"That won't be necessary, Pat. This job can get pretty boring. Scott just made my day. He has your smarts."

"No. He has his mother's smarts." Pat winked at him.

The private looked at Pat's pretty wife, "If you are as smart as your husband, then your son is going to brilliant."

Dale laughed. Mark joined in.

After meeting the gate guard, Dale felt a lot calmer as they walked into the embassy. She realized that was why Pat took the extra time socializing. He seemed calmer, too. Entertaining a child can have that effect.

Pat walked directly up to and into Andy's office. He saw Andy's daughter and put Scott down in the doorway to let him walk in on his own.

Scott saw Jenifer and ran to her when she spread her arms.

Andy smiled. So did Nasser.

Jenifer said, "Scott, I want to show you something. Will you come with me?"

Scott looked at his mother. Dale smiled and nodded.

Scott said a perky, "Okay."

She took his hand and led him out of the room.

Pat took Amanda from Dale.

Pat looked at Ambassador Sullivan and then at Colonel Neal Williams. Neal had a smug look on his face. He seemed happy that Pat was in trouble. Pat knew he had made his choice not to work with Pat as a friend, but against him as a superior officer.

Pat said, "Good morning, Nasser."

"Hello, Pat."

"Jamil." Pat nodded at the SAVAK agent.

Nasser spun his head and looked at Jamil and asked in Farsi, "You know O'Sheen?"

Caleb explained in Farsi, "I only know him as my neighbor Pat. I didn't recognize the name Major O'Sheen."

Pat said in Farsi, "Nasser, Jamil is one of my neighbors. Why are you here?"

"We are investigating a crime last night." He answered in Farsi.

Pat said in English, "Jamil, do you speak English?"

Jamil answered, "I understand. Not speak so good."

Pat nodded. "Gentleman, this is my wife, Dale. She doesn't understand Farsi, so we need to continue in English."

Nasser did a slight bow toward Pat's beautiful wife and asked Pat why she was here.

"Nasser, my question is why are you here?"

Neal said, "Major, just answer his question, Why is Dale here?"

Pat ignored Neal and repeated, "Why are you here, Nasser?"

Dale stepped back and glared at Neal. He averted his eyes from her glare.

Nasser said, "We are investigating a crime that occurred last night."

"And you think this embassy was involved?"

"No, Pat. I'm here to ask if you were involved."

"Why would you think that I was involved in a crime last night?"

Neal barked, **"Answer his question, O'Sheen."**

Pat glared for about six seconds at Andy instead of Neal.

Then Pat smiled at Nasser and calmly said. "Did someone report that I committed a crime last night?"

Neal said, "You put two guys in a hospital."

Pat turned slightly towards Neal and glared at him, "Colonel, were you a witness to that."

Neal said nothing.

"Andy, would you ask Neal if he witnessed me committing a crime last night."

Neal answered, "I was not a witness."

Dale couldn't believe that Neal had turned against Pat. She knew where Pat was going with this, which made her very, very nervous.

Pat turned back to Nasser, "If you are referring to the slight altercation I had with three men last night, my wife was a witness. You need to ask her what happened."

Nasser said, "She is your wife. She will say what you told her to say."

Dale had heard enough, **"That is not true."** She stepped forward, "I begged him to tell me what to say on the walk over here. He just kept telling me to answer your questions honestly about what I saw."

Nasser stared at Pat's beautiful wife. He was the director of SAVAK because he could read people. Dale was telling the truth.

Nasser bowed slightly, "What did you witness, Mrs. O'Sheen?"

"We left a restaurant after a great meal. As we were approaching the corner at the end of the block, Pat stopped me and asked me to move behind him. I didn't, so he stepped in front of me as three men came around the corner. Pat said something to them in Farsi. They spread out to attack us. I learned later that Pat believed that they were a father and two sons.

"The older son moved around Pat toward me at the same time his father tried to sucker punch Pat. Pat blocked the punch and side-kicked the older son knocking him into the street where he was hit by a car as I looked on horrified. When I looked back at Pat, the big man who tried to sucker punch him was sitting down holding his throat, and his younger son was kneeling next to his dad. Pat said something in Farsi to the younger son, who looked up at his brother and ran to the street to help him. Pat grabbed my arm and we left."

Nasser looked at Pat, "All three of them said you attacked them."

Pat said, "Nasser, do you really believe that I would attack three men, while I'm leaving a restaurant with my wife?"

When Nasser didn't answer, Pat asked, "Who is the big man, and how did he know my name?"

Nasser replied, "I don't know how he knew you. Aren't you curious how badly they are hurt."

"I'm sure they only stayed in the hospital long enough to set the older brother's broken arm and perhaps put a few stitches in his head. I purposely didn't hit the father hard enough to crush his larynx. I could have.

"Who is he, Nasser?"

"He is the head representative for the Steel and Truck Drivers Association."

Pat looked at the ambassador, "Andy, how would he know me?"

"I have no idea."

Nasser said, "What makes you think he knew you?"

"He glared at me when he first came into the restaurant. He almost attacked me inside while we were talking to Youssef's wife. Youssef ordered him out of the restaurant. Youssef can verify the big man's hostility towards us."

"Okay, Pat. I'm sorry we had to bother you and your family."

He asked one more question, "Why did you leave the scene?"

"To get my wife home safely. I figured the police would take me in for questioning, leaving my wife alone on the street. I couldn't allow that."

Nasser smiled, "They probably would have."

He offered his hand. Pat shook it and smiled.

Nasser turned and said, "See you later, Andy." He ignored Neal, a definite show of displeasure.

Jamil stepped forward and shook Pat's hand. He spoke very softly in Farsi, "Pat, you should consider taking a vacation away from Tehran to let things cool down."

Pat whispered in Farsi, "Thank you, Jamil. I think I can arrange that."

Pat asked in a soft voice, "Jamil, what is the name of the big guy who attacked me?"

He whispered into Pat's ear, obviously desiring deniability.

When the Iranians were gone, Pat turned to Andy.

Andy said, "I'm sorry, Pat. I knew you would have an explanation. You handled that expertly."

Pat nodded, "Jamil suggested that I take a vacation away from here to let things cool down. Apparently, the guy I hit is like a union boss in Iran and knows a lot of thugs. The Army owes me a lot of leave. I think I'll take a week."

Pat glared at Neal, "A week should give the two of you time to decide if I should be reassigned to some other embassy." Neal couldn't hold Pat's glare.

Pat continued, "I've completed my research for General Haig, so I won't object if I am reassigned."

Andy said, "Where will you go on leave?"

"Australia. Can you arrange for visas for us?"

Dale said, "Australia?"

Pat turned to Dale, "We have an open invitation from the Webb family. How does that sound to you?"

She smiled for the first time since entering Andy's office, "Fantastic."

Andy said, "When do you want to leave?"

"How soon can you get the visas?"

"I'll file it as a diplomatic trip to our embassy down there and have them for you this afternoon. Uncle Sam will pay the airfare. The government assigned you here and is responsible for keeping you and your family safe. Write down what flights you want, and I'll get someone to make your reservations."

"Thanks, Andy. We'll go down to my office and make some calls to set it up. It's late afternoon Down Under in Australia."

Chapter 33
Retreat

Pat called Cory Webb's house from his office. Teresa answered the phone.

Pat hit the speaker button, "Hello, Teresa. It's Pat O'Sheen. I have you on speaker with Dale."

"Wonderful. Hello, Dale. I hope you are calling to tell us you are coming to visit."

Dale said, "Hi, Teresa. As a matter of fact, that is why we are calling."

"Really! When?"

Pat said, "We hope to leave Iran tomorrow. We wanted to make sure you both will be there."

"I will be here. Cory is not here now. Let me switch phones and pick up in his office. He keeps a calendar in there. Hold on."

A minute later, they heard the extension pick up. "Are you still there?"

Pat said, "Yes."

"It looks like Cory is tied up on Monday. But all he has is a ton of phone calls to make on the calendar for the rest of the week. It is probably too late to reschedule his Monday appointments."

Pat said, "That's fine. My government is paying for the flight. Our embassy is in Canberra, which I am sure you know is closer to Sydney. We will probably get into Sydney Monday, spend Monday night in Sydney, and then fly into Melbourne on Tuesday afternoon."

"How long can you stay?"

"We will probably fly out on Friday. We don't want to overstay our welcome."

"Poppycock. Plan to stay at least till Sunday. Friday is a holiday here and there will a lot happening in Melbourne on Friday and Saturday."

Pat looked at Dale, who nodded her approval with a big smile. He said, "Okay. We'll plan to fly out on Sunday."

Dale asked about the weather, and what clothes to bring, and a multitude of other things.

When they disconnected, Dale said, "I can't believe it. A government paid vacation to Australia."

Pat smiled and took her into his arms. The tension of the morning and the fight the night before retreated into the background.

Pat said, "Do you remember how to get to the ambassador's family quarters?"

"I think so. If I get lost, I can ask someone."

"You check on Scott while I check on flight schedules."

She took Amanda from Pat.

***

Dale rang the doorbell to the private quarters. An embassy employee opened the door.

"I'm Dale O'Sheen. I'm here to pick up my son."

"Come in." After closing the door, she said, "Please wait here."

A couple of minutes later the Ambassador came out, "Dale, I'm sorry about all of this ugly mess."

"Thank you. But I don't see how you could have prevented it."

"Well. I'm sorry about the way Colonel Williams acted in there this morning. He thinks he's Pat's boss."

Dale said, "Neal is a colonel and Pat is a major. I'm pretty sure in the military that makes Neal his boss."

Andy chuckled, "You might want to remind your husband of that fact. Although, I must say that Pat could be a good diplomat. Pat has a knack for winning people over to his way of thinking."

It was Dale's turn to chuckle, "I am very aware of that."

Andy laughed. Dale joined in.

"Thank you, Andy. I really appreciate your support for him."

The ambassador's wife came around the corner. Dale saw her first, "Hi, Jane. How are you?"

"I'm fine, Dale. How are you? I heard about your harrowing experience. Do you have time for a cup of coffee or tea so you can tell me about it?"

"Tea sounds wonderful." The three of them went into a parlor. Jane told the lady who let Dale into the quarters what they wanted in Farsi. They all sat down.

Jane said, "Andy told me that you were attacked by three men?"

"That's right. I've known Pat since we were sixteen. I've never seen him in a fight before—if you can call it a fight. He had two of the men down and the third backing away in surrender in less than five seconds. I was shocked."

Jane said, "Good God."

"Good God is right." Dale added, "It helped me appreciate why our government wants to keep my husband in the Army."

Andy smiled. It was the same story that he heard this morning, but the emphasis was totally different when it was girl talk.

Jane said, "It must have been frightening."

"The big guy berated us as we were finishing our meal in the restaurant. The restaurant owner kicked him out. When we left, they came around a corner and Eddie moved me behind him and warned them not to mess with him. He said it in Farsi, so I didn't know what he said until he told me later.

"Anyway, the biggest guy tried to sucker punch Pat. Pat blocked it and then it was over before I knew what was happening. I didn't have time to get frightened."

Jane said, "And he put two of them in the hospital?"

Dale shrugged, "I just heard that this morning. He kicked one of them into the street and he was hit by a slow moving car. I think he hit the older one in the throat because I could tell that he was having trouble breathing."

Andy said, "Pat was smart to bring you here this morning as a witness. He nipped it the bud before the Iranians could blow it out of proportion."

The doorbell rang.

Dale said, "We are going to Australia on vacation if we can get flights there."

"Why Australia?" Jane was curious.

"Friends of Pat invited us. I've talked to them on the phone a few times. Pat said that we are a lot closer to Australia here than in America. I really don't like to fly."

174

Pat looked in from the hallway, "There you are."

He stepped in through the doorway, "How are you, Jane?"

"Fine. We were just talking about your heroics."

"It wasn't heroics. It wasn't even fair. I was trained in Army Special Forces. The thugs had no training at all."

Andy chuckled. Haig told him that Pat was reluctant to accept accolades.

Pat heard Scott running up from behind and turned. Scott launched before Pat bent over, but Pat caught him. "Hello, little buddy. Have you been having fun with Jenifer?"

"Yes."

Pat smiled at the grinning Jenifer.

Andy said, "Jenifer, come in and sit down."

Pat put Scott next to Dale, pulled a paper from his pocket, and handed it to Andy with a look of doubt on his face. "Here's the best flight schedule that I could find."

While Andy reached for his reading glasses to look at the schedule, Dale asked, "When are we leaving?"

Pat told her, "Seven-thirty tomorrow morning if we can go."

Andy said, "Good, you're flying into Sydney. Is that where your friends live?"

"No. They live in Melbourne. They are not available until Tuesday. Our embassy is near Sydney and I want to visit it. I will pay for our flight down to Melbourne. It's not on that schedule.

"Read further down and you'll see that we are flying back out of Melbourne on Monday."

Andy grimaced, "Is this the total price down here at the bottom?"

"Yes sir. Unless diplomats get a special rate."

"We can get a special rate for you, but not for your family."

Andy soured, "Pat, I can't justify this. Why don't you vacation in Egypt, or somewhere in Europe?"

"That is what I thought, Andy. I didn't realize that Australia was that far from here and that the cost would be so high. We'll go back to my office and come up with a different vacation plan."

Andy said, "Apologize to your friends in Australia for me."

"They will understand, Andy." Pat walked over to Dale and saw her disappointment.

"I'm sorry, Dale. I need to study my world geography. We are not much closer to Australia here than we were in America. We wouldn't get to Sydney until seven-thirty Monday morning.

Dale's eyes widened, "Almost a whole day in the air?"

"Sixteen hours in the air and we'd lose seven and a half hours in time zones."

Dale shook her head, "I'm not up for that. We need to call Teresa."

Pat picked Scott up.

Jenifer said, "Can you leave Scott here while you figure this out?"

Scott smiled up at his dad and nodded. Pat put him down.

Dale and Pat left for his office with Mandy in Pat's arms.

Chapter 34
Insubordination

The O'Sheens decided to let things cool down in Iran while taking their vacation in Italy.

On the plane ride across the Mediterranean Sea, when Scott fell asleep on Pat's lap, Dale said, "Eddie, can I talk to you about your career?"

He said, "Sure."

She took a deep breath for courage, "Yesterday morning, while you were checking plane flights to Australia, Andy apologized to me for Neal's attitude in the meeting with SAVAK and the police."

"Neal's attitude wasn't Andy's fault."

Dale didn't want Pat to take over, "Andy said that Neal thought he was your boss. I was surprised at the way he said it. I said you were a major and Neal was a colonel and in the military that makes Neal your boss."

Eddie had looked down at Scott on his lap. When she didn't continue, he looked back into her eyes.

Dale continued, "Eddie, Andy told me, that I should remind you of that."

She watched his eyes to see if Pat was going to take over at the criticism. Eddie didn't reply or divert his eyes from hers. Dale waited, her heart rate increased. She could almost visualize the mental conflict in her husband's mind.

His eyes softened, "Pat is still learning."

Dale smiled at the fact that Eddie maintained control. "Pat needs to understand the military command structure and his place in it, or he is going to ruin your career."

Pat said, "I was surprised when Neal turned back into an asshole."

Dale worried that Pat might have taken over. Eddie had rarely used a curse word from the day they first met. She reached deep in her soul and prayed for the right words. "Do you remember when I worked for Dr. Liesec at Auburn? He was an asshole. You begged me to put up with him because we needed the money for you to graduate." She let that sink in.

"Eddie, you cared about your career back then."

He said, "That was before the war. We were kids . . . and very naive."

Dale tried a different approach, "You cared about your career because you loved me."

Dale could see that approach hit a nerve. "You recently told me that Pat was only five years old and was learning fast. You are much older. Why can't you control him? I don't understand."

Eddie didn't respond. She was used to that. Eddie always selected his words very carefully.

She interrupted his thought process, "You told me that you know what Pat does and thinks, and that you couldn't do what Pat does. When Pat does screw up, you say he is a just a kid and still learning. Why do you let Pat run your life?"

Eddie listened, but was still searching for the right words to respond. This time Dale waited him out. She worried about what was going on in Eddie's head. She didn't want to drive him crazy. Cap said that creating a war personality to deal with the horrors of war made perfect sense. Dr. Creighton at Cap's psych ward agreed with him. Dale should have asked Dr. Creighton how she could remain sane being married to a man with two personalities.

Eddie finally spoke, "Pat thinks that I'm a pussy."

"What is that supposed to mean?"

"That I have the heart of a woman; sweet and kind, but unable to handle the ugly realities of life."

Dale stared at her husband. Pat had never criticized Eddie in any way to her.

"What do you think about Pat?"

"He is much more of a man than I am. I guess that is why I let him take control."

Dale argued, "A real man has a heart and can be a gentleman instead of going macho at every confrontation. I think Pat used excessive force on the street in Iran the other night to impress me."

"Dale, Pat could have easily killed the big man with the shot to his larynx. He held back for your sake."

"Did he hold back, or did you hold him back?"

Eddie shrugged. He wasn't sure. Dale had given Eddie and Pat a lot to think about.

***

The O'Sheen family loved Rome and Venice and almost everything in between. Pierre and Kathie Boudreaux drove down from Paris and spent two days with them in Venice. Pat got a good grasp of the Italian language while in Italy. Dale complained that the food was so good that she put on five pounds in the week that they vacationed in Italy. Scott was an angel for most of the trip. Pat carried him for two miles one day while he slept with his head on Pat's shoulder. Dale couldn't imagine how anyone could carry a kid as big as Scott that far. Pat couldn't help but remember carrying Craig Dolly, who weighed two hundred pounds, that far in Nam. That time Pat almost died from heat stroke. Pierre and Kathie took turns helping Dale push Amanda's stroller.

They got back to Tehran on Sunday. Pat went to the embassy on Monday morning. Cleo was happy that Pat was back. Colonel Neal Williams was no longer working at the embassy. Friday had been his last day, and he had already left Tehran for Cairo. Eddie would have liked to have tried to smooth some ruffled feathers before he left.

Cleo told Pat that he was supposed to report to the ambassador's office at nine. Pat went up to the second floor early to talk with Kay and Hal Middleton, Omid and Amir. They all asked Pat about the attack against him and Dale on the street. He downplayed it as a minor incident.

The ambassador called him into the office along with Hal Middleton, the station chief, and closed the door. They sat on the couch and chairs.

The ambassador said cordially, "Pat, how was your vacation in Italy?"

"Very good, Sir. Dale and Scott enjoyed it. Dale would like to take Scott back there when he gets older because he didn't understand most of what we saw indoors, but he loved the statues, the outdoor scenery, and the unique buildings."

Pat appreciated the ambassador's soft introduction to a confrontational issue that needed to be addressed. Pat broke the ice, "Andy, am I still welcome by the powers-to-be in Iran?"

Andy smiled, appreciating that Pat went to the meat of the issue. "Nasser wants you to stay. Fahad does not."

"What do you want me to do, Andy?"

Andy looked at the station chief, passing the buck.

Hal said, "Pat, We recommended to General Haig that you be reassigned." He said it apologetically.

Pat smiled, "Thank you, Hal. Dale and I are ready to leave here after the attack on us by the labor thugs. I have learned enough to believe that I have finished my assignment here for General Haig."

Andy was worried that Pat would be upset at the embassy's recommendation. He wanted Pat on his side. He said, "Pat, the new military attaché won't be here until next week. I would like you to stay until he gets here."

Andy added, "Al wants you to call him tonight."

Pat was anxious to talk to General Haig.

Andy added, "Nasser wants to talk to you as soon as possible."

Pat was concerned that the director of SAVAK made the request again to the ambassador while he was gone. "Is it about the attack on Dale and me?"

"He didn't say. Call him and let me know what he wants." Andy's comment wasn't a request.

Pat nodded, "I will. But, he will probably want to talk to me in person, off the record. So don't expect an answer until after we meet."

Hal said, "Pat, Nasser is a very shrewd man. You impressed him by your incursion into Iraq. But be careful what you say around him."

Pat respected the station chief, "I will Hal. Would you brief me on your concerns?"

Hal smiled at O'Sheen's willingness to cooperate. "Let's go to my office."

In his office, Hal moved behind his desk. He had not dealt with Pat very much based on his instructions to give Pat a free rein. Pat sat down in a chair across the desk from him.

Hal opened the conversation when Pat didn't speak, "Pat, you chose a bad guy to pick a fight with and put in the hospital."

Pat said nothing, which was a bit unnerving to Hal.

Hal tried to recover from a bad start to the conversation, "Nasser explained to you who the Union boss was. He was not someone to mess with in Iran."

Pat responded, "Hal, if you believe I picked a fight with him, there is no need to continue this conversation."

Hal returned Pat's stare that locked onto his eyes. "Pat, I don't believe that you started it, but I think you used excessive force, particularly in a friendly country."

Pat said in his defense, "I was protecting my wife. I could have easily killed all three of them. That would have been excessive force. And dead people could not have identified me and none of this would be an issue."

Hal noticed that Pat's stare got more forceful. He could no longer hold it and looked down, and picked up a paper off his desk. He said while handing it to Pat, "This is a formal complaint against you."

Pat read the complaint from the labor thug and looked up at Hal, "I'm not surprised, what do you suggest?"

"Pat, I suggested that they not bring you back here from Italy. Andy wants you to stay until the new military attaché arrives, but I will support you if you want to get your family out of here immediately."

Pat liked Hal, "And if I decide not to retreat, what do you recommend?"

"Watch your back and make sure no one follows you home."

Pat chuckled, "Hal, I've done that since my first day here. I'll stay as long as Andy wants me here."

Hal nodded, "I expected you to say that. I can assign two men to cover you to make sure that no one follows you home."

Pat knew how much Hal and his wife Kay cared about Dale. He didn't totally reject the offer. "Hal, no one will ever succeed in following me home. They might find my home by following your men who are following me. I can take care of myself. But if you think my family might be in danger, I would appreciate you covering Dale and my kids when I am not with them."

Hal agreed.

Pat waited until eight p.m., nine-thirty a.m. EST, to call General Haig's office.

"Hi, Debbie."

She recognized his voice, "Hi, Pat. General Haig is expecting your call. Hold on."

Haig got on the phone in command mode, "Major O'Sheen, you have attracted a lot of negative attention over there."

"I was protecting my wife, sir."

"Everyone over there believes that you used excessive force."

Pat was not in the mood to go through this again, "I have learned from the experience."

"I hope so."

Pat shocked the general, "I won't show mercy the next time. I will make sure that all of the witnesses that can identify me are dead."

The line was silent.

Pat smiled. Then he remembered Dale's warning about him ruining Eddie's military career. Pat added, "Or I could try to put them down without putting them in the hospital. General, the degree of the threat will determine which outcome prevails."

The general smiled, but he remained silent.

Pat understood his silent technique. "Sir, I would like to go to Cairo next to learn how President Sadat and the Egyptians view Saddam Hussein and Khomeini."

Haig accepted Pat's redirection of the conversation. He didn't want to chastise Pat anymore for protecting his wife. "Pat, no one agrees with you that Khomeini is a major player."

Pat said, "They will by the end of this year. I need to follow up in Cairo to convince you from a different perspective. I have learned that President Sadat in Egypt is a close friend of the Shah."

General Haig said, "Pat, Colonel Williams just took over at our Cairo embassy as the Military Attaché."

"I am aware of that."

"Pat, he has been very critical of your performance in Iran."

"I am aware of that. His wife will be in Cairo. My wife and his wife, Rita, will become close friends, and Neal and I will settle our differences in the first few days."

Haig said, "Pat, I will consider your request." He disconnected abruptly without amenities.

On Tuesday, Pat's phone rang. Cloe told him that a Colonel Kramer was calling. Pat accepted the call.

"Hello, Colonel, congratulations on your promotion. I hadn't heard."

"Thanks, Pat."

"To whom do I owe this unexpected pleasure of your call?"

Ray smiled. Pat knew this wasn't a cordial call. "General Haig asked me to call you."

"Are you working at the Pentagon?"

"No. Haig just knows that we go way back as friends, and . . ."

Pat interrupted, knowing why Ray was calling. "And he wants you to lecture me about my insolence."

Ray laughed. He wasn't surprised when Pat didn't join in his laugh. "I told General Haig that it would be a waste of time. But I agreed to call you. Life isn't as exciting without you around here. I just want to talk. How is your family?" Ray knew Pat's motivation better than anyone in the army now that Burkowski was gone.

Pat loved Ray. "Scott is learning Farsi. Dale was starting to enjoy Iran until we were attacked. Amanda has started talking a lot."

Pat changed the subject. "Ray, are you calling about my next assignment?"

"No. I was calling about your insolence. Am I wasting my time?"

"No, Ray, you are not. Dale and Ambassador Sullivan, whom I have learned to respect, have chastised me for it." Pat was prepared for the lecture.

"Pat, you are the best warrior and military strategist I have ever met. You intimidate your superiors."

"Did I ever intimidate you, Ray?"

"No. But I knew you before you became Pat."

Silence followed. Ray was used to the tactic and waited Pat out.

Pat finally said, "Ray, you were the first one to ever call me Pat."

"I remember. It was on your birthday in the community shower in Saigon. Did I create a monster?"

Pat was surprised that Ray remembered. He sighed again. "I created my 'Pat' persona, Ray. You just gave him a name. Pat helped me survive the war and has helped me survive many conflicts since then. Do you think that Pat is a monster?"

Ray sighed, "Pat, my lecture is over. Take care of yourself and your family over there."

"I will, Ray. Thank you." They disconnected. Pat was inspired to try to become a great military commander like Colonel Ray Kramer.

No one tried to follow Pat home until Wednesday, the day he met with Nasser. Nasser gave Pat the same type of warning to watch his back while in Iran that Hal had, but his motive was different. He wanted to follow Pat with a small force to kill the labor boss and his anti-Shah supporters when they attack Pat. Nasser didn't use the word "if"; he used the word "when". Nasser had no doubt that Pat would be attacked again.

Pat declined his offer, but made his own offer, "Nasser, if that S-O-B attacks me again, I promise that I won't spare his life like I did the first time."

Nasser smiled. And then he switched the subject to Khomeini. Pat shared his Saddam Hussein and Khomeini theory with him.

Pat was followed when he left Nasser's office. He assumed that Nasser knew where he lived and would have no reason to follow him, so Pat knew the thugs were at work again. He shook the tail before returning home.

Pat called Hal Middleton at the embassy the next morning and told him the situation and about Nasser's offer.

They agreed that Pat should not come into the embassy unless it became necessary.

Pat told Dale that he was being reassigned, possibly to Cairo. Dale was relieved. She was afraid to leave the house. They spent the day packing.

Pat went to the embassy on Friday. Omid and Amir made excuses to not accompany Pat to midday prayers at the mosque. Eddie let Pat take complete control.

None of Pat's Muslim friends talked to him after prayers in the mosque. He was followed to Youssef's restaurant. The two men who were following him ate in the restaurant. Pat considered that they might have just been coming from the mosque to eat there and were not following him. A slight cramp attacked Pat's abdomen.

After lunch, the two men continued following Pat. Pat walked three blocks out of his way and approached SAVAC Agent Jamil's house. He saw six men turn a corner toward him from two blocks ahead. The same big guy was leading them, his oldest son was next to him with a cast on his left arm.

Pat saw Jamil and his father sitting on the front porch. He hurried forward and waved. Jamil's father waved and Jamil smiled.

Pat pointed down the road at the six men approaching. Jamil recognized the labor leader leading the group, "Pat, come into the house."

Pat replied in Farsi, "Jamil, I will not put your family in jeopardy. Call for several ambulances."

Jamil tried to grab his father's arm to pull him into the house. His dad liked Pat and shrugged him off and said in Arabic, "I want to witness this."

Jamil ran into the house to get his gun, explained what was about to happen out on the street to his wife, and ordered her to call for ambulances and to call Nasser at SAVAK headquarters.

Chapter 35
Holocaust

Pat took a peek at the two men behind him and then turned toward his main adversary and the five men approaching with him. The big man had a weapon held to his right thigh. Pat moved to the left to put the two men approaching from behind him in the line of fire. He yelled in Farsi, **"I already warned you once not to mess with me."**

The big man pulled the weapon from his thigh. Pat smiled, it was a combat knife the size of a butcher knife. His son with the cast on his left arm showed a smaller knife.

Pat yelled, **"I don't want to kill any of you."**

Three of the men slowed at the warning and at Pat's lack of fear. The big man, the man to his right, and the son on his left didn't slow.

Pat took two fast, aggressive steps toward the big man, surprising him. Pat had noticed that he held the large knife underhanded, in a defensive position. The big man thrust the knife forward at Pat's abdomen as Pat expected.

Pat jumped to his left and swung his right hand up from below his right hip and grabbed the big guy's wrist and the hand holding the knife. He threw a powerful left-footed kick out and into the man's groin to the left as he executed a Karate chop down into the crook of the big man's arm while forcing his hand upward. Pat used his right hand to guide the knife up into the big man's throat and up though his tongue and into to roof of his mouth.

Pat saw the son coming at him with the other knife. He rotated his dad to block his approach and pulled the knife from the dad's throat. He swiped the big knife across the son's throat, and the big, sharp knife almost severed off his head.

Pat sensed the two men closing in behind him. He ducked and a punch ricocheted off of the top of his head and into the nose of the big man who was still standing and holding his throat. The hard blow that ricocheted off of Pat's head and into the nose of the big man, knocked him down on his back onto the street.

Pat flipped the knife in his hand and thrust it up behind him into the puncher's abdomen.

Pat saw a punch coming toward his left eye. It was too late for him to block it so he spun to his right to reduce the effect of the blow. The blow caused a few starbursts in his head, but he accelerated his spin while raising the knife. The point of the knife entered the man's right temple and penetrated six inches into his brain.

Pat pulled the knife out and jumped over the bodies in front of him and spun to face the three remaining men. One moved at him aggressively, encouraging the other two. Pat threw the knife five feet across the prone bodies and it penetrated through the man's breastplate up to the hilt.

The other two men turned to run. Pat jumped forward and yanked the hunting knife out of the man's chest as he was falling, and he threw it fifteen feet at the older of the retreating men. It stuck in his right kidney, and he went down. The eighth man ran and escaped Pat's wrath.

The man who Pat kicked in the groin was struggling to get up from his hands and knees. Pat kicked his head like it was a football and he was the team punter, breaking his neck.

He picked up the smaller knife the son had dropped. The whole conflict had only lasted about two minutes. He approached the father, who was lying on his back holding his throat. Pat looked down into his eyes. The man's eyes widened in terror, shocked that his foe had survived. O'Sheen's red eyes looked down at him as he showed him his son's knife.

Pat stood in a position to block the view of Jamil's father from the porch. He said, "I told you twice that you didn't want to mess with me. Now your wife's beloved oldest son is dead."

Pat saw the pain in the big man's understanding. "She will know that you are to blame and will want you dead, so I am going to kill your sorry ass for her." He threw the smaller knife down and it penetrated the big man's heart.

***

Jamil ran from inside the house out onto the porch with pistol in hand. He saw Pat standing in the street, his back to the house . . . and saw no one else. The four foot wooden fence blocked most of his view of the pavement in the street. He did see one man down with a big knife in his back. He jumped down the three steps to the yard with his boots landing loudly on the sidewalk. Pat pulled the smaller knife from the big man's heart and spun defensively when Jamil landed.

Jamil realized that Pat spun around to evaluate if he was a threat. Jamil pointed the barrel of his pistol up at the sky as he ran to the fence. He froze at the site of the holocaust. He had assumed that Pat scared most of the men away, but the street was covered with bodies and blood. The scene was unfathomable. Jamil had grabbed his gun from inside the house and returned to his porch in two minutes or less.

Jamil went through the gate and examined the bodies. Five were dead. The two live ones, one with a knife wound to the abdomen and the one with the large knife still imbedded in his kidney would die soon without quick medical attention.

While Jamil was assessing the casualties, Pat approached Jamil's father who was standing behind the fence taking in the carnage. Pat handed him a business card, "Abad, would you please call this number at my embassy, ask for Cloe, and tell her what happened here?"

Abad took the card, nodded, and hurried into the house.

Pat heard distant sirens.

Jamil said, "Pat, sit up on my porch until the police get here."

Pat appreciated the offer, "Thank you, Jamil."

Two police cars arrived first, followed by two ambulances.

Jamil tucked the gun under his belt and showed his SAVAK identification to the first policeman that approached him.

The officer asked, "What happened here?"

Jamil said, "All of these men attacked the American soldier sitting on my porch." Jamil pointed at Pat. Abad was handing Pat a wet rag to wipe the blood from his face and hands.

The officer looked at Pat incredulously, "Are you saying that one man did all of this?"

"Yes. I went inside to get my gun. When I came out, this is what I found." Jamil waved Pat off the porch.

Pat came through the gate as paramedics jumped out of the two ambulances. He handed the officer his diplomat ID.

The cop said, "Do you know why these men attacked you?"

Pat pointed, "The big man and his son—the one with the cast on his arm—attacked me and my wife a couple weeks ago. I put both of them in the hospital. I have no idea why they attacked me the first time."

Jamil said, "I was one of the SAVAK agents with your Captain Hanif who investigated the first attack."

The cop nodded and addressed Pat, "Are either of the knives yours?"

"No. The father came at me with the big knife. The son had the smaller knife."

The cop was amazed, "Where did you learn to fight?"

"U. S. Army Special Forces—and in Vietnam."

The cop replied, "You sound like an Iranian, not an American. How long have you been in Tehran?"

"Almost two months."

An embassy pool car sped up to the scene as the ambulances left with the two that were still alive. Hal Middleton jumped out and showed his ID. As he walked up to Pat, he surveyed the scene and exclaimed, "Holy shit!"

He recognized the SAVAK officer, "Jamil, how many casualties?"

"Five dead and two on the way to the hospital."

Hal looked at O'Sheen, saw the blood covering him, and said with concern, "Pat, are you hurt?"

"A nick on my left eye and a bruise on the top of my head."

"You took on seven men and that's all they did to you?"

Pat said, "Eight men. One of them got away."

"Holy shit. Why did they attack you?"

Pat pointed, "The dead big man and his dead son with the cast on his arm are the two who attacked Dale and me two weeks ago. **If I had used excessive force then, this would never have happened**." He wanted Hal to understand what he considered to be excessive force.

Hal went to the pool car and retrieved a Polaroid camera.

A van and a sedan pulled up to the scene. A man in a suit got out of the Sedan followed by Nasser, the SAVAK director. Two technicians, one with a camera, got out of the van. The man in the suit pointed out specific areas on each body to the camera man.

Nasser nodded at Pat and stopped to look down at the big man and his son. He failed to hide a slight smile and then surveyed the other three men and approached O'Sheen, "Pat, it looks like you did use excessive force this time."

A voice from the other side of the fence said, "He had no choice, Director."

Everyone turned to Jamil's father.

Abad said, "I watched the whole fight from my porch. When I saw the big man and the one with the cast coming at Pat with knives while all of the others converged on him, I thought for sure they would kill Pat. I've never seen anyone move so fast or fight so precisely. It was all over in less than two minutes."

Nasser turned to his employee, "Where were you, Jamil?"

Jamil started at the beginning, "Pat stopped at my gate and told me to call for several ambulances. O'Sheen pointed down the street and I saw six laborers coming from that way and two coming up from behind Pat. I told Pat to come into my house. Pat said he didn't want to put my family in jeopardy and turned to face the six men. I ran in the house to get my gun and told my wife to call for the ambulances and to call your office. When I came back out, Pat was standing and seven men were down."

"Seven?"

"Yes. Ambulances took two to the hospital. One was stabbed in the stomach, and I don't think that he will survive."

Jamil's dad, Abad, said, "One man ran away. You should arrest him for attempted murder."

Nasser turned to Pat with a smile on his face, "You told me you would handle them for me if they attacked you again. Our file on you suggests that your warrior skills were exaggerated. I guess I can remove that doubt from our file."

Pat said, "Nasser, I'm sorry about all of this. Did the investigation explain why they attacked me the first time?"

"It seems that the father hated Americans."

Pat remarked, "He told me that in the restaurant before their first attack. There must be more reason than that."

"Well, with all of them dead, I guess we will never know."

A flash bulb went off in Pat's brain, and he thought he knew why he was targeted. He didn't share his suspicion with Nasser.

Chapter 36
Cairo

Hal drove Pat home. Fortunately, Dale wasn't at home. Pat took a shower and dressed in his army uniform. Hal waited and took Pat to the embassy. Pat threw his bloody clothes in a dumpster at the embassy and followed Hal into the embassy. Hal showed the ambassador the Polaroid pictures. Andy shook his head in amazement that approached shock and told Pat that he would send a fax to Haig explaining what had happened.

Pat expressed his desire not to disclose the outcome of the encounter to anyone in the embassy or to his wife.

Andy couldn't believe how calm Pat was—just another day on a battlefield.

Back in his office, Pat dialed the number his wife gave him a week earlier. He recognized the voice that answered and asked the kid if he knew the labor boss without disclosing that he had killed him. The silence that followed answered Pat's question.

Pat said, "Al-Rashid, I got you out of prison, why do you want to harm me?"

Silence.

Pat said, "If you won't talk to me, I will talk to your father."

Al-Rashid answered, "I disclosed to our backer that you are against our Islamic revolution. I had no idea that they would attack you and your wife. I am sorry."

It was clear that al-Rashid didn't yet know about today's events. "They attacked me again today. Your backer, his son, and four more of the labor thugs are dead. Their blood is on your hands."

Al-Rashid gasped.

Pat said nothing to console the kid.

The kid finally replied, "If you killed them then they are martyrs in paradise, each with seventy-two vestal virgins." He disconnected.

Pat was stunned. *Martyrs in Paradise with seventy-two vestal virgins?* The disclosure was new to Pat and idiotic. *Seventy-two vestal virgins.* He didn't know what a *vestal* virgin was. The kid was apparently on drugs with raging male hormones after spending so much time in prison.

Pat called Haig at eight p.m., nine-thirty a.m. on Friday morning in D.C. After Pat's report on the attack, Haig agreed to send Pat to Cairo on a trial basis. If Pat could not get along with Colonel Williams after two weeks, they would move him to the embassy in Morocco, Pat's second choice. Pat agreed.

When Pat got home, he downplayed the attack and told Dale about the transfer to Cairo.

Dale asked, "Isn't Cairo in Egypt?"

"Yes. Scott will get to see the pyramids, and you and I can take a romantic cruise on the Nile River." He knew that after the second attack today that she was anxious to get out of Iran. Norma Jean had told her that Pat had killed men during the attack to protect himself. Pat refused to elaborate when Dale asked about the attack. She was used to that. Pat never talked about his combat. She was glad that they were leaving Iran.

On Sunday they flew to Cairo.

An Egyptian, who introduced himself as a low level diplomat, picked them up at the Cairo International Airport. Pat remembered Jim Reese calling himself a low-level diplomat when he picked them up when they first arrived in Tehran. Jim Reese was CIA. Pat was on a steep learning curve, and he was enjoying it.

They were shown to a fourth floor furnished apartment owned by the embassy. While they were getting settled as much as possible without their possessions from their home in Tehran, there was a knock on the door. Pat opened it to a pretty woman in her mid-forties.

She asked, "Are you Major O'Sheen?"

"Yes, Ma'am."

Dale was approaching the door.

The woman threw her arms around Pat in a hug, shocking him. "Thank you for saving my marriage."

When Eddie was speechless, Dale asked, "Are you Rita Williams?"

She released Eddie's hard, sexy body, and looked at the woman behind him. "Yes. You must be Dale."

After a few amenities, Eddie knew that he had lost Dale to Rita for the next few hours. Eddie and Scott walked the neighborhood and found a park with a large swing set, a slide, and a sand box. Pat tried to teach Scott how to swing himself. He concluded that Scott wasn't heavy enough or strong enough to bend the long chains to keep the seat swinging. Scott kept begging his dad to push him higher and higher. Eddie decided that he was already pushing him too high.

Rita was gone when Pat and Scott got back to their new apartment home. Scott ran and started telling his mother about the park, and how his daddy had pushed him so high on the swings.

Dale smiled at Eddie with a little more than just admiration expressed in her eyes.

Scott yawned, as if on cue.

Dale told Scott, "I borrowed sheets from Aunt Rita and put them on your bed."

She looked at Eddie, "I haven't put any on our bed yet."

Eddie smiled, "We don't need sheets. We don't even need a bed."

She knew he understood her intentions.

She took Scott by the hand and led him to his new bedroom. They both put him down for his nap. When they left his room, Dale said, "I guess you know that he won't be taking naps for very much longer?"

Eddie nodded as he headed to their new bedroom. Dale followed him.

Thirty minutes later, Dale kissed Eddie on his naked shoulder and hugged his side. "Rita believes that God sent you to Iran to save her marriage. I understand why she hugged you at the door."

Eddie didn't know what to say.

She said, "Eddie, you are too modest."

He chuckled, "How can you say that when I'm lying here on my back naked on a bed with no sheet to cover me."

Dale raised up on her elbow and scanned his naked body. "Wow! You are naked. How did that happen?"

194

He chuckled, "I have no idea."

He rolled her on her back and scanned her body, "I do believe that you are naked, too. How did that happen?"

She said, "You took my clothes off. Now you are going to pay."

"I thought I already did."

"That was just a down payment." She rolled him on his back and sat on his abdomen, pinning his shoulders to the mattress with both hands. She smiled down into his beautiful hazel eyes that were more brown than green in the tan room.

She said, "I want you to remember something."

Eddie slid a hand from her thigh up to her breast. "What is that?"

She slid her butt lower, confirming that her antics were effective. "Rita is not the only one that thinks you hung the moon." She leaned down and kissed him passionately.

The next morning, Eddie fed Amanda and put her in the stroller. He took the family out to eat at a neighborhood restaurant that Rita had recommended. Dale explained that she didn't need to wear a scarf to cover her hair in Egypt—that their economy relied on tourists from Europe, Asia, and America. Eddie smiled at her quick acceptance of their assignment in a new country.

Eddie was able to understand the Egyptian Arabic of the waiter, but knew he was recognized as a foreigner. He vowed to correct that quickly. Scott, Dale and he enjoyed their food.

The next morning, Eddie walked to a nearby bank and transferred the money from his bank account in Iran. They all went shopping with Rita to buy groceries, paper products, and wine. They found some puzzles for Scott and even managed to buy a couple bottles of bourbon— the only two in the store.

Chapter 37
New bosses

Pat reported to the embassy on Thursday morning in his formal military uniform that Dale ordered him to wear. A marine private escorted him to Colonel Neal William's assistant, a clean-shaven Egyptian man in his fifties. Pat was already missing Cloe and regretted that he was not able to go to her wedding in Iran.

The assistant stood and introduced himself as Omar Bashara. Pat smiled and shook his hand.

Omar said, "Colonel Williams wanted you to report to him as soon as you arrive." He sat down at his desk and dialed a three number extension and announced Pat's arrival.

Pat wondered if Neal was going to make him wait for twenty minutes like he did for their first meeting in Iran.

Omar stood up and approached a closed door . . . the fact that it was closed was not a good sign.

He opened the door and waved Pat in.

Colonel Williams was walking around from behind his desk. He was in uniform.

O'Sheen took two steps into the room, snapped to attention and saluted. Eddie was still in control.

Neal was surprised. He returned the salute. "Pat, please sit down."

O'Sheen said, "Before I sit down, I want to apologize for my behavior in Iran."

Neal looked into Pat's eyes and saw sincerity. He gave Pat an excuse. "General Haig expected too much from you. You had no diplomatic experience and were under a lot of pressure."

O'Sheen didn't respond immediately. Unlike Pat, Eddie always selected his words carefully.

Neal repeated, "Please, sit down."

Eddie was surprised that Neal was being so friendly. He sat down, and Neal sat down on the chair next to him instead of behind his desk.

Pat surmised, "Have you talked to General Haig?"

Neal smiled at Pat's perception. "He called me because I filed a complaint against you."

"Neal, I don't blame you." Eddie said no more.

Neal made eye contact with O'Sheen. "Are you not curious what Haig said to me?"

Eddie shrugged. "I have no right to ask what my superior officers are saying about me." Eddie looked down, deflecting from Neal's eye contact.

Neal was surprised at O'Sheen's supplication. He fought against his inclination to be in control. "Pat, General Haig told me that if I felt the need to control you because of my higher rank, he could bust me back to your rank as a major."

Eddie looked up into Neal's eyes, "Is that why you are treating me differently—to further your career?"

Neal admitted, "That was my reasoning before your family arrived in Cairo. But after Rita met Dale, she gave me no choice. She already believes that Dale will be her best friend here.

"Pat, I have to admit that I am jealous of you. Andy told me about the last attack against you in Tehran, that you killed six of the men in the attack. You are an amazing warrior, which is what every young soldier aspires to be when he joins the armed forces. I've never been in a fight outside of training. My strength is that I have language skills, but even your language skills put mine to shame."

Eddie said, "Neil, I'm not proud of my warrior talents. My plan when I married Dale was to be an engineer with a stable job in my home town and to live in a nice house with a white picket fence. I didn't want to join the army. My birthdate lottery number was thirty-three—meaning I was sure to be drafted. I volunteered when the Army agreed to let me finish my engineering degree.

"Neal, Vietnam changed me. It turned me into a warrior, and that part of me can be an asshole at times." Eddie managed to hide the pain that attacked his stomach. "I regret being so rude to you at our last assignment together. I was going to apologize when I got back from Italy, but you had already left Iran."

Neal was too surprised to respond. He smiled at Pat.

Neal stood and picked up the handset on his desk phone, dialed three numbers, and waited. He said, "Alfred, Major O'Sheen has arrived. . . . Yes, sir. We will come right up."

O'Sheen followed Colonel Williams to the ambassador's office. Eddie was nervous, but he didn't let Pat take over.

The ambassador met them inside his office door. "Major O'Sheen, welcome aboard."

Eddie shook the offered hand of a man in his fifties who was about Pat's height and thirty pounds overweight, "Thank you, Ambassador Atherton." Pat would have something clever to say. Eddie remained silent.

The ambassador said, "May I call you Pat?"

"Yes sir. I would like that. Thank you for your warm reception."

The ambassador smiled. O'Sheen did not come across as trouble maker. "You can call me Alfred when only supervisors are near."

Eddie smiled and nodded once.

The ambassador led O'Sheen to a couch and asked him to sit. He retrieved a manila file from his desk and sat down on the chair nearest to Pat. The ambassador's office was arranged the same as Ambassador Sullivan's office in Tehran. Pat surmised the design was dictated by the State Department. Neal sat on the other chair.

Alfred pulled an eight-by-ten faxed picture from the folder and handed it to Pat. O'Sheen recognized the picture that Hal Middleton took of all the corpses on the street in Tehran. Pat tried to take over, but Eddie set the picture on the coffee table and leaned back on the couch without comment or a challenging glare at the ambassador or Neal.

Atherton said, "I don't want a scene like that repeated here under my watch."

Eddie explained, "My wife and I went out to a restaurant here last night and thoroughly enjoyed ourselves. I don't think the Egyptians hate Americans like many anti-Shah Iranians."

Neal jumped in, "Why do you think your attackers were anti-Shah?"

Eddie prevented Pat from taking over, "The labor boss that attacked me was backing students at the university in Tehran to organize anti-Shah protests."

Neal challenged, "That is just conjecture on your part. You were in Iran for less than two months."

Pat glared at Neal.

Neal averted the glare. O'Sheen's friendly demeanor had changed in a heartbeat. He did not want to get into another confrontation with O'Sheen that he would probably lose again.

Pat accepted Neal's retreat and justified his analysis. "Neal, I talked to the student who gave the labor boss my name. The student's father is a close friend of mine. With SAVAC director's Nasser's help, I managed to get the student out of prison. The student apologized and didn't realize that disclosing my name might result in an attack on my wife and me. When I told him that I was attacked again and killed six of his backers, he was shocked into silence. Then he told me that the six men I killed were martyrs in Paradise, each with seventy-two vestal virgins. Then he hung up on me. I haven't a clue what he meant by seventy-two vestal virgins." Pat picked up the picture to emphasize the result of the second attack against him.

Neal knew that Pat attended midday prayers with the Iranians in the Tehran embassy. But based on Pat's statement, he realized that he had more knowledge of Islam than O'Sheen. "Pat, the promises for sexual pleasure for men in Paradise is well documented in the Quran, and in the Islamic hadith teachings that interpret the life of Mohammad. There is a considerable promise of many houri—vestal virgins—wives who return as virgins after each time you screw them."

Pat had a new respect for Neal's knowledge. "But, seventy-two? I'm thrilled that I can keep my one woman happy."

Neal chuckled, "Some of the hadith scholars explain that a man in paradise will have an eternal erection—always willing and able."

Eddie was surprised. He looked at the ambassador, "Alfred, does that sound like paradise to you?"

Alfred chuckled, "Not to me. Maybe to a sex pervert." Considering that he was in a Muslim country, he took it back, "I will deny that I ever said that."

Pat laughed. He was already starting to like the ambassador.

Neal said, "Pat, I've studied Muslim scholars' interpretations of the Quran. If you read the early Arabic Quran, the Prophet Mohammed left the door open for that interpretation."

Eddie said, "They hide their women under burqas and chadors without realizing that it doesn't teach them how to control their God-given male urges."

Neal injected, "The men do interact with their sisters and female cousins, and over fifty percent of the Muslim men marry their first or second cousin, because they are the only women that they are allowed to be around on a regular basis."

Eddie groaned almost silently. Neal, whom he had alienated in Iran, was a wealth of knowledge that he had not tapped into. A pain hit his stomach like he had been kicked. He didn't let Pat take over. An involuntary smile spread across his face. Eddie was learning how to fight back against Pat.

Neal saw the smile, "Do you find that amusing?"

"It's not that, Neal. I just realized that because I was such an ass to you in Iran, I failed to realize how much your knowledge could have contributed to my efforts there."

Neal was shocked that Pat would admit that in front of the ambassador on his first day in Egypt. He was incapable of anticipating Pat.

Pat looked at the ambassador when he let out a big sigh of relief. Pat addressed the issue directly, "Alfred, General Haig expressed his concern to me about Neal and I getting along. When we arrived, Rita, Neal's wife, hugged me. Rita and my wife, Dale, became instant friends and spent two hours together. Last night Dale made her opinion very clear that I was at fault for Neal's bad feelings toward me. Dale told me that if Neal and I don't get along, we will have to look forward to sex with vestal virgins in paradise, because we will never have sex here with our wives on earth again."

Neal burst out laughing. Between his guffaws, he admitted that Rita had made the same threat.

Ambassador Allerton joined in the laughter. General Haig had advised him on how to handle the difficult policing of the conflict between Williams and O'Sheen. Dale and Rita had diffused the conflict without him having to threaten any disciplinary action. He had read

O'Sheen's file, the small parts that Haig sent to him. A significant portion of the abbreviated file was redacted. He was worried about controlling such a clandestine warrior; a warrior whom his new military attaché, Neal Williams, didn't want at the embassy. He was relieved that Neal was accepting O'Sheen.

The ambassador said, "Haig didn't explain why you are being assigned here."

Pat wasn't sure of Haig's purpose. He pointed to the picture of the dead bodies in the street. "I needed to get out of Iran, but stay close to hot spots that might develop in the Middle East. I want to learn to speak like an Egyptian and get the pulse of their feelings about Anwar Sadat signing the peace treaty with Israel and determine if his regime is stable. I also want to go into neighboring Libya and Tunisia to learn their local dialects.

Alfred said, "Why?"

Pat answered honestly, "In case I have to infiltrate one of those countries in the future with the need to pass as a local."

That made sense to Alfred, "So you will be here for a long time."

Pat clarified, "For at least a few months."

The ambassador was shocked that O'Sheen thought he could accomplish such lofty goals so quickly and looked at Neal.

Neal was supportive, "Pat learned to speak Farsi in Iran like a local in a few weeks."

The ambassador suggested, "Pat, you should seek input from my staff before you go out into the streets." He stood up and punched three numbers on his phone.

When his call was answered, he said, "Have Milton come to my office."

Pat knew that Milton was the Station Chief . . . and was most likely CIA.

Pat said, "Alfred, getting the opinion of Americans in theater is not the way I approach my research. I will request your staff's input after I formulate my independent opinion."

Neal scoffed, "Like your opinion that the Shah of Iran is in trouble? No one agrees with that."

Pat started getting a little testy, "And no one agrees with me that Saddam Hussein will be running Iraq before the end of the summer. And no one is concerned about Khomeini. Neal, everyone will agree with me before the end of the year."

The ambassador worried about the conflict redeveloping between the two and interrupted. "Pat, what are your immediate plans?"

Pat was pleased at the intrusion, "Alfred, after the first attack on us, my wife was anxious to get out of Iran. We took a family vacation to Italy. Dale will freak when she learns that I killed so many men during the second attack on me. She needs another vacation. The Army owes me more than three weeks leave. I plan to take my wife and kids on a vacation to see the pyramids so that we will learn how to enjoy our assignment in Egypt. I will be out of your hair for at least a week and learn how to speak like a local while I'm vacationing."

Alfred smiled, "The locals exploit foreign visitors to the pyramids. Naferet in Administrative Services advises American visitors on the best way to circumvent their scams. You should talk to her."

Pat smiled, "Thank you. I will."

The station chief, who was shorter than Pat and fifty pounds overweight came through the door. Pat stood up to greet him. Alfred handled the introduction.

The station chief didn't offer his hand. Milton McGregor said, "Major O'Sheen, your insolent reputation precedes you."

Pat didn't like his attitude, or his attempt to intimidate. "McGregor. You don't need to worry. I don't want your job." He locked eyes with a potential new adversary.

McGregor snarled, "You are not to do any intelligence investigations in Egypt without clearing it with me first."

Neal rolled his eyes. He had warned Milton not to confront O'Sheen.

Pat took over from Eddie with an aggressive step toward Milton, their eyes still locked.

Milton was alarmed and retreated a step.

Pat's voice was calm, "Milton, you don't want to mess with me. I haven't been informed that I have to answer to you."

"I am the station chief. You follow my orders unless the ambassador overrides them."

Pat took another threatening step forward. McGregor tried to retreat another step, but his back hit the wall. Panic crossed his face.

The ambassador yelled, **"Major O'Sheen, back away from him."**

Pat glared into McGregor's eyes for another ten seconds. The ugly station chief was too fearful to cause Pat any future problems. Eddie hurt Pat's stomach. Pat backed up two steps and turned to face the ambassador.

The ambassador tried to remain calm and friendly, "Pat, Milton and Neal answer directly to me and you answer to both of them."

Pat pointed his thumb over his shoulder at McGregor, "Alfred, you need to teach this asshole some manners if you expect me to answer to him."

Milton stepped aggressively toward Pat's back. Pat saw him in his peripheral vision, rotated, and started to step toward the station chief, his foot landed on McGregor's foot and his left shoulder contacted his chest. Pat caught him by his shirt to keep him from falling to the floor and possibly hitting his head on the wall.

Pat said, "I'm sorry, Milton. I didn't realize that you sneaked up behind me."

Neal managed to hide his smile. *Déjà vu!* O'Sheen had confronted Neal when he tried to put Pat under his thumb when they first met in the Iranian Embassy. O'Sheen would never be under anyone's thumb. Neal didn't like the station chief, but he had warned him not to try to dominate Pat. The chief had apparently taken his advice as a challenge rather than a warning.

Pat warned McGregor, "I think you should leave this office while you still can."

Milton started to step forward, but O'Sheen's glare froze him. He looked at the ambassador.

Alfred said, "Milton, I suggest you leave and let me handle this."

Milton left the room.

Alfred took a deep breath as O'Sheen turned back to him. He said, "Pat, I understand why Neal didn't want you here. I . . ."

Neal interrupted, "I retracted my objection. I suggest we give Pat the two weeks that General Haig requested."

The ambassador looked at Neal with surprise. He had just witnessed O'Sheen's insolence that Neal had complained about.

Pat let Eddie take over. Eddie was pleased that Neal was on his side.

Eddie stepped over, picked up the picture of the holocaust on the streets of Iran, and looked at the bodies in the street. "I'm sorry, Alfred. My wife and I are still stressed out after this." Pat handed the photo to the ambassador. "I should have handled Milton more diplomatically."

Neal chuckled under his breath. He was enjoying watching O'Sheen's manipulations.

O'Sheen said, "I will get Neferet's advice for my family's visit to the pyramids. After mid-day prayers, I will get out of your hair for a week. You can decide if you want me here or not while I am on vacation." Pat left the room without requesting permission.

Chapter 38
Reprieve

The ambassador looked at Neal, "Mid-day prayers? Is Pat a Muslim?"

"He often went to mid-day prayers with the Iranians in the embassy in Tehran. I don't think he is a Muslim—yet."

"Neal, Pat's insolence with Milton gave us all the reason we need to reject his assignment here. Why are you suddenly supporting him?"

Neal picked up the picture and studied it, "Alfred. I'd be up tight for several months, or maybe years if I had done something like this, which I am not capable of doing. General Haig called me. In Vietnam, O'Sheen pulled off two POW rescues without any casualties to over two hundred prisoners-of-war that he rescued. In the largest rescue of almost two hundred prisoners, Pat planned the rescue, which had to be approved by the top brass of the three military branches in the Pacific theater. Pat and his sniper partner killed all but nine of more than sixty prison guards before the Special Forces units arrived to secure the camp."

Alfred said, "Just the two of them? You have got to be kidding me."

Neal shook his head, "Haig said that Pat killed most of them by infiltrating the camp in the middle of the night and planting explosives at two of the three guard barracks. When the explosives went off, he took over a guard tower and took out most of the guards in the middle barracks with grenades and a Soviet 50 caliber machine gun mounted on the guard tower.

"The reason I bring this up is that Haig also told me that during one of the planning meetings with the top level brass in the Pacific Theater, O'Sheen chastised the top brass to their faces for their poor management of the Vietnam War and for letting politicians run it. He was just a lieutenant then. Somehow, he still made it to the rank of major in record time.

"Haig's point was that O'Sheen is very opinionated, and that no one will ever be able to stop him from expressing his opinion. He emphasized that Pat is too valuable of an asset to be discarded because of his outspokenness and lack of finesse."

The ambassador said, "What do you suggest?"

"O'Sheen is a very nice guy as long as you don't try to bully him. I suggest that you tell Milton that O'Sheen will be answering to you directly. General Haig warned me that if I felt the need to control Pat because of my higher rank, he would have to consider the option of busting me back to a major."

Alfred sighed. O'Sheen had connections at very high levels.

Neal read apprehension in the sigh. "Alfred, I could tell that Pat liked you. He will cooperate as long as you keep treating him with respect. The bigger question is can you convince Milton to back off without ruining his morale."

That was the big question. The ambassador appreciated Neal's perception.

***

Naferet was a gorgeous Egyptian woman with a long, thin nose, dark brown eyes, and a captivating smile. She didn't cover her shiny, long, coal-black hair that hung below her shoulders. Pat introduced himself in Arabic.

She was thrilled to advise Pat on visiting the pyramids, and she gave him more brochures than Dale could read in a week.

Pat asked, "Do you have Dhuhr prayers in the embassy?"

"Yes."

"Who do you suggest I talk to about them?"

"What do you want to know?"

Pat was in uniform, "I want to know if anyone will object if I pray with them."

Naferet was surprised. No other American had ever prayed with them.

She jumped out of her chair so quickly that Pat stepped back, "Follow me."

She introduced Pat to Khalid Masri. Masri talked to him for quite a while to get acquainted and about the prayer service. Pat had to ask language questions about many of the Egyptian Arabic colloquialisms he was using. Khalid was patient and very helpful. Pat arranged to meet him before noon.

Pat went back to Neal's office. He was getting acquainted with Neal's aide, Omar Bashara, when Neal's office door opened.

Neal said, "Pat, I thought I heard you out here."

Pat said, "I hope I wasn't disturbing you."

"Of course not. Did Naferet help with your trip to the pyramids?"

"Yes. She was very helpful."

"I hope you can stay on here when you get back and advise Rita and me on the best way to visit the pyramids."

Pat said, "Neal, have you got a couple of minutes?"

"Sure. Come into my office."

After Neal closed the door, Pat went straight to the point, "Neal, I'm sorry if I put you in a bad spot with Milton. Can you share Alfred's attitude after I left the office?"

"He was ready to file an objection to your assignment here. I suggested that he give you the two weeks that Haig requested."

"How did he respond?"

Neal shrugged, "He is talking to Milton now. It could go either way."

"Thanks for your honesty, Neal."

Pat looked at his watch. "It's almost time for midday prayers. I don't want to know anything more about my status until I get back from vacation. Dale deserves a vacation without the stress of having to think about having to move again.

"Neal, can you keep this from Rita until after we leave tomorrow morning? She won't be able to keep it from Dale."

"Yes. Will you be able to keep it from Dale?"

Pat chuckled at Neal's perception, "I can't lie to her. But I think I can cushion it enough for her to enjoy our vacation."

Neal smiled as Pat trotted out of the office toward the Muslim prayer room in the embassy.

Neal mused, *the Muslim prayer room.* Perhaps he should learn the Muslim prayers.

When Pat arrived at their fourth story apartment, Scott heard him enter and ran toward the front door. Dale had given up on outrunning him to the door two years ago. She followed at a walking pace and reveled in the love shared between Scott and his dad.

She loved the man who came through the door. It no longer mattered very much whether he was in a Pat or Eddie mode. She loved him both ways. But if he came home as Pat, she would know that his first day at the embassy didn't go well.

Pat put Scott on his left hip, hugged and kissed Dale. He smiled. "They approved our vacation to the pyramids."

Her face lit up, "When?"

"We can leave tomorrow morning. We need to be back next Monday morning."

Dale threw up a barrier, "We don't have enough clean clothes to travel for a week."

Eddie had spent two weeks in the same clothes in the jungle. That was why God invented lakes and streams. But he had anticipated her concern. "There is a dry cleaner a block from here. Bag the dirty clothes up, and I'll run them over there."

Dale objected, "They won't have them ready by tomorrow."

Pat smiled, "We can drive down to the largest pyramids near Giza for two days and drive back here to pick up our laundry for the rest of our vacation."

"Rita heard that we should hire a guide to take us to the pyramids—to avoid all the tourist scams."

Pat could see her excitement, "I have hired the cousin of Naferet at the embassy."

"Who is Naferet?"

"A beautiful Egyptian woman in Administrative Services."

Dale's eyebrows raised. "How beautiful?"

"Cleopatra beautiful." Pat grinned at her concern. "Almost as beautiful as you."

Dale laughed. She finally knew which husband came home. Pat wasn't very good at disguising his false flattery.

She sighed, "Your first day at the embassy didn't go so well, did it?"

Pat didn't reply.

Dale pressed with malice, "Pat, did you have problems with Neal?"

"No. Neal and I got along fine."

"The ambassador?"

Dale was too perceptive. "I really like the ambassador."

Dale glared at him, waiting.

Pat couldn't lie, "I got crossways with the station chief, Milton McGregor."

Dale got inches from his face, "Why didn't you let Eddie handle him?"

Scott started squirming in Pat's arms to be let down. Pat lowered him to the floor without diverting his eyes from Dale. He noticed Scott running to his bedroom and knew that he was upset. He knew that he was at fault. He yielded to Dale's glare. "I'm sorry, Dale. I was wrong. I'll let Eddie patch things up when we get back from vacation."

Pat looked down the hall, "Scott is upset. I don't think he has ever seen us argue before. May I go apologize to him?"

Dale moved to the side to let Pat pass. She smiled as she watched him hurrying to Scott's room.

She sighed. She was close to getting Pat to understand that he needed to let Eddie use his excellent social skills in disagreeable situations. She walked down the hallway and peeked in Scott's doorway. Scott was lying on his bed. He rolled on his side and turned his back to his daddy as Pat sat down on the edge of the bed.

Pat said, "Are you mad at me, Scott?"

"Mommy's mad at you."

"You are right. I made her mad."

Scott was stone still, anxious to hear his dad's explanation.

"Scott, do you remember in our last house making your mommy mad when you dumped your plate of food on the floor because you didn't like it?"

Scott didn't respond.

Pat pressed, "Do you remember that?"

Scott pulled his knees up into a fetal position, "Yes."

"Mommy is not still mad at you for that. She still loves you."

Scott didn't respond.

Pat said, "I did something worse than dumping food on the floor, and your mother got mad at me. I just told her that I am sorry, and she stills loves me."

Scott rolled onto his back and looked up into his daddy's eyes.

Pat continued his lesson, "I am sorry that I made you mad. Do you still love me?"

Scott climbed up to his knees and threw himself into his daddy's open arms.

In the hallway, Dale had to flick a few tears off her cheeks. There was no difference between Pat and Eddie in how they dealt with their kids.

Chapter 39
Pyramids

The O'Sheen family met Neferet's cousin, Kara, south of Cairo in a market parking lot at eight a.m. Her car was set up like a taxi, and she started a mileage meter and a time clock. It was good that Dale could understand her English because Kara was like a fountain spewing knowledge about the pyramids. After parking in Giza, they pushed Amanda's stroller past dozens of camel owners aggressively soliciting them. Scott was fascinated by the camels and wanted to ride one. They stopped at a camel owner that Kara knew (probably a cousin). Pat agreed on a price with Kara's help. The price included two camels, a trip around the back of the pyramids, out across the sand to an excellent photo viewpoint, and back to the Great Sphinx in front of the pyramid. The ride took about 35 minutes. The camels were led by 2 teenage boys. Pat tipped them generously before they climbed on the camels' backs, which brought big smiles to the teenagers' faces. They took lots of photos of the O'Sheens and showed them how to pose for pictures at the best angles.

Kara took them to the oldest and biggest pyramid, Cheops, one of the only intact manmade seven wonders of the ancient world. Pat paid for a guided tour inside. Dale suffered from a slight case of claustrophobia in the small, steeply-sloped passageways that were only about three-feet square and some that were more than 300 feet long. They were rewarded when they exited the Ascending Passage into the beautiful Grand Gallery and then through a flat passage into the Queen's chamber, both rooms were wide and over 20 feet high. They finally ascended over 150 feet through the Grand Gallery into the King's chamber, which was about 17 by 34 feet, and 20 feet high. The chamber walls were faced with smooth granite stone. The only object in the King's Chamber was a lidless, rectangular granite sarcophagus, one corner of which was broken. The sarcophagus was larger than the Ascending

Passage, which indicated that it must have been placed in the chamber before the top of the pyramid was built in place. Eddie marveled at the architecture skills that existed over 4000 years ago.

Scott just marveled at everything.

They had an early lunch to beat the crowds at a place Kara recommended. She knew the owners, *probably relatives*.

When they were seated in the restaurant, Dale pulled out all of the pyramid brochures that Naferet gave Pat and requested, "Kara, will you recommend what we should see in the next couple of days?"

"Yes." She sifted through the brochures quickly, selecting only four. She rearranged the order of the selection and opened the top one.

She began, "Let us spend a couple more hours here visiting the Sphinx and the Valley Temple. Then I can take you to your car. I suggest you drive toward Memphis and find a hotel for the night. She opened the second pamphlet. Tomorrow you should see the Step Pyramid of Zoser, and then drive down toward Dashur." She mapped out the second day.

Kara smiled, "To be honest, I think you will be tired of Pyramids after two days. I know Scott and Amanda will be. If you want to vacation more, I would take the kids up to Alexandria on the Mediterranean Sea. Scott is not old enough to enjoy the museums, shrines, and mosques in Cairo."

Kara's instincts were right: Scott was tired of pyramids by early-afternoon the next day. They drove home and picked up their clothes from the cleaners on the way. They beat the worst of the rush hour traffic in Cairo, but it was still bad. Scott took a short nap in the car while Amanda slept on Dale's lap. Everyone was glad to be back at their apartment. Their boxes had arrived from Tehran.

Dale cooked a simple tuna fish casserole. Pat made drinks and talked to Dale about the pyramids and the people they encountered as he helped Scott with a puzzle on the dinette table.

During dinner Dale said, "I don't think Scott is up for going to Alexandria tomorrow." *Meaning that she wasn't.*

Pat needed to talk to Neal. He didn't want Dale talking to Rita and worrying about having to move again so soon.

Dale had Rita's phone number. After dinner, while Dale was doing the dishes, Pat called Neal at home. Rita answered.

"Hi, Rita. This is Pat. Can I talk to Neal?"

"Sure."

He heard her call, "Neal, it is Pat O'Sheen."

After a few seconds, "Hello, Pat. Where are you calling from?"

"Neal, we saw all of the pyramids the kids could handle, and we are back at home. What is my situation at the embassy?"

"Alfred is willing to let you try to work it out with Milton one-on-one. They are expecting you back on Monday."

"Thank you, Neal. The vacation helped. I will apologize to Milton and Alfred. I appreciate your support."

Neal offered, "Pat, most of the time, you are a very nice guy."

Pat said, "You are too . . . most of the time." Neal would understand the return dig.

Dale was tugging at Eddie's shirt sleeve. Pat said, "Dale is anxious to talk to Rita."

Neal laughed, "Rita is breathing down my neck, wanting to talk to Dale. I'm handing the phone to her."

Pat handed the phone to Dale. After a few short amenities, Dale said, "It's early. Can you and Neal come up and have a drink. We can tell you about visiting the pyramids." The Williams lived on the second floor of the large apartment building.

Rita consulted Neal on Dale's offer. He shook his head. She glared at him and nodded her head up and down threateningly.

Neal shrugged and said loud enough for Dale to hear, "I'd love to. Give us ten minutes." He remembered Pat telling the ambassador that if he and Pat didn't get along that their wives would cut them off and they would have to hope that there would be vestal virgins in heaven. That was before Milton entered the ambassador's office and everything went sour.

Pat put Amanda to bed while Dale freshened up.

Dale welcomed Rita and Neal Williams with hugs. Pat poured them wine while Scott made slow progress with the puzzle on the dinette table.

Neal walked over and looked at the puzzle, "That looks like a tough puzzle, Scott."

"It is." Scott smiled up at him, putting a longing into Neal's heart: Neal's kids were still at Rita's parent's house in Georgia until the school year finished at the end of next week.

Neal looked at the picture on top of the puzzle box and suggested, "Scott, look for this dark red color on the puzzle pieces, and try to put them together to make this red school house here." He pointed at the bottom left corner of the picture on top of the box. Neal had taught his kids how to work puzzles when they were Scott's age.

Scott started searching through the pieces for the color. Dale smiled. Scott liked Neal. She liked Neal.

Dale suggested, "Let's sit down in the family room. My legs are tired. I think we walked at least six miles in the last two days around the pyramids." Dale sat down where she could see Scott in their small apartment.

When they sat down, Dale guided the conversation to their childhoods. Everyone was soon getting comfortable with each other. Pat poured them another drink.

Scott walked into the room and stood in front of Neal. He waited patiently until Neal looked at him. Scott pointed to the dinette table, "I did it."

Neal jumped to his feet, "Show me." Pat, Dale, and Rita followed.

Scott ran to the table, climbed up on a wooden dinette chair on his knees and said, "Look." He pointed to the completed red school house on the puzzle pieces.

Neal said, "Wow! Scott, you did do it."

Scott beamed and looked at the picture on the box cover. "What should I do next?"

Dale looked at Pat wondering how he ever got crossways with a nice man like Neal. Pat smiled at her having read her thoughts.

Neal suggested, "Do you see all this brown ground down here and the black horse?"

Scott started searching the puzzle pieces for the colors.

With Scott occupied, they sat back down, and Dale started sharing their experiences at the pyramids. Rita had a lot of questions. Dale sought Pat's agreement with her opinions once in a while. He always agreed with her.

Scott walked into the room and climbed up into his dad's lap, facing him. Everyone watched.

Pat said, "Are you getting tired?"

"Yes," He rubbed his eyes with the back of his wrists,

"Do you want me to put you to bed?"

"No." Scott laid his left ear against his daddy's chest.

Rita smiled.

Dale smiled and resumed her conversation where Scott's entrance interrupted it.

Scott was asleep a few minutes later. Pat shook the ice in his dry glass, getting Dale's attention. She noticed that Rita's wine glass was empty and Neal's was still half full.

She picked up Rita's wine glass, took Pat's, and went into the kitchen.

Pat asked Rita, "How are your children getting over here after they finish the school year?"

Rita smiled, "I'm flying home next Thursday to pick them up."

Pat asked for Dale's sake. "How long will you be gone?"

Rita looked at Dale, "A week."

Pat looked at his wife, "Dale, do you want to go with Rita and take the kids home to see your parents."

Dale ran out of the kitchen excited. "Are you serious?"

Pat took her enthusiasm as a "Yes".

Pat put up a barrier, "I will miss all of you." He knew exactly what Dale would say.

"Well, you go off on your missions sometime for months at a time, and we miss you something awful. It's your turn to sit at home missing us."

Pat turned his head and smiled at Neal.

Rita jumped up. "Dale, I think Pat is serious?"

Pat said, "I am very serious."

Neal warned, "Pat, the army won't pay for their flights."

Dale chimed in, "My mom and dad will help pay if necessary. They are dying to see their grandkids."

Rita said, "My family is in Laverne, Georgia. It couldn't be more than a three hour drive from Birmingham."

Rita ran into the kitchen and started plotting with Dale.

Neal smiled at Pat. They both knew that their wives were going to be friends for life. He would fight tooth and nail to keep Pat in the Cairo embassy for more than two weeks. He wondered if Pat was using Dale's trip home as a manipulation. He concluded that he didn't care—their wives were happy.

Chapter 40
Apology

On Monday morning, Pat wore a suit instead of his military uniform to the embassy. He was provided with a little windowless office near Neal's office. Pat called Donya, the ambassador and the station chief's administrative assistant, and asked her to try to get him an appointment with Milton.

Twenty minutes later, Pat answered his phone. It was Milton.

"O'Sheen, you don't need to meet with me. You answer directly to the ambassador, now." Milton's tone was gruff.

Pat bit his tongue, "I was hoping to talk to you."

"About what?"

"I want to apologize for my abhorrent behavior and ask you for some advice."

Milton was curious about the request for advice.

Pat waited through a long minute in silence.

Finally, Milton said, "Come up to my office."

"Thank you, Sir." Pat disconnected.

Milton was surprised by the "sir".

On the second floor, Pat said hello to Donya, who was at the dhuhr prayers he attended in the embassy. She smiled a hello and said, "Chief McGregor is expecting you."

The door was open so Pat stuck his head in. Milton waved him in.

Pat asked politely, "May I close the door?"

Milton was apprehensive because O'Sheen was so lethal, but he nodded because Pat's request was friendly.

Milton didn't offer Pat a seat, so Pat stood behind a chair in front of Milton's desk.

"Chief McGregor, I'm not making excuses, but a part of me turned into an asshole during the Vietnam War." Eddie was surprised that he didn't get a pain in his stomach from Pat. He continued, "I thought I had that part of me under control. A few weeks, ago my wife and I were attacked as we left a restaurant a few blocks from our home near our embassy in Iran. The week before I arrived here, I was attacked by eight anti-Shah union thugs on a street in Tehran. I think those incidents unleashed that asshole warrior attitude I developed in Vietnam. I'm sorry that I took it out on you. The vacation to the pyramids put me back in control."

Milton stared at O'Sheen. O'Sheen didn't avert his eyes. Milton could read his sincerity.

Milton admitted, "Alfred showed me the picture of the bloody corpses in the street in Tehran. I can't believe that one man could kill so many men."

Pat said, "Milton, it really wasn't a fair fight."

"Seven against one is never fair."

Pat countered, "Those men were labor thugs. I was trained in Army Special Forces and honed my skills to survive the Vietnam War." Pat expected Milton's look of surprise.

Pat said, "Two of the dead men were the ones who attacked my wife and me, and they brought knives to the second fight. I don't regret killing the two of them. I took their knives away from them and the warrior in me reacted like he did in the jungles of Nam. I used the knives that I took from them to defend myself against the rest of the men.

"I was still very stressed out about killing so many men in Iran when I arrived at the embassy here. I'm sorry that I took my stress out on you."

O'Sheen turned away and said softly, "I regret that I killed so many of them." Pat started to retreat from the office.

Milton was overwhelmed. He had never met a warrior like O'Sheen before. He wasn't sure how to react. He could see the pain of remorse in O'Sheen's face.

"Pat?" He phrased the address sympathetically.

O'Sheen turned back to him.

Milton offered, "I have never been in a war. I don't have any experience to relate to yours, and I've never dealt with a decorated war hero before."

218

O'Sheen said sadly, "Milton, I am not a hero. The soldiers who died in the war were the heroes."

Milton offered, "Please, sit down."

Pat didn't react.

Milton argued, "I agreed to see you because you said you wanted my advice."

Pat sat down in a chair across the desk from the station chief. He looked into Milton's eyes trying to determine if the timing was right to press forward.

Pat pressed Eddie forward without taking over. "Milton, what can you tell me about the Egyptian Islamic Jihad?"

Milton leaned back in his chair. He reversed the question, "What do you know about the term jihad?"

Pat knew it was a fair question. "My interpretation in the Quran is that jihad is the religious duty of Muslims to maintain their religion, striving to serve the purpose of Allah on this earth. I understand that refers to the 'higher' or 'greater' jihad. The other meaning of jihad is an outer struggle against the enemies of Islam—the 'lesser jihad', which may take a violent or a non-violent form. My fear is that the violent form is starting to take control of the Muslim world."

Milton leaned forward in his chair. O'Sheen had a realistic grasp of Islam for a military intelligence officer who had only been in the Middle East for a few months. He said, "I heard that you prayed with our embassy Muslims at noon on your first day here. Are you a Muslim?"

Pat skirted the question, "Christians and Jews could learn a lot from the Muslims on how to praise God. We all worship the same God. All three religions believe that God chose their ancestor, Abraham, to introduce Himself to the human species. We all believe in the teachings of what Christians call the Old Testament. Muslim hadith writings portray Jesus as one of the major prophets of Allah—almost on a par with Mohammad."

Milton said, "I've never heard that."

Pat elaborated, "On Muhammed's celebrated Midnight Journey, the Archangel Gabriel took Mohammed to heaven from the rubble of the destroyed Second Jewish Temple Mount in Jerusalem. In heaven, he met with Jesus and John the Baptist, Moses, Abraham and others."

Milton raised both hands, palms facing O'Sheen, "Okay. You obviously understand Islam better than I do. Most Americans that come to Middle East don't have a clue. Why are you asking about the Egyptian Islamic Jihad?"

"Milton, I was attacked in Iran by a 'lesser jihad' group. One of my goals is to figure out why so many Muslims are suddenly turning to violent jihad."

"Pat, we haven't seen that violence in Egypt."

Pat nodded, "Not yet. That is why I want to infiltrate the Egyptian Islamic Jihad—to see if they are being recruited into violent jihad."

Milton returned to the attitude when they first met, "I can't let you compromise this embassy by trying to infiltrate them."

Pat tried to take over, but Eddie managed to keep him at bay. He reached into the inner pocket of his suit coat and retrieved his fake IDs. "I won't infiltrate them as an American. I will infiltrate them as this Syrian." Pat put the passport ID on the desk in front of Milton.

Milton stared at O'Sheen and met unflinching eyes. He picked up the ID and gave them a cursory view, "Who is this?"

"That is me in the disguise I used when I infiltrated Iraq recently."

Milton was starting to realize that he was dealing with a very skilled covert operative, "Are you saying that you can disguise yourself to look like the man on this passport?"

Pat nodded, "I passed through Iranian, Syrian, and Iraqi customs looking like that."

Milton argued, "But if they remove your disguise, they will identify you as an American."

Pat smiled at Milton, "The Army and CIA can come up with a credible cover that I was turning to the other side—a traitor committed to Islamic Jihad who regularly prayed with the Muslims in the embassies in Iran and Egypt."

Milton was alarmed, "That could remain your legacy in your file forever."

Pat shrugged, "I won't care. If my true identity is exposed, I'll be dead. I trust the CIA to keep that legacy from being disclosed to my family."

Milton argued, "I don't think that you could possibly learn anything significant enough that would deserve risking your life like you propose." He was starting to admire O'Sheen.

"Milton, I believe that there is a radical, militant, Islamic movement afoot that is going to kick America and the whole world in the butt if we don't recognize its threat and quell it before it starts to gain momentum. None of the brass in America believe me. I need more facts. All I want from you is the intelligence gathered on the Egyptian Islamic Jihad."

Milton admitted, "The information on them is classified. I will try to get you clearance."

Pat stood up, "Thank you for accepting my apology. I am sure that you will be able to get me clearance."

Milton said, "That may take some time."

Pat smiled, "I understand."

Pat gnawed at Eddie's insides. Eddie knew that Milton was going to resist giving him clearance, but he bought Pat time to plan a strategy that Milton couldn't anticipate. Pat understood and quit gnawing.

Milton watched the warrior stride athletically out of his office. He was going to have to go way up the ladder in the CIA to rein O'Sheen in. O'Sheen could upset the hard earned status-quo in the embassy's diplomatic relationship with Egypt.

Pat organized his office to his satisfaction and was warmly welcomed at midday prayers in the embassy. He was getting acquainted with many of the Muslims on the large embassy staff—three times bigger than the Muslim staff in the embassy in Iran.

That evening, Pat called CIA headquarters and consulted with his high level CIA friend, Pete—it was morning in Langley. He convinced Pete of his need to infiltrate the Egyptian Islamic Jihad (EIJ). He trusted Pete to convince his superiors to get him the clearance he needed and CIA contacts in Egypt that could help him.

Chapter 41
EIJ

The next afternoon, Pete called Pat and gave him the contact information for another Caleb (no last name), the CIA undercover agent in Cairo that had the most knowledge about the EIJ. Pat made contact with Caleb a few minutes later and arranged a dinner meeting. Pat called Dale and explained he would be home late after a dinner meeting.

At dinner, Caleb agreed to introduce Pat to an EIJ member after the mid-day prayers at the Mosque on Friday, but advised that he would not hang around after the introduction. Pat showed Caleb his Syrian ID, so that Caleb would recognize him at the Mosque. Caleb was impressed.

The next morning, Pat had a message to come to the station chief's office. He anticipated a confrontation for contacting Caleb without Milton's approval, but Pat let Eddie maintain control. Pat was realizing that Dale was right, Eddie was better at dealing with bureaucrats.

When Eddie entered Milton's office, he was asked to close the door.

When he turned to face the station chief, Milton was miffed and said, "Pat I thought that you agreed not to infiltrate the EIJ until I gave you clearance."

Pat said, "I didn't say that I would not make preparations to infiltrate." He pulled a chair back from the front of Milton's desk. "Milton, who do you think gave me Caleb's name?" He sat in the chair.

Pat's question confirmed Milton's suspicion that O'Sheen was well connected high up in the CIA. O'Sheen's insight that Caleb had reported to Milton about his meeting with Pat was impressive. Milton said, "I still don't have clearance to allow you to infiltrate the EIJ."

Pat said confidently, "You will have it before the end of the day. What are you willing to tell me about the jihad group now?"

Milton turned the question around, "Tell me why you plan to infiltrate the EIJ as a Syrian." Caleb's report to Milton had been thorough."

Eddie nodded at the fair question. "Syrian President Assad was opposed to Egyptian President Anwar Sadat's signing of the peace treaty with Israel at Camp David in America. Anwar Sadat has become very friendly with the Shah of Iran. Syrian President Assad will support any attempts to remove the Shah and President Sadat from power. I want to find out if the EIJ will welcome Assad's support, or if they already have it." Pat knew the danger to himself if the Syrians had already approached the EIJ.

Milton surmised from Pat's firm grasp on the Middle East situation that Pat's mission was probably way above his security clearance level. Pat was in a class of his own. During the next hour, he shared every file he had on the Egyptian Islamic Jihad with Pat. Pat absorbed the intelligence amazingly quickly without asking many questions.

After mid-day prayers at the embassy and lunch in the cafeteria with his new Muslim friends, Pat walked to his bank. He made a withdrawal from his slush funds in Switzerland and deposited some of the money in a bank in Cairo. He called from a pay phone and made reservations for Sayid Hanna at the Marriot Omar Khayyam Hotel in Cairo.

Back in his office, Pat returned a call to General Haig at his home. Pat explained his plan. It was in line with Haig's objectives for O'Sheen and he approved.

That night, Dale made love to her husband and later helped put the finishing touches on Pat's disguise. She still found it hard to believe that she was married to a spy. Pat told her he would be in Cairo, and that the embassy would be able to get a message to him in case of an emergency.

The next morning, Thursday, Pat said his goodbyes to Dale and Scott. He hugged and kissed Amanda and was rewarded with a huge smile, despite his disguise. Neal drove Rita, Dale, and the kids to the Airport. Pat watched from a distance as Neal got them safely onto the plane that was their first leg of their flights to America to retrieve Rita's kids and for their kids to visit their grandparents.

Pat flew to Damascus using his Iranian fake ID. He spoke to enough workers in the airport to refresh his Syrian accent, swapped IDs, and flew right back to Cairo using his Syrian papers. He had to assume the EIJ would check his arrival as stamped on his passport.

He caught a limo to the most expensive hotel in Cairo and had dinner in the fanciest restaurant in the hotel.

After breakfast the next morning, he arrived at the Great Mosque of Muhammad Ali Pasha almost two hours before the first call to prayers so that he could tour one of the most visited sites in Cairo. The mosque could be seen when entering the city from any direction.

He met Caleb at the prearranged corner of the mosque ten minutes before the mid-day prayer service. They shook hands as if meeting for the first time and made their way into the mosque at the first adhan (call to prayer). Pat followed Caleb who made his way purposefully through the crowd and placed his prayer rug on the floor. Pat put his prayer rug down next to him.

When the prayers were over, Caleb turned around and Pat turned to follow his lead.

Caleb said to a man Pat recognized from the files Milton showed him, "Hello, Khalid. Do you have a minute?"

"I've got a meeting, Caleb. But I can give you a minute."

"This is Sayid Hanna from Syria. He is a friend of one of my cousins. He was hoping to meet someone in the EIJ today."

"Why?" Khalid was alarmed.

"I just met him and didn't ask, because I really don't want to know. I will leave the two of you alone." Caleb turned and walked away leaving Pat in an awkward situation.

Pat answered the 'why' question, "My Syrian government would like to offer financial support to your organization."

Khalid was surprised and skeptical, "What do you do for the Syrian government."

"I'd rather not say at this time."

"Then you are wasting my time."

Pat expected the reaction. He looked around to see if anyone was within hearing range and said softly, "I work for the Syrian External Security Division of the General Security Directorate."

When Khalid's eyebrows raised, Pat said, "We need to talk in private."

Khalid's eyes remained locked with Pat's while he took his time making a decision. "Do you have your passport and visa with you?"

"Yes."

"Follow me."

They went through a closed door that led toward the back of the mosque. Khalid closed the door and asked Pat for his papers. Pat handed them to him. The Egyptian compared the photo on the passport to Sayid's face. He noticed the custom's stamp, "You arrived in Egypt three days ago?"

"No. I arrived yesterday." Pat hadn't looked that closely at the custom agent's stamp. But he assumed the question was a test.

"Who got you with Caleb to contact us?"

"I assume it was a cousin of his. I didn't arrange the meeting. I just followed the instructions I was given by my government and met him at the corner of the Mosque ten minutes before Jumu'ah prayers today."

"How did you recognize him?"

"I was given his picture." Pat was starting to worry that he was getting Caleb in trouble. The EIJ was very security conscious.

"Let me see it."

"I trashed it. I have a good memory for faces."

Khalid studied Pat's eyes. He accepted what he read in the eyes, turned, and walked almost a hundred feet down the circular hallway that skirted behind the huge prayer room. Pat followed. The doorways on both sides were almost thirty feet apart indicating large meeting rooms. All of the doors had key entries. The last door on the right side of the hallway was only twenty feet down from the previous door, indicating that it was smaller room. It had a numeric keypad entry.

Khalid instructed Pat to sit down on the chair at the end of the hallway. He used his body to block Pat from seeing the numbers he punched on the keypad. He looked at Pat, "This may take a while. I assume that you are not in a hurry."

Pat smiled, "I've already toured your beautiful mosque. I have no other plans for today. I'm comfortable sitting here for as long as it takes."

Khalid liked Sayid. He pointed up at a camera on the wall as a warning and entered the room. Pat had already noticed the camera.

A minute after Khalid entered the room, a bull of a man exited. He nodded at Pat and leaned against the door, his huge arms crossed in front of his large chest. It was obvious to Pat that the EIJ was not a social organization.

Twenty minutes later, the door opened, and the bull got instructions, and the door closed again.

The bull explained politely, "I need to search you for weapons."

Pat smiled, happy that he was granted a meeting. He stood up, turned around, spread his legs, and leaned his palms against the wall. The search was thorough, but gentle. Pat was slightly offended when his wallet was extracted from his back pocket. Pat saw several men exiting the next door down the hallway.

The bull knocked three times on the door, waited five seconds, and knocked two more times. The door opened. Pat knew that he wasn't entering a room full of boy scouts.

As it turned out, there were only two men seated in the room; Abbud al-Zumar, who Pat recognized from a file Milton shared with him, and a man Pat had never seen before. Khalid entered through a side door on the right.

Pat was directed to sit at the end of the table, opposite Abbud. Bull walked the fifteen feet to the other end of the table and handed Pat's wallet to Abbud. Abbud removed everything from the wallet and spread the items on the table.

Abbud looked up at Pat, "No credit cards or other identification."

Pat nodded, "My boss doesn't like paper trails on his foreign agents that can be followed back to him. I pay for everything in cash. That is why there is so much cash in my wallet."

Abbud spread out the money. The man's eyes next to him widened in surprise—or perhaps greed.

Abbud opened the passport, "Sayid, why do you carry your passport and visa and no other identification?"

A glimmer of a smile passed across Pat's face, "Abbud, passports and visas are easy to forge."

226

Abbud leaned forward in his chair, "You know who I am?"

"Yes. You are Abbud Al-Zumar. My External Security Division in Syria doesn't have the resources of the Mossad or the CIA, but we try to keep track of our neighbors, as your Egyptian GID keeps track of us."

"What is in my file in Syria?"

"I'm a young agent and my security clearance is too low to know what is in your file. I was instructed to try to make contact with you or Khalid Islambouli." Pat looked at Khalid. "I expected it might take weeks to make contact with either one of you. My handler is going to be impressed that I made contact so soon."

"What is the name of your handler?"

Pat shook his head, "I doubt that the name I know him by is his real name."

Khalid interrupted, "Is Sayid Hanna your real name?"

"It is as far as anyone in Egypt is concerned."

Abbud motioned to the bull. He started to approach Pat.

Pat locked eyes with Abbud. The bull put two hands on Pat shoulders and started to press down. Pat kept his eyes locked on the leader, "Abbud, I was ordered not to harm anyone in the EIJ unless it was for self-preservation. I'm not concerned about the pistol on your lap, but get this ape off me."

The offended bull started painfully squeezing Pat's clavicles.

Abbud was surprised that the agent knew there was a pistol on his lap. He saw no fear in Sayid's eyes. He had no doubt that Sayid was a foreign agent. His Arabic accent was definitely Syrian. He waved the bull off and raised his pistol up and pointed it at Pat's chest.

Pat kept his eyes locked on Abbud's and stood up slowly in place. "Khalid, please slide my wallet and its contents down to me.

"Abbud, I will tell my government that you are not interested in their support."

Abbud was surprised that the agent had the guts to stand up with a gun aimed at his chest, and he laid the pistol on the desk, "Sit back down, Sayid. I was just trying to determine if you are who you say you are."

Pat said, "You can check my arrival on flight 1492 from Damascus." Pat assumed that they already had confirmed that fact.

Pat sat back down. Khalid slid Pat's stuff to him. Pat smiled at him in appreciation. He was winning Khalid's trust.

"Abbud, I know my arrival and my government's offer is not something that you expected." Pat slowly put everything back in his wallet except for a yellow piece of paper. "I will be in town for a few days. The name of my hotel and my suite number is on this piece of paper. If you are interested in another meeting, you can contact me there."

Khalid said, "What does your government expect in return for their generosity?"

"I haven't been given any specifics. I know that my country isn't happy with your country's peace treaty with Israel. My guess is that they suspect that you feel the same way. I'm just here to see if you are interested in starting a dialogue. I was told that this first encounter might be dangerous. I am young and expendable. If my government wants to work with you, I'm sure they will send someone with more experience to handle any future business."

Pat stood up. "You know where to reach me." He left the room unimpeded.

The bull followed him until he left the mosque.

Chapter 42
Success

Milton answered his phone in the embassy saying, "Chief McGregor?"

Caleb reported, "O'Sheen met with EIJ for over an hour. He left the mosque an hour ago in a cab. He was followed from his meeting back to the Marriot on the Nile."

Milton asked, "How was his demeanor when he left the mosque?"

Caleb described it as perky.

Milton added the words 'left the meeting with EIJ perky' to the bottom of his list. He read down from the top of the list; 'arrived at the airport from Damascus on flight 1492', 'wore a very expensive suit', 'checked into the most expensive hotel on the Nile at seven p.m.', "limo to the mosque at nine a.m.', 'said noon prayers impeccably', 'handled the introduction to Khalid comfortably', over an hour in meeting with EIJ', 'left the meeting with EIJ perky'. He added to the bottom of the list 'took a cab back to the most expensive hotel in town and was followed by EIJ'.

Milton said, "Caleb, O'Sheen is above our league. Perhaps we should back away."

Caleb suggested, "Perhaps he is a double agent. That might explain how he can afford to operate at such a high-class level— throwing around so much money."

"I don't buy that, Caleb. He is an American hero. But, stay with him a little while longer."

***

When Sayid Hanna left the room in the back of the mosque, Abbud looked at Khalid, "What do you think?"

229

Khalid said, "I'm impressed with him. He was not intimidated by Jaeden's size pressing down on his shoulders or even with your pistol. We know he arrived on flight 1492 as he said. He answered all your question honestly, even my question if Sayid Hanna was his real name."

Abbud looked to the older man to his right, "Muhammed, what do you think?"

Muhammed sighed, "That young man has been battle hardened to the point that he has no fear. His accent was Syrian, but I picked up some Farsi in it."

"Is he an Israeli Mossad agent?"

"No."

"American CIA?"

Muhammed hesitated, "Possibly. But I don't think so. Although that could explain the Farsi in his accent."

Abbud looked back at Khalid.

Khalid offered, "He is old enough to have fought for Syria in the Yom-Kippur War and in lots of skirmishes against Israel since then. It is not uncommon to become battle hardened in the Middle East.

"As far as the Farsi is concerned, Iran shares a border with Syria. Syria probably has several agents in Iran, and he is polished enough that he was probably one of them."

Abbud respected Khalid's opinion. "So you believe him?"

"Abbud, Syrian President Assad has not been shy about expressing his opposition to Egypt's peace treaty with Israel. Our relations with the other Arab countries is deteriorating. We have been seeking funding to overthrow Sadat and bring Egypt back into its rightful place in the Arab community. I think we have to consider Sayid's overtures seriously."

Muhammed said, "Saudi Arabia has promised us funding."

Khalid fired back, "They have been promising that for almost a year. They have so many Americans crawling across their country that they can't fart without an American smelling it."

Muhammed replied testily, "Egypt isn't much different. Sayid might be an American agent."

Abbud looked at Khalid, "You need to have Sayid followed."

Khalid smirked, "I already have men following him."

***

Pat noticed the tails following him from the mosque. He expected one of the tails, but he was disturbed by the other.

He checked for messages at the front desk, had none, and punched a code on the elevator keyboard to allow him access to his suite on the top floor. He changed into his gym shorts, a T-shirt, and running shoes. He packed the sack on a small running belt with his visa, change for a pay phone, a small folding knife, and a two-shot, over-and-under, two-barreled derringer that was advertised as only accurate from five feet—maybe ten feet for Pat.

Pat hurried through the lobby not noticeably identifying the people who were following him. He surveyed the street for a threat as he exited, leaned against the wall of the building next to the front door and stretched his calves like any runner should.

He trotted down the sidewalk to the left slowly enough to give time for the surveillance car to pull away from the curb to follow him. After a quarter mile, he picked up his pace. The surveillance vehicle couldn't keep up with him in the heavy traffic. One man was trying to keep up with him on foot. Pat was almost sure it was Caleb. He picked up his pace even more and left the man far behind. He left the river road and snaked through several blocks, ran another mile, and then stopped at a pay phone. He called the embassy and asked for Milton.

"Chief McGregor."

"Milton, it's Pat."

"Where are you?"

"I have lost the surveillance from the EIJ and Caleb. I'm calling from a pay phone."

Milton was speechless about O'Sheen picking up on Caleb tailing him.

Pat pressed, "What is Caleb going to tell the EIJ if they stop him and ask why he is following me?"

Pat was not surprised that Milton didn't have an answer. "I don't have a problem with him following me if you are sure that they don't know he is working for America. I can't think of a good explanation that he can give the EIJ for why he would be following me."

Milton's response was what Pat wanted to hear. "Pat, I'll pull all surveillance off of you."

"Thank you, Milton. I will be back in the office in a few days and give you an update." Pat disconnected.

Pat ran back to the Nile River and ran at a ten mile-per-hour pace the two miles back toward his hotel. He slowed to a trot for a quarter mile and walked the last two-hundred yards to catch his breath. His clandestine operations were interfering with his conditioning. He was dripping with sweat as he passed through the lobby. Only one man watched him walk to the elevator.

After his shower, he did some repairs to his disguise and called the front desk. He had no messages and asked to talk to the concierge. After discussing what Pat had already visited, the concierge recommend that he visit the Al-Hussein Mosque. Pat told the concierge to have a limo waiting for him at nine the next morning.

Pat ate dinner at an expensive restaurant a few blocks away that the concierge recommended. Pat was followed as he walked to and from the restaurant.

The next morning, Pat arrived in the lobby for the first time in casual clothes. The concierge smiled his approval. Pat discreetly handed him a large tip as he was escorted to his limo.

The limo driver opened the back door for Pat to enter. Pat stopped and introduced himself to the driver. The driver said his name was Muhammed. Pat shook his hand before climbing into the back seat. The driver looked at the concierge whose nod conveyed that special treatment would be financially rewarding.

Two blocks down the road, Pat said in Arabic, "Muhammed, I need to stop to buy a pack of cigarettes."

"Yes sir." Three blocks later he pulled over to the curb.

Pat said, "Stay behind the wheel." Pat exited the limo, entered the store while noticing out of the corner of his eye the car following him pull over to the curb a block back. Pat bought a pack of Turkish cigarettes.

The Al-Hussein mosque was one of the most sacred Muslim sites in Cairo for Shia Muslims, a place that any Muslim from Syria would want to visit. Pat paid the limo driver generously and asked to be picked up in two hours. He toured the mosque and talked to several local smokers. He maintained his Syrian accent and had to ask for interpretations of some of the Egyptian phrases. He was quickly learning the local dialect.

Forty minutes after he returned to his hotel room, Pat walked to same restaurant he had eaten at the night before and ate a late lunch.

On the walk back from the restaurant, Pat stopped at a phone booth and called the embassy.

"Neal, it's me. Did everyone get home to the States okay?"

"Yes. Where are you?"

"Milton knows. I don't mind if he tells you. Tell him the EIJ has not reestablished contact. He will understand my message.

"Neal, hang up. I am being watched and I'm going to pretend to talk on this pay phone for a while longer."

The next morning, Pat went for a five mile run along the river bank. An hour after he got back to his room and had his shower, the phone rang and he was informed that he had a visitor in the lobby. He rode the elevator down and recognized Khalid Islambouli of the EIJ. He walked across the lobby and shook his hand.

"Khalid, it is good to see you. Can I buy your lunch?" By his presence, Pat knew Khalid was willing to discuss the Syrian offer. Which meant that they wanted to overthrow Anwar Sadat. Mission accomplished.

Khalid said, "Yes. But we need some privacy."

"I'm sure I can arrange that in the dining room." Pat did so with the appropriate tip.

They talked over lunch. Khalid gave Pat a phone number to make future contact.

Pat made two separate calls from his room to make plane reservations under two different names, one flight to Damascus, one back to Cairo.

Pat flew to Syria and spent the night in Damascus and arranged for a rental car for seven in the morning. He socialized in the hotel bar before going to bed, ate dinner alone, and called Dale's parent's house from his room. It was noon in Alabama.

"Hello?"

"Hi, Griff. How are you?"

"Hi, Eddie. I'm great. Your kids are growing like weeds. I sure wish you would get an assignment stateside. How are you doing?"

"Good, except that I miss y'all, Dale, and the kids."

"Of course you do. Mary wants to say hello before Dale gets on."

Pat talked to his mother-in-law and then Dale got on.

"Hello."

"Hey, Hon." Eddie had taken over.

She said, "Hey. Are you at home?"

"No. I'm calling from a hotel in Damascus, Syria. I'm flying back to Cairo tomorrow."

Dale informed him. "We are flying out of Atlanta on Friday afternoon, which means with the time change we will be arriving in Cairo on Saturday afternoon.

Pat approved and talked to Scott for a couple minutes. Then he and Dale talked for another five minutes before disconnecting.

The next morning, Pat drove to Lebanon and used his Syrian passport to cross the border. With Dale in America, he was in no hurry to get back to Cairo. He got stuck in the morning rush hour traffic driving into Beirut. He drove around the American embassy twice and then admired the Mediterranean and the sea-side resorts while driving down the Minet El-Hosn road. He got a feel for the lay of the land and the attitude of the people.

He drove back across the border to the airport in Damascus and caught his afternoon flight to Cairo using his Iranian passport. He was gaining confidence in traveling the Middle East without worrying about drawing attention.

He removed his disguise in the bathroom at the Cairo airport and caught a cab to his vacant apartment. The fact that Scott or Dale didn't greet him at the door was more depressing than he anticipated.

He showered and made a drink. His thoughts drifted to Mike Burkowski. A tear ran down his cheek. He chugged his drink and made another with his hands shaking. He knew he needed help. Pat refused to take over—it was time for Eddie to face the pain.

He picked up the phone and dialed the number Dale had given him for Rita. Neal answered the phone.

"Neal, I'm back in my apartment."

"Was your mission successful?"

"Yes." Pat diverted, "I'm not used to coming home without Dale and Scott being here. I need someone to talk to. Can you come up and have a drink?"

Neal sensed Pat's funk. "I can be up there in ten minutes."

"Thanks, Neal."

Pat led Neal to the kitchen, "I've got wine, beer, and Bourbon."

Neal was alarmed when he saw how Pat's hands were shaking. He realized that Pat was on the edge.

"Pat, are you alright? What happened on your mission?"

"The mission went fine." Pat took a big gulp of his drink, "Neal, I need to talk to someone about Mike Burkowski and the Vietnam War." A tear ran down Pat's cheek. "It all hit me like a freight train when I came home to an empty apartment."

Pat sighed deeply, "I wouldn't blame you if you turned and ran out of here as quickly as possible."

Neal grabbed the bourbon bottle, "I think I'll need whisky for this conversation."

Pat stumbled quickly through his and Mike's background together; becoming like brothers as they went through Sniper, Special Forces, and OCS training and their first tour-of-duty in Nam. Then he got into the second tour and being approached by the CIA for a POW rescue.

Neal forced Pat to provide more detail on the POW rescues and how important Mike Burkowski was to Pat's success.

Two drinks later, Neal had to press hard to get Pat to talk through the final hour of the embassy evacuation. Moisture filled Neal's eyes as Pat blubbered through the scenes when his snipers failed to report in, and when he watched from his tree as Burkowski was shredded to pieces by a half-dozen AK-47s.

Neal was seeing a totally different side of O'Sheen.

He worried as Pat laid his head on the back of the couch. He was shocked when Pat started snoring. His blame for Burkowski's death was apparently off Pat's shoulders—at least for now.

Neil didn't awake Pat and left the apartment. He was still in shock with what Pat shared with him. He suspected that he and Pat would be friends for life.

Chapter 43
Report

The next morning Pat wore khaki pants and a polo shirt to the embassy. Neal's door was open, and he waved Pat in.

Neal said, "You look much better this morning."

"Thanks, Neal. I really appreciate your help last night. That is the first time I've ever told that whole story to anyone. The memory has always been too painful. I felt the need to tell it so that I can get past it. I'm sorry I put you through that."

"I'm just glad I was there to help. Sometime soon, I would like you to tell me how in the hell you managed to get out of Vietnam."

"How about tonight?"

"I'm game if you are."

Pat changed the subject, "Do you think you could arrange a meeting with Milton and Alfred? I would like some input on my analysis on the EIJ before I report to General Haig."

The earliest Neal could arrange the meeting was at three that afternoon. Pat hated paperwork, but he hand-wrote an eight-page report, leaving space for the embassy's input. He went to mid-day prayers at the embassy and then walked out to have lunch in town. No one followed him. He talked with several locals, practicing his Egyptian Arabic dialect, and was back in his small office in the embassy by two-thirty.

He and Neal walked up to the ambassador's office together.

Pat showed the ambassador his Iranian passport first.

Alfred looked at the picture, "Whose passport is this?"

"It's mine. That is me in disguise. Milton stamped the first arrival date in Cairo for me. I flew to Damascus with that passport."

"Then I flew back to Cairo with this one." Pat handed Alfred the Syrian passport.

Alfred looked at the custom stamps. "And then you flew back to Damascus with this Sayid passport?"

"Yes, and then flew back to Cairo with the other one yesterday."

Alfred looked at the custom stamp on the other one. He looked at Milton.

Milton knew what Alfred wanted to hear. "There is no way the EIJ can trace Pat back to this embassy."

Alfred smiled at Pat, "What did you learn?"

Pat related his story, making light of Abbud's pistol threat. He told of being followed by the EIJ, and of Khalid showing up at his hotel, which confirmed Pat's suspicion that they wanted to oust Anwar Sadat. No one in the room disagreed with him.

Alfred asked, "How far do you think they will go to try to oust Sadat?"

Pat answered immediately, "Assassination."

Alfred gasped, "Are they that well-funded?"

"Apparently, not yet. That is why they went for my bait of Syrian money."

Milton jumped in, "Who told you to go in with that offer?"

"Milton. I didn't discuss my strategy with anybody. I trusted my instincts."

Neal said, "Your strategy could have gotten you killed."

Alfred said, "Or embarrassed our embassy."

Pat laughed. The laugh came out involuntarily and it echoed with insolence. He had already explained to Alfred how he protected the embassy and the State Department. Diplomats didn't have a clue.

Alfred was offended by his laughter.

Eddie said, "Alfred, Milton has already agreed that I didn't compromise your embassy."

Alfred was worried about Pat's conduct for a minute. But after the laughter, Pat seemed normal.

Alfred asked, "Should we warn President Sadat?"

Pat shrugged, "That is a diplomatic decision."

Milton pressed, "Pat, what is your recommendation?"

Pat said, "We have time—perhaps several months before we have to take any action."

"Pat, what are you going to recommend to Haig?" Alfred was starting to understand why General Haig was allowing Major O'Sheen to operate outside of embassy control.

"I don't have a recommendation at this time. I'm still trying to put all of this Middle East mess together in my mind. It saddened me to learn that Egypt is not as stable as I had hoped."

Milton asked, "Are you going to make further contact with the EIJ?"

"Not unless I am ordered to. And in that case, I will need to work with someone who can also pass as a Syrian."

Pat added, "I don't think protecting President Sadat is a priority. I think Saddam Hussein and Khomeini are our first priority."

Neal bowed his head when Alfred looked at him. He still thought O'Sheen's Khomeini theory was off the wall.

Pat didn't press. "I can deal with Khomeini later. General Haig and I agreed that I should learn the Arabic dialects in Libya."

Alfred injected, "So what are your immediate plans?"

"Unless you have something you want me to do here, I plan to finish learning the local Egyptian Arabic dialect this week until my family gets back, and then fly to Tunisia and then to Tripoli."

Pat considered, "I may reverse that order. But, I want to learn both dialects."

Alfred advised, "You can go to Tunisia as an American. But you probably should use your fake IDs to go into Libya. Our relations with General Gadhafi are not good."

Dale, Rita, and the kids got in safely on Saturday. Pat followed Neal as they drove to the airport. On the way home from the airport, they all stopped at a local restaurant that Neal recommended for an early dinner together. Pat liked Neal's kids.

When they got to their apartment, Dale was exhausted, apologized, and went straight to bed. Pat was expecting it, knowing that Dale couldn't sleep on airplanes. Pat put Amanda to bed, played with Scott for an hour, and put him to bed.

Pat and Dale woke up early on Sunday. They lingered in bed without getting bored for an hour before the kids awoke.

Chapter 44
Routine

Pat decided to go to Benghazi, Libya from Damascus and then on to Tripoli. In Benghazi, the Arabic was close to Egyptian and it only took him two days to feel comfortable enough with the dialect to sound like a local. But, it took him a full week in Tripoli. Pat was shocked at the difference between east and west Libya. He was able to understand most of the words, but had to ask a lot of questions about terminology. Speaking like a local was more difficult because it seemed that all of the vowels were long and many words had emphasis on different syllables or no emphasis at all. But after a week of talking to the locals, Pat was able to think and speak in their dialect. He learned from the locals that Muammar Gadhafi was in firm control of the country. Dissidents were not tolerated and several thousand were imprisoned.

Pat called Dale as soon as he got to the hotel in Tunis, the American friendly capital of Tunisia, to tell her he might run a few days behind his planned schedule to return home. Two days later, Pat knew that it would take him months to be able to pass as a local in Tunisia. The locals used a lot of French phrases. Years ago, Tunisia was a protectorate of France for twenty-five years and speaking French was imposed on the citizens through the public institutions. Pat's fluency in French helped him converse, but he was unable to see enough patterns to know when to inject the French phrases.

As Pat had discovered in Tripoli, most Tunisian locals couldn't understand his Syrian or Egyptian Arabic, so he had to use the Libyan dialect (darija) that he worked so hard to learn in Tripoli.

Pat flew back to Damascus the next morning and then back to Cairo.

After spending two hours of quality time with Scott and an hour of rapturous time with Dale, Pat walked to the embassy. It was almost midnight in Egypt.

Pat recognized the voice that answered the phone. "Debbie, are you always cheerful?"

"Pat? Is that you?"

Pat chuckled, "Yes. How is little Gregory?"

"Great. He'd probably be better if I spent more time with him. How are your kids?"

"Great. They might be better if I could spend more time with them." Pat considered saying that they were doing great because of their mother, but that would probably make Debbie feel guilty. He couldn't think of anything else to say.

She saved him. "General Haig told me to put you straight through." Pat was put on hold.

She came back on, "Pat, I'd like to meet Dale and your kids."

"I'd love to meet Gregory and your husband." Pat hesitated, "I can't remember his name."

"That's because I never told you my husband's name." The line clicked over to a different ring. Pat realized that her husband was probably CIA.

General Haig picked up.

Pat updated him on his progress. Haig seemed to be most interested in his success in learning to speak like a local in Tripoli.

At the embassy the next day, Pat split his time between helping Neal with military attaché duties and helping to gather intelligence for Milton and the CIA. He was worried that his job was getting too routine for his tastes.

On the first Sunday back from his trip across North Africa, Pat took his family to the Saint Mark Coptic Orthodox Cathedral for Mass. He had explained to Dale that the Coptic churches didn't recognize the Vatican's authority, but the Vatican recognized their apostolic succession, just as the Vatican recognized the Eastern Orthodox religion in Eastern Europe and Asia—meaning the bread and wine was consecrated into the Body and Blood of Christ.

When Pat parked, Dale pointed, "Is that where we are going to Mass?" Dale was overwhelmed by the magnificent architecture of the cathedral. She knew Egypt was a Muslim country and was expecting to go to Mass in a low profile warehouse like they had in Tehran.

Pat returned her smile, "Yes. I didn't expect the church to be so beautiful."

Pat watched the women approaching the church with scarves wrapped around their hair. He was about to suggest that Dale do the same, but Dale had already grabbed a scarf and started copying their hair wrapping style. She was adapting to life in Muslim countries.

Pat got out of the embassy pool car and opened the passenger door for Dale. Scott climbed out first.

Pat picked up Amanda. Dale got out of the car and gave Pat a slight hug. "I like Egypt a lot better than Iran."

Scott said, "Me too."

Pat's heart was warmed by their comments. He smiled. There was no better joy in life for a father than for his wife and kids to be happy.

They weren't late for Mass, so unlike the Mass in the warehouse in Iran, they were hardly noticed, except for the men admiring Dale's natural beauty.

An elderly lady approached Dale as they entered the lobby of the church and handed her a bulletin. She asked in Arabic, "Are you new to the Parish or just visiting."

Before Pat could interpret, to his surprise, Scott interpreted in English for Dale what the lady had said.

The lady smiled at Scott. She switched to barely understandable English, "What an adorable child." She looked at Dale, "Are you American?"

When Dale hesitated, Pat answered, speaking English slowly and clearly, "Yes. My wife is American. We just recently moved to Cairo."

A church bell rang. She spoke to Pat rapidly in Arabic, "My husband is an usher today. I hope that you can stay for a while after Mass and meet him."

Pat smiled, "We can."

Dale expected to follow her husband up to one of the pews near the front as usual, but they sat near the back of the large church. She didn't understand the language of the Mass, but she knew most of the

242

prayers and was able to covert some of the words over to the prayers she knew so well in English.

After Mass, the same woman was waiting for them in the lobby. Her fifty-something-year-old husband stood beside her with a forced smile on his face. Pat could tell immediately that he was military, or ex-military. The way he studied Pat made him suspect that the man worked in intelligence, probably the GID. Pat knew that there was no way to guide Dale gracefully past the couple.

Dale recognized the friendly lady and stopped to talk to her.

The lady said to her husband in Arabic, "Saleh, this is the new family that just arrived in Cairo."

Pat recognized him as the usher that escorted the late arrivals down the center isle to pews with a few empty seats. Pat was impressed that the large Coptic Church was so crowded. The priest's homily, that Dale couldn't understand, addressed the need for Christians to have the courage to stand up for Christ. Perhaps in contrast, he closed the ceremony with a prayer to keep the parish's Christians safe.

Pat smiled and accepted the extended hand. He said in English, "Saleh, my name is Eddie."

The guy who was introduced by his wife as Saleh, didn't try to hide his GID role, "Major O'Sheen, I've seen you in the mosque a couple of times." His English was excellent.

Pat wasn't surprised that Saleh knew who he was, "Like you, I praise God in public whenever I can find the time. It encourages other less ardent believers to commit to God when they have a lot of company joining them in their praise. Don't you agree?"

Dale picked up Scott when the man addressed her husband as Major O'Sheen out of the blue. She knew Pat took over from Eddie and she listened to his logical, but challenging response.

Saleh replied, "People feel freer to share their honest opinions at a mosque or church."

"Saleh, I agree. What is your full name?"

"Saleh Mulita."

Dale asked the lady in Arabic where the lady's room was.

Scott said loudly in Arabic, "I have to go, too."

Pat said to Saleh, "Perhaps our families can share a meal at a restaurant after Mass next week?"

"Why not today?"

Pat smiled and switched to Arabic, "You have me at a disadvantage. You know who I am. By next week, I will know who you are, and we will be playing on a level field. I'm sure you can understand my point of view."

Saleh smiled and nodded. Pat handed Amanda to Dale and took Scott to the toilet.

On the way back to their apartment, Pat pulled unexpectedly into a crowded parking lot of a restaurant.

Dale suggested, "This place is too crowded. There are people waiting outside."

Pat offered, "It wouldn't be crowded if the food wasn't good. Do you have somewhere you need to be?"

Dale shrugged and smiled. She had learned not to argue with her husband when he was in his Pat mode.

Pat said as he got out of the car, "Stay in the car. I'll put our name on the waiting list and see how long the wait will be."

Dale locked the doors and admired her husband's graceful strides as he half trotted to the front door. She still couldn't believe that her teenage heartthrob had become an international spy.

Pat returned to the car and said it would only be ten minutes.

Dale complained, "They usually underestimate."

"It gives us time to talk about our first Mass in Cairo." Pat knew what was on her mind.

Dale jumped on the opening, "Can we talk about what happened after Mass? How did that man know you as Major O'Sheen? You just introduced yourself as Eddie. Did you know him?"

Pat squelched his chuckle at Dale's multiple questions. He knew that she did that to jump start Eddie. Pat didn't need a jump start and answered her questions in reverse. "I don't know him. He must be connected to Egyptian intelligence. I will know more about him by the time we have a meal with him and his wife after Mass next Sunday."

"What?" Her eyebrows raised. "You must be joking."

"Not at all. He suggested we join him for lunch today."

Dale said, "I'm not sure that I want to join in your spy games, especially not with our children present."

Scott chimed in, "Daddy, are you a spy?"

Pat and Dale shared a look. Scott was getting too old to talk around openly.

Pat forced a chuckle, "Scott, do you know what a spy is?"

"Yes."

Pat pressed, "Tell me what a spy is?"

"Bond. James Bond. Double-O-Seven."

Dale burst out laughing.

Pat glared at Dale.

She handled the glare and explained, "We have a Beta tape player in our apartment. Rita gave me a list of movies we can get free from the embassy. I got 'Gold Finger' while you were travelling North Africa."

Pat recalled the line Scott quoted from the movie. He was getting more convinced that Scott inherited his audio-recall.

He reminded Dale, "We already saw that movie together."

Dale chided, "We didn't. I watched it with Eddie. This time I watched it from a totally different perspective—your perspective." Dale smiled at Pat.

Pat understood. Dale knew when she was talking to him and not Eddie. He let Eddie take over.

Chapter 45
The Mulitas

Pat approached whom he had learned was the Egyptian deputy director of domestic intelligence (of the General Intelligence Directorate—GID), Saleh Mulita, at the mosque on Friday after midday Jumu'ah prayers.

Saleh smiled as Pat approached him. He introduced Pat to the four men gathered around him, explaining that Pat worked at the U.S. embassy. Pat assumed they were all GID. Pat conversed with them in their local Egyptian Arabic dialect. He knew Saleh had already recognized his linguistic talents, and Dale was convinced that Egyptians were friendly to Americans.

Pat tried unsuccessfully to goad them into a conversation on Sadat's treaty with Israel. Their avoidance of the subject told Pat more than an honest conversation about the subject could. Saleh made a covert motion that Pat caught, and the four men bowed away with best wishes to Pat.

Saleh was about to speak, but Pat preempted him, "I look forward to sharing a meal with your family after Mass on Sunday."

Saleh smiled, "I hope my son and granddaughter will be able to join us. She is about Scott's age."

Pat locked eyes with Saleh, "That would be great." They both knew they were using each other, and that developing a friendship could be valuable if the diplomatic relationships between their governments became strained.

On their way to Saint Mark's on Sunday, Pat said, "Dale, we are going to eat with Saleh and his family after Mass if he shows up."

Dale looked over at her husband, who didn't look at her as he concentrated on driving through the horrendous traffic. "Are you talking about the older couple we met at Mass last Sunday?"

"Yes. Saleh is a deputy director in Egypt's intelligence agency."

Dale objected, "I don't think I like the idea of you involving me and the kids in your covert operations."

"This has nothing to do with covert operations. It has to do with befriending important diplomatic contacts. You and I together are better than me or Pat alone."

Dale thought about it. She trusted that Eddie wouldn't put his family in jeopardy.

"Are you asking for me to collaborate with you on Pat's intelligence operations?"

Eddie nodded, "Only with friendly assets."

"Assets?"

Eddie didn't respond.

Dale pressed, "Do you mean assets that Pat can use in the future?"

Eddie smiled and nodded.

Dale returned the smile. Her heart rate accelerated. The thought of helping her husband with his covert operations was exhilarating.

After Mass, Saleh introduced his son to Dale and Pat, and then his granddaughter to Scott. Al-Saleh was Pat's age—in his early-thirties—and his daughter, Nevera, was four or five. Based on his demeanor, Pat assumed Saleh's son also worked for the GID but didn't ask. Saleh recommended that they eat at the same restaurant that Pat had pulled into on impulse the week before. Saleh said that the owners were members of the Coptic parish, which explained why it was so crowded after Mass last Sunday.

The meal went well. Dale made friends with al-Saleh and asked about Nevera's mother, as Scott made friends with Nevera. All of the adults spoke English the whole meal. Scott and Nevera sometimes talked in Arabic. No business was discussed, but a mutually beneficial bond of friendship was initiated, satisfying the objective of both Pat and Saleh.

On the drive back to their apartment, Pat said, "Scott, why did you tell Nevera that I was a spy?"

Dale jumped to Scott's defense, "He never said that."

"He said it in Arabic and everyone at the table but you understood it." Pat repeated, "Scott, why did you tell Nevera that I was I spy?"

Scott sensed that he had done something wrong. He shrugged as he looked up into his daddy's eyes.

Pat smiled at his innocence, "Scott, I am not a spy; not like 'Bond . . . James Bond'.

Scott chuckled and added, "Double-O-Seven."

Dale said, "That was a movie, Scott. Your daddy is not a spy. He is in the army." She looked over at Pat apologetically.

Pat smiled at her. "Dale, did you learn anything about Nevera's mother?" Saleh had kept Pat pretty occupied.

"She died. I don't know when or how. I don't think al-Saleh wanted to talk about it in front of Nevera."

Monday was a normal day at the embassy. But on Tuesday morning, Neal Williams greeted Pat as he approached his own small office in the embassy and Neal asked him to come into his office.

Pat turned and looked at Neal when he closed the door after they entered. He knew there was an issue.

Neal got right to it. "The director of the General Intelligence Directorate (GID) wants to meet with you and Milton. Milton wants to know why he specifically asked for you."

Pat didn't hide his suspicion. "Neal, my family and I had a friendly lunch with Saleh Mulita and his wife and son after Mass at Saint Mark's Cathedral on Sunday. We didn't talk shop at all."

"Did you invite Saleh?"

"He invited me last Sunday. I declined because he called me Major O'Sheen, and I didn't know who he was until Milton told me.

"Neal, what do you suggest?"

Neal appreciated O'Sheen asking him for advice, but he suspected that Pat was three steps ahead of him. "Milton wants to meet with us."

"Okay. When?"

Neal picked up phone receiver and dialed three numbers. When it was answered he said, "O'Sheen is here." Neal listened. "We will be right up."

Pat explained to Milton his three encounters with Saleh Mulita.

Milton asked with an attitude, "Do you know who al-Saleh Mulita is?"

248

Pat's dander got up. "No. But, I'm sure you are about to tell me."

"He is an assistant director over foreign intelligence in the GID."

Pat smiled, "I thought he was probably GID. Is he a friend of yours?"

Milton didn't answer.

Pat said, "He is young to be an assistant deputy director. Is that due to his father's position?"

"I'm sure that helped, but the son is brilliant and devious. Was he at the Mass the previous Sunday?"

"I didn't see him there."

Milton ran his hand back through his thinning hair. "It seems to me that he had his dad arrange the lunch to meet you. What did you tell him about yourself?"

"Not much. I sat next to his father and talked mostly to him. Al-Saleh sat next to my wife. They both had kids between them. They talked a lot."

"You need to call your wife and see what she told him about you."

Pat said, "That won't be necessary. I listened to every word of their conversation."

"You just said that you were talking to the father?"

"Milton, I'm capable of doing both at the same time. Didn't they stress the importance of learning to do that in your CIA training?"

Milton nodded. "So what did she tell him?"

"That we fell in love as teenagers, married young, that I joined the army to finish college, and served in Vietnam, and that after the war I was recruited into military intelligence because of my foreign language skills."

Pat added, "When al-Saleh asked her if we had served in other countries, she told him we were in Iran for a short time."

Milton brightened at the last comment. "Pat, did you know Nasser Moghadam in Iran."

"Yes. We were becoming friends. He investigated both attacks against me."

"Bingo. Al-Saleh and Nasser were roommates in college."

Pat said, "In England."

Milton was surprised, "You already knew that?"

"No. But they both speak English with the same accent."

Pat filled in the blanks, "So Milton, you think al-Saleh talked with Nasser about me."

"Yes, and learned about your big massacre."

Pat glared at Milton for his nomenclature, but controlled his anger. Eddie was proud of him. "When are we meeting with the director?"

"Eleven o'clock. I want you to wear your dress uniform with every decoration you ever earned on it."

Pat agreed with Milton's reasoning. "Where are we meeting?"

"At their offices. Meet me in the lobby at ten-thirty."

Chapter 46
An Accounting

The first surprise to GID Director Ameen Nummur was Major O'Sheen's youth and his average size. The second was the number of medal insignias and service decorations that were displayed on his uniform—more like one would expect on a general's uniform. The erect posture and direct eye contact did not surprise him.

Milton handled the introductions in Arabic in the director's office. They sat around a coffee table, Milton and Pat on the couch, with the director and al-Saleh sitting in higher chairs. There was coffee and tea on the table, but everyone passed.

The director started in Arabic, "Major O'Sheen, I'm sure you are wondering why we called you here."

"Yes sir. I am curious, but I am also honored."

A slight smile crossed Nummur's mustached lips.

"Major, I understand that you were in Iran before coming here?"

Milton looked at O'Sheen. They had assumed correctly.

Pat's eyes didn't leave the director's. "Yes sir. My wife and I were attacked by three labor thugs after leaving a restaurant in Tehran one night. Two of the thugs had to be treated at a hospital. After I was attacked a second time, my wife no longer felt safe in Iran. I requested a reassignment to Cairo."

"What did you do to instigate the attacks?" The director was intentionally accusatory.

Pat didn't fall for the bait, "None of the attackers were in a condition to tell me what I did to provoke them."

Al-Saleh unintentionally laughed. "It is hard to get answers out of dead men."

Pat locked eyes with al-Saleh, "I do have a good idea why they attacked me."

Al-Saleh waved his hand for Pat to continue.

"During the second attack, when I saw men following me, I tried to make it to a friend's house who works for SAVAK and for your college roommate, Nasser. Eight men cornered me before I could get through my friend's gate. The two men who attacked me and my wife brought knives to the fight this time. I used those knives to fight them all off me. I regret that so many of them were killed."

Al-Saleh said, "Six of the eight died, a seventh almost died in the hospital."

Pat rubbed the scar on his chin, "It wasn't a fair fight."

"Eight against one rarely is."

Quoting from a previous report he had made, Pat said, "They were street fighters at best. I was trained in Army Special Forces and fought in the jungles of Vietnam. If they hadn't brought the knives to the fight, more of them would have survived."

Al-Saleh was speechless.

The GID director asked, "You said that you have a good idea why they attacked you."

Pat nodded, "I made a good friend in Tehran whose son is in the university there. I talked with the student after the second attack. He admitted telling the labor thug who first attacked me and my wife that I was snooping around looking for anti-shah dissidents and Ruhollah Khomeini supporters. The attackers were financially backing student protests against the Shah. I guess they thought I threatened their security."

"Did you threaten their security?" Al-Saleh had found his tongue.

"I didn't until after the first attack."

Nummur changed the subject, "Major O'Sheen, I'm not familiar with that award on your purple heart."

Pat assumed that he was satisfied with the explanation of what happened in Iran. "It means that I have more than one Purple Heart. Please call me Pat, Director Nummur."

"Okay, if you will call me Ameen."

Pat smiled and nodded.

Milton spoke up for the first time. "A bronze oak leaf cluster is worn for each Purple Heart earned after the first. The silver cluster is worn in place of five bronze. It means that Pat was injured by the enemy six different times in combat. Three times he almost died."

Pat looked down at his lap for the first time.

"Pat, you are lucky to be alive."

Pat looked back up, "I agree, Ameen."

"So what will you be doing for your embassy here, Pat?"

Milton got nervous.

Pat said, "Like military intelligence officers in all countries, I hope to meet my counterparts in your military so in case of disagreement we can help smooth ruffled feathers or help clear up misunderstandings before our superiors get mad and cut diplomatic ties."

Milton smiled. *What a perfect answer.*

The director said, "Pat, I will put in a good word for you with our defense minister."

"Thank you, Ameen. I would very much appreciate that."

Ameen stood up, so they all stood up. Ameen extended his hand, "Welcome to Egypt, Pat."

"Thank you, Sir." He shook the offered hand.

Pat stepped over to shake Mulita's hand, "Al-Saleh, please don't bring up the second attack to my wife. She knows I was attacked, but she doesn't know that I killed so many men."

He nodded. "I understand, Pat."

With the Americans gone, the director asked, "Are you satisfied, al-Saleh?"

"Yes sir. Just remind me to send at least a dozen men in full body armor if we ever have to pick him up against his will."

Ameen chuckled and nodded his agreement. "He would make a formidable enemy. And he already speaks Egyptian Arabic like a local." Nummur added, "He is very intelligent, al-Saleh. I threw him a curve ball with the question about what he will be doing at the embassy. The question made Milton nervous but not Pat. His answer was brilliant. He is able to think quickly on his feet."

"Or more than likely, he was three steps ahead of us and expected the question, Ameen."

In the car, Milton said, "You handled that expertly, Pat."

"Thank you, Milton."

Milton gave Ambassador Atherton a blow-by-blow accounting of the meeting.

Alfred said, "You sound like you are starting to admire Pat."

"I do, Alfred. After hearing him explain the attacks on him in Iran, I can understand why he was still wound up so tight when he first got here to the embassy. I think he will be a very valuable asset to us here in Egypt."

Chapter 47
New Friends

Two weeks later, over drinks on Thursday night, Pat said, "Dale, I have to go on a trip next week. I think you might enjoy going with me."

"Where are you going?"

"Casablanca."

Dale's eyes lit up, "Humphrey Bogart's Casablanca? Where is it? How far is it?"

Pat chuckled, "Yes. Humphrey Bogart's Casablanca. It's in Morocco, which is on the west African coast on the Atlantic Ocean, not too far from the Mediterranean Sea: about two-thousand miles from here: maybe five hours air time."

Dale said, "About like flying from Washington to L.A.? Yes, I want to go."

Pat smiled. "Don't forget that in the movie, Ingrid Bergman hated Casablanca until she met Humphrey Bogart at Rick's bar."

Dale glowed, "Do you know if Rick's Bar is still there? Maybe they have a colored piano player named Sam, and I can say, 'play it again, Sam'." She giggled.

"I doubt that there ever was a Rick's bar in Casablanca, except in the movie."

Pat stood up from the couch, went to the kitchen phone, and dialed 0. He spoke in Arabic asking for an information operator in Casablanca.

Dale smiled at her incredibly confident, sexy man. Pat reached out his drink, and she tapped her glass against his.

Pat was distracted from his sexy wife when a woman came on the line. He had difficulty understanding her. He drove his mind to the Arabic spoken in Tunisia and replayed her words in his mind. He changed his Arabic dialect, "Can you connect me to Rick's Bar in Casablanca?"

He waited ten seconds. She came back, "I cannot find a listing for a Rick's in Casablanca."

He said, "Thank you." He shook his head informing Dale of the result.

Dale said. "I still want to go. When will we leave?"

Pat was enthused. "I will ask Neferet, in administrative services, for her advice in the morning. I'm targeting Wednesday as the debarkation day. You do understand that it will be a working trip for me?"

"Why are you going?"

"To learn to speak the dialect in Morocco like a local."

"Why?"

"Because General Haig knows that I am capable of learning all of the local Arabic dialects in North Africa. One never knows what the future might bring."

That made sense to Dale.

Pat and his family flew from Cairo to Rabat, the capital of Morocco. Neferet suggested they stay in hotels there. Casablanca was just an hour drive down the coast. She also recommended spending a day and a night in Marrakesh, a two-to-three hour drive southeast of Casablanca.

In Rabat, their first stop in the rental car was at the American Embassy. Pat had called ahead and talked to Colonel Steve Windsor, the Military Attaché. Steve had someone prepare a recommended itinerary for their visit, including marked maps. Even though Dale wore a modest dress, Steve had trouble keeping his eyes off her. Pat and Dale were both used to that from military men.

All of the Moroccan women were enthralled with Scott and his short blond hair and over Amanda's smile while Pat had a short private meeting with the ambassador, the station chief, and Steve Windsor. Steve had already explained to them Pat's reason for coming to Morocco. The last five minutes of the meeting was conducted in Arabic. The ambassador expressed skepticism that Pat could learn to speak like a local after just one week.

Pat stopped and bought a bottle of bourbon, a pack of cigarettes, a six-pack of cokes, and snacks. Then they checked into the hotel. The

256

room that Neferet reserved for them had a view of the Atlantic Ocean, and the sun was starting to set over the water. Pat found an ice machine, and Dale made drinks as Scott started in on the snacks. They watched in awe as the large orange sun dipped into the Atlantic Ocean.

They ate in the restaurant in the hotel. The food was good but bland. The bar adjoining the dining area was almost full.

When they got back up to the room, Dale and the kids were tired and ready for bed, so Pat left them in the room and went down to the bar. Now the bar was less than half full. He saw two men about his age meet in the lobby and go into the bar. He recognized their local dialect.

They sat on stools at the far end of the bar. Pat took the one stool that was available to their immediate right. The bartender brought the two men drinks without taking their order . . . meaning that they were regulars. Pat smelled vermouth in the clear drinks.

The bartender asked Pat for his order.

Pat pointed to their drinks and said, "I'll have the same drink that they are having."

The guy next to him looked momentarily at Pat, probably because of his accent. Pat pretended not to notice. When the guy pulled out a cigarette, Pat pulled a cigarette out of his pack and asked him for a light.

The guy flicked the lighter again, lit Pat's, and said, "Where are from?"

"Cairo. Are you two from around here?" That started the conversation. The guy on the end couldn't hear and suggested that they move down to a table.

Ten minutes later, they were better able to understand Pat, partly because the noise level in the bar had decreased as men left. They were patient with Pat as he asked in French what some of their phrases meant. In Morocco, French was a bridge language between people of different Arabic dialects. Morocco had also been a French Protectorate, like Tunisia and Algeria.

Pat bought the next round of drinks. The conversation went to international politics. The two Moroccans were impressed with Pat's viewpoints.

After an hour, Pat motioned for his bill.

They objected and insisted on buying him a drink.

Pat agreed, "Are you brothers?"

"Our wives are sisters. They won't let us drink around our neighbors at home, so we come here on Wednesday nights."

By the time the brothers-in-law left the bar, Pat was able to think with the Moroccan dialect in his head. He hoped that after another eight to ten hours of conversations with locals he could master it. His week-long effort at learning the dialect in Tripoli and two days in Tunis were paying dividends here.

The next morning, the O'Sheens toured the Chellah Necropolis in Rabat, which had Roman ruins dating back to the first century. After lunch, they toured the Mohamed V mausoleum. As they exited the mosque, Pat started talking to a local before they encountered a tour group from Texas. Actually, Dale and Pat didn't find them. Scott was already bored with historic sites and ran over to a group and to a girl about his age because he recognized their American English. Dale gasped when she realized Scott had gotten away and saw Pat running after him.

The group was alarmed when they saw Pat running toward them. A really big guy stepped forward to confront Pat as the rest of the group gathered around their children. Pat recognized the Texas accent of the girl that Scott was talking to.

Pat slowed to a stop ten feet from the big guy who definitely had a military demeanor. Pat spoke in his Alabama accent while pointing to his son, "I'm sorry if I alarmed y'all. My son, Scott, got away from us."

Dale caught up and ran past Pat pushing Amanda in the stroller. She grabbed her son up into her arms.

Pat walked past the big soldier without interference and calmed Dale, who was scolding Scott for running away from them.

The big guy approached Pat, "You look familiar. Were you Army Special Forces?"

Pat replied, "I still am. You look familiar. What are you?"

"I was a Navy Seal."

Pat made the connection with the scar that ran from his temple down below his right ear that cosmetic surgeons hid as well as they ever could. He remembered his arm was also injured as he climbed aboard an evacuation helicopter during the second POW rescue.

Pat offered his hand, "I'm Eddie O'Sheen." He hoped that the Navy Seal wouldn't recognize the first name and make the connection.

"Jim Turner." The Navy Seal shook the offered hand.

Jim made the connection. "Aren't you Captain Pat O'Sheen?"

Pat didn't want Dale to learn too many details about the POW rescue. "No."

Dale stepped forward, "He is Major Pat O'Sheen, now." She looked at Pat wondering why he was hedging.

Still trying to deflect away from the rescue, Pat said, "Jim, this is my wife, Dale, son, Scott, and daughter, Amanda."

The big Navy Seal smiled at Dale and turned, "Honey, come up here." His pretty wife approached with their five year old girl in her arms.

Turner said, "Sally, this is Major Pat O'Sheen."

She said, "The one at the POW camp in North Vietnam?" Based on the unbelievable story her husband had told her about Pat O'Sheen, he should be eight feet tall and three feet wide, with a thirty inch waist. She gave Pat a beautiful smile.

Jim said, "Yes. He and his sniper partner were the ones who rescued almost two-hundred POWs in North Vietnam."

Pat started backing away. Dale put a hand on his back and held him in place. She wanted to hear this.

Pat tried to deflect again, "Jim, isn't that where you got the scar on your face?"

"Yes."

Pat addressed Sally. "Your husband's Seal unit had the hard part—keeping the Cong from their base a half mile away out of the POW camp so my partner and I, and all the POWs could be evacuated." Pat was trying to back Turner off from saying what he didn't want Dale to hear.

Jim failed to recognize Pat's intent. "Bullshit. You and your sniper partner killed most of the sixty guards at the POW camp before we arrived. Somehow you accomplished that without one POW casualty."

Dale looked at her husband incredulously. *Killed sixty guards! Rescued almost two-hundred POWs?*

Pat looked warily over as Dale stepped forward. She said with ire, "When you called me from the aircraft carrier, you said that you and Mike rescued a few POWs. Two-hundred is a hell of a lot more than a few."

Turner realized that Pat's wife was in the dark about the details of the rescue, and that he had screwed up by saying too much. He offered, "Pat, I did hear that you had thirty South Vietnamese soldiers with you."

Pat looked into the soldier's eyes with appreciation for getting him halfway off the hook.

Pat finished getting off the hook. "Jim, my best friend and sniper partner in Nam was Mike Burkowski. After that rescue, he got killed over there and I don't like to talk about the war, not even with my wife."

Jim nodded in understanding.

Pat changed the subject, "Are you still in the Navy?"

"Retired."

"You look too young to be retired."

"I was given a medical retirement. When I got this . . ." Jim ran his index finger down the scar on his face. " . . . I also took a bullet in the shoulder. After six surgeries I can only raise my arm up to here." He raised his left arm and hand up to almost shoulder level. "I work with my dad and these guys in our oil business in Texas, now."

Jim introduced the other two families.

A Limo pulled into the nearby parking lot.

Jim instructed, "Carl. Go hold our Limo."

He turned back to O'Sheen. "Pat, what are y'all doing for dinner tonight?"

When Pat shrugged, Jim suggested, "Why don't you and your family join us for dinner at the Hotel Sofitel Rabat? We have reservations at eight."

Pat looked at Dale, who smiled and nodded her approval.

He said. "Sounds great, Jim."

"Why don't you come to my suite at seven, and we'll have cocktails first and get better acquainted." He looked at Pat's pretty wife, knowing that she would have the final say.

Dale said, "Thank you, Jim. We'd love to."

In Turners' suite, Pat explained to Jim that he worked at the embassy in Cairo, and that he was on a working vacation to learn the local dialect. Pat was not surprised that Dale and Sally hit it off while talking at a little kitchenette type table.

260

The wives joined their husbands and they shared vacation plans in Morocco, which were very similar. Scott helped the younger Carol with a puzzle on the coffee table.

Jim made a motion to his wife and she stood up and opened one of the doors on the three bedroom suite. Two pretty teenage girls walked out.

Sally introduced Jim's nieces.

After courtesies, Denise, the older one went back and stood where she could see through the opened bedroom door. The younger one, Deidra, sat down next to Pat and Amanda on the couch and watched Scott hand Carol the last piece of the puzzle. Carol spun it around and tried it different ways. She finally made it fit and glowed a smile at Scott. They said, almost in unison, "We did it!"

Deidra praised, "Scott, you are good at puzzles."

Scott turned around and smiled at her.

She said, "Scott, my name is Deidra."

"Hi, Deidra. You are pretty."

She was surprised. "Thank you. How old are you?"

"Six."

Deidra looked up at Dale, "Six going on eighteen. He is very smart."

Pat knew what Dale was going to say and preempted her. "Deidra, he gets that from his mother."

Dale shared a look with Pat and chuckled.

The other four kids ran out of the bedroom past Denise. One of the older kids, a boy perhaps eight-years-old said, "The movie is over."

The kids all handled Sally's introduction to the O'Sheen's politely and patiently.

Sally said to Dale, "We are going to order room service for Jim's nieces and the kids. You are welcome to bring your kids with you to dinner in the restaurant if you are not comfortable with that."

Dale looked at Deidra.

Deidra said, "I won't let Scott or Amanda out of my sight."

Dale said, "Scott."

He turned around.

"Do you want to eat dinner with us in the restaurant, or eat up here?"

261

Deidra threw in the enticement, "Up here with all of the other kids."

Dale looked at Pat. He nodded his approval but said, "Let's take Amanda with us. She has already eaten and will fall asleep."

After dinner, and by the end of the evening, they decided to vacation together. Jim had the concierge make another room reservation for the O'Sheens in the hotel that they were staying in Marrakesh for the next night. They agreed to meet at the Hassan II Mosque for the group's ten o'clock tour in Casablanca. The O'Sheens thanked Jim for the drinks and for paying for the meal, which Pat knew was very expensive for the large group.

Chapter 48
Moving forward

The next morning they all toured the mosque together. The Hassan II Mosque was advertised to be the biggest mosque in the world outside of Saudi Arabia and had the tallest minaret on earth. (Minaret is a tall slender tower, typically part of a mosque, with a platform near the top from which a muezzin in earlier centuries called Muslims to prayer.) Pat was realizing that all of the tourist mosques claimed to be the biggest or best in one way or another.

Dale was comfortable with the group of Americans, which allowed Pat to slip off to talk to the locals. The tour was over before the first call to Jumu'ah prayers. Pat met them as they came out of the mosque. Pat pulled a long item out of the back pocket of Amanda's stroller and put it under his arm.

Jim looked at Pat, "What is that under your arm?"

"A Muslim prayer rug. I'm going to mid-day prayers in the mosque."

Pat pointed to a street, "The restaurant is two blocks down that street and a half a block to the right. I'll catch up with you there."

Pat had a thought, "Have any of you ever heard a Muslim call to prayers?"

They all shook their heads.

Pat looked at his watch. "It is quite impressive. You should hang around for at least the adhan, the first call to prayers. I'm going in for prayers after that. What you will hear is the *Takbir* where the muezzin chants 'God is greatest' followed by the *Shahada* where he chants 'There is no God but Allah' and chants again 'Muhammad is the messenger of Allah."

The adhan started four minutes later. Pat interpreted the Arabic chants. He had to add at the end, "Hasten to prayers" which he hadn't told them earlier.

Pat went into the mosque.

Jim looked at Dale, "Is Pat a Muslim?"

"No. We are Catholics. He is just blending in, learning the local customs."

"Is he a spy?"

"Not like James Bond. He . . ."

Scott heard James Bond and interrupted, "Bond, James Bond. Double-O-seven."

Everyone laughed.

Dale continued, "Pat is in military intelligence."

Jim chuckled, "My dad thinks military and intelligence are contradictory terms."

Dale laughed, "Pat's dad called it an oxymoron when Pat told him that he was going into military intelligence."

Jim laughed, "Yes, oxymoron was the word I was looking for."

At lunch, Jim apologized that there wasn't enough room for the O'Sheens to fly with them to Marrakesh on the Gulfstream jet.

Pat waved off his apology. "I want to learn the countryside. That is hard to do from the air. Marrakesh is only about a two hour drive. We'll catch up with y'all at the hotel before dinner."

Marrakesh was great, especially the atmosphere at dusk. The street food carts served all kinds of delicacies with mouth-watering aromas filling the air, surrounded by what could only be described as a medieval circus with a myriad of storytellers, fire-eaters, jugglers, and skilled acrobats. They watched snake-charmers and saw herbalists dispensing mystical remedies, and heard a variety of musical troupes.

The kids enjoyed a fifteen minute tale about a Barbary pirate, told in English by a flamboyant story teller wearing a black patch over one eye and old pirate garb.

Eddie explained after the tale that centuries ago along the coast from Rabat to Tripoli the Muslim states supported their governments by sponsoring piracy. The baby sitters and older kids gathered around him to hear.

Eddie gave a lesson on early American history. "When America won its independence from Britain over two hundred years ago, our new nation had to pay a lot of money in tribute to the Barbary pirates, the same pirates that the storyteller was talking about, to keep them from attacking American merchant ships carrying American goods to sell and trade to the rich countries on the Mediterranean Sea. Our new country didn't have a big Navy with warships yet.

"By the time Thomas Jefferson became our third president, the United States of America was developing a respectable Navy. Thomas Jefferson refused to pay the tribute to the pirates, and Tripoli declared war on America. Congress declared war on Tripoli. Our ships and our marines won the war. That is why the United States Marine's theme song still begins with 'from the halls of Montezuma to the shores of Tripoli'."

Dale sang it for the kids, "From the halls of Montezuma, to the shores of Tripoli. We fight our country's battles, in the air, on land, and sea.

Jim joined in with a beautiful baritone voice.

"First to fight for right and freedom. And to keep our honor clean. We are proud to claim the title of United States Marine."

Everyone in the group clapped.

Pat smiled at Dale in admiration.

Dale smiled at Jim in admiration.

Jim laughed with joy.

Dale asked Pat, "Where did 'halls of Montezuma' come from?"

"The Mexican-American War, I think."

Dale leaned up and kissed him on the cheek. "You are so smart."

At dinner, the waiter came up and asked for drink orders in Arabic.

Pat said in Arabic, "Do you have a waiter who speaks English? I'm the only one who understands Arabic."

The waiter said in French, "Do you understand French?"

Pat looked at the blank looks around the table and answered in French. "Apparently, I'm the only one at the table who speaks French."

Pat could tell that the waiter didn't want to lose a large table of wealthy Americans.

The waiter said, "You could interpret for me."

Pat almost chided him that he would have to split the tip with him if he did that. He considered asking to talk to the manager. Instead, he suggested in Arabic, "Have a waiter who speaks English take everyone's order and interpret it for you. I will serve as an interpreter on all other matters."

The waiter smiled, "I can arrange that." The waiter left the table.

Jim asked Pat, "What was that all about?"

"He didn't speak English. He wanted me to be his interpreter. We worked out a compromise."

"Did you speak to him in French?"

"Yes. Morocco was a French Protectorate until 1956. French is still a second language and is used as a lingua franca—a bridge language between Arabic dialects that can't communicate well."

Jim cocked his head. "Didn't I hear in Nam that you were fluent in Vietnamese?"

Pat nodded.

Jim shook his head. "How many languages do you speak?"

Pat shrugged, "That depends on what you call a language. The Arabic spoken here in Morocco isn't intelligible to an Egyptian who speaks Arabic. They might as well be different languages."

Jim smiled, "I can see why the military assigned you to foreign intelligence."

The meal was fabulous. Jim insisted on picking up the whole tab again. Pat couldn't imagine how much this whole trip from America was costing Jim's oil company.

As they were waiting on the check, Pat asked Jim, "Where are you going after Morocco?"

"To visit the pyramids and then to Jerusalem and the Holy land."

Pat pulled a paper from his pocket and asked Jim for a pen. He wrote Kara's name and telephone number. "This lady was our tour guide to the pyramids. She was wonderful in getting us around all the scams. If you decide to call her, use my name. She is the cousin of a grand lady who works in my embassy in Cairo."

Pat wrote down the number of the embassy and the phone number in his apartment, "Call me at these numbers if you need help."

They had all enjoyed Marrakesh and each other's company so much that they all decided to spend another night there.

On the second night, the older kids wanted to listen to same pirate story from the same storyteller. The storyteller was glad to oblige

266

because of Pat's generous tip the night before. The older kids had a better understanding of the Barbary pirates the storyteller was mimicking after Pat's history lesson the night before.

Scott and Amanda were fascinated by the fire-eaters, jugglers, and acrobats.

The next morning, the group from Texas flew up to Meknes, a town filled with historic sites. Pat drove a different route back to Casablanca so he could see a different part of the country.

They rented a room in a hotel in Casablanca. Dale wanted to go to at least one bar there. The concierge at their hotel directed Pat to a piano bar, and after an adequate tip, the owner of the bar agreed to let them bring the kids in for ten minutes—Amanda was asleep in her stroller. Another tip got them a seat by the piano. The Arab piano player was talented.

Pat grew up with musicians in his family. He spent his time playing sports, but when his sister or mother sat down at the piano or the organ in their living room, he always came in to watch and listen. His mother taught him chords on the piano, and he learned to play a few songs by ear. But he had too many other interests to take the time to learn how to coordinate his eyes on the notes on a page of music to his fingers on the keyboard.

Listening to and watching the talented piano player, and after his last year of intensive training in learning Arabic, Farsi, and Urdu, he realized that music was a language. To master music, one needs to think in that language.

Their vodka martinis arrived and Pat pulled away from his flashbacks.

The piano player finished a song and looked up at Dale, possibly hoping for a song request, but most likely just to admire her beauty.

Dale smiled at him and said, "Play it again, Sam."

The dark-skinned Arab laughed joyously and nodded. To Dale's astonishment, he started playing the theme song from the movie, Casablanca. Scott, who sat on Pat's lap, started thumping the beat on the edge of the piano. Dale was in heaven.

Pat was in heaven seeing the enjoyment expressed on the faces of his wife and son. The entire patronage in the bar picked up on the

Americans' excitement and gathered around the O'Sheens at the piano. Amanda was awakened by the excitement, and Pat lifted her out the stroller. The piano player smiled at Amanda without missing a cord on the piano. Amanda returned his smile.

The owner let the O'Sheen family stay for longer than ten minutes—they were good for business. But the O'Sheens left after their second drink. Dale was satisfied that she could tell her family and friends that she went to a bar in Casablanca and told the piano player, "Play it again. Sam".

On Monday morning, they drove back to the American Embassy in the Moroccan capital of Rabat. Colonel Windsor invited the whole O'Sheen family into his office and asked Dale how their vacation went. The question was a good way for him to admire her beauty without being obvious.

When Colonel Windsor walked Pat into the ambassador's office for a private meeting, the Moroccan women workers in the embassy took Dale and her kids under their wings again.

The ambassador started the interview in Moroccan Arabic. "I hope your family enjoyed Morocco."

Pat knew he was being tested. He replied in a long dialogue in the local Arabic. "Ambassador, my family enjoyed our short time in Morocco more than our total time in any other foreign country. We met a group from Texas, toured with them, and had a fantastic time. The local people seem to like Americans."

The ambassador offered some history. "When America first gained its independence, it signed a treaty with Morocco. It was the first international treaty for America. That treaty has been honored ever since, for over two hundred years now."

They talked in Arabic for another five minutes.

The ambassador said, "Major, I underestimated your linguistic skills. Somehow you managed to master the local dialect in a week."

Pat wasn't about to tell them about his audio-graphic memory. He simply said, "Thank you, Sir."

The O'Sheens flew to Algiers as planned. It was the only African country on the Mediterranean coast Pat had not visited. Based on the hotel concierge's recommendation, they took a cable car from the hotel to Notre Dame d'Afrique. The Catholic basilica was over a hundred years old and had over forty huge, stained-glass windows. The view of the Mediterranean Sea and the coast of Algiers from the church's back yard was breathtaking. Even Amanda gasped at the view.

The basilica was built under French occupation. Its symbolic and religious importance was summed up by the inscription on the apse: *Notre Dame d'Afrique priez pour nous et pour les Musulmans* ("Our Lady of Africa, pray for us and for the Muslims.").

The locals spoke a mixture of Arabic and French like in Tunisia. Pat could communicate with the locals, but like in Tunisia, Pat knew it would take a long time to sound like a local, to learn when to inject French phrases. The O'Sheens flew back to Cairo the next morning.

When they got back to their apartment, Scott ran to the bathroom.

Dale said, "I think he has to poo. It's your turn."

Pat smiled. "Okay." He had slept on the plane, and knew that Dale was not able to sleep in the air where any serious mechanical failure would mean certain death. He waited at the partially opened bathroom door for Scott to call for help to use the toilet paper.

Dale called Rita Williams and told her that they were back home.

Rita ran up the stairs and was there minutes later. She was all smile when she hugged Dale, anxious to hear about the trip.

Pat heard the excited girls' reunion through the bathroom door as he was trying to teach Scott how to wipe his butt. After he finished, Scott pulled up his pants and ran out of the bathroom, "Aunt Rita! Aunt Rita!"

Rita squatted down and her face glowed as Scott ran into her arms.

Pat watched with surprise. He didn't realize that Scott loved Rita so much. He knew that Rita and Dale had formed a bond that would last a lifetime. He knew that nurturing his friendship with Colonel Neal Williams was imperative. Rita was a blessing to Neal. Dale was a Godsend to Pat.

Rita looked up at Pat and smiled at the exceptional man. Dale had told her what Pat was doing in the bathroom for Scott. It was hard to fuse her idea of Pat as a decorated war hero who rescued hundreds of POWs behind enemy lines, with a man who would wipe his son's butt when his wife was available to perform the smelly, nasty chore. Dale's husband was becoming more attractive and more lovable at each encounter. She couldn't imagine how her husband had ever gotten crossways with Pat O'Sheen.

Chapter 49
Iranian History

Pat started to adapt to the normal embassy functions. Eddie forced Pat to accept a normal happy life without any dangerous threats arising. Pat was losing his dominance over Eddie, but he didn't mind: Dale and Scott were very happy. Amanda would be talking up a storm soon. The embassy was happy. The Egyptian diplomats were happy. Pat shared Eddie's happiness and was content to be in the background until the next crisis arose. He expected that crises would come very soon.

The downturn started in Iran, in September, 1978, on Eid-e-Fitr, the holiday celebrating the end of the month of Ramadan, the month of Muslim fasting, which is much stricter than the Christian time of Lent. In Tehran, a permit for an open air prayer was granted with expectation of a controllable crowd of ten to twenty thousand. Instead, the crowd estimates were up to 500,000. The clergy led the crowd on a large march through the center of Tehran. A few days later, more large marches took place, and for the first time, protesters openly vocalized their demand for Khomeini's return to Iran and the establishment of an Islamic republic.

Pat's phone rang in his small office in Cairo. It was Hal Middleton, the station chief at the Tehran embassy.

"Pat, Hal Middleton here."

Pat was surprised. He said, "To what do I owe this honor, Hal?"

Hal chuckled. O'Sheen wasn't honored. "Andy (the ambassador in Iran) wants you to come back to our embassy to help deal with this crisis."

"Why me?"

Hal answered honestly, "Nasser (the director of the Iranian secret police, SAVAK) wants you back here."

Pat had the highest level of respect for the secret police director, Nasser Moghadam. He answered honestly. "I'm not bringing my family back to Iran, Hal."

"Pat, you predicted this revolution. Nasser believes that you might be able to help avert it from escalating more."

"It is too late for that, Hal. I tried to warn everyone months ago—no one believed me. There is nothing that I can do to prevent the revolution. Give Nasser my phone number."

Pat waited, but Hal didn't respond. Pat knew that he was letting down his friends in the Iranian embassy. He advised, "Hal, send your wife and kids home to America for Thanksgiving and Christmas. Advise Andy and all the other Americans who have wives and kids there to do the same."

Hal objected. "We can't do that."

"You must. And never bring them back to Iran."

Hal offered, "Andy believes the Shah will maintain control."

Pat didn't respond.

Hal understood the meaning of the silence—Pat believed in his doomsday prophecy and had nothing more to offer.

Pat knew he had made his point. "Hal, you know how to contact me." Pat disconnected. He hoped his warning would be taken seriously.

At midnight on September 8, the Shah declared martial law in Tehran and eleven other major cities throughout the country. All street demonstrations were banned, and a night-time curfew was established. However, in Tehran 5,000 protesters took to the streets, either in defiance or because they had missed hearing the declaration of the ban, and the protesters faced off with soldiers in Jalen Square. After the firing of warning shots failed to disperse the crowd, troops fired directly into the mob, killing 64. Additional clashes throughout the day (a day which would be called Black Friday by the Shah's opposition) brought the opposition death toll to 89. The deaths shocked the country, like the shooting of the anti-Vietnam protesters at Kent State University in Ohio had shocked Dale and Eddie a decade before, which added fuel to the anti-Vietnam War protests back then. In Iran, the death of student protestors damaged any attempt at reconciliation between the Shah of Iran and the opposition.

In Iraq, Khomeini immediately declared that "4,000 innocent protesters were massacred by Zionists". *Zionists? Israelis?* Israel had nothing to do with the problems in Iran.

Hoping to break Khomeini's contacts with the opposition, the Shah of Iran pressured the Iraqi government to expel Khomeini from Najaf, Iraq. Saddam Hussein didn't need coaxing. On October 3, Khomeini tried to go into exile in Kuwait, but the Sunni Muslim government wouldn't let him in. He obtained a tourist visa to France and on October 8 he moved into a house bought by Iranian exiles in Neauphle-le-Château, a village southwest of Paris. The Shah hoped that Khomeini, being cut off from the mosques in Najaf, Iraq, would cut him off from the protest movement. Instead, the plan backfired. With superior French telephone and postal connections (compared to communications in Iraq), supporters started flooding Iran with recordings of Khomeini' sermons and his philosophy of forming an Islamic State.

A few weeks later, Neal Williams walked into Pat's office in the embassy in Cairo and put a copy of the London Times on his desk. He pointed to a headline, **BBC interviews Khomeini**. The article began, "In a British Broadcasting Corporation (BBC) interview with Ruhollah Khomeini outside a mosque in Paris this morning, the Iranian cleric portrayed himself as an "Eastern mystic who did not seek power, but instead sought to free the Iranian people from oppression by the Shah". Pat scanned through the article. He looked up at Neal.

Neal said, "No one believed your Khomeini theory, including me. It is happening."

At nine o'clock that night, Dale answered the phone in her nightgown. A deep male voice came across, "Is Major O'Sheen there?"

Dale thought she knew but asked, "May I tell him whose is calling?"

"General Haig."

Dale was wary of his unfriendliness. "Hi, Al. Is something wrong?"

The answer came back with authority, "Dale, I need to talk to Pat."

Dale was shocked by the urgency and the rudeness. "Yes . . . yes sir. Just a minute." Dale heard the shower turn off. She ran into the bathroom.

Her eyes were wide. "General Haig is on the phone. He was very rude to me. There must be a serious crisis."

Pat grimaced. He dried his naked body as he walked to the kitchen to pick up the phone. "Good morning, sir."

Haig almost grinned. It was night in Cairo, but Pat knew it was morning in Washington. "Pat, I need you to catch the first commercial flight available to Berlin. We have an F-15 waiting there to bring you to Washington."

Pat waited patiently. No explanation followed. He said, "May I ask what this is about?"

General Haig noted O'Sheen's calm response, apparently he was not impressed by the F-15 urgency.

"President Carter wants to talk to you about Iran and Khomeini. Saddam Hussein has expelled Khomeini from Iraq."

Pat responded calmly, "I am aware of that, Sir."

Haig had expected an 'I told you so'.

"Pat, nobody believed you about Hussein and Khomeini. Everyone in D.C. is willing to listen to you now."

Pat said, "Al, you have frightened Dale by your attitude when she answered the phone. Give me something to comfort her."

Haig wasn't surprised by Pat's criticism. Pat was more focused on his wife's concerns than the concerns of the president of the United States. "Let me talk to her."

Pat offered her the phone. She shook her head—she heard the Iranian references and did not want Eddie to go back into Iran.

To comfort her, Pat said, "They want me to come to Washington." Pat handed the phone to Dale and wrapped the towel around his waist.

Dale accepted the phone. "General Haig, Eddie says that you just want him to come to D.C."

"That's right, Dale. I am sorry that I alarmed you with this urgent request. President Carter wants to meet with your husband."

Dale was shocked, "I guess that you won't tell me why?"

"I can't even tell Pat much over an insecure phone line."

274

"Thank you for talking to me and calming my fears, Al." Dale handed the phone receiver back to Eddie. She was wide-eyed. "President Carter wants to meet with you?"

Pat nodded calmly, like it was no big deal. She was starting to realize that her husband was becoming a very big deal.

She had tried to ignore her libido reacting to his lean, muscular almost naked body while he talked on the phone. She wished that he hadn't wrapped the towel around him after he handed the phone back to her. She couldn't believe that the president—the President of the United States—wanted to meet with her husband. "When are you leaving?"

"I have to fly to Berlin on the first plane out to Berlin. Then an F-15 is taking me to Washington."

Dale was alarmed. "An F-15 fighter jet? Why?"

Pat wasn't sure how to phrase it to ease Dale's alarm. "President Carter wants to meet with me tomorrow. The F-15 flies at Mach 2.5. It is the fastest way they can get me to Washington."

"What is Mach 2.5?"

"Two and a half times the speed of sound: about two thousand miles per hour."

Dale's jaw dropped. "Have you ever been in one?"

"No." He smiled. "I am looking forward to it."

Dale was incredulous. "Why does the president want to meet with you so quickly?"

"I'm not sure. But I think it has something to do with Iraq exiling Khomeini to France."

Pat held up his palm toward her to delay more questions, "I've got to make a plane reservation to Berlin. Will you make me a drink?"

Dale was hyper and needed to calm down. She made two drinks.

Pat made a reservation on the first flight to Berlin at six a.m.

While Dale made the two drinks, she peeked periodically at her husband: *Who was he that the president would so aggressively seek his advice? An F15!* Her alarm grew. *What was the immediate threat? Was her family safe in Cairo?*

When Pat got off the phone, he saw Dale's alarm and knew he would have to explain. "Let's sit on the couch while I tell you what I think is going on."

Dale's alarm subsided with Eddie's calm demeanor. If there was a life threatening crisis, Pat would have already taken over from Eddie.

Eddie reminded her of his theory about Saddam Hussein taking over Iraq, exiling Khomeini, and Khomeini orchestrating an Islamic revolution in Iran. He said, "Dale, no one believed my analysis. Khomeini wasn't even on their radar screens. But now, Saddam has taken control of Iraq and has exiled Khomeini as I predicted.

"Neal showed me an article this morning quoting a BBC news interview with Khomeini in Paris that warned that the Islamic revolution is gaining momentum in Iran. I think that BBC interview with Khomeini has convinced the powers in America that my analysis many months ago was correct. They finally want to consider the intelligence I have gathered."

Dale had no idea who the BBC was. She didn't want to waste time finding out. "How long are you going to be gone?"

"I have no idea."

She scanned his almost naked body again, leaned toward him, and put her hand on his bare chest. "I'm so proud of you. Ten years ago, I could never have imagined that a United States President would so urgently seek advice from my teenage heartthrob to fly you home in an F-15 fighter jet at Mach 2.5."

Pat approved where she was leading. They might be apart for a while. "Teenage heartthrob?"

Dale noticed him scanning her body in her conservative nightgown. She wished it wasn't so modest. "Yes, my teenage heartthrob. You were seventeen years old when you first tried to feel my breasts while we were kissing at a drive-in theater."

"I remember. It was an Elvis Presley movie. You froze. I knew that I had offended you when a tear escaped from your right eye. I was ashamed of myself."

Dale wasn't surprised that he remembered every detail of that night. She did too.

She said, "After I rejected your first effort, you didn't try to fondle my breasts again until many years later."

Pat smiled, "During some of that time, I was still considering becoming a priest."

"What changed your mind?" She knew the answer.

"I fell in love with you."

Dale leaned against him and pecked a kiss on his lips, "And for all of the time we dated you still dreamed about feeling my breasts?"

Pat chuckled. "My imagination went a lot further than just feeling your breasts."

Dale noticed the towel rising on his lap.

She smiled, "You respected me too much to venture much further. There were several times that you could have had me completely, but you always held back."

Pat countered, "There were hundreds of times you could have had me and didn't try."

Dale countered, "If I had, you would have thought that I was a slut. A southern, Catholic girl's reputation was ruined if they initiated sex. You were too holy to go past petting."

Eddie still cherished the memory of that intimacy. "I had to confess our inappropriate touching in confession many times."

Dale recoiled, "I hope you didn't use my name in the confessional?"

Eddie eyes gleamed into hers. "Father Muller probably knew who I was touching inappropriately in my confessions, and who was touching me inappropriately."

Dale's face blanched. "I can never face Father Muller again."

"Dale, I think he admired our restraint compared to other confessions he was hearing. Our petting was the least of Father Muller's concerns in the confessional. He did ask me one time in the confessional if I was still considering becoming a priest."

Dale's eyes widened, "So he does know it was me that was . . . that was . . ."

Pat finished for her. "The girl who was touching me sinfully. Yes. But I'm sure he was impressed that we never fornicated."

"What did you tell him when he asked if you still wanted to be a priest?"

"I told him that I wanted to marry the girl who I let touch me sinfully, and that I would enter the priesthood if she decided to dump me."

Dale paled, "Father Muller must hate me. God must hate me for stealing you away from Him."

Pat chuckled, "I was still a kid when you overwhelmed my libido and captured my heart. I have never doubted that God put you in my life."

Dale kissed him tenderly on his lips. "We did fornicate a few weeks before we were married. Did you tell Father Muller that in confession?"

"Yes. He asked me if that was the first time. I'm sure he was surprised that we waited so long."

"Sheez! How can I ever face him again?"

"I'm sure he admires your control over my hormones. I'm sure he hears confessions on murder, rape, incest, adultery, and blow jobs. Teenagers petting is not something that would shock him."

Chapter 50
The President

Pat walked into the White House in his full-dress military uniform. He wasn't as nervous as the first time he was scheduled to meet with a president until he followed General Haig and the CIA director down an elevator to super-high security level and passed through two more security check points.

Pat came to a dead stop in a doorway to a meeting room. The whole presidential cabinet was assembled. He took a deep breath and followed the general and the CIA director into the room. No one stood up to greet them.

The CIA director led Pat and Al to three empty seats and sat down in a chair next to Pat with Haig to on Pat's right. Haig's demeanor was comforting.

A minute later, everyone stood up and looked past O'Sheen toward the door.

Pat turned and saw President Carter's entrance, accompanied by a Secret Service agent and his chief of staff, Hamilton Jordon.

The president made a beeline straight toward Major O'Sheen, followed closely by the SS agent.

Haig stood up and stepped forward, "Good morning, Mr. President, this is Major Pat O'Sheen."

Pat had stood up with Haig and snapped to attention and saluted his commander in chief.

His respectful gesture was rewarded with a toothy smile.

President Carter graduated from the Naval Academy and served in the Navy until his father's death. He resigned his commission in the Navy to manage his family peanut business in Georgia. The first thing the president noted was that O'Sheen's uniform decorations were almost equal to General Haig's. Then he noticed the silver maple leaves on his

Purple Heart medal. He was briefed on O'Sheen's POW rescues and his Saigon evacuation survival. He wasn't told that O'Sheen was wounded during six separate combat operations.

The president stepped forward and offered his hand. "Major O'Sheen, your reputation precedes you."

Pat smiled and shook the offered hand. "I hope you won't hold that against me, Mister President."

The president's smile faded in confusion, saw the amusement in Pat's eyes, and he laughed. Most people who meet him for the first time were intimidated. The president was impressed that O'Sheen, a young major, was so calm that he could joke. Carter was already starting to understand why Haig was so high on Major O'Sheen.

Carter and his chief of staff took the two empty seats. The Secret Service agent stood five feet behind O'Sheen because he was the only possible threat to the president in the room.

Carter turned presidential. "Major O'Sheen, I was told that you were the only one to predict the unexpected recent developments in the Middle East."

Pat responded with only a slight nod.

Carter pressed, "Do you really believe the Shah's control of Iran is in jeopardy?"

Pat answered forcefully, making sure that everyone on the president's cabinet would understand his conviction. "Yes sir. My initial concern was that Saddam Hussein was taking control of Iraq, and that he would exile Ruhollah Khomeini. When I served as a military intelligence officer in Iran, student protests in Tehran were based around Khomeini's teaching. Now that Khomeini is in France after Saddam forced him to leave Iraq, I expect the protests in Iran to escalate and become more violent. Shah Pahlavi exiled Khomeini from Iran fourteen years ago. Despite that length of time, I learned that Khomeini is still revered in Iran. Khomeini was comfortable with his Shia congregation in Iraq. Now that he is a man without a country, he will be more aggressive in fermenting revolution in Iran. I suggest . . ."

The Secretary of State interrupted. "The Shah's military is too powerful to allow a revolution to gain any momentum in Iran."

The CIA Director spoke up, "When I first presented O'Sheen's theory in this room, none of us gave it much credibility. Hussein's expelling Khomeini from Iraq has proven O'Sheen's credibility. We brought him all the way from Egypt, and I suggest that we hear him out before we start criticizing each part of his opinion."

The Secretary of State amicably nodded in agreement. The CIA director looked up at Pat. "Please continue, Major."

Pat smiled at the director. He had supporters in the room.

He looked at the president for permission to continue.

Carter said, "Pat, I believe that you were about to make a suggestion."

Pat didn't cushion it with any lead up. "If we want the Shah to remain in power, Khomeini must be compromised." He expected everyone in the room to object.

Even Al Haig gasped in a deep breath.

Carter heard Haig and looked at him, "Al, are you recommending that we assassinate Khomeini?"

Haig said defensively, "O'Sheen has never suggested that to me, Jimmy." He turned to glare at Pat. Pat ignored him and kept looking at the president.

Carter returned O'Sheen stare. "Major, are you recommending that we assassinate Khomeini?"

"Yes sir. If that is the only way to negate his influence."

The president replied, "Do you really believe that Khomeini is that big of a threat?"

Pat nodded, "Yes I do, Mister President. In the two months I was in Iran, I talked to several hundred Iranians. None of them are happy with the Shah. Most of them knew who Khomeini is, and they blame the Shah for the murder of Khomeini's son a year ago. I have no doubt that Khomeini has the influence to ferment a successful revolution against the Shah. Now that Saddam Hussein has exiled him from Iraq, he has the motivation."

The Secretary of State reiterated, "The Shah's military is strong enough to put down a revolution."

Pat addressed him, "Mister Secretary, you are underestimating the fervor of the Islamists. I was attacked twice in Tehran for discouraging student protests against the Shah. A student, who is the son of a very close Iranian friend of mine, confirmed that my support of the Shah was the reason for the two attacks against me. The student is an avid follower of Khomeini and a believer in Islamic cleric rule in Iran. After I was forced to kill in self-defense during the second attack against me, I called the student and accused him of identifying me. He admitted it. I blamed him for the attack and told him that the blood of the men I killed was on his hands. He told me that the men I killed were now martyrs living in paradise, reaping the martyr's reward of seventy-two vestal virgins."

Pat paused to let that thought sink in. He wasn't going to explain its meaning. He continued, "Gentlemen, that level of fanaticism shocked me. Muslims are required to defend their faith. Defending the faith is called jihad. It is a not much different than Christians being willing to die as martyrs rather than deny Christ. In Islam, there are three levels of jihad. The first level is similar to the Christian level of refusing to deny their faith. The second level is peaceful civil disobedience. The third level adheres to violence. Khomeini's goal is to form an Islamic state controlled by the clerics. His teachings are radicalizing the jihadists to resort to violence. We have to nip this in the bud. Khomeini is the bud. He should be compromised."

Grumbling started around the table. Pat wasn't surprised. American diplomats could never agree on a plan to win a war . . . or to prevent one.

Haig was shocked at O'Sheen's outspoken frontal assault to the president and his cabinet.

The president spoke to O'Sheen. "How did you become an expert on Islam, Pat?"

Pat appreciated the informal address. "When General Haig asked me to learn Arabic and Farsi, I learned the Muslim daily prayers from my teacher at CIA headquarters. I have been going to midday prayers in mosques for almost a year. My teacher recommended the Quran and many hadiths to help me become proficient in reading and writing Arabic. I learned more from the hadiths than I did from the Quran."

Carter didn't understand, "What is a hadith?"

Pat explained, "Hadiths are the collections of reports claiming to quote what the prophet Mohammad said verbatim on many political and religious matters."

Carter's eyes were still locked on Pat's, sizing him up. "Pat, are you a Muslim?"

"I am a Christian, Sir, but I love to praise God in the prayers of Islam. Christians could learn a lot from Muslims about how to praise our God."

Pat knew that his knowledge of Islam was important to make his argument clear. "Muslims, Jews, and Christians all recognize Abraham as their founding father. The Muslims recognize Moses, John the Baptist, and Jesus as prophets almost on a par with Mohammed."

The president's eye contact with Pat's eyes radiated approval, but he looked at his watch, trying to stay on schedule for his busy day. "Very interesting. Do you have any other suggestions, Pat?"

Pat could tell that his time was about up. "Yes sir. We must scale back the number of American personnel in the embassy in Tehran, particularly personnel with families over there. And our State Department needs to start courting Saddam Hussein in Iraq. He is almost in total control of Iraq now. And he will not like the idea of a radical Shia Islamic state on his border. Saddam is a Sunni Muslim. A majority of the Muslims in Iraq are Shia. If we let Khomeini continue the revolution and take over Iran, we can expect a full-scale war between Iraq and Iran within the next year."

The Secretary of State was impressed with O'Sheen. He took charge of the briefing. "Major O'Sheen, Ambassador Sullivan wants you to come back to the embassy in Tehran. The Iranian ambassador here in Washington has made the same request."

Pat had to reconsider his earlier refusal. "I will not take my family back to Iran. I will go back to update my evaluation. I may have to go in disguised to avoid being attacked again. I may be able to convince the SAVAC director in Iran to send assassins to Paris to compromise Khomeini."

President Carter grimaced, "Any other recommendations, Pat?"

"Mr. President, I am concerned for the safety of Anwar Sadat. Our State department should cultivate a good relationship with his potential successors, particularly vice president Hosni Mubarak."

The president was surprised by the departure from the Iran and Iraq crisis. But he nodded, "Thank you for your candid report, Major O'Sheen."

Pat recognized the words of dismissal. "It was an honor to meet you, President Carter." He stood up saluted, did a formal half turn, and left the room followed by the Secret Service agent.

General Haig looked to the president for instructions.

Carter said, "Al, he is a very unique young man. Thank you for bringing him here. Give him transportation and time off to visit his family while he is in the States. I may want to talk with him again before he goes back to Cairo. And Al, let me know if you come up with any ideas on compromising Khomeini short of assassination. I won't allow assassinations on my watch."

Pat spent two nights with Dale's family and visited with his friends and Dale's friends in Alabama. He flew back to D.C. on a Monday morning in an F-4 Phantom fighter jet piloted by an Alabama National Guardsman who needed the flight hours. He was chauffeured from Andrews Air Force base to General Haig's office in the Pentagon.

General Haig greeted him with a smile. After amenities, Haig said, "Pat, the president wants you to go back into Iran to give us an update."

Pat said, "Al, I was hoping to have permission to go to Paris."

Haig understood, "The president said that no assassinations would be approved under his watch."

"So Carter would prefer to go to war down the road and sacrifice the lives of tens of thousands of American soldiers instead of killing one fanatical cleric?"

Haig understood Pat's motivation, "He doesn't see it as an either-or scenario. I know you passionately believe in what you are predicting, Pat. But I agree with the president. If I were in his shoes, and based on what we know so far, I could not authorize assassinating Khomeini at this time."

Pat nodded once, "The people in America can't yet fathom the havoc that Khomeini can cause in the world. So I will go back into Iran. I'll need a week to grow a beard first and come up with a disguise. Maybe I can avoid another attack on me.

"I will also need a bedroom in the embassy. I don't want to be seen walking near the embassy. And if Ambassador Sullivan wants me to meet with Iranian officials, it will have to be at our embassy in secret."

284

Haig was surprised by all of the demands, "Pat, are you that nervous about going back into Iran."

"Cautious is a better word, Al. As the situation in Iran deteriorates, fewer Iranian government officials will be trustworthy. I don't want to be involved in another major lethal incident on the streets of Tehran.

Chapter 51
Surprise

Pat went straight to his office in the embassy after his commercial flights from D.C. landed at the Cairo airport. He called Andrew Sullivan in Tehran.

The phone was answered, "Ambassador Sullivan."

"Hi, Andy. How are you?" He assumed Kay told him who was calling.

"Hi, Pat. I'm okay. I'm a little nervous that your prediction on Hussein expelling Khomeini from Iraq came true. When are you coming over?"

"The first part of next week. I want to get a decent beard growing first. I don't want to be easily recognizable."

"I doubt anyone here will want to mess with you again."

"Maybe not. But I don't want to have to kill any more Iranians.

"Andy, I hope that you talked to General Haig?"

"Yes. We'll have a room for you here at the embassy."

"Good, I'll let Hal know my flight schedule."

Pat added, "Let me know if anything serious happens in the meantime."

Pat updated the Cairo station chief, Milton, on his plans to visit Iran and then drove home.

Milton no longer doubted that the young major had connections at the very highest levels of the American government.

Dale beat Scott to the door and threw herself into Pat's arms. She rubbed the stubble on his right cheek.

When he hugged Scott, Scott rubbed his left cheek, "You need to shave."

Pat laughed and rubbed Scott's cheek, "You are the one who needs to shave."

Scott laughed, "Uh-Uh."

Dale laughed.

Pat sighed. *There is no place like home.*

Dale asked, "Are you exhausted?"

"No, I slept on the planes."

Dale wasn't surprised. "Do you want to shower and shave or do you want a drink first?"

"A drink. Make two."

Two drinks? Dale knew that he wanted to talk about something serious.

Pat lowered Scott to the floor and Scott ran toward the living room yelling, "I've got something to show you."

Pat followed his son.

Scott pointed to the top of a coffee table.

Pat approached and said in Farsi. "Wow! That is a forty piece puzzle."

Scott answered in English, "Fifty pieces."

Pat continued in Farsi, "There are not many large structures with the same colors."

"Huh?"

Pat repeated the sentence in English, and continued, "This is a hard puzzle. I am so proud of you."

Scott glowed and then admitted, "Uncle Neal helped a little."

Pat said, "Neal is a good teacher. Scott, I am still learning from my teachers."

Scott's eyes widened, "You still go to school?"

"Sometimes. But Uncle Neal didn't teach you how to do puzzles in school. If you can't figure out how to do something, ask people for help. Someone will teach you."

Pat smiled at Dale's glow.

He looked back at his son, "Scott, do you know what?"

"What?"

"You can teach your little sister a lot of things." As if on cue, Amanda yelled from her crib.

Pat went into the kid's bedroom and turned on the light. Amanda's face lit up when she saw her daddy.

287

She stole most of her dad's time while Dale prepared supper. Scott didn't seem to be jealous.

They ate tuna salad sandwiches, and later, after Pat put Amanda to bed, he jumped in the shower while Dale put Scott to bed. When he came out of the bathroom, Dale was sitting on the side of the bed in her sheerest white-laced negligee.

She looked at Pat, "You forgot to shave."

"I didn't forget. I need to explain why I'm growing a beard."

Dale suspected that she was not going to like the explanation. "I'll make us another drink."

She opened one of her dresser drawers. "Put these on in case Scott wakes up."

Pat caught the gray briefs that she threw at him and stretched them out. "I didn't know they made them this small."

Dale snickered, "It's a new European male fashion."

She watched him put them on.

She approved, "Very sexy. Don't put on anything else."

"Yes ma'am." He approved where she was leading.

With drinks in hand, they sat on the couch.

Dale was worried. Pat's tiny European briefs weren't bulging in anticipation, despite her shear negligee. She guessed, "When are you going back into Iran?"

Pat was glad that she addressed the controversy so quickly and without objection. "Next week. I shouldn't be there more than two weeks."

She sighed and snuggled up next to him. She put her hand on his naked thigh as his arm went around her shoulders. The tiny European briefs awakened.

288

Chapter 52
Iran

Pat got out of the cab wearing a dark grey suit and carried his suitcase into the U.S. embassy in Tehran.

He walked around to the military attaché's office. Cloe looked up from her desk when he approached. "May I help . . .?"

She looked closer at the grinning man and squealed, "Pat?"

Pat took off his rose colored glasses, flashed a big smile and said in Farsi. "'I' have missed you, Cloe."

She jumped to her feet with a big, beautiful smile. "Praise be to Allah. What are you doing here?"

"I'm just visiting. How are you? Did you get married?"

"Yes. I hate that you missed my wedding."

"I hate that I missed it, too. I'm sure you were a beautiful bride."

A colonel walked out of the military attaché's office and asked in English. "Who is this that has you so excited, Cloe?"

"Major Pat O'Sheen, Sir. He used to work here."

The colonel walked past her desk and offered his hand. "I'm Leland Holland, Major. I've heard a lot about you from the people in this embassy."

Pat shook the hand, "I hope it wasn't all bad, Colonel. I'm pleased to meet you."

Cloe couldn't hold her tongue. She asked, "Pat, how long are you going to be here?"

"About a week or possibly two."

"Where are you staying?"

"I believe they have a room for me here at the embassy."

Holland confirmed, "We do, Major."

Cloe looked at the colonel. "You knew he was coming and didn't tell me?" The colonel chuckled. He'd never seen Cloe so happy to see someone. "Yes. If I had known you were so fond of him, I would have mentioned it."

"Can I take him upstairs? I want to see the looks on everyone's faces."

"Sure. I'll go with you." Leland wondered if Major O'Sheen was as popular with the other embassy employees.

When Kay Middleton ran around her desk to hug him, and everyone else gathered around to welcome him, he had his answer. Even the station chief, Hal Middleton, came out of his office to greet him.

Pat heard a recognizable voice call out, **"What's all the commotion out here?"**

Pat slipped the rose-colored glasses from his shirt pocket and put them on as the people parted.

He said in Farsi in a high-pitched voice, "My apology for disturbing you, Ambassador Sullivan."

The ambassador stared from his doorway, then walked a few steps closer, "Pat?"

Pat took off the glasses and donned a big smile. They both took two steps forward and shook hands. Pat said, "How are you, Sir?"

"Concerned, Pat. You sure look different with a beard, and particularly when you are wearing those funky, rose-colored glasses. What poor hippie in California did you mug to get those glasses?"

Pat laughed, "I found them in a store in Cairo, and I couldn't resist buying them."

Pat met with Andy, Hal, and Leland in the Ambassadors office. He explained that his mission was to follow up on his earlier research to update Washington. He restated his theory that Khomeini would intensify his efforts to overthrow the Shah after being exiled from Iraq by Saddam Hussein.

Pat addressed the ambassador, "Andy. Hal said Nasser Moghadam *(director of SAVAK)* asked to see me?"

"Yes. I'll call him and tell him that you have arrived."

"Andy, let me call him. He may want to meet with me off the record."

Colonel Leland Holland interrupted, "Major, you are not to have any contact with Iranian officials without my approval."

Leland was shocked by O'Sheen's icy glare.

Milton attempted to defuse O'Sheen, "Lee, I explained to you that Pat doesn't have to play by the normal rules."

Lee said, "Hal, all soldiers have to follow military protocol."

Andy was impressed at Pat's restraint when he remained calm and looked to him for help. Andy said, "Lee, Pat was the only one to predict that Saddam Hussein would kick Khomeini out of Iraq, and that Khomeini would try to ferment a revolution against the Shah here. When the BBC printed an interview with Khomeini in Paris, President Carter ordered General Haig to fly Pat to a cabinet meeting at the White House. Haig told me that President Carter sent Pat here. We have orders to give O'Sheen our full cooperation."

The colonel shifted in his seat, "Hal, were you aware of that?"

"No, I'm not surprised about Haig's involvement, but I wasn't aware of the president's involvement."

The two men looked at the ambassador.

"That information about the president is confidential, need-to-know." The ambassador looked at the station chief. "Hal, didn't you warn Lee not to pull rank on Pat?"

"Andy, like I said earlier, I told Lee that Pat doesn't have to play by the normal rules."

Colonel Holland jumped up, "I don't guess I'm needed in this meeting." He turned to leave.

Pat said, "Lee?"

Andy groaned when Lee spun back and glared at Pat. "That is **Colonel** Holland to you, Major."

Pat's return eye contact was soft, his voice was respectful. "Colonel Holland, I could tell that Cloe likes you and has the highest level of respect for you."

The unrelated comment threw Holland off stride. The confused shake of his head was almost invisible. "What does she have to do with this?"

"Cloe has great instincts on people's character, and I trust everyone who she likes and respects."

Andy leaned back in his chair. Lee was very high on Cloe. Cloe was very high on Pat. Pat's invocation of her into the conflict was fascinating. Pat's diplomacy had greatly improved since he had worked in the Iranian embassy less than a year ago.

Pat stood up, "Colonel, I regret that my mission here is an affront to the normal military chain of command. I would really appreciate your help." He slowly approached Lee and offered his hand.

The colonel saw the sincerity in the major's eyes. He accepted the handshake. "Okay, Pat, you can call me Lee."

Everyone in the room smiled.

Chapter 53
Assassins

Pat was temporarily assigned to his old office. It was tiny, but it was all he needed, and Cloe's desk was right outside his door. He called SAVAK headquarters.

After passing through two screeners, Nasser Moghadam answered his extension, "Hello, Pat."

"Hello, Nasser. How are you?"

"Worried. Are you in Tehran?"

"Yes. I just got here a couple hours ago. How can I be of service?"

"Are you free tomorrow morning?"

"Yes. Did Andy tell you I didn't want to go where I could be recognized?"

"I understand, Pat. Do you know where Laleh Park is located?"

"Yes I do. What time?" Pat used to go there to research the opinions of common Iranian citizens.

"How about seven-thirty at the fountain?"

"I look forward to seeing you there, Nasser."

Pat's next call was to his good friend, Rashid. Rashid was thrilled to meet with Pat that evening. Nasser had helped Pat get Rashid's son released from of a Tehran prison.

Pat said, "Rashid do you remember where we first met?"

"Yes, outside a women's clothing store."

Pat advised him about his beard, and that he looked different. Rashid understood Pat's caution after the attacks against him when he was last in Iran.

That evening, Pat dressed in casual clothes and drove from the embassy in a pool car. He diverted several times to make sure he wasn't followed. He arrived at the rendezvous point early and canvassed the area. He watched from a distance as his friend Rashid arrived. When he was sure that Rashid had not been followed, Pat approached the bench.

Rashid stood as Pat approached and smiled in recognition. He spoke in Farsi. "Hello, Pat. I like your beard."

"Thank you, Rashid. How are you?" They gripped each other's hand, a close friendship conveyed from eye to eye.

Rashid said, "Pat, I called to talk to you at the embassy after I heard about the second attack against you. They told me that you no longer worked there."

Pat nodded, "I got my family out of Iran in a hurry after the second attack. They reassigned me to the embassy in Egypt. I am back to visit friends like you."

Pat answered some questions about the attacks without implicating Rashid's son.

"The newspapers reported that you killed six of the men who attacked you." His eyes widened when Pat didn't deny the newspaper report.

Pat switched to a more personal subject. "Rashid, are you a grandfather, yet?"

Rashid face lit up, he understood that his American friend didn't want to talk about the attacks. "Yes, my first grandson was born two weeks ago."

Pat enjoyed his long story about the early arrival of his grandson. Pat said, "Congratulations. How are your sons?"

"They are okay, Pat. I'm worried about their future and the future of Iran."

Pat nodded in understanding, "Is al-Rashid still at the university and staying out of trouble?"

"So far. I know he is involved in student anti-government protests. But there are student protests all over Iran. Most of them have been peaceful. But as more and more students get involved, I'm afraid it will soon get out of hand."

Pat went to the crux of his questioning. "Do you think Khomeini is behind the protests?"

"According to my sons, he is definitely behind them, and his influence in Iran is growing rapidly."

The answer confirmed Pat's expectations. He talked with his friend Rashid for another hour about the attitude of the people in Iran.

The next morning, Pat drove to Laleh Park to meet the director of the Shah's secret police. He arrived before daylight. He carefully selected a properly positioned tree, threw a rope over the lowest limb, climbed the rope to the branch, and climbed high up into the tree. While climbing the tree, he couldn't help but think of his best friend ever, Mike Burkowski—deceased. He managed to handle the painful memory of seeing Mike being shredded apart by North Vietnamese AK-47s as Mike rappelled from his sniper tree.

Pat didn't see any threat during the next hour. He watched as Nasser approached the fountain on foot with four security guards. Pat expected the guards. But then he saw four men trailing far behind Nasser, all wearing black and staying in the trees.

Pat rappelled down the tree. The rope burned his left palm a little as he rappelled from the lowest branch. He looked at his palms—they were no longer calloused like they were in Nam. Diplomatic duty was making him soft.

He approached the fountain. Nasser was sitting on a bench under the shade of trees about thirty feet from the fountains edge. One of his guards was sitting on the bench with him. Pat noticed a family resemblance. When a guard stopped Pat's approach, Nasser saw him. Pat smiled and nodded. Nasser said something to the guard sitting next to him.

The guard got up and approached Pat. Instead of frisking him, the guard simply asked Pat if he had any weapons. Pat handed him a four-inch folded knife from his pocket, and he joined Nasser on the bench. Nasser expressed his approval of Pat's beard.

Pat disclosed immediately, "Four men dressed in black followed you into the park. Are they yours?"

"No. But they were probably just coming to visit the park."

Pat shook his head, "Two on each side of the walkway, staying in the trees and keeping their distance behind you so that you could not see them."

Nasser called his guards over. They hurried him back into the trees and three of them set up a perimeter around him and Pat. The fourth guard faced Pat, almost nose to nose. He had Nasser's eyes.

Pat asked the guard if he had a spare gun. When the answer was negative, Pat asked for his knife. The guard didn't trust Pat.

When Nasser intervened, the guard handed the knife to O'Sheen. A bullet hit a tree next to the guard closest to the fountain. The gun report echoed through the park. The careless shot telegraphed their intention, which convinced Pat that the assassins were amateurs.

Pat said to Nasser as he opened the small folding knife, "I am going to circle to the right."

Nasser said, "No, Pat. The police will be on the way."

"The assassins will know that and will move in quickly." Pat smiled, "I'm an expert at fighting in trees and jungles." He moved away silently.

About twenty yards into his circle, Pat saw a man moving toward Nasser to his left. He moved to an interception point and waited behind a tree trunk. When the guy passed five feet from him, he took two quick silent steps and snatched the Luger pistol from the assassin's right hand. When the man spun toward him in shock, Pat thrust the knife with his left hand through his right carotid artery and into his larynx. Blood from the artery squirted all over the front of Pat's shirt. When he grabbed the guy's black shirt to lower him to the ground as silently as possible, he felt a bullet proof vest under the black shirt. *Head shots will be required.* Pat moved forward with his victim's pistol.

He heard another guy moving through the trees to his right. He hurried as fast as could without making noise. He saw the man thirty feet away moving toward Nasser and knew he could not intercept him with the knife in time. He raised the Luger he had snatched from the other assassin, anticipated the assassin's movement between trees, and shot him in the back of the head.

Nasser heard a single shot in the woods where Pat had gone. His heart sank, Pat didn't have a gun.

Pat ran at full speed around the perimeter without worrying about being heard. He expected that the other two assassins had circled to the other side of Nasser. He ran across the wide sidewalks of the main entrance leading to the fountain and ran into the trees on the other side. The assassin he encountered twenty feet into the trees was as surprised as Pat was. They both raised their pistols toward each other at the same time. Pat slowed and veered to his left as both pistols fired at the same time. Pat's bullet pierced the assassin above his right eyebrow. The assassin's bullet hit the edge of a tree a foot to the right of Pat's head and a foot in front. Splinters slammed against the right side of Pat's forehead and face and one splinter pierced his right eyeball.

Pat heard sirens in the distance and tried to keep running in pursuit of the fourth assassin, but both eyes were watering and his vision was too blurry. He had to slow. He wasn't going to catch up with the fourth assassin.

Pat stopped and yelled in Farsi as loud as he could manage, **"Nasser, three of them are down. The fourth is coming around on your left side."**

Nasser sighed his relief that Pat was still alive as his guards moved toward his left.

Pat hoped the fourth assassin would flee after hearing his warning. Pat knew the park well and hurried as fast as he could, with his blurred vision to block his retreat. He wiped the tears from his uninjured left eye and moved faster as the vision in that eye started to clear. He heard the assassin running. He ran an intercept course, knowing the assassin was making too much noise to hear him.

Pat raised the Luger as they converged. The man ran across twenty feet in front of Pat. Pat fired a bullet into the man's right hip, and the assassin collapsed to the ground with his arms in front of him to break his fall. This assassin was well trained and didn't drop his Luger pistol. He started to swing the Luger toward Pat. Pat shot it from his hand, and one of his fingers flew away with the Luger. *This assassin was not an amateur.*

Pat approached the man with the Luger aimed at his head. The man sneered at him with hatred filling his eyes. Not a reactive hatred at being defeated, but a chilling evil-ingrained hatred aimed at him personally.

Pat smiled at him with admiration. The assassin was one tough S-O-B. When the man saw the smile, he lowered his forehead to the

297

ground in resignation and moaned as his adrenaline waned and pain kicked in.

Pat moved forward and kicked the man's gun farther away from him.

Pat yelled, **"Nasser, the fourth man is down. I could use some help over here."**

Nasser ran toward Pat's voice. At first he was outrunning his guards and his guards forced him to slow. When they cautiously approached, they saw Pat standing over a body with a pistol aimed at the prone man.

Nasser was concerned about Pat's red eyes and all of the blood covering him.

Pat heard boots running toward the fountain. One of the guards went to meet the approaching police. The guard who looked like Nasser's relative approached Pat as the two other guards approached the assassin on the ground to secure him. Nasser's relative extended his right hand, palm up. Pat waited until he was sure the assassin was no longer a threat, spun the pistol in his hand, and put it in the guard's outstretched hand with the barrel facing sideways in a non-threatening position.

The guard appreciated the professional, non-threatening surrender of the weapon. He switched the pistol to his left hand and extended his right hand again. "Thank you, Major O'Sheen."

Pat shook the offered hand and said, "I didn't kill this one so that you could interrogate him."

Nasser saw the blood covering the front of Pat's shirt and on the right side of his face and despite the frightening red eyes, he rushed forward.

Pat gave him a half-assed smile. "I'm fine, Nasser. Superficial wounds."

Pat followed Nasser's eyes and looked down at his blood soaked shirt. He touched his shirt, "This is not my blood."

Nasser saw the splinters piercing the right side of his face and realized that Pat was fine until he looked closely into Pat's red eyes. "Pat, you have an inch-long splinter stuck in your right eyeball. We need to get you to a hospital."

A police captain and three officers, who were following Nasser's guard approached.

Nasser turned toward them.

The police captain said, "Nasser, are you all right?"

Nasser nodded, "Yes. Thanks to Major O'Sheen." He explained Pat's warning about four men following him into the park. He introduced Pat to the captain and explained his embassy connection.

The captain looked at Pat's shirt and face, "Are you okay, Major?"

Pat nodded, "I just need to get all of these splinters out of my face and my right eye."

The captain noticed that the major spoke Farsi like he was raised locally. "An ambulance should be here in a few minutes. Are you the same major who fought off the attack a while back?"

Nasser answered for Pat, "He's the same one." He addressed Pat, "Where are the other three bodies?"

"One is out toward the main entrance, two are on the other side. I'll show you." Pat started walking toward the fountain, followed by all but two of the policemen who stayed to guard the assassin.

As they passed the fountain, two paramedics ran up to them carrying a stretcher. One of the policemen following Pat peeled off to lead them to the injured man. Another ambulance pulled up the sidewalk and parked beside the first. Two paramedics jumped out and ran toward Pat because he was covered in blood.

Pat pointed to his left. "Nasser, one of the dead assassins is about twenty feet into those trees."

Nasser told one of his guards to stay with Pat, and the others and a policeman followed him into the trees. The first paramedic to reach Pat looked for a chest injury.

Pat said, "That is not my blood. Can you get these splinters out?" He pointed to his face.

The second, an older paramedic, took a closer look. He said, "Keep looking straight ahead." He looked at the splinter in the eye from the side and said, "I can get them all. Get into the back of the ambulance."

Five minutes later, the splinters were out. The paramedic put antiseptic drops in Pat's eye and rubbed antiseptic cream on the side of his face where he removed the other splinters. He reached up and turned off the bright light.

Nasser stuck his head in the back of the ambulance, "Does he need to go to the hospital?"

The paramedic shook his head, "Only if gets an infection. He should get some antibiotics."

Pat sat up on the side of the gurney. The paramedic gave Pat the small bottle of antiseptic drops. Pat smiled and thanked him. Nasser helped him step down from the back of the ambulance. Only Pat's right eye was red, now.

Pat led the police to other two bodies. When they got to the last body, who was the first man he killed, Pat pulled the blood-covered folded knife from his pocket with right hand. He looked at the police captain, "Do you need this for evidence?"

The captain shook his head and looked at a policeman beside him and told him to note it in the report.

Pat pointed to the guy with the slit throat on the ground, "I used his gun to shoot the other three."

The savvy police captain already had that gun in an evidence bag. He looked in Pat's eyes, "Did you learn how to fight in the jungles of Vietnam?"

Pat nodded.

Chapter 54
The Embassy

Nasser's limo pulled up to guard gate at the embassy. Pat rolled down his back window and the guard recognized Pat and approached. He saw the blood covering him. "Good God, Major O'Sheen. Are you all right?"

"I'm fine, Jim. The other guys are not. Do you recognize Director Moghadam?"

"Yes sir."

"One of his guards is driving our pool car behind us. Let us through."

"Yes sir." He pointed his thumb up to the guard in the gate shack and the gate opened.

Cloe saw the Limo pull up and walked to the window to see what important man was arriving in a Limo.

She gasped when Pat climbed out of the Limo covered with blood.

She ran into Colonel Holland's office, "Major O'Sheen is out front and he is covered in blood." She ran to the front door, with tears streaming down her cheeks and arrived as Pat was walking in. She croaked through her tears, "Pat, are you okay?"

Lee Holland ran up behind her. He slowed when he saw Nasser follow Pat in.

Pat gave Cloe a reassuring smile, "I'm fine, Cloe. The blood is not mine."

"What happened to your eye and face?"

"Splinters. Nothing serious."

Lee turned to the gaping receptionist, "Call up to Kay. Tell her that I'm bringing Director Moghadam and Pat up to the ambassador and try to describe Pat's appearance to her."

Lee turned back toward the door. One of Nasser's guards had entered and was closing the door. Lee looked at the SAVAK director, "Hello, Nasser." He knew better than to say *good* morning.

"Hello, Colonel. Let's go upstairs."

Hal Middleton, the station chief, stood in his office door and his wife, Kay, was walking out of the ambassador's office as Pat was entering the outer room. She froze and paled as her hand went up to her mouth. A collective gasp went through the large multi-desk room.

The ambassador froze behind Kay.

Pat announced loudly, "I'm fine everyone. The blood is not mine. There was an incident. I tried to help." His injured right eye belied his simple explanation.

The ambassador moved around Kay and motioned them into his office. Hal was the last one to enter and closed the ambassador's door.

Andy looked at Pat, "Why don't you use my bathroom to clean up."

Pat nodded, "Thank you, Sir."

Pat gasped when he looked in the mirror. He had no idea that he looked so bad. He had blood splotches and blood smears all over his face, and blood splatters in his hair and on his eyelids and ears. He knew the assassin's jugular had sprayed all over him as he lowered him silently to the ground. The paramedic could have been kind enough to clean him up a little. The only clean spot was where the paramedic wiped the antiseptic cream on his cheek after removing the splinters.

It took Pat five minutes and a half-roll of toilet paper to look halfway presentable. Pat took his shirt off to reverse it inside out, but it was soaked through. He put it back on normally. The vision was blurry in his right eye, but at least he wasn't blind. He put in two antiseptic drops from the small bottle the paramedic gave him.

The five minutes Pat took to clean up was long enough for Nasser to tell his version of the story.

Andy turned as Pat walked out of the bathroom. "You look a little better."

Pat said, "I'm sorry, Andy. If I had known that I looked this bad, I would have insisted on stopping at my room downstairs." He glared at Nasser.

Nasser said unapologetically, "Pat, I wanted your embassy people to see you like that. It illustrated how great of a warrior you truly are, and the risk you took to save my life."

His guard chimed in an analysis of the attack. "Major O'Sheen prevented any of us from getting injured or killed. I could not believe that he went out into the trees against four armed assassins with just a folding knife and somehow managed to put all four of them down."

The embassy personnel were surprised that Nasser's guard so openly expressed his opinion. Pat approached him with hand extended, "What is your name?"

The guard accepted Pat's hand. They shook American style for the second time. He replied, "Saleh."

Pat filled in his last name, "Saleh Moghadam?"

The guard looked at the director. When Nasser smiled, Saleh admitted, "Yes. Saleh Moghadam."

Pat added, "Nasser's younger brother?"

Saleh smiled as he looked into Pat's clear left eye, "I am his older half-brother."

Nasser's pager buzzed. Nasser looked at the number and then at the ambassador, "Andy, it's the police captain that came onto the scene."

Andy said, "There is a phone on the table next to the couch."

When the director hesitated, Hal offered, "You can use the phone in my office."

Nasser looked at Pat.

Pat read something in his eyes that explained the reason why Nasser wanted to meet with him privately in the remote park. Pat stepped toward him, "Nasser, I trust everyone in this room. You can too. Use the phone in here."

Nasser looked at his half-brother, who sighed and then nodded, knowing they were starting to cross an invisible line of trust. He trusted Pat.

Nasser looked back at Pat. He trusted Pat and sat down in an arm chair next to the phone. He picked up the receiver.

303

Hal explained, "Dial nine for an outside line and wait for a dial tone."

Nasser connected to the police captain. He explained that he was in the American ambassador's office. Nasser listened for over a minute. He said, "Are you sure that he said Major O'Sheen?" Nasser listened for another thirty seconds and said, "Thank you, Captain." Nasser looked up at Pat.

Pat said, "Don't tell me they coerced the surviving assassin into talking already?"

Nasser did a slight shrug, "He asked about his brother in the ambulance. Apparently, his brother was the one you killed by the main entrance. When the policeman in the ambulance told him that his three comrades were all killed, he told the policemen that he was hired to kill me and the American, Major O'Sheen. He asked if you were dead.

"The policeman told him that you were the one who shot him and killed the three other assassins. The assassin declared that you had to have luck to kill his brother, and then he bragged about several high-level government officials his brother had killed."

Pat's mind replayed the scene of running at full speed across the main sidewalks near the entrance to the fountain and into the trees, his shock at seeing the assassin, and the assassin's shock at seeing him running toward him. Pat had assumed that the other two assassins had circled away from the entrance to the other side of Nasser. But the big brother sent the two least experienced men one way as a diversion, and his experienced brother the other way to kill him and Nasser, while he waited in reserve at the exit in the unlikely case that the other three failed with their advantage of surprise—a surprise that was thwarted by Pat seeing them following Nasser from his vantage point in a tree.

Pat raised his index finger and felt his right eyelid as he closed it over his aching eyeball. He realized that if he hadn't slowed and veered to his left, the bullet from the assassin would have hit him in the head instead of hitting the tree. He recalled shooting the survivor in his hip, and the guy maintaining his hold on the Luger as he crashed to ground while swinging the pistol toward him. Pat realized that the two brothers were at least as good as him; maybe the older brother was better. Perhaps the best he had ever encountered. He was lucky to be alive.

Nasser had never witnessed Pat going into a reverie before, connecting his audio-graphic memory to his visual memory. "Pat, are you okay?"

Pat didn't answer. *Why were hired assassins after him in Iran?* "Pat?"

Pat looked at the director, "Nasser, how did they know you were meeting me in the park? I didn't tell anyone that I was meeting you. Not even Andy."

Nasser looked at Ambassador Sullivan and the embassy personnel one at a time and they all confirmed Pat's claim. He suggested, "Pat, maybe they followed you from the embassy."

Pat shook his head, "I made sure I wasn't followed. I got to the park before daylight so that I could find a good vantage point to observe who was coming and going. That is why I saw the four assassins following you in. If they had followed me, they could have attacked me while I was alone in the park. Nasser, you have a traitor who knew you were meeting with me and knew where we were meeting. If I hadn't spotted them following you, they could have pulled off a surprise attack while we were out in the open by the fountain, and we might have all been killed."

Nasser nodded, and diverted. "Pat, we never did get to talk."

Pat realized that Nasser had met him away from the embassy to discuss something that was related to what happened this morning. "Nasser, if you can give me ten minutes to take a quick shower and change clothes, we can talk in my office or out in the embassy yard."

Forty minutes later, after Pat and Nasser talked in the embassy yard, Nasser's limo pulled out of the embassy. When Andy asked what Nasser wanted to discuss, Pat declined to answer, explaining that he needed General Haig to clear its disclosure. While Pat attended midday prayers with the Muslims in the embassy, Kay typed a report written by her husband on the incident. She faxed signed copies to the CIA, the State Department, and to General Haig. It was the middle of the night in Washington, D.C.

That afternoon, at eight a.m. Eastern Standard time in America, the phone in Pat's bedroom in the embassy rang. Pat picked it up, "Hello?"

"Pat, it is General Haig."

"Good morning, Sir. I was going to call you in another hour."

"Pat, Andy faxed me a report on the assassination attempt. Have you read the report?"

"No sir."

Haig read it word for word. "Is this report accurate? You went after four assassins with a pocket knife?"

"Yes sir. The report is a well-written summary of what happened. But I only went after one of them with my pocket knife. I used his gun against the other three."

"Pat, are you sure that you were the one targeted?"

"General, the surviving assassin knew my name and rank, and knew that I was in the country. I didn't tell a soul that I was meeting Director Moghadam in the park. No one followed me there. The leak had to come from Nasser's end. Nasser was also a target in the assassination attempt."

Haig was quiet.

"Sir, my mission here is complete. I don't believe the Shah will last until spring. The reason Director Moghadam wanted to meet with me privately was to get my help in seeking asylum in America for him and his family. He believes that Khomeini will have him and his family executed when he gets total control of Iran."

The general sighed. O'Sheen had been right all along. "Have you told anyone else about his request?"

"No sir."

"Well don't. I'll handle it from my end. Pat, do you think Khomeini was behind the assassination attempt?"

"Nasser and I both think that is a possibility. When I was assigned to the embassy here, I talked to a lot people in Iran about Khomeini. After I killed the six labor thugs, he might view me as a threat and doesn't want me in Iran."

"Pat, I want you out of Iran immediately. Do you need help in getting back to Cairo?"

"No sir. I'll be fine. I have enough cash. But I will need some long overdue expense reimbursements very soon."

Haig smiled. "I'll take care of that today, Pat." The prod was the closest comment to a complaint ever expressed to him by Major

O'Sheen. He knew Pat went deep into his own finances to conduct his covert operations, and wondered how a major was able to self-finance the amounts already turned in on his expense accounts. Perhaps the CIA provided cash advances. He didn't want to know. He knew Pat up close and personal and doubted that O'Sheen had ever tried to cheat the government out of one dollar on any of his tax returns. Haig wanted Pat to be able to react immediately without having to wait for cash advances from the Army. Haig could overrule the bean-counters in the Army who had already complained about some of the major's extraordinary expenses during his incursion into Iraq and his latest extraordinary expenses in Cairo to infiltrate the EIJ.

"Pat, call and let me know when you get back to Cairo safely."

"I will, Sir."

Pat took cab to Tehran airport to fly back to Cairo.

He told the cab driver to turn right toward the mosque, and then told him to find a place where he could buy cigarettes. His cabwas not being followed.

Chapter 55
Cairo

It was almost dark when Pat got home to their fourth floor apartment. Scott beat Dale to the door as Pat walked through the front door. Pat dropped his suitcase and caught Scott in midair, lifted him up and hugged him.

Scott's smile waned, "What's wrong with your eye?"

"I hurt it."

"Do you want me to kiss it and make it better?"

"Yes." Pat turned his head and closed his eyelid. Scott kissed it gently.

"Thank you, Scott. It feels better, now." Somehow it did.

Dale handed Amanda to her husband, and looked at his eye with more concern. "It doesn't look better. It looks a lot worse than you described on the phone. Have you seen a doctor?"

Pat shook his head, "Just a paramedic."

"Well I'm going to call Rita to see if Neil can find an eye doctor here."

Pat deflected her concern, "Can I have a hug first?"

Dale smiled and moved under his right arm. They hugged as she raised her face up and kissed him. She rubbed the tickle from her chin, "I hope that you will get rid of that beard soon."

Pat chuckled, "Tonight."

Scott disagreed, "I like it."

"Well then, I'll keep it."

Dale said, "Oh no you won't, unless you want to sleep on the couch." Dale laughed. Life was so much more fun when her man was home.

After the kids were in bed and he made love to Dale, Pat had the embassy fax a message to General Haig that he was back in Cairo.

The next morning, Pat went to an eye doctor. They gave him a shot of penicillin, some prescription eye drops, and told him to come back in a week if the vision in his right eye hadn't cleared.

When Pat got to the embassy, the military attaché, Neal Williams, asked him to come into his office.

Neal closed the door. He inspected Pat's eye and said, "Hal Middleton called me this morning."

Pat sighed and rolled his eyes, "I guess he told you about the assassination attempt."

"Yes." Neal chuckled at Pat's frustration. If Neal had a heroic encounter to brag about, he would want his fellow officers to know all about it. "Hal said the Iranian people are safer with you out of the country."

The attempt at humor didn't raise Pat's spirit. "Pat, do you have any idea why you were attacked this time?"

"Neal, apparently, someone has put out a fatwa on me. The surviving assassin said they were hired to kill me and Nasser."

Neal knew what an Islamic fatwa was—a license to kill. "Why?"

"Probably for the same reason the labor thugs attacked me—to stop me from meddling in their revolution. I think that I may have asked at least one too many Iranians about Khomeini.

"Neal, have you told anyone in the embassy about the attack against me and Nasser?"

"Not yet."

"I'd prefer that you keep the assassination attempt confidential— at least while I'm still here in Cairo."

Neal agreed with the condition that Pat tell him the details. It was obvious that Pat was a hero again in preventing the assassination attempt against the SAVAC director in Iran. Neal had never had the opportunity to do anything heroic. If he had just thwarted an assignation attempt against a high level official in Iran, he would want his heroics shouted from the rooftops. O'Sheen was just the opposite—he wanted his heroics kept secret.

Pat told Neal the details of the assassination attempt. Neal promised not to disclose them to his wife, Rita.

At his Cairo apartment that evening, with Dale's sleepy head on Pat's shoulder at ten-thirty, the phone rang.

Dale said, "I wonder who's calling this late?"

Pat got up from the couch, "I'll find out."

When the caller identified himself, Pat smiled at Dale and said. "Good afternoon, General Haig."

Haig assumed that O'Sheen was identifying the late night caller to his wife. He was happy that Dale was still awake. "Pat, would you and your family like to move back to America?"

"We are happy in Cairo, Sir." Pat smiled at Dale. "But I'm sure my family would love to move back to America."

Dale's jaw dropped, and then her face lit up as she ran toward him.

Haig said, "Pat, you will be working directly for me at the Pentagon, but you might be spending a good bit of time at Langley, so you will want to find a place to live on that side of town. Like always, any work for the CIA is need-to-know."

"Yes sir. When do you want me in D.C.?"

"Don't kill yourself and your family packing, but don't drag your feet either. I am concerned about your safety in the Middle East for now."

"I understand, Sir. I'll keep Debbie informed on my progress."

Dale was getting two glasses out of a cabinet as Pat disconnected. She turned around wide-eyed. "Tell me I heard you right. We are moving home?"

Pat chuckled, "Yes. If you consider D.C. home."

"I consider anywhere in America home." She threw her arms around him. "I wish we had some champagne."

Pat unbuttoned two top buttons on her blouse, "I like wine better than champagne. It tastes better on your lips and tongue." He turned away from her and pulled an open bottle of white wine out of the refrigerator, removed the cork, and slowly poured two glasses as Dale unbuttoned all of the buttons on his shirt. He reached for one of the glasses of wine.

Dale blocked his hand, reached up, and pulled the shirt off his shoulders and sighed as it dropped to the floor. She started unbuttoning her blouse below where Pat quit. Pat helped her from the bottom button up.

310

He ran his hands up over her bra and pulled the blouse off her shoulders and let it fall to the floor.

Dale reached for her glass of wine. He blocked her hand, reached around her and had the clasp on her bra unhooked in a second. She was surprised when he stepped back and picked up his wine glass without removing her bra.

She moved forward and tried to unbuckle his belt. When he helped, she knew Pat was in control. She smiled as his pants fell to the floor around his feet, grabbed his briefs, and started pulling them down. Eddie would have objected—Pat didn't. They sat naked with their glasses of wine on the couch. The couch had a blanket on it that they could use to cover their nakedness if Scott woke up and walked into the den. Pat would hear him get up. Pat admired Dale's naked body clearly with his left eye. Scott didn't interrupt their hour of passion.

After the passion subsided, Dale asked, "What kind of conflict did you encounter in Iran this time?"

"Let's don't go there. I don't want you to think of me as a lethal warrior. I just want you to think of me as a loving husband and father." His declaration earned a loving smile from Dale.

They spent the next two days packing. Pat was granted two days of leave so they could stop in Paris to visit with Pierre and Kathy Boudreaux on the way back to America. Dale was afraid that it might be long time before she would get back on this side of the Atlantic Ocean to see Kathy again.

Chapter 56
D.C.

The O'Sheens arrived in D.C. on a Monday. Pat reported to the Pentagon on Wednesday, November 1, 1978. He rode the Metro into D.C. so Dale could use the car to look for an apartment, and also because parking near the Pentagon was almost impossible unless you had an assigned parking space. They had already learned that two apartments were available for sublease in Georgetown where they stayed when Pat was learning Farsi and Arabic at CIA headquarters in Langley, but none of their friends still lived in the apartment complex, and they could afford a nicer apartment on his major's salary.

Pat was assigned to a small windowless office in the same wing of the Pentagon as General Haig. The office had a desktop computer monitor and a computer terminal under the desk that was tied to the Pentagon's network of IBM mainframes. Pat hadn't used a computer since college where programs were entered into an IBM 360 with punch cards using FORTRAN programming language. Pat couldn't type—he had to hunt and peck. The Pentagon put on one-week-long computer training classes that began on the first Monday of every month. Pat was scheduled for the next week.

Dale found an apartment that she liked near Georgetown University, about halfway between the Pentagon and Langley, and only about five blocks from a Metro station. She wanted Pat to see it before signing a lease. She didn't realize that if she found a place to live that would make her happy, he would be happy, even if it was purple and green and surrounded by stuffy intellectual professors. Pat caught the Metro out to the Georgetown station. The complex had a swimming pool, an exercise room, and was priced below the level of status seeking professors. They signed the lease.

Pat rented a U-Haul truck and they drove to North Carolina to pick up the meager furniture that they had put in storage at Fort Bragg when they moved overseas.

Pat started computer training on Monday, November 6, 1978, the day after demonstrations at University of Tehran in Iran became deadly when a fight broke out with armed soldiers. Tehran broke out into a full-scale riot. Block after block of Western symbols such as movie theaters and department stores, as well as government and police buildings, were seized, looted, and burned. The British embassy in Tehran was partially burned and vandalized. The American embassy was threatened as well, but SAVAK Director Nasser Moghadam made sure it was protected. The event became known to foreign observers as "The Day Tehran Burned".

The Shah of Iran appointed a military prime minister. Khomeini condemned the military government and called for continued protests and for "rivers of blood" to be spilled. The military authorities banned street demonstrations and extended the curfew.

The next week, Pat got a call from Detective Pierre Boudreaux in Paris. The French foreign intelligence had learned of a possible jihadist terrorist attack. They had put an agent undercover working with North African Muslims in the vineyards, but his Arabic was traditional. Most of the immigrants were from Tunisia, Algeria, and Morocco and the agent couldn't communicate very well with them.

Pierre explained, "Pat, my C-O remembers you for helping us compromise the assassin Diffley just south of Paris." (That was day Pat met Pierre, the day Pierre got shot, and the beginning of their very close friendship.)

"Pat, I told my C-O that you could speak all the Arabic dialects. He was impressed."

"Pierre, are you asking for me to infiltrate the Muslims in France?"

Pierre said apologetically, "I wouldn't put you at risk like that, Pat. But my boss went to a big secret meeting this morning, and he suggested that we ask for help from the CIA. I'm sorry I brought your name up because the French intelligence is going to request that the CIA send you to France. I am really sorry, Pat."

Pat knew that Khomeini was living southwest of Paris. "Pierre, when is the end of grape picking season?"

"Three to four weeks from now. Why?" Pierre could never understand how Pat's mind always jumped ahead.

"Isn't that where most of the Muslims live and work?"

"Yes."

"Pierre, is there a large vineyard area southwest of Paris?"

"Yes. The Loire River area."

Pat said, "Find out if there are a lot of Muslims picking there this year."

"I already know that they are there. What are you thinking, Pat?"

Pat chuckled, "Supplementing my military pay by picking grapes."

Pat called Haig's secretary, "Hello, Debbie."

"Hi, Pat."

Pat challenged, "How did you know it was me. Your voice recognition skills cannot be that good."

"Only for you, Pat."

"Bull. . . " Eddie didn't finish the expletive. He rarely cursed.

Debbie laughed, "Pat, your extension is listed now. If you call any extension in the Pentagon, your name and extension is displayed."

Pat appreciated the disclosure, "Thanks for the heads up, Debbie. I believe I already owed you one. Now I owe you two."

She chuckled, "Pretty soon I will own you." She wished she could own him, but knew she couldn't because of Dale. *But a lady can enjoy her fantasies.*

She was alarmed that her flirtation might have stepped over a line when Pat didn't have a comeback. She recovered from her fantasy, "Pat, did you call to talk to me or General Haig?"

Pat sensed her discomfort, "Heh, heh. I'd much rather talk to you, but I really need to talk to Al."

"He will be back in an hour. I'll tell the **general**, that a **major** wants to talk to **Al**."

"Debbie, are you going to help me get a change of rank?" Pat laughed, "Back to captain?"

Debbie giggled, "I'm sure that I can help you achieve your goal, **Captain** O'Sheen." She wondered how talking to such an unassuming, highly-decorated, American hero could be so enjoyable. It already made her day special.

An hour later, Pat answered his phone, "Major O'Sheen."

"Guess who?"

Pat recognized Debbie's voice and answered, "Raquel Welch. Sweetheart, I told you to never call me at the Pentagon." Raquel Welch's name didn't just pop in Pat's mind. If Debbie used Raquel's hairdresser, makeup artist, and costume designer, she could be her double in movies.

Debbie burst out laughing. Pat was totally unpredictable. "**Captain**, Al wants you to come up to his office immediately. Pat, immediately means without delay, not even a bathroom stop to unzip your pants."

Unzip your pants! Pat wasn't naive. Father Muller would be very disappointed in Pat for what he was thinking. Dale should want to kill him for how his body reacted to Debbie's invitation. He realized that he needed to tone back what started as a friendly flirtation with a woman that he had bantered with over the phone for many years, but whom he had not worked close to before. "Tell the General that I will be right up."

Pat was greeted with a warm, enticing smile from Debbie. Haig's door was opened. Pat gave Debbie a timid smile as he walked past her desk and stopped in the general's doorway. The general was on the phone, but he waved Pat in.

Haig put the phone down on the receiver. "Pat, close the door."

When he did, Haig continued. "Pat, have you ever met Pierre Lacoste?"

"No sir."

"Do you know who he is?"

"Yes sir. He is the head of foreign intelligence in Paris."

Haig stared at Pat. Pat stared back without breaking eye contact.

Haig sensed that Pat was already three steps ahead of him. He challenged, "Do you know why I brought up his name?"

Pat nodded, "He wants me to go undercover with the Muslims in France to help uncover a terrorist plot."

Haig's jaw almost dropped. He sat up and slid his chair forward and planted his elbows on the desk, "How in the hell do you know that?"

Pat was not offended by the general's attitude. "A man in France told me."

Haig saw O'Sheen's insolent attitude surfacing. "Told you what, Major?"

"That the French intelligence had been warned about a terrorist plot, and that they could use my North African language skills to infiltrate the Muslims in France to help uncover the plot."

Haig stared at O'Sheen who was barely over thirty years old. Haig couldn't imagine how Pat had high level intelligence contacts in France. "What man in France told you that?"

"I won't expose his identity, Sir."

"You will if I order you to."

Pat broke eye contact, looked out the window at the Washington Monument and said nothing.

Haig knew O'Sheen wasn't admiring the view—his eyes weren't focused. He could imagine the wheels turning in the major's brain. He patiently waited.

Pat looked back at him and continued the conversation as if there had not been a two minute pause, "General Haig, my sources are not the issue. You wanted me to learn Farsi and the Arabic dialects to allow me to infiltrate the Middle East and North Africa. But because of my lack of experience, you didn't want me to infiltrate Iraq, a hostile country. I have to admit that I was nervous passing through customs into Iraq with false IDs that the SAVAC in Iran forged. I learned a lot on that infiltration. I was more comfortable entering Libya with the forged documents. My covert insertion talents can only improve with experience. What better place to gain experience than in France—a friendly country."

Haig leaned back in his chair. The major had accurately summarized his vision for developing military insertion specialists. "What do have in mind, Pat?"

Pat didn't hesitate, "Flying into Morocco, Applying a disguise, and flying from Rabat to Paris as a Moroccan immigrant to pick grapes in the vineyards near Orleans, France."

Haig tried to conceal his smile. O'Sheen was thinking more than three moves ahead. He wondered if O'Sheen would proceed without

316

authorization—or against orders as he was prepared to do when he went undercover into Iraq. His encounter in Iraq with the defense minister was pure luck. But very few seasoned covert agents could have turned the chance encounter from the threat of exposure into valuable intelligence like Pat had.

"Pat, what do hope to accomplish?"

Pat allowed a slight smile to escape. He knew he had gained the general's support. "I hope to learn the terrorists' target, their plan of attack, and if I am right about who is behind it."

Haig suddenly understood Pat's fervor. O'Sheen was thinking six moves ahead of him. "Do you hope to prove that Khomeini is behind the terrorist plot?"

Pat nodded, "Proving that would be a bonus, Sir. It could turn the European press against Khomeini and possibly thwart his attempt to take control of Iran."

Haig didn't try to conceal his smile, "What can I do to help?"

Pat was ready to proceed, "I need to talk to the French intelligence, preferably to the agent who learned of the terrorist plot."

Haig looked at his watch and stood up. "Pat, plan to report to CIA headquarters in Langley tomorrow."

Pat stood up. General Haig offered his hand across the desk without considering military protocol.

Pat shook his hand, "Thank you, Sir. I won't let you down."

Haig squeezed Pat's hand a little harder, "I'll remember that promise, Major."

Chapter 57
The Plot

Pat moved into southern France as a Muslim migrant worker from Morocco. His tanned skin, short beard, and hazel eyes allowed him to pass as a Moroccan. France's undercover intelligence agent in the area worked as a supervisor in the largest winery in the Loire River valley, and Pat was hired as a grape picker.

Pat quickly realized that the North African workers had trouble communicating with each other, and he served as an interpreter. As a result, Pat made friends quickly. A week into his stay, the French vineyard supervisor asked Pat to act as an interpreter in disputes among the Muslim factions, sometimes as many as two or three a day—a Muslims' honor is easily offended. Pat always stopped picking at noon to say his midday prayers in the field. The foreman didn't mind because Pat still managed to pick his quota of grapes each day.

When a new foreman took over the crew, he challenged Pat at noon when he stopped working and prostrated himself in the field in prayer. Pat explained to him in French that he would resume work after he finished his prayers. Pat put his forehead back to the ground. A few minutes later, a whip cracked above his back. Pat didn't flinch and said his Arabic prayers louder. A minute later, the whip cut into his back. Pat prayed louder. A loud protest arose from the rest of the Muslim pickers. The foreman didn't crack the whip again.

Pat stood up and told the foreman in French, "I've finished my prayers, I will return to work now."

At the end of the day, Pat exceeded his quota despite serving as interpreter for a dispute. The new foreman made Pat his assistant foreman.

A week later, after evening prayers in the Orleans mosque, the imam approached Pat and asked that he follow him. Pat nodded, rolled up his prayer rug, put it under his arm and followed him to a large back room. In less than five minutes, the room was filled with forty to fifty men. Pat recognized two leaders from the mosque.

A Persian (Iranian) approached the front-center of the room and addressed the assembly. When he finished his monologue in a Farsi Arabic dialect, an angry murmur started through the crowd. Pat realized that his words had been misinterpreted. Pat slowly approached the front of the room. The Persian looked at him defensively. Pat said to him in his native Farsi, "Let me interpret your message." The Iranian didn't object.

Pat bowed to a leader whom he recognized and addressed him by name in his Libyan dialect asking for permission to speak. Pat hoped that Abu recognized him. Abu hesitated for effect, and he motioned with his hand for Pat to speak. Pat interpreted the Iranian's monologue, and the cooperation he was seeking from the assembly. Abu nodded.

Pat turned to another chieftain who had grumbled loudly. He bowed and asked for permission to address him. He nodded immediately. Pat addressed him in his Moroccan dialect and repeated the Iranian's request.

Pat repeated that three more times to the chieftains around the room in their native dialect.

Pat served as interpreter for arguments late into the evening. The basic message was that Khomeini wanted the Muslim factions to unite and begin observing Sharia law in France. Pat knew what the Iranian meant by Sharia law, but he didn't define it to the North African Muslims in the room.

The next morning, Pat was conveying the essence of the meeting to France's undercover agent as they walked toward the town center where transportation would take them to the vineyard. A black Mercedes skidded up next to them and three heavily armed men exited.

Pat whispered to the French agent, "Don't offer any resistance. I will be fine. This is what I have been hoping for."

One of the armed men escorted Pat's cohort forward down the sidewalk. The two other men ordered Pat into the backseat of the car in Farsi. Pat bowed slightly and voluntarily entered the back seat of the sedan. The two men got in the back seat with Pat in the middle. A black eyeless hood was pulled down over his head. Pat did not object. The third man jumped into the front passenger seat, and the Mercedes took off with a jerk with one wheel peeling rubber.

The hood wasn't removed until thirty minutes later. Pat was only slightly surprised that he was standing in the presence of Ruhollah Khomeini. Pat stood motionless . . . in awe, actually. Two of the large men from the Mercedes had a hard grip on both of Pat's upper arms, so hard that Pat's forearms and hands were going numb. A minute later, the Ayatollah finally looked up. Pat met his eyes.

Khomeini asked Pat in broken French, "Are you ready to die for Allah?"

Pat gave him a short nod.

Khomeini raised a Luger and aimed it at Pat's chest. He ordered his henchman to release Pat. He repeated his question, "Are you ready to die for Allah?"

Pat's eyes never left Khomeini's as he stepped slightly forward toward the threatening nine millimeter pistol and answered in Khomeini in his native **Farsi**, "Yes. If that is what my Supreme Leader wants of me."

Khomeini stared into Pat's fearless eyes, and he slowly reached down to the floor behind his desk. He said in Farsi, "Put on this suicide vest to see if it fits."

Pat did. It fit.

Khomeini pointed the Luger at Pat and asked again, "Are you willing to die for Allah?"

A slight grin passed fleetingly across Pat face, "I am. But I believe that Allah gave me extraordinary language skills and has more important plans for me than suicide."

Pat took a half a step closer to him without breaking eye contact. Khomeini didn't look comfortable with a weapon in his hand. He had not released the safety on the revolver. Pat was close enough to snatch the Luger and shoot him before his men could react. But Pat would die seconds later. President Carter and General Haig were opposed to him assassinating Khomeini. And he could not complete his mission to uncover the terrorist plot if he was killed.

He bowed slightly again and spoke to Khomeini, still in his Iranian Farsi, "What is it that my Supreme Leader would have me do?"

Khomeini lowered the pistol and asked Pat if he could speak Italian.

Pat answered, "I can speak it fluently."

"Why is an educated man like you picking grapes in France?"

"It was the only job that I could find. I send most of my earnings to my destitute family in Morocco."

Khomeini accepted his lie. "Let me see your visa."

Pat pulled it from his back pocket and handed it to a man wearing spectacles, who moved up without being beckoned.

The man looked at the visa and said to Khomeini, "It is an open Visa, good anywhere in Europe."

Two days later, Pat was in Venice, Italy, serving as an interpreter between Iranians and executives from an Italian contractor. He had not been allowed to report back to the vineyard or have contact with anyone.

The French undercover agent reported that Pat had been taken away by armed men and had not been heard from since. That word got back to Pierre Boudreaux. Pierre and Kathy were alarmed. Pierre felt bad about getting Pat into this. Kathy wanted to call Dale. Pierre expressed his belief in Pat's unique talents and dissuaded her from panicking Dale just yet.

Two days later, Pat knew the details of the terrorist plot. The plan was to bring explosives through the Italian firm contracted to work on the Eiffel Tower in preparation for their annual celebration ceremony of France's most important historical man-made icon. The Eiffel Tower had been built for the 1889 world's fair.

Pat wrote a short note to Pierre Boudreaux, put it in a small addressed envelope, and covertly handed it to the concierge at his hotel in Italy whom he had befriended. He trusted the concierge to mail it covertly. He wanted Pierre to have the intelligence if he didn't get out of Italy alive.

Before sunrise, Pat disguised his appearance and snuck out of the hotel with his suitcase and climbed behind the wheel of a non-descript small Fiat rental car the concierge had waiting for him.

Pat didn't breathe easy until he removed his disguise and drove across the border into Switzerland. He stopped and called his slush fund banker in Zurich. The banker knew Pat and granted him access to his safe deposit box despite his lack of proper identification as Pat O'Sheen. Pat retrieved his American "Edward Brown" papers and enough money from the box to fly back to America.

The next evening, Kathie Boudreaux sat down next to Pierre on the couch. Pierre was watching a France versus German futball (soccer) game. She handed him a small note she had retrieved from an envelope that came through the mail.

Pierre read the note.

"Target: Eiffel Tower

90 year anniversary celebration

Explosives will be brought into France by an Italian subcontractor working on the tower."

The note was signed with an artistic scripted "P".

Pierre smiled. "I told you not to panic Dale."

Kathie handed Pierre the opened envelope without a return address. The postmark was from Venice, Italy, five days after Pat's abduction. She wasn't convinced, "Why did he send us such a short note and not a letter. And why hasn't he contacted us since he mailed it?"

Pierre shrugged, "I don't know. But he was obviously still alive five days after his abduction and was still gathering intelligence. He is probably still deep undercover."

Kathie moaned, "So he risked sending you this short note in case he doesn't get out alive."

Pierre sighed. He had no comeback to negate her logic.

Two hours later, Pat and Dale called Pierre and Kathy from Washington. Pat gave Pierre the name of the Italian subcontractor that was working with Khomeini's terrorists. Pat requested that Pierre expose that Khomeini was behind the terrorist plot.

Part Three
The History of what happened

Chapter 58
Ayatollah

The Shah granted amnesty to dissidents living abroad, including Khomeini. As the end of 1978 approached, the Shah's power was crumbling. Because he had been a leader in the resistance, the Shah chose Shapour Bakhtiar to help in the creation of a civilian government in place of the military one. Bakhtiar was appointed to the position of Prime Minister by the Shah as a concession to his opponents, especially the followers of Khomeini. Although this caused him to be expelled from the National Front, Bakhtiar accepted the appointment because he feared that the communists and mullahs would take over the country, which he thought would lead to the ruin of the Iran he loved.

Strikes were paralyzing the country, and in early December, six to nine million people—more than 10% of the country—marched against the Shah throughout Iran.

In his 36 days as prime minister of Iran, Bakhtiar ordered all political prisoners to be freed, lifted censorship of newspapers (whose staff had up until then had been on strike), relaxed martial law, ordered the dissolving of SAVAK (the regime's secret police), and requested that the opposition give him three months to hold elections for a constitutional convention assembly that would decide the fate of the monarchy and determine the future form of government for Iran. Despite these conciliatory gestures, Khomeini refused to collaborate with Bakhtiar, denouncing the prime minister as a traitor for siding with the Shah, labeling his government "illegitimate" and "illegal" and calling for the overthrow of the monarchy.

With the SAVAK secret police in Iran dissolved, and at Pat O'Sheens insistence, the United States granted asylum to SAVAK Director Nasser Moghadam and his family.

Pat's friend, Ambassador Sullivan, recommended that America accept the fact that a revolution would be successful and should seek to use America's considerable influence to steer the revolution's success toward its more moderate protagonists. It was made clear to him that his view was not shared by President Carter's regime in Washington.

Ambassador Sullivan cabled Washington that it might be necessary to plan policy options if the Iranian military proved unable to assure the Shah's continuance in power. In January 1979, the White House instructed Sullivan to inform the Shah that the U.S. government felt he should leave the country. Ambassador Sullivan ignored the request.

On January16, 1979, Shah Reza Pahlavi left Iran at the behest of Prime Minister Shapour Bakhtiar who sought to calm the revolution. After Shah Pahlavi left Iran, spontaneous attacks on statues of the Pahlavi monarchs' decades of rule followed, and within hours, almost all evidence of the Pahlavi four decade dynasty was destroyed.

On February 1, 1979, the exiled Khomeini returned to Tehran. The BBC reported that over five million people lined the road from the airport into Tehran, cheering loudly as Khomeini's parade of limos to celebrate his return.

Days later, with Tehran in the throes of revolution, under Secretary of State David D. Newsom called Ambassador Sullivan from the White House Situation Room and said, "The National Security Advisor, Brzezinski has asked for your view of the possibility of a coup d'état by the Iranian military to take over from the Bakhtiar government, which is clearly faltering."

Andy Sullivan knew the request was idiotic and replied, "Tell Brzezinski to fuck off."

Newsom said, "Andy, that's not a very helpful comment."

"Do you want me to translate into Polish?" Sullivan hung up.

On the morning of February 14, 1979, the same day that the US Ambassador to Afghanistan, Adolph Dubs, was kidnapped and fatally shot by Muslim extremists in Kabul, Afghanistan. Marxist Fedayeen militants stormed the U.S. embassy in Tehran and took a U.S. Marine named Kenneth Kraus hostage. The incident became known as 'The Valentine's Day Open House'. Ambassador Sullivan surrendered the Embassy to save lives, and with the assistance of the Iranian Foreign

Minister Fahad, secured the embassy back into U.S. hands within three hours. Kraus was injured in the attack, kidnapped by the militants, tortured, and was tried and convicted of murder. He was sentenced to death by his accusers. But President Carter and Ambassador Sullivan secured his release.

After the incident, and to O'Sheen's relief, the embassy staff and their American families were finally reduced from about a thousand to about one-hundred.

Andy Sullivan's exchanges with the White House became increasingly bitter and he resigned. He left Iran and retired from government service later that year. (A year after he left Iran, the ambassador wrote that he received "a most unpleasant and abrasive cable that contained unacceptable aspersions upon my loyalty." He wrote, "When I was told by telephone from the State Department that the insulting message had originated at the White House, I thought that I no longer had a useful function to perform on behalf of President Carter in Tehran."

At the end of March, Pat was called into the CIA Director's office. Pat's CIA handler, Gene Tanner (Gene finally had a last name), accompanied Pat.

The CIA director walked around his desk as Pat entered. He said, "Good morning, Major." He offered Pat his hand.

"Good morning, Sir." Pat shook the offered hand.

The director smiled, "President Carter got a call from the president of France. Based on the intelligence you uncovered on your mission over there, France foiled a terrorist plot to bring down the Eiffel Tower. The president of France thanked Carter for your service to their country. Congratulations, Pat."

"Thank you, Sir." Pat had already heard from Pierre that the plot was foiled.

The director continued, "And President Carter wanted me to tell you that he has not forgotten your early warning about Ayatollah Khomeini taking over Iran. A warning that nobody in his cabinet agreed with."

Chapter 59
Theocracy

On April 1, 1979, April fool's day, Iran officially became an Islamic Republic—less than a year after Pat started warning anyone who would listen, and only a few months after the top brass and politicians in America finally started to believe in the intelligence he gathered. Ayatollah Khomeini was the supreme leader of the theocracy and instituted Sharia law. Dale watched the announcement on NBC Sunday Night News on the couch with her husband.

Dale knew her husband was not happy at the disclosure, but was surprised when he jumped up off the couch cursing under his breath and made a drink. Dale stood up a bit warily and walked into the kitchen. She knew that Pat spent the last year trying to prevent what was just announced on the news.

She knew that Pat took over and tried to calm him, "Pat, you did all you could do—you warned everyone."

Pat looked at her with cold, cold eyes, "I could have done much more." She had no doubt that it was Pat, and not Eddie in control. Pat opened a drawer in the kitchen and pulled out a pack of cigarettes and a zippo lighter. He turned away from her toward the back deck to smoke.

Dale grabbed his left arm. When he turned, Dale said, "What more could you have done?"

Pat's eyes were cold as ice, "I could have killed Khomeini. I had the opportunity. Our government and your teenage heartthrob, Eddie, wouldn't let me."

Dale's jaw dropped.

Pat walked out on the back porch, ashamed of himself for alarming Dale. He lit up a cigarette and plopped down despondently on a cheap aluminum and fabric chair. He drank a third of his drink and took a long drag on his cigarette, sucked the smoke in and held it in for a long time to get the maximum dose of nicotine into his bloodstream. His mind replayed the black hood coming off his head and seeing Khomeini sitting in front of him across a desk.

Dale came out with a drink in her hand. She plopped down in a cheap chair next to him. She didn't speak. Pat didn't speak.

She finally said, "You met Khomeini?"

Pat gave her a quick version of his abduction, the black hood, the hood taken off, and Khomeini sitting at a desk in front of him. He explained that when Khomeini aimed the pistol at him, that he could have grabbed the pistol and killed him. Pat looked away from her and chugged half of the remaining drink in his hand.

Dale would have been mortified at Pat's inclination to kill a few years ago. She managed to say calmly, "Why didn't you kill him?"

Pat was surprised by the calm question. He looked into Dale's eyes and for the first time couldn't read them. He said, "My mission was to uncover a terrorist plot. If I had killed him, I would have failed my mission."

"What was the plot?"

"Bringing down the Eiffel Tower with explosives."

Dale's eyes widened, "The attack the French foiled last week? That made international news. That was one of your missions?"

Pat told her about Khomeini sending him to Italy to serve as interpreter and about his note to Pierre.

Dale was confused, "That was last year. Why is France just now reporting it?"

"The ninetieth anniversary celebration of the tower's construction was last week, March 31. I guess the French were watching the contractor and caught them smuggling in the explosives."

She placed her hand on his, "It seems to me that your help in stopping the terrorist attack was more important than killing Khomeini. By the time you went on that mission, the revolution in Iran was unstoppable."

Pat sighed and then nodded. "I worry about what havoc the Ayatollah might wreak on the world down the road. I have a lot of friends in Iran."

Dale grimaced and patted his hand in understanding.

Haig told Pat to wear his dress uniform with all his decorations to the Pentagon to take pictures, and if possible, to bring Dale and his kids for a family picture. It was a pretty spring day. Dale wore a nice dress that showed a little cleavage, and high-heeled shoes. Scott wore a coat and tie. Amanda wore a pretty new dress that she loved.

In the Pentagon, Pat took them to his office first. Scott sat down in his daddy's chair while his dad called up to General Haig's office. Debbie put him on hold. When she picked back up, she told Pat to bring his family up in twenty minutes.

Dale pointed to the computer terminal, "Are you learning to use that?"

Pat turned it on and connected to ARPANET, which was a large wide-area network created by the United States Department of Defense Advanced Research Project Agency (ARPA). ARPANET served as a testbed for new networking technologies, linking the Pentagon to many universities and research centers. *It would eventually develop into the internet and the World Wide Web.*

In General Haig's reception area, Debbie jumped up and ran around the desk to meet Pat's wife and kids. She was surprised at how gorgeous that Dale was. Then she escorted them into the general's office. Pat carried Amanda, and Scott was holding Dale's hand. A camera flash went off as Pat entered. Pat froze when he saw General John Swanson, Colonel Jerry Swayze, Major Ray Kramer, and Major John (Cap) Romano mingling with General Haig. *What was going on?*

Scott saw Cap, let go of his mother's hand and yelled, "Uncle John, Uncle John"

Cap bent down as Scott ran to him. "Hi, Scott." He picked Scott up and hugged him. Everyone smiled. The cameraman flashed several pictures.

Cap said, "Wow. You are getting so big."

Scott smiled.

Pat wondered if Kramer or Romano was getting a promotion. Pat knew he didn't have anywhere close to enough time-in-grade (TIG) as a major to meet Army protocol for a promotion.

Pat was a bit surprised when Dale moved forward alone with all the brass in the room and hugged Cap, and took Scott in her arms. Cap introduced Dale and Scott to General Swanson, and then to Colonel Swayze. She already knew Major Kramer and General Haig. Dale knew that Pat had worked under all of them—and had impressed them all.

Cap said, "Dale, you stand right here with Scott for a picture"

He looked at Major O'Sheen, "Pat you stand here."

Pat looked at General Haig, who nodded for him to follow Cap's direction.

Cap grabbed Pat's shoulders, moved him a half step forward and turned him so that he was at a right angle to Dale and slightly left of her. Cap looked at the cameraman who nodded his approval. Cap moved across from Pat and turned around.

Seconds later, Pat was shocked to be facing the five officers who merged into a straight line, shoulder to shoulder facing Pat. Cap yelled, **"Attention."**

Pat habitually snapped to attention, but he looked over at Dale, who had a smirk on her face that said, *I can keep a secret from you, too.* The cameraman flashed a picture.

General Haig said, "Eyes front, Major O'Sheen."

Pat snapped his face forward and stared into Haig's bemused eyes. The cameraman standing ten feet to Pat's left snapped several pictures.

Haig stepped forward and pinned a medal next to the Distinguished Service Cross already on Pat's chest as Cap read from a small notebook, "The Distinguished Service Medal is awarded to any person who while serving in any capacity with the United States Army, has distinguished himself or herself by exceptionally meritorious service to the government in a duty of great responsibility. The performance must be such as to merit recognition for service which is clearly exceptional."

A tear escaped from Dale's eye. She flipped it away with a thumbnail.

Haig shook O'Sheen's hand, "Pat, President Carter wanted you to have the medal. Everyone in this room agrees that you deserve it. It will be the last honor I will give you. I am announcing my retirement next week."

Pat said, "I hate to hear that, Sir."

"Thank you, Pat. It has been quite an experience working with you. Everything you predicted in the Middle East has come true. You are an invaluable asset to our country and our army.

"Next week, you will start reporting to Colonel Swayze and General Swanson who have been transferred to Military Intelligence. I hope that you will retire from the army as an old general like me."

Dale ran across and jumped into Pat's arms and kissed him barely short of passionately while Scott and Amanda hugged his legs.

Pat's face glowed. *Life doesn't get any better than this.*

Pat loved his job, and said a short prayer to God thanking Him for the talent He gave him. But Pat was still concerned that he was prevented from doing enough to prevent Khomeini from taking over Iran.

THE END

Author's note to my many loyal readers:

I hope you enjoyed this historical thriller. But I couldn't leave the historical Iranian crisis unfinished. So below, I have added a preview of Spy Hostages, which leads into to the 444 days that Iranian students held American Embassy personnel hostages in Iran, and Pat O'Sheens efforts to free them. Read the preview below.

Please go to my website edsheehan.com. If this is my first novel that you have read, please read my first novel in my Pat O'Sheen thriller series, *A Spy is Born*. You can order off Amazon at https://www.amazon.com/Spy-Born-Pat-OSheen-Novel-ebook/dp/B08K63NN2M

Preview to *Spy Hostages*, a Pat O'Sheen thriller.

Chapter One
Embassy takeover

Amanda had just fallen asleep in Dale O'Sheen's lap when the TV program Dale was watching was interrupted by a special news bulletin. *The American Embassy in Iran has been taken over by a group of students. We don't yet know why. As ABC News learns more, we will keep you advised.* It was November 4, 1979.

Her husband was kneeling on the floor at Dale's feet teaching their seven-year-old son, Scott, how to play checkers on the coffee table. Pat jumped up after hearing the news bulletin. He cursed underneath his breath.

Scott complained, "We haven't finished the game."

He told his son, "I have to go the bathroom."

Dale knew that her husband was upset by the news bulletin.

The kitchen phone rang. Dale O'Sheen answered with three-year-old Amanda held on her hip. The deep voice that came through was authoritative and asked to speak to Major O'Sheen.

She wasn't surprised by the authoritative voice on the call—just surprised that it came so quickly. Dale asked, "May I tell him who is calling?" She knew it wasn't Alexander Haig, her husband's main mentor had retired from the army.

"Dale, this is General John Swanson. Is Pat there?"

"Hello, John." She was surprised that the call came from a general she had met when Pat was awarded his Distinguished Service Medal. "Let me get him."

She walked to the door of their hallway bathroom. "Eddie, General Swanson is on the phone."

He came out of the bathroom and smiled at her, "You call General Swanson, John?"

She gave him a wry smile, "I do when he calls me, Dale."

Pat picked up the phone, "Good evening, Sir."

"Hello, Pat. Have you heard the news from Iran?"

"Yes sir. I'm not surprised. I recommended that we close our embassy when Khomeini took over. General Swanson, I want to go back into Iran as soon as possible. A lot of the Iranian embassy hostages are my friends."

General Swanson smiled. He wasn't surprised that the American hero was anxious to help his friends in the American embassy in Iran—many of them soldiers. "Pat, meet me at Langley at nine a.m."

"Yes sir." Pat hung up and looked at Dale. Worry was written all over her face.

She objected, "Eddie, please don't volunteer to go back into Iran?"

Her husband smiled. Eddie, the teenager she had fallen in love with, would not have smiled. She wasn't surprised that Eddie's warrior persona, Pat, had taken over after hearing the news about his friends in the embassy being taken hostage. Her husband's Pat persona that he developed during the war in Vietnam to deal with the killing had stayed in the background since they returned to America from Iran and Egypt a year ago. Dale thought he was out of their lives forever. Obviously not. She grimaced.

Pat saw Dale's concern, "Dale, you and I were assigned to embassies in the Middle East so that I could develop the expertise to handle a crisis just like this. I have to go back into Iran."

Dale argued, "The last two times you were in Iran they tried to kill you."

Pat understood her fear, "That was because I was opposed to Ayatollah Khomeini taking over Iran back then. Now that he has taken over, I am no longer a threat." Pat wasn't sure what else to say to calm her fear and didn't try. "Dale, I have to go back into Iran for my friends and for America. It is my duty . . . it is what I have been trained to do."

Dale objected, "Let someone else handle Iran. The kid's and I need you here." She knew her objection was in vain by the look in Pat's eyes. A tear rolled down her cheek.

Pat moved toward his short, pretty, blond wife. She moved away with Amada in her arms, holding her protectively.

Pat stopped his advance and cocked his head. "Dale, are you afraid of me?"

She saw the pain in his eyes. She said too loudly, **"Pat, I thought you were gone—that Eddie didn't need you anymore."**

Scott ran from the family room up to his daddy with his hands raised. Pat lifted him up and stared lovingly into Dale's beautiful, light brown eyes. Scott glared at his mother for getting cross with his daddy.

Dale was surprised by her son's disapproval. The last time she and Pat argued—a long time ago, Scott took her side and was angry at his daddy. She looked back into her husband's eyes that expressed love. She melted. There was no question that General Haig had her husband trained to handle this type of crisis in the Middle East. She was just shocked and dismayed at Pat's sudden reemergence.

Something that she didn't totally understand moved inside her. "I'm sorry, Pat. I was shocked. I thought you had left us." She stepped forward and hugged him. She said, "I **have** missed you."

Pat glowed at her acceptance. He kissed her lips tenderly when she turned her face up to him. "Dale, I never left. I have enjoyed every loving moment that you and Eddie have shared with our kids. But Eddie and our country need me again."

The worried look invaded her face again, but acceptance took control. She was married to an extraordinary thirty-three-year-old soldier with a duel personality. The teenage heartthrob whom she married created his "Pat" persona to deal with the guilt of killing so many enemy soldiers in Vietnam. Pat was an American war hero and had met with three U.S. presidents and many of the top military officers in all three branches of the military. "I understand, Pat. Promise me that you will come back home to us, and bring Eddie home with you."

Pat smiled, "I promise. We'll be back. This type of operation is in my area of expertise."

They put the kids to bed. They made drinks and sat on the couch. Pat put his right arm around her and kissed her tenderly again—like Eddie would kiss her.

She looked up into loving eyes, wondering if they were Eddie's or Pat's loving eyes. Pat had become good at imitating Eddie over the years since the Vietnam War was over.

When he started unbuttoning her blouse, she knew it was Pat. Eddie would have let her start the foreplay.

She reluctantly stopped him. "I'm not sure that Eddie would approve." Her juices were flowing and making her feel guilty . . . like she was cheating on Eddie.

Pat explained, "Dale, Eddie and I share the same body. You should have noticed that he has initiated sex a lot more than he used to? Eddie would patiently wait for you to initiate it. I taught him that you enjoyed being coveted."

Dale looked up into Pat's lustful eyes with surprise, "You've encouraged Eddie to make love to me this last year . . . while you were gone?"

"Dale, I was never gone. Eddie is encouraging me to make love to you now, so that you will accept me back into your life."

Dale sighed at the absurdity, "How can I be sure?"

Pat took her hand and placed it on his lap. "Eddie wouldn't let this happen unless he approved."

Dale felt the swelling and smiled. Something felt different through his shorts. She unzipped his pants and slid her hand inside and confirmed her surprise. "You are not wearing underpants." She did not withdraw her hand. She was seduced.

Pat smiled. "I took them off in the bathroom. I can teach Eddie a few tricks that turn you on." He resumed unbuttoning her blouse without objection.

She hadn't made love to Pat for a long time. Pat wasn't as reserved as Eddie. She felt a little guilty as her passion took over as he removed her blouse. He raised his butt as she pulled off his shorts. She removed her bra.

The next morning, Pat hugged Dale to wake her up. She looked into his eyes, the memory of last night still flowing through her veins. She put her arms around him and they kissed.

"I've got to get ready to go, Hon."

She smiled. Pat didn't call her "Hon". She confessed to Eddie, "I made love to Pat last night."

"I know. You were incredible." Eddie rarely talked about sex.

She grinned, "Pat thought so."

Eddie said, "Dale, a man has no right to demand sex from his wife unless he wants to have children. If a husband and wife love each other, they want to please each other in every way possible. God made sex pleasurable to encourage procreation, and intimacy, and passion helps fuel marital bliss. Children are the result of the passion, and they give their parents the ultimate joy."

Dale put her elbow on his chest and looked deeply into the beautiful hazel eyes that she fell in love with when she was seventeen-years-old. "I wish I had recorded that."

"I can repeat it."

She knew her husband had an audio-graphic memory and said, "I won't forget it. Particularly the first part about a man's right to demand sex to have children. Does a woman have a right to demand sex from her husband if she wants children?"

Eddie smiled, "I don't think God's principals are sexist."

She smiled, "Then I am demanding my rights."

She looked down into his dreamy hazel eyes, and then moved the sheet aside, scanned his naked body, lied down next to him and rolled into his arms.

She whispered, "I'm addicted to your body."

He chuckled.

She pushed back and looked into his eyes, "What's so funny?"

"I am the one addicted. You have a gorgeous, sexy body that any man would become addicted to. God didn't give men sexy bodies—just a . . . a functional appendage."

She scanned his naked body again. "Your appendage is cute and incredibly functional, but it is just a small part of why your body is so extremely sexy."

"A **small** part?" Pat put his hand on his heart like it was aching.

Dale laughed. She had heard that men were sensitive about their size. She leaned down and kissed his lips. "If it were any bigger, I would have run away from you the first time I saw it."

Pat laughed, "You are such a good liar that I must agree to succumb to your marital demands."

THE END

If you liked this novel, please write a review on Amazon

Coming in the autumn of 2021
Spy Hostages

Readers who like action thrillers and like to follow action characters like Jason Bourne, Mitch Rapp, and Jack Reacher through many novels, will enjoy following legendary covert operative, Pat O'Sheen, and his loving family through this and other perilous journeys. *Spy Hostages* is a military, historical thriller staged around Washington, D.C. and in Iran.

Pat is a religious family man whose love for his wife and high school sweetheart, Dale, and their two kids are his top priorities along with God and country. Life is great until students take over the embassy in Iran. Pat had recommended closing the embassy when Ayatollah Khomeini and Islamic zealots took over the country from the Shah.

Pat knows that he will have to go into Iran covertly to figure out how to free the hostages. He had served as a military attaché in the embassy and knew Iran and the language very well. He saved POWs from behind North Vietnam lines during that war but he knows that this rescue will be much more difficult. Can he get the hostages out of Iran without getting them and himself killed?